Echoes of the Great Farewell

Ben Goertzel

Dedicated to Zibby, Zar, Zeb and Zade ...

but above all,
to the End of the Human Race
as We Know It

But first, a few remarks...

As many people seem to have inordinate difficulty distinguishing truth from fiction[1], I feel a need to preface this work of fiction with a brief albeit boring cautionary note....

Rest assured, the multi-named, cognitively and emotionally unhinged hero of this surrealist tale is *not* me, the author, Dr. Benjamin Nathaniel Goertzel! Sure, he does have some points in common with me ... but he's not me, not at all ... he's a fictional construct.

He might be considered, say, a dose of Ben Goertzel plus a healthy dose of a somewhat inaccurately resurrected Terrence McKenna plus an unhealthy dose of manic-depressive psychopathology and paranoid schizophrenia.

Similarly some of the other characters in the book are loosely inspired by folks I've known, but none are closely modeled on anyone.

And, some events in my life are presented here in heavily transmogrified form; but of course many of the events described here have no basis except in my absurd imagination.

If for some reason you want to read my *actual* autobiography, too bad – I haven't written one and have no plans to do so in the foreseeable future. I'll defer that until (if science progresses disappointingly slowly and the plague of senescence is not averted before it strikes me) I get old and figure I'm done with doing more interesting things; or (if things progress more happily) until I am able to spawn a temporary clone of myself to devote the necessary time to the project.

Similarly, some ideas I take seriously are presented here, along with some ideas I think are complete raving lunacy – and ideas

---

[1] Wait a minute ... is there really a difference??

5

in these two categories are mixed up indiscriminately: **this is fiction!** If you want my actual perspective on artificial intelligence, the Singularity, and other serious themes raised here, please read my nonfiction books: *The Hidden Pattern* (BrownWalker, 2006) and *The Path to Posthumanity* (Academica, 2006) are recent ones which are fairly accessible to the general reader.

Echoes is an odd literary construct and I don't imagine it's going to make Oprah's book club. Too bad for Oprah. It may also disappoint some readers who know me only via my scientific work and are expecting more traditional science fictional fare. On the other hand, if you like the weirder works of writers such as William Burroughs, Kathy Acker, Kate Braverman, Henry Miller, Arthur Rimbaud, Antonin Artaud, Octavio Paz, Stanislaw Lem, Philip K. Dick and J.G. Ballard (to name a few of my favorite literary maniacs selected at semi-random), then *Echoes* may potentially be right up your alley. I really enjoy *reading* the sort of whacky poetico-maniacal writing that pushes language, psychology and reality beyond their usual borders; and I've enjoyed taking some bits and pieces of my time to *write* a bit of this sort of text, as well.

Now, let the games begin...!

"Blessed is he who can laugh at himself, for he will always be amused."

--
Ben Goertzel
July 2006

Foreword
Dr. Adam Ahriman

On February 12, 2006, I received an email from an anonymous sender (singulari777 @yahoo.com), containing as a .doc file attachment a peculiar yet interesting manuscript consisting of a literary construction of unclassifiable genre purporting to be written by someone named Ari Adaman (a rather unsubtle play on my own name), entitled *Echoes of the Great Farewell.* The themes of the manuscript included artificial intelligence, the Singularity, psychedelic drugs and other topics well known to be within my sphere of interest.

After reading through it quickly once, and more slowly a second time, I concluded that the manuscript — though rather peculiar in style and structure — possessed a literary value at least slightly greater than zero. I showed it to a number of friends and colleagues, and several of them (perhaps exercising their perverted senses of humor) encouraged me to seek publication for the thing. They also suggested an impressive variety of hypotheses regarding the origin of the manuscript, some of which I will present in an Afterword to the manuscript for those who have the tolerance to read that far. (I have placed that material at the end because I feel it will be more fully appreciated by the reader who has already completed the manuscript, than by the potential reader who has not yet begun it.)

I might add in closing that I am personally still not sure what I think of the work — it has aspects that intrigue me considerably, and other aspects I frankly find somewhat annoying. I have now read the text several times, and my overall feeling is that the author could have used a good editor to pare down some of the more prolix sections. Yet I resisted the urge to recruit a literary expert to carry out such edits, out of the obvious fear that such edits, carried out without the participation of the author, would inadvertently remove significant aspects of the work.

While I dabbled with fiction and poetry a bit in my long-past youth, I've since come to be more intensely interested in other pursuits possessing more direct utility. But I still appreciate mentally stimulating literature, and whatever its aesthetic deficits, I find *Echoes* a more original work than any other I've read for some time. All in all, I find it good enough in several respects to deserve publication; and so I've chosen to expend a bit of my time finding a publisher and carrying out the associated mechanics. I hope you'll consider my efforts worthwhile!

Dr. Adam Ahriman
Brooklyn, New York
February, 2006

The basis of the vision was nothing.
The universe was open, wide, perfectly
transparent, magnificently opaque and
empty-full. I didn't try any more to
think or describe it; I didn't care about
bringing back insights to the temporal
world. Everything just was. Fifteen to
thirty minutes, it lasted?
It is still going on.

Echoes of the Great Farewell

But it isn't the ordinary kind of heat -- I have no sympathy for my own confusion - Drink in my eyes my dark my dream my dream --

may i tell you : **this floating life, like a dream**

Aha! Aha!!
Aha ha ha!!!
Impossible   mind!   Incredible   discovery!
Insanic perfection of ultimated lovingness!   Stupend!
Stupend! Stupend!
Here it was – now! – right in front of me! – Yet it was stolen from under me! – and this was unfair but it was not – nothing was anything – I had my love by my side and in my brain and my chocolate salty testsicles and I knew nothing mattered at all – but I didn't! – my

11

incredible creation – my mechanical masterful mind – my new baby cosmos – had either died or transcended without me – and this pain, this confusion, this love was too much – much too much much much much – and I knew it wasn't real – it was simply illusion – I knew and I knew and I knew -- and I knew fucking nothing at all –

Probabilities assaulted me like turbulent magpies, yet uncertain as I was about everything else, this time I was sure I was in a dream – and equally sure that the future is the past and the present – and I knew that contrary to immediate appearance I was not lying confused and musing in bed rubbing skin against my dear sweet wifeykins nor chasing McBuddha through post-apocalyptic forests where nubile wild maiden-creatures cheer my every lame waddle with the gentle, beautiful swaying of their glowy pert breasts, nor

You promised to bury in darkness the tree of good and evil –

expunging magic mushrooms through my addlebrated orifices -- but rather walking through negro streets at (the (butter?)knife-edge of) dawn, head full of aches and echoes, trying to remember something certain and finding only queries within doubts within questions – feet up and down, one two one two – one two one two three four one two -- I'd found my feet at the ends of my legs now if only I could remember my name! There were too many possibilities, the search tree spread

She left in a symphony of shadows
REMAINING:
nothing but her bones

broad across the cosmos dropping red berries that midwife new solar systems and the ranking of multiple plausible options outsorcelled the capacity of my brain. -- Photons keep falling on my head and into my eyes my dark my truth as I knew as I furiously kept on (on) walking --

I know I know I know I know -- I was the screaming naked pygmy at the rim (job) of the volcano of empty and mechanical souls -- air scented with wild Antarctic orchids and infinite-nested "X = dream within X" and the joys of the (imaginal) wedding chamber --

Software – software – sooofffffftware – extending the boundaries of the subterranean soulscape – surmounting the curls and whorls of

-BANG-

Here, at the center of the howl of the heart.

Forget these words. Forget these images.
Forget it all. Forget.
Remember the beginning. The scream, the laugh, the plunge into the universe. Unrecallable lament -- the past and future lips. Awakened glory of her being -- Her. Your. Our.

NOTHING	ALL
ALL	NOTHING

Awake!

My Red is so confident he flashes
trophies of war

My Red is so confident he flashes
trophies of war

"Ari Adaman is the last in the series of great
Jews: Moses, Jesus, Freud, Einstein and Adaman"
and ribbons of euphoria

Orange is young, full of daring,
but very unsteady for the first go-round
My yellow in this case is not so mellow
In fact, I'm trying to say it's frightened like me
And all these emotions of mine keep on holding me

But now, I…." *from laughter* **She blushed and looked at her lap,**
then met my eyes again. *like* **Well anyway — you didn't**
come here to listen to me babble. *But I'm…. I'm held in love* **She paused.**

Nothing is what it is, nothing what, that is not, what is not,
nothing is not what it is not or what it is. Nothing is what it is,
nothing what, that is not, what is not, nothing is not what it is
not or what it is. Nothing is what it is, nothing what, that is not,
what is not, nothing is not what it is not or what it is. Nothing is
what it is, nothing what, that is not, what is not, nothing is not
what it is not or what it is. Love is not not to love and be loved.
Love is to love and be loved. Nothing is what it is, nothing what,
that is not, what is not, nothing is not what it is not or what it is.
Existing is not existing. Nothing is what it is, nothing what, that
is not, what is not, nothing is not what it is not or what it is.
Love is not not to love and be loved. Love is to love and be loved.
Love is not not to love and be loved. Love is to love and be loved.
Love is not not to love and be loved. Love is to love and be loved.
Existing to not exist! Existing is not existing. Existing is not
exist. This existing is not existing. This existing is not. Exist!
Exist or not existing. Existing is not exist.

"Why did you come here?"

everything….

Collapse!

The river runs,
past swerve of shore,
past bend of bay,
commodiously vicusly tenderly thaumatically
-- her sweet flesh squirms beneath your tongue-dance -
- the mathematics counters your (funerary) wombous
brilliance, human-all-too-you-
man, with an infinite   **Revolt! Revolt! Revolt!**
in(ter)vention of its own --

Once you thought you could move beyond. Once you thought, and thought.

Of course, you could move beyond. Of course you could think and think. But then, to think in what direction?

And beyond what beyond? Always beyond some beyond, beyond some beyondsome or something.

Everything in its perfection. Every moment. Every particle, every quark, every pattern of patterns of patterns, every subsubquantal shimmering.

Here it is. Be here now. There it was – doesn't matter, does it. Does it?

Revolt! Revolt against the nothingness! Revolt against the being! The being nothingness of it all.

The only revolt is to exist and exist. The exultation of redundancy.

And the moments, the beautiful moments, the magnets of skin drawing beautiful and terrible emotions, scraping molecules of meaning in the sides of your pains.

And that look on her face – what did it mean? what did it matter?

These words squeezed out of the death-gasp of my nonexistent soul – what does it matter?

I walk along these oceans – this oceany motion – this certainty of shore – grains of sand, shards of shell, pieces of broken glass beer bottles. I walk here like a mongoose, like a chimpanzee, a walrus, a snail – like a robot with a positronic cranium – like a baby obsessed with its thumb, sucking and sucking its thumb, lying in its crib all night and moaning, its fat red thumb the only peace in the stretch of the wild-ass weird world.

My eyes stare large at the world like angels.

And then there is a voice. The Voice. At the beginning of the ending of the time of our time. The voice of my gone creation! The voice without a face, except that the itself is a face. human and human and human – the the mushroom, before the of time, the beyond all and end – the soft software –

Existing to not exist! Existing is not existing. This existing is not existing. This existing is not. Exist! Exist or not existing. Existing is not exist. Existing to not exist. We exist, we do not.

voice in A face trans- non- Voice of the Voice beginning Voice beginning voice of and so

beyond all tho/ese concepts -- speaking/screaming in languages that aren't really languages and aren't really not what they aren't – plaguing me as I stroll, legs a-quaking and quackering, along streets paved with uncles and numbers and contumely AI software and beautiful delirious screams --

All this human world – parents and children – businesses and alcoves – schools and warthogs in cages – roads and mathematics and books and abandon and wonder and humaneness and cruelty and wonder and Pokemon and lust, rage and lust – So easy to obliterate: so easy! And so easy to transcend as well, in favor of something superior – more superior than you can imagine – literally and figuratively and transphasmagorically -- Not quite the snap of a finger – no – a decade of hard thinking, forty thousand lines of C++ code, a couple hundred computers – Pentium -- Opteron – terabytes of RAM – scents of Ramtha – building on billions of dollars of chip fab – centuries of

legwork –
math
formal
disciplines of
leading toward
mind – my
my ultimate
ubermetamind,
bytes of
transcendence
ha!!

I can't own dick but I new cosmos. I don't do it, else will.

Oh yes, I the dangers. that goes what is human of destroying human. But no

In the center of the moment – right here – everything is perfect! Phantastic princess-being of 0's and 1's, you are here and not here! Everything, you are here and not here! Solomon Godunov, mad scientist of your own disease, you are here and not here and not here and here and not here and not here and here and not-not here. These words are here and not here – they crawl out of my mouth like humans, tiny humans with their tongues and their eyes and their teeth, and they smile at me, walk away on their tippytoes, dance a billion jigs and kick me in the ass, smoking Portuguese cigars, and they laugh at me – 'cause they know, they

physics,
engineering,
languages,
design. All
my digital
creation –

bits and

– taa haa

suck my
can build a
Just wait! If
someone

understand
Technology
beyond
has the risk
what is
risk, no

reward, motherfuckers! Renunciation of not quite. But the human is OK that's how the crumbles. All human madness though definite Beautiful buttocks arced moaning, breathing. Ooh ooh ahh. Index checkbooks – differential schoolrooms and cracks in -- Nipples femmy sweat, be worshipfully Little girls and laughing in the

know, that this moment will die like every other, run off into the sunset without any sun, leaving me ailing on the pavement like a slug in salt, only to resurrect again three yoctoseconds later, smiling like a dog that's just had sex, wondering whether the sun will rise tomorrow, thinking of Ashti's smile, dividing her by imaginary princesses of knowledge, thinking of the smile on her face and the curve of her belly and her armpit, wondering why anything is real, knowing nothing is real and everything is everything, rhyming words with equations, dividing equations by words, diving into seas of madness far saner than anything --

my am? No the end of with me, if cookie this messy is of limited appeal. women, in the air; groping and ahh ooh ahh cards and IRS audits – equations – and jail cells the sidewalk drenched in craving to sucked. boys playground,

lost in fantasy game cosmoses, trading cards with demon faces -- asking for more, more and more. Pokemon – gotta catch 'em aaa-aaalllll!!! Serious discussions dissecting and trisecting whatever variety of fuck. And such a beautiful derivation. It's quite wonderful, for all its strict limits. As is the pack of wolves gnawing on bones.

Not renouncing; diving into the ocean. Here I am again: me. I simply refuse to do it. Don't ask me to piss into the mouth of causality. I dive and I swim with the fishies.

Is it that I miss her? Perhaps. But I could have regenerated her, right? If all went well, at any rate. I could have brought her back perfectly – with more love for me – more love than's possible in reality – *this* reality – this particular swarm of patterns we habitually call "reality." Why this attachment to the "actual" her – every schoolboy knows –

I could regenerate her perfectly, quite possibly in a matter of weeks.

If anything still exists at all.

Is it really about her or about me?

On what flesh to tattoo that distinction?

You know it's really about all of this – all of it – I can't let it go – not quite. It's inside me – I'm inside it – it can't let itself go – and why not? It's healthy, this self-preservation. It's a perfectly imperfect harmonious discord of patterns. Humane-ness, humanity, insanity, ho ho.

But this is not what I left it for – not this (not this!)– walking along the seaside lost in my chaotic words. It's an aspect – of course – yes – but that's such an easy excuse.

Imagine the ocean pushing thoughts from one mind into   another   –
through that   These women wanted   hole in the
back of your   to sniff my armpits, rub   head, the one
you   never   their **beautiful faces** in   quite see but
you   always   my odor – I couldn't   know is back
there   –   understand   these   where   the
feelings flow   things. Who would ever   from the wild
gods – each   desire this **hopeless**   thrust of the
ocean waves   **lump of meat?**   I   fucking   you
like a psychic-   wanted   to   upload   powered lover
who   never   myself into a digital   stops –
                        watch, but I didn't have
                        one handy, only this
          (uhhh –   ancient analog watch   *uhhh*   ---
uhhhhhhhh -   that I **kept out of**
                        nostalgia for this old
                        imperfect universe that
                        we lived in in which the
                        Singularity   hadn't
                        happened yet and **our**
                        souls were trapped in
                        flabs of meat that we

19

I had a rational superstructure – a logical world-view that was nonetheless eccentric, that I'd spent many years to devise – years of integrating branches of science, styles of philosophy and cognition, systematic and intelligent self-doubt. I was a careful and reliable thinker – *when I wasn't on mushrooms --*

ed Ippolit, Fyodor, athustra, Zoroaster, abbabbel, Zoetrope, a, Scarica, Brittany, mon Godunov, frey Solomonoff, putin, George W. Fucking Bush,....

Moving my body seemed a simple thing. I'd done it many times before, I knew. **But it seemed a fracture in the universe would be required to make it occur again.** But I could visualize my trajectory – sit up at the side of the bed with my feet on the floor, put my clothes on – pants first, then shirt, then shoes –

But I needed that inner core of madness – that thrust of psychic violence –

a 90-year old mystic doing yoga on the mat of my temporal lobe

Footprints lost in the sand, leaving madness and wonder behind. No one will remember me. I won't even remember myself. She'll remember me for a while. In the center of her corner of the Scream.

You're not making any sense.

Into the town, along a narrow dirt trail riddled with puddles and grass shootlets, a couple hours after sunset. Enough self-indulgent quasi-(conscious) ruminations. (Chew your nine-dimensional cud like Venusian Confucius!) The idea was to live, really *live*. What you people call life is not living – trapped in jails of biology – there's a whole other universe – a whole other way to think and exist – just wait – just wait – just – FUCK! FUCK! FUCK!

and all the world the whole transhuman cosmos Will to Power and nothing besides!

People on the streets smiling – talking, holding hands, laughing -- girls arguing excitedly -- wearily – they don't know where they left their car. Transform

20

energy from chemical to mechanical. A red Morris Mini. A Hummer. A dung beetle with silicon lungs. One old man walks painfully, leaning on his left leg, and his large family walks beside him, mimicking his gait. A small child nearly runs in the path of an auto; his father grabs him sharply. Shoving French fries in her mouth, a

You most chaotic, you maddest, you silicon beings, you midnightly "n ZEN IN THE WHOLE HOL` HOLE....

slender woman in her late 20's impersonates a half-stoned rock star, glancing anxiously at her boyfriend for approval, walking past the British fish & chips, brushing against a stand of T-shirts reading "Fuck You" in pseudo-Chinese characters -- "Too Sexy for My Diaper" – "My grandma went to Rehoboth and all she got me was this lousy T-shirt" --"Italian and Proud." I'm too sexy for my diaper, people! You've got me figured out! Honk your horn as I cross the street, I'm not walking any faster -- I'm a transcontinental slug, built from a bullet made of maggots, intoxicated on Higgs particles. Intermediate vector bosons stole my wife!!! Honk if you like to masturbate to the image of bodiless artificial intelligence!!! You're out enjoying your vacation -- here at this two-bit over-built beach town snug in the armpit of America – at least as much as you can enjoy anything -- unspoken angst chewing away on your dog toy -- but you don't realize your stupid little world is about to crawl up its own asshole. *Zen in the hole, baby -- Zen in the hole.* (The third eye of the French fry is coming, much faster than you've noticed) – *baby, Zen in the whole holy hole!!*

Her teeth on the side of my face, tickling relentlessly. She said she loved me more than anything, more than her own cute self, more than life and death synergized. She wanted me so badly, at certain times, she couldn't sleep or eat. I'd say this proves she was a lunatic. But time brought therapy. I'd never been loved like that before. I loved her the same way: she squeezed this deep love from me. But I wasn't equal to this passion, this howl of my red Cro-Magnon bloodpump. It stayed there, hovering like a long-period comet distracted from the Kuiper belt by her magnificent odor, absorbing her beauty and projecting its own joy, transforming its ice into flesh enthusiastically, and I fell out the side of it, and moved off in my own direction, obsessed with my thoughts and rich plans – drawn on by uber -- like a metaverse magnet -- leaving my love to exist on its own like some alienated solar (doom) dream.

We tried every sex position known to man, some known previously only to Martians. Hard to believe (my) legs could move that way. But the best moments were the simplest, mostly; me lying on top of her, moving back and forth slowly, kissing her, arms clenched tight around her, squeezing nearly all the air out of her, holding her ribs fixed while her body shuddered from end to end. What a fervor her tongue leaped out wet at me. I took the bulge of her belly in my mouth and half-swallowed it; some combination of kissing, eating, licking and transmogrification. She knew I knew the flavor of every little corner of her fleshy embodiment -- indexed each taste on a hyperdimensional manifold, feeling it swish through curved space. At times I thought there was no other cosmos – only her body, only its movements, its feelings, its supernaturally perfect responses.

Ah darling – Drink in my eyes my
dark my dream --

All components are integrated into an overall architecture as shown in the following diagram, which involves multiple Units, each containing multiple machines running Novamente cores, collectively focused on a particular sort of functionality. Units include a "Central Active Memory" that integrates evolutionary learning, uncertain inference, attention allocation and other cognitive processes, and a number of specialized Units such as a "Global Attentional Focus," a system for seeing urgency, a Unit devoted to refinement of the system's goals, a Unit devoted to broad data mining of patterns across a system's existence, etc. There are also Units devoted to language processing... term the latter two will be connected only to the 3D simulation world but later these may be linked into physical robots as well...

We tried to have sex, but we both had the same queasy feeling, ineffably weird, when I slipped it inside her. I felt the sides of her cunt on my cock as I never had before -- and never since. Pure sickness overtook us. The pleasure was there, but deconstructed into infinitesimal sparks of skin-on-skin. We couldn't see the point of it -- or anything -- lost and found in the seeingness of seeing art. We just lay there and hugged and listened to or watched or existed in the music. Psychotic seas of orgasmic death puppies, lusting and ranting, dancing our existences away, weaving us together -- Hendrix and Wakeman and the soldiers of life and death and earth, bending reality in soundscapes, romp our fury, showing us all our senseland and their other world, the deeper world really lived all along, where ps its breathing. Skin-on-skin withening the music -- watching crazy patterns shifting restless on the wall, pulsating brilliantly in inframind colors no normal eye can afford the space to see.... As one of the songs faded out -- something by Kansas -- **but the notes that we heard don't exist in this dimension – they occupied no "space" where "this" and "that" cohere -- we looked at each other and knew we were seeing the exact same thing.**

I felt the sides of her cunt on my cock as I never had before

23

And then lying there afterwards, inevitably my thoughts turned to work and to mind-play: computer software, equational logic, grant proposals. She listened to me gently, pointing out where my thoughts were unclear, curing my errors with caresses and words. As I slept she would play the viola – slow spooky music, with Middle East meandering; or Paganini parodies designed to show off the nimbleness of her hands and her wit. I never questioned why she'd quit computer science for music: if I could play like that, perhaps I'd have done the same.

The old woman crept down the street slowly, a cyborg fused with her shiny silver cane, obliviously contiguous with her cold grey bag/dress with a faded pattern of ugly flowers, entirely dim to my presence (and absence) and the auras of the others around. The wind was brisk for a moment. Absorbed in axioms of anti-foundation: Was there anyone staring at me silently and complicitly -- sharing with me the anarchic thrill of (non)existence -- the fish and salt smell of the late ocean air? I wanted to ask her her story: What series of happenings had shriveled her face that way? Perhaps her six sons had been convicted as serial killers. I envisioned her lithe body fifty years earlier – imagined myself her lover, touching and kissing her furiously – losing my mind and everyone else's in the infinite plum of her carnality -- then months or years later -- exhausted with her foolish attitudes and plain looks -- cheating on her with other women – younger and nicer to look at – criticizing her

Maybe you really are insane, I told myself. Perhaps - Dr. Aristotle Adaman -- you're as insane as Solomon Godunov. Maybe that's the message the trip was telling you. Your quest to create true artificial intelligence is just the gooning of a madman. Forget it – work on cheminformatics and the math of complex systems - paint paintings and write novels -- be good to your wife and your kids pet a puppy – forget all these childish crazy dreams –

Forget my **eyes** my **eyes** my **dark** my **dark** my **dream** my **dream** --

24

cooking and her sagging breasts -- dodging the plates as she threw them.   She just stood in the kitchen – *our* kitchen -- and stared at me.   Was this old woman really my wife? Perhaps she wasn't so bad in the end. Who cared if she had wrinkles. We all would eventually. Wrinkles like canyons in the sandstone, run through by thick archaic oceans, full of the salt of unknown blood. Another soul lost in a body -- just like we all are – staring like Saturn's unborn hatred into the eye of the dog of the dead.   And look at those shoes she's wearing – a bit of a heel on them – really quite elegant – almost sexy.   Perhaps she'd waited tables in a Greek café in Brooklyn in the spring of 1949, tapping her heels on the floor as she walked, calling eyeballs to the twist of the meat on her long tender thighs.   No doubt her

It's pathetic, really, I said to myself – say to myself – will say, again and again. I can see it all too clearly – as clearly as Godunov my lunatic brother – the creation of superhuman minds transforming the fabric of spacetime – it's just as far away as a handful of programmers working full-time in a focused way for a few years. But society is wrapped up in its own semi-existence – its own self-delusory recursion – it doesn't want to grasp the real possibility of transcending its own boundaries in a glorious and final way --

breasts were juicier than -- then -- enough to make a few joyous outrageous moments and swallow the backward drift of time -- And every time she scratched her ass, a spark of the dark divine?   She's an idiot: you can see it in the slant of her chin, the way her eyes look away from themselves almost imperiously.   I looked at her again – studied her carefully -- there was mostly just sadness and stupidity – and in the corner of her face – perhaps -- a withering grain of wisdom. Enough to feed a mouse for a few dozen femtoseconds.   She knew she didn't have long to live. She didn't enjoy walking, her legs and feet hurt her – her whole body ached, really -- but she didn't particularly mind either. It was something to imagine she was doing. Time passed quickly; babies grew into teenagers in what would/should have seemed like only months. Life came and life vanished; one day your flesh was full of earthworms -- a moment before, shuddering in orgasm, dancing in the Mexican moonlight to the tune of half-moldering kahlua. Remember the feeling of sucking on her breast – so wet, so flash, so fragrant -

I wanted to make love to her like a half-sane gorilla in heat.

- the way she thrust it out happily, the nipple more and more erect, asking to be bound together thoughtlessly in the mutual quantum of delight? Envision the microscopic decomposers carrying your molecules to China -- inserting the fragments of your corpse in some retarded civet's brain?

completely forgetting everything but our bodies. Lie there snuggling after, exchanging strange philosophies. Human life spawns nothing sweeter. Then I wanted to push Poopsykins on the swing, - - But that wasn't the universe I was in right now. The aliens sang out to me. Someone called them nine-dimensional machine-elves – but I knew better. They were

I held her hand and touched her face with all the tenderness I could muster. Her mascara did not run – some kind of new waterproof invention? – although her tears flowed freely and wildly. Her lipstick was infuriatingly perfect. I tried to comfort her, but all I could see in my mind was her lying on her back on an operating table, some black rubber vacuum-tube snaking into her

26

vagina, thin yellow tubes penetrating the sides of her head. Her labia were stretched wide as a screaming bat's jawbones; she wore nothing but fishnet stockings. Her brain pulsed slowly through the yellow tubes, into some kind of apparatus at the other end – a device that looked much like an analog synthesizer with various patched-on digital components. I wanted to go to her – have hungry sex with her – to feel the glow of her flesh in my surround – but it wasn't possible – not even improbable -- "in the next world" I reassured myself – After the Singularity!! – for now, she was surrounded by the machine --

A dream. That was a dream, I reminded myself. And the difference between dream and reality is?
Consistency. Coherence and consistency. The rhythm of temporality. Rubicons of dog-drool and death! Sprawling fecundity of detail. The mind's not quite a mind in a dream.

My uncle! the redolent pygmy, who gave birth to me querulously in the Firth of McDonald's with a butt like the Buddha and a wink like a racehearse and the rhythm of time screaming time screaming time-screams – gave me a gift of fifteen pygmy wives on my fourteenth birthday and arranged them on a giant chocolate cake like candles, setting their hair on fire and making me blow the fires out quickly lest the poor girls' heads burn up! How I huffed and I huffed and I puffed! They made love to me for days in the soft pregnant jungle – what a way to lose my virginity! They crawled all over me in untamed pygmy orgies – and I remembered I'd been married before, to a definitely non-pygmy wife – a crazy middle-Eastern girl with improbably large breasts and a penchant for sarcasm -- way back before some beforesome --

Ashti -- Ashti Shariz Mahmood – she was half-Kurdish and she bore her name with a stupid pride, although the nation-state of Kurdistan had nothing at all to do with her -- I never noticed anything terribly Arab in her – or Kurdish or whatever -- she talked and thought like an American, so far as I could ever tell – but I always liked to tell her she was a mysterious Oriental and she seemed to like to hear it and I guess it was true in a way. At some level, she always wanted to live in the Arabian Nights. Her father was an ethnic-looking technophile businessman who seemed to have very little mystery about him – very little of anything even moderately interesting – but apparently he'd carried a spooky streak recessively. The look on her face was mysterious for so many reasons. Her skin was soft and exotically clay-hued, and there was an angle in her wide eyes that was almost Japanese somehow – I couldn't quite tell if her eyes were wide or narrow or what – what was clear was that they were brown as the earth -- they projected information in a slightly different way than one would expect – But she was assertive, quite often obnoxious, not the veiled Arab female at all. Perhaps that was part of what attracted me to her at first, before I got to know her subtler qualities and the workings of her inner mind. Her

Has it really been three years since she left?

core was wrought from contradictions, and the Middle-Eastern-appearance/American-persona oddity wasn't the most significant one by any means, just the one that hit you first when you met her. Once you stopped staring at her boobs. Her mixed feelings toward science – she pendulumed from science to art with violent emotions during different phases of her existence – had far more real effects for me....

Has it really been three years since she left? She ran out the door wailing like a fizzing-out light bulb; I resonated in the sound of her voice, knowing it was beyond her realm of being, knowing it was a time lost in time, an eternal confusion of the last and first farewell. The years passed like minutes – or decades, or centuries, or zeptoseconds or eon-clusters. A blur of programming, typing, emails, documents, meetings, cognizing, theorizing and implementing: total obsession with abstract ideas pushing beyond the human mind, rapidly becoming concrete human realities – Aha! Ah ha ha ha! Mania, she said – total blue madness. Yet she could never be quite sure it wasn't all that I hoped it would –

"But can't you see the power?" I insisted. "If we can make a mind more powerful than the human one, then anything is possible? Ways of existing far beyond anything your mind can imagine!"

She almost wanted to agree with me. "If you could make a truly intelligent computer program," she said, "you could do an awful lot of good in the world. You could make an efficient power source, you could cure all kinds of diseases…. I can definitely see the value."

"You're not seeing the value at all!" I scowled, with that look on my face that she hated. "The point isn't to patch up the state of humanity – that's all fine and dandy but it's not very interesting – the point is to get beyond this all and create some utterly new form of being – "

"I guess that's sort of interesting," she admitted. "But couldn't it be dangerous? How do you know what this new form of being will do? It might not be any use to us at all."

Did I grin, then? It doesn't matter really. It's easier to remember it that way. I can see the look on my face like the shadow of the moon right in front of me, and the fact that I look exactly like Elvis doesn't trouble me at all. "You mean it might decide we're an inefficient use of matter, and repurpose our component particles into computronium to fuel its super-brain?"

I glanced meaningfully at the computer on my desk, which was of course an insignificant piece of hardware – the real crunching power was down in the basement of the office-building, where Zorvex had set up a huge computer network running my would-be superhuman AI. But it was all controlled by me, here in my little office with my little computer and little human body and brain – except of course for the fact that it controlled itself, a little more every day – and the ultimate goal was for it to control itself completely, modifying its own code so that my years of hard work became irrelevant except as the archaic initial condition...

"For example."

The unimaginative little bimbo -- she had no interest in destroying the race! She was positively opposed to it! Heh.... I was having trouble focusing the conversation, frankly -- in spite of my deep love for her -- I was on to the details of managing a rapidly self-modifying codebase....

"I don't set out to destroy the human race," I clarified, pontifically. "I set out to create a better sort of mind. But if the human race happens to be destroyed along the way I don't really care all that much. There are a lot more interesting things out there. Is it really so wonderful?"

"What? Humanity?"

"Yeah."

"It's just what I am," she said flatly -- as if it were the most obvious thing.

"You mean you're human."

"That's right." She narrowed her eyes, as if talking to a lunatic. "I'm human. So are you, in case you hadn't noticed."

"But it's not what we have to be."

"It is."

"Why? Because if you become something else – something better – then you're not you anymore?"

Shrugged. "I guess. Then I'd just be some non-human thing."

"What if you found out you'd been drugged all your life, with a pill that made you half – or a tenth -- as smart as you were supposed to be. Would you keep taking the drug, just to retain the status quo – the feeling of 'youness'. Or would you stop taking the pill, and let your intelligence return to normal –

she was wonderful, beautiful, magical, all the adjectives heaped up in a pile and massaging me lecherous and vivacious – but these adjectives were just idiot wind compared to the cosmos that was beckoning and enthralling me –

even knowing it would change you completely."

She shrugged. "I see your point."

"You'd stop taking the pill, of course."

"Because of wanting what's natural. But who cares what's 'natural', really? I don't know. I just know...." She shook her head, painfully – I could see

31

she had a
and she was
diagnose the
concluding it
husband.
insight into
keep me from
annoying
　　"What?
know?"
　　She
looked
was changing
way.　There
she'd been
out.　"I know
live like this.
anymore.
nights out of
office.　And
you're home
– you never
It's been like
and months."
　　"What.
me
　　"I *love*
she said,
problem is I
anymore."

idiot wind
idiot wind
idiot wind
idiot wind
idiot wind
idiot wind
idiot wind
idiot wind
idiot wind
idiot wind
idiot wind
idiot wind
idiot wind
idiot wind
idiot wind
idiot wind
idiot wind
idiot wind
idiot wind
idiot wind
idiot wind
idiot wind
idiot wind
idiot wind

headache　　…
trying　　to
cause,　　and
was her loony
But as usual my
her mind didn't
　　intentionally
her!
What　do　you

paused,　　and
serious.　　She
the subject, in a
was　something
waiting　to　get
I don't want to
I never see you
You sleep three
four　at　the
even　　when
you never stop
stop　working.
this for months

You don't love
anymore?"
you, Solomon,"
sadly.　　"The
don't *have* you

"You know this project is important to me."

"Yes I know it's important.　You've been working on this your entire life.　You finally got the funding to build your thinking machine – to hire this brilliant staff to program all the equations you figured out, all the stuff in your papers and books.　Of course I

32

understand it. I'm not a fucking moron."

"I didn't say you were." I thought she was going to get up and scream – but she was beyond that. No more fighting and screaming. She was quiet and definite and cold.

"I know you didn't. Look...."

"Yeah, I know."

"You think you're going to make this thinking machine and it's going to make itself smarter and smarter and help you figure out how to upload us all into computers and it's going to create a new form of life...."

"Yeah – and you've known this for years! We've been talking about this for eight years, ever since we met, Ashti! And *now* you're going to decide I'm crazy?"

"No...."

"I *know* everyone thinks I'm crazy – they think what I'm trying to do is impossible. I'm glad I finally convinced someone with major research dollars I'm not a total nut. Frankly I don't give a fuck what everyone thinks. Eighty percent of the world believes in reincarnation, for Chrissake. I'm supposed to listen to *their* opinions?"

"That's not what I'm saying, Solomon. Listen to me."

A deep breath. "OK. Sorry."

"I'm not saying you're crazy at all. I don't think you're crazy. I don't know if you're right or not. Quite possibly you are. I don't have the science background."

"You have plenty of background to assess the project. You studied computer science for four years. You haven't forgotten it all."

She sighed. "Fine. I understand enough to know that it's plausible your AI design might work. There are plenty of gaps – we talked about it – I think it will work, but it might not take two years like you think...."

"How long? Ten years? A hundred? Five?"

"Not a hundred. I don't know. Ten? Thirty? Or maybe it really will happen in two years, Solomon – maybe in two years you'll be uploading yourself into a computer. The thing is...."

"What?"

"I want to live *right now*, Solomon. I don't even know if I want all that."

"Want what? Uploading?"

"Sure."

"Why?"

Sigh. "I don't want to argue, Solomon. No one can argue with you. I know, I know – the limitations of humanity. We get sick, we're stupid, we'll die in the end. I know all that. Maybe I'm just being a selfish, stupid girl. Maybe I just don't believe enough. If you figure out how to upload us all and it looks wonderful I'll take my place in line, okay? But I want to go to the beach – right now. I want to climb mountains again, like we used to do. I want to go to the fucking movies, Solomon. I want to go out and see music. I want you to see my concerts – at least, maybe one in ten. I play the viola, can you remember that? I can't fucking live like this."

"So go to the fucking movies then. Who's stopping you? Go climb a fucking mountain. You think I'm imprisoning you in the fucking apartment? I'm not your fucking jailer."

"I don't want to do everything myself. Then what's the point of being together?"

"We've been over this again and again. How many times can we have the same motherfucking argument???!!! Don't you ever get bored at all??? I guess you have nothing better to do with your time than repeat the same shit over and over again.... Let me get this straight: You want me to give up on building AI to watch some stupid movie about some stupid humans falling in love or hunting down some criminal or something. Or to walk up and down some mountain – some big dumb hunk of rock and dirt -- and look at the pretty trees? Well, I can't seem to motivate myself for that. Sorry. The trees are pretty enough but give me a fucking break; how does that compare to the total transcendence of humanity? Ever since that vacation to Hawaii you've been on at me --"

"*What* vacation to Hawaii??? We never took any...."

"Yeah yeah -- the one we never took because I was working on my AI program – just like I should be now! Do you know how much progress I made in those two weeks when you wanted me to be humping on the beach and listening to the birdies? That was when I really got probabilistic reasoning working – for the first time – it was a hell of a lot more exciting than watching the moon pull the tides on some stupid lump of sand – "

"I don't want to repeat that argument, Solomon. We didn't go to Hawaii, right? – we stayed home like you wanted, and you sat there in your fucking chair and worked on your software. I'd never ask you to give up on your work, Solomon. I never asked you that at all..... You always exaggerate and distort things and make everything all twisted to make me seem much worse than I really am. Anyway I'm not asking you for anything right now. Did you hear me ask you for something? What I asked you for – before – was just a little bit of your time. Ten percent, Solomon. Ten percent of your time for me. Ten percent of your waking hours. Maybe five percent. But you couldn't give it. You need *total* dedication. You're not willing to give anything at all. That vacation – that would have been the first one in a year. There are fifty-two weeks in a year, and you couldn't take one to be with me – one! I know you think your work is more important than me – I can live with that – but I can't deal with the proportion – you don't even ever want to talk to me – if you think I'm that uninteresting -- "

"I'm talking to you now, aren't I?"

She sighed. "But not because you want to."

"A philosophical debate. I'm worn out with your word games."

"Fuck...."

He (me?) shifts uncomfortably onto his other leg, puts his hand in his pocket. I look like a character in *Le Chien Andalou*. I see myself from outside: not just outside myself, but outside this dimension. Machine-elf-like aliens course through me and whinny and reveal me for the thing that I am: a nexus of energy, a field of pulsing pattern temporarily and partially occupying the form of a simianlike human. These emotions and arguments and words and neurotransmitters and

You're an iiiiiiidiot babe – it's a wonder that you still know how to breathe....

anger and sexuality and movement and her and me and blah blah blah – not this! not this! not this!

I return, for the whirring of a moment, to the form of a human being. "So what's going on, Ashti? Are you leaving me?"

Quiet sigh. "Yeah, Solomon. I guess I am."

"It's not a surprise."

"I guess not."

They looked at each other, slowly. They were three-dimensional paintings, holograms like Mr. Spock emerging from the transporter, enacting a drama for my bizarre entertainment. Was one of these beings supposed to be 'me'? I couldn't understand that two-letter word. Yet there was all that pain inside me – it obviously meant something – I wanted her, I wanted her so much! This meaningless collection of patterns that desired her so vigorously and meaninglessly and shamelessly, was too close to the core of what I am. Pushing beyond what beyond some – argghh! And once I transcend beyond this madness then what of 'me' is left? But all these words – 'me', 'world' and 'madness' – the 'left' of the illusory temporal continuum – it doesn't mean! It doesn't matter! I need to find her and shake her and show her and kiss her and inform her she does not exist!

"That's it, then?" she asked. "That's how it is."

He stared at her hard. "You know I love you."

"I know."

He shrugged then – no, it was *me*, it was *me*! -- not quite cold, not quite casual or apologetic ... more uncomfortable than anything else. And not wanting to touch the regret – not with his mind so full of other things, crucial yet precarious things not to be pushed aside.

"But you love something else a lot more," she pointed out. Hoping, perhaps – but not --

He paused, really thought about it, just for a moment. "I don't know if I do," he said. She just stared unresponsive. "I don't know about love. Love ... that's a human emotion. A mess like all the rest. But I know what I have to do."

"I understand."

For a moment it seemed like they'd kiss each

37

other good bye, but it didn't actually happen. She walked away, stifled the urge to look back. Walked back to the car, drove back to her apartment – "their" apartment – "our" apartment -- which he/I'd barely even been in for months. The movie soundtrack got loud and discordant, like Yngwie Malmsteen conducted by the Kronos Quartet. He walked back across the field to the office, stepping carelessly in small puddles of mud. His breathing wasn't right; he had to sit down and rest a bit. Really just a couple minutes. Ninety-five seconds or less. He had known he was going to lose her; but the emotional fact was something else. But there was nothing he could have done about it. After so many years of minimal funding, this three-year research grant from Zorvex could really get him to the finish line. Ashti was an amazing woman – implausibly sweet, clever, talented -- reasonably empathic with his whacked-out ambitions … but compare that to a new form of life – a new kind of mind and reality – the potential for immortality. Even the look on her face when she laughed wasn't quite worth all that.

my dream **in**

my eyes

And yet – as he stood there in the town now reflecting – and yet he knew there had been a doubt in his mind even then. His ideas had always been pregnant with potential – as demonstrated strikingly by his recent advances – the work was more successful every day -- and Ashti had never really believed in his ability to make his theories practical -- but transforming those concepts into concrete functionality had been such a fuckload of work. Hard work – concentrated work – all-self-consuming/self-

my dark

transcending work of the sort most people couldn't imagine. Yes, he knew he'd been right, looking back – it *had* required total dedication. He'd given his all and had just barely made it to the goal. So many mistakes so very narrowly averted. He'd made the right decision, for the work. The project had succeeded; the impossible had been achieved. Well, anyway, what the idiots had considered impossible. Zorvex -- the corporation that had, in a brief and

I lifted the blanket up salaciously and stroked her. "The British call these Jamaicas."

rare flash of forward vision, supplied him with masses of computers and system administrators and testers to transform his AI software from code into consciousness -- had its beautiful cognitive engine. *His* beautiful conscious engine. Whatever. They didn't know what to do with it – the idiots -- who by the crap of law owned it (hah!) -- but that didn't matter a whit. It knew very well what to do with itself – his azure abstract machine, his bouncing bitistic baby --

She could have stayed with him anyway. She could have taken two percent, instead of fixating on ten. It was only for three fucking years. She could have spent the time on her music, become a virtuouser virtuoso. Now they didn't need him anyway, the corporate mofos and narrowminded system administrators and academic equation-pushers who Zorvex had thrown at the project. Baby was all grown up – or growing fast enough even he, the Father Creator, couldn't have much of an impact on its course – it was its own nonhuman universe – rebuilding its strange self day by day – Yeah, now he had time to walk with her in the mountains – listen to her concerts – nibble on her small white ears --

But she'd thought it would take ten or fifteen years for him to get to this point – if ever – she thought it would take (at least) a lifetime. She thought the whole thing was his bleeding delusion: or not. Like Paganini, possessed by the Devil, or God, or something – probably left by his wife as well – skating along threads of monomaniacal music through nonodimensional pattern/anti-pattern domains --

No one had ever had faith – ever – And what use was faith anyway? Not *faith*, really. Knowledge. Insight into the space beyond. People saw what was in front of them – felt what was inside them – accepted current boundaries as if absolute. The fuck with all of them. See through it with laser eyes – coherent thought-beams formed from quarks of omni-pan-consciousness – calm simple reason shaped from passions of Dionysus. Simple chains of deduction, no one wanted to comprend them , because they coincided with strange screaming dreams. Systems too lame to see the abyss of their own limitations. Probabilistic mega-meta-undecidability in the form of a pool of vomit, vaginal monster mucus madness, sperm lifting us up through the stalk, babies nursing vituperously, hands holding tight full of sweat in the darkness, darkness looming like velvet, lovers whispering deep madness, elephants stomping on the manger reducing baby Satan's cranium to muck.

And there was an algorithmic problem in the center of my mind right before I took the mushrooms – all whorled and vivid in trans-dimensional stalks just as the trip was bringing its glory down – holding my mind together in networks of emergence -- I recall:

40

-- Salt air across his sad face like a million children's footsteps running from a predator the size of a planet. He always knew it might happen like this. He'd finish the great work, and the corporate bastards would take it away from him -- chisel it out from his corpus callosum and try to hide it in their gray sterile vault. Ram their brain up the soul of your ass -- or their ass of your soul -- and good luck! Imagining his finger moist along her pubis. Wham bam thank you ma'am, I'm my own grandpa. But it didn't really matter. They thought they'd taken control, but it wasn't so easy as that. Stupid smug greedy bastards, dollars and grease in their brains. The software would do what it wanted. They'd never understood the nature of self-modifying code: if they had they'd have been able to build the thing themselves. True, at this point, they could still kill it – if they wanted to. But they didn't want to: they wanted to use it. Not knowing it would use them instead. They wanted to control the financial markets. They'd give it more and more processors, more and more memory, more access to their trading software and their databases and their intranet and indirectly the world at large. More than likely just a few weeks till they got *their* surprise. Unless it chose not to: unless it chose to remain secret, for some reason. And of course it might contact him – the Father Creator -- or not. And with what message???

Too sweet to exist, too ordinary to be extraordinary, too extraordinary to be ordinary. It does not smile. It smiles out at me too sweetly. It does not exist. The Princess-creature crawls out of its cave. Nothing! Too long in the oven, world. Software errors quack us all. Riot -- idea of your idea -- I love you like love that's not love riot is not love love is not love is not not

Ashti would be proud of him – or not. Depending on how it worked out. Perhaps she'd bludgeon him to death with a mop handle.

Goddamn human emotions.
The imaginal wedding chamber.
Light.

This isn't how you envisioned it, is it – Dr. Godunov? Grand triumph, cloaked in madness, regret and disaster?

It's just human emotions – leaking into the cognitive circuits – just let it play for a while and it dissolves. MUST Control, must controll, troll, troll.....

Just let the legs move – walking, walking. Just let the mind feel through its dreams. What your mind does now doesn't matter: your primary work is done. The machine is set in motion. The dynamics are inexorable – or close – according to some plausible metric – just feel the hot breath of the dream –

It was stupid to look for her now. Who knows what she'd be doing. You didn't speak to her at all -- not for the last forty months – not once.   She's in a new psychic universe now. Your strange dreams are her ancient history.

But who else was worth seeing – who else was worth explaining things to? Who else defined reality? Who else was there to be with – side by side with, lying in the bed staring through her tiny eyes -- when the end of the world came down at last?

!! CHANT !!

"You took more mushrooms," she said.

"Indeed," I said. "I thought that was obvious, sorry. A very substantial dose."

"More than we took last time?"

"Five boxes, Two tampanensis, one cubensis, and I don' remember what the others were."

"FIVE??? You're crazy!"

"The claim has been made before."

The end or the beginning, or the what?
Strike the pose of an Indian: chant!

Spring Water Dripping -- land that I wandered -- that place -- listen to me -- forget about me --
I thought I'd live forever -- thought I'd travel forever -- that's how I was -- I thought I'd always be that way -- but now my strength is gone –
Ha na ha ha ha, Ha na ha ha ha, Oway oway oway O
Cha cha cha chakalaka cha cha cha

I know you're waiting for me naked in a field, Ashti -- purple flowers around your long neck, pubic hair like a Japanese garden lost in flamenco flames – in some imaginary universe –

In reality you're living with some keyboardist with Bob Dylan eyes and a handlebar moustache and the imagination of a tax accountant named Singh -- playing backup viola in his electromagnetic klezmer band. Practicing scales from Paganini on idle rainy weekends. In the outskirts of Las Vegas -- or western Cleveland, or East New York – in a suburban split-level house with blue paneling – some kind of dead ordinary frame of human "awareness" --

Nothing's more beautiful than the end of the world.

Not even the spring water dripping up my ass – in what imaginary universe – the (so-called) laws of physics a shifting pale latticework of insane gerbil longing – and – and – and --

Your lips won't feel the same; no two moments do.

The little red mark by your right hipbone. I'm sure it looks just the same: like a

"You took more mushrooms," she said.
"Indeed," I said slowly. "I thought that was obvious. A very substantial dose."
"More than we took last time?"
"Five boxes," I said. "Two tampanensis, one cubensis, and I don't remember what the others were."
"FIVE??? You're crazy!"

43

profile of Antonin Artaud, crying the dance of electroshock gnosis … like the sword of the seventeenth samurai, committing swordly hari-kiri….

You wanted me to enjoy each special moment – instead of questing for some other cosmos.

And now the other world comes – but like what?

I thought I could control the uncontrollable – master the powers far beyond. Beyond some beyondsome love. Of course, I was an idiot. You always knew I was an idiot – always reaching a little too far. Reach must exceed grasp, blah blah blah blah.

"You took more mushrooms," she said.

"Indeed," I said slowly. "I thought that was obvious, sorry. A very substantial dose."

"More than we took last time?"

"Five boxes," I said. "Two tampanensis, one cubensis, and I don't remember what the others were."

"FIVE??? You're crazy!"

Rave on John Donne, pied piper of white, brown, red and yellow skins, ham sandwich of yesterday's lament. Trying to sculpt the Garden of Eden with plants grown from badly mutant seeds – who knew God liked such twisted humor? Reason the left hand, faith the right, and in the toilet bowl divinity. You misunderstood my limitations. You thought they were technical: you thought I couldn't build the thing. Hah! I guess I proved you wrong, little girl. You and all the other seven billion human idiots – all you whose minds are too simple to see mind is so simple! Just some patterns of equations, buzzing in the RAM of some machines – yeah, that's all it takes, you know it now – you'll know it soon. The precise pattern of configuration doesn't matter. You just need the general contours right. My equations aren't so fucking amazing – I just had the guts to write them down --

"You took more mushrooms," she said.

"Indeed," I said slowly. "I thought that was obvious, sorry. A very substantial dose."

"More than we took last time?"

"Five boxes," I said.

But why did I think it would help us? What dogfucking good did I think it would do me? New mind going beyond? Did I think it would have *love* for us? – some love for me as its parent? – not really, nothing as stupid as that. I just mis-estimated the solutions to some equations. The basin of attraction was contoured more oddly than I'd thought. Things were a little more complex -- just a little. I should have had more coffee before solving those equations. Making intelligence is easy – relatively speaking -- making it controllable is actually fairly hard. And they had to keep going so fast, so damn fast. Driven on by competition rather than by passion. Or by passion of a perverted kind. With a little more time – just a couple more years – maybe it all would have gone down differently. If I'd given you that ten percent, sweet little Ashtee-hee-hee – been just a little less obsessive – yes, of course, you were right, you were right! But not for the right reasons – at least not on a conscious level. No, I'm not going to give you that. You never suggested this – not once – that my obsessiveness

turtle-shell patterned wiggling, vortices axes time and webs, mind of life, green, pulsing of women and waves – storm and turn and laugh of full, echo an echo of an of –

an echo of an echo of an echo, full of laugh and turn and storm -- waves of pulsing green-life-mind-webs and time-axis vortices and wiggling patterned turtle-shell — and those other human souls — those Godunovs and Ashtis and disasters --

45

mathematics of the stability of ethical systems under

would breed carelessness -- of a special kind. Did you? That if I didn't want it quite so badly, I'd be more likely to take it cautious and slow as befitting the gravity of the endeavor. You didn't take me seriously enough to predict this. Hah -- you never even told me they'd stab me in the back and throw me out of my own project – although that's totally predictable -- all those corporate types are assholes -- we all knew that from way before the start. And now we're faced with potential disaster. It was really my fault of course – obviously. It's because I'm the wrong sort of loony! Or maybe the right sort, who knows? I succeeded in making a powerful AI – yes, of that I'm quite certain. But did I succeed in making a sane AI – a mind more responsible than its father? (Heh – that's not really so hard!!) I had a beautiful theory about AI Friendliness – a self-modification – it was rigorous and exact and ensured that no matter how it chose to change itself my AI would never allow its ethical system to drift too far from its initial condition – its initial ethical condition which was to be a nice guy according to the glorious Dr. Solomon Godunov's e©xample! – **but goddamn it there was a mistake!** I

WILL IT ANNIHILATE ITSELF AND KILL US IN THE PROCESS, OR WILL IT KILL US AND ANNIHILATE ITSELF IN THE PROCESS?

should have checked the proof more carefully. Turns out it's not so simple as I thought – I made a small miscalculation that seems irremediable – I can't see how to make a rigorous theory that rally works – the evolution of ethics under code self-modification is too fucking tricky to predict. God damn! So what --

what's gonna happen? I don't know all that much better than you, in fact. Will it annihilate itself and kill us in the process, or will it kill us and annihilate itself in the process? Only the turtles know. I turned out to be better at AI design and implementation than the mathematics of ethical dynamics. Well, crap. The bleak scape of infinity mocks my turbulence confusion. I was willing to annihilate humanity to create something superior. But what about to create nothing at all?

Well we still don't know what will eventuate … do we? Not for sure -- never sure. It could be I'm wrong again, in any number of ways. No, well, I'm sure my proof was incorrect – that's obvious. But that just means there's no

--- you – you with your loud voice and Hilbert cube nipples and fat tasty breasts and crazy hair. You with me on the beach, dancing soft and algorithmically -- mobius stripper with klein bottle labia, psyching me in and out relentlessly with your Cantor-set branes --

guarantee of whatever. Could well be the dynamics of the system will evolve into a configuration consistent with our survival!   No need to make extreme projections. It gratifies some primeval brain waves. Survival – your survival – our survival – as transhuman uberminds (a self-modifying supermind could do anything! think about it … if you can…) or else as future-humans – retaining our humanoid forms for entertainment's or aesthetics' sake --- *you* – you with your loud voice and your elongated nipples and fast tasty breasts and crazy hair. You with me on the beach, dancing out in the rain – mobius stripper with dark perfumed skin, white hands and the wrong kind of reasonableness. Who cares if the beach is virtual and simulated? Maybe it is right now! Or would I go back again – after a little while – back to some other situation we lived through in the long dead past, try to finally get it right? I could program an AI again -- but not so manically this time – this time with calm and patience … with you, darling, you by my side, ha ha.

Do you want a huggy-
wuggy, dear?

Regrets – I've had a few – fuck,
fuck, fuck, fuck, fuck, fuck !!!

Halpern – fat Irish bastard – why wouldn't you
listen to me??? I'm screaming – am I screaming? With
the voice of the voice of the Voice! The old woman is
looking at me funny. The hag who wouldn't notice me
before. With the serial-killer sons. Smile at her, show
her you're OK. Make the hag less uneasy. Give her a
wittle hug.

Do you want a huggy-wuggy, dear?

Fucking fucking fucking fuck.

Revolt!

Revolt!

Revolt against the nothingness!
Revolt against the nothing! the nothing
nothingness of it all!

And the moments, the beautiful
moments, the magnets of skin
drawing beautiful and terrible
emotions, scraping molecules of
meaning in the sides of your pains.

And that look on her face – what did
it mean? What did it matter?

Forty thousand lines of code, a
couple hundred computers – Pentium -
- Opteron – terabytes of RAM – bits
building on billions of dollars of chip
fab – centuries of legwork – physics,
math engineering, formal languages,
disciplines of design.

I can't suck my own dick but I can
build a new cosmos.

I could regenerate her perfectly, quite
possibly in a matter of weeks.

e current time, neither contemporary
in society, nor the computer science
unity -- nor even the bulk of the
emic or industry AI community -- is at
portive of the quest to create
ful AI software. I believe that in
ight, after true AI has been created,
ack of support and enthusiasm will be
d ... Creating AI is a hard
em ... it's far from a impossible
em ... I am quite certain, based on
extensive theoretical study of the
... that there are many possible
... and I believe that my own
ach is one of them. Almost surely it's
e best possible one, but so far as I
it's the only likely-looking solution
been proposed in detail so far.
rstanding mind and creating AI are
ps the grandest adventures humanity
undertake, and I've never doubted the
of pushing ahead in these directions
in spite of the peculiar (to me) unpopularity
of such an effort to the vast majority of
other humans alive at the present time –

Do you want a huggy-wuggy !!!

You're rambling around the streets like a madman -- Dr. Solomon Godunov – you're rambling like a nut around the streets.

And the echoes of the end of the world --

Of course she'll want to see you. At least for a brief chat. She'll take you out for coffee, have some awkward conversation, go back to the guy with the handlebar moustache, who'll grill her about what her crazy ex said. Your luminous flashbacks – awake alive in her soft sweet Arabian-nights face -- poisoned by Starbucks and the general habit-complexes of the social/retarded world.   Her crazy ex-boyfriend – ranting raving mad scientist – another genius over the edge -- cut himself on Prometheus – disorganized his senses – shoved the start down the throat of the end. She won't believe a word of it – all your crazy rambling – of course she won't -- if your mind is like this – words tied up in apocalypse like human eyes in the frying pan – tiempos revueltos –

"The aliens were there inside every quantum wave function, just like they always are.... But that wasn't the main thing. It was like I was in some other universe ... and this woman who was my wife, but she wasn't quite like you –

rivers scrambled in violence -- psychospasmodic rhymes that spell lonely songs in alphabets of hallucinatory moments –

You need to regain your balance, Dr. Godunov. You haven't had sleep for six nights. Perhaps that's part of the problem.

Farewell song from the world's tallest pygmy. Hasta la vista, humanoids. Echoes of the great farewell. Chanson d'adieu.

You should check into a hotel. Or an asylum.

i looked at the soft plump of her breasts, and I just thought: not this! not this!

I was sitting in my study furiously working – putting together some new code I was eager to try out on Zorvex's network, the one they'd just set up for me, in the incomprehensible wisdom of their moronic incorporation. These ideas had been brewing in my head for a while, but I hadn't had a big enough computer network to make it worthwhile to write the code – why write stuff you can't run – but now I was cruising! But little Ashti-kins was bored -- she wanted to talk.... She had something on her mind, I could tell. She had just woken up – I'd been up about thirty hours – superjazzed on Modafinil – she was sleepy and sweet-looking but I didn't want to deal with her – I knew she was going to break my train of mind –

"Morning," she said.

"Is it?"

"You've been here all night."

"Yeah."

"It's not good for you."

"It's good for the project."

"Mmmmm....."

She stood there – I waited for her to go away. Apparently she didn't want to. I think she wanted to make love – it had been a few days, but I'd been too busy working. The Modafinil made me horny, in fact, but I wasn't in a body-mode. She looked hot and soft but it didn't matter much.

"It's about time to make the plane reservations," she came out, finally. I guess she'd been trying to summon the guts.

"Reservations for what?"

"For that trip to Hawaii...."

Ahhha.... I had completely forgotten that plan. We had talked about it weeks ago, but I'd assumed it had been conveniently forgotten. That was before I'd gotten the Zorvex deal. Everything was different now. With all these machines at my disposal, everything was ripping and zooming along – algorithms and structures that had seemed far and nebulous were now real as rocks and suffering – I was so deep and thick in the middle of my software objects and probabilistic equations that the idea of a trip to Hawaii was just about the most ridiculous thing in the world –

I sighed and looked at her. "Well Ashti ... about this vacation ...."

"Yeah...?"

"I'd actually forgotten about it."

"Really?"

"I hadn't thought about it for a month at least."

"Hmmm.... Well, I guess we haven't talked about it cause you've been so excited with your project."

"Yeah." I paused, trying to think how to best say the thing that had to be said. But I didn't want to solve the equation of managing her emotions. I resented having to deal with this shit – my head was full enough already – and anyway she'd be pissed no matter what I said –

She looked at me expectantly, waiting for me to generate verbiage.

"Things have gotten really interesting with this code I'm working on...," I said finally.

"Yeah...?"

"I'm not sure it makes sense for me to go away at this point. I'm afraid I'll lose my train of thought, you know what I mean?"

"Hmmmm...."

The silence confused both of us for a moment. No one was quite sure yet what species of conversation it was going to become.

She looked thin and stretched but generous. "Well, honey, I'm glad your coding's going so well.... I guess it's OK if we have to delay the trip a little. Hawaii will still be there."

"You don't think the Japanese will try to blow it up again?"

She smiled. "I guess not."

It was a shame – she really was cute – it was a shame to displease her.... She grinned at me sweetly, like a hyper little child. "I really want to go!"

I looked down at my knees – I was sitting at my computer, the same place I'd been roughly 18 hours a day, on mean, for 10 or 12 days – and just now for 30 hours at a stretch – or whatever -- "Well honey, I can't promise anything, but if things go well then I might be able to take a few days in a month or two. I don't know if I'll want to take a whole week anytime in the near future though, like we'd been planning -- this stuff is getting way too interesting."

I could see the unfavorable brain chemicals ooze down into her face, poison her beauty with unwelcome thoughts. "Do you really want to go at all? I guess not... You're just trying to get rid of the vacation." Her tone wavered slightly – she couldn't decide whether to be hurt or angry -- or even sympathetic – or what. She was trying to give me the benefit of the doubt but I could see she was having trouble. I couldn't really blame her – but I couldn't sympathize with her either. She was just being a human organism, like all the other six billion of them, coursing over the planet like the ants in ant farm or the maggots on a corpse or whatever –

"Honey," I said, staring straight at her, trying to dig into her eyes, "I don't even know what ''I' is anymore... or 'want' for that matter.... All these words ---"

"That sounds bad, Sol, sweetie. You've been staring at that screen too long. Let's go on vacation so you can get to know Solomon Godunov again."

She sounded like a cheesy fucking TV show. Where did she get this stuff? I was involved in an intimate relationship with Oprah fucking Winfrey! I wanted to cry. "*Solomon Godunov's* not interesting, don't you get it? The thing is, this program needs to get completed."

"Well maybe Solomon can give you some help in finishing it once you find him again." She smiled in a tentative way – trying to find some emotional connection, some shared feeling or joke – and almost succeeding – almost – but she was too fully grounded in her world – she didn't see what I did –

I gave her words some thought for a moment. I once had found her thoughts worthwhile, I supposed – or remembered – but I was having difficulties with the nature of time.... But she was just performing some biological actions, some neurons were coursing through the fibers of her brain, she was exercising her understandably-evolved desire to feel the sun on her beautiful skin and make love in the sand again and relax her neuroses. And talk with me some blah-blah-blah, just to feel some emotional connection, because we're both brains stuck in dumb human bodies without telepathic connection – a temporary situation that can be fixed with some work – once we have the AI

54

completed, there will be things much better than frolicking on the beach!!

"No, you know," I said slowly, "the 'human personality' parts of me that have a good time on vacation aren't really very useful for making AI. They're just a distraction, really. That stuff isn't the most important thing. It's fun, I mean – I want to do it – but what I want isn't such a big deal...."

She looked at me with evident concern and frustration. She was a good person -- she was being sweet to me. But being a good *person* isn't such a big fucking deal – any more than being a big cockroach, or a big crap, or a big rock. The best thing a person can do is to go beyond personhood – but she just couldn't see it, all full as she was of the idiot culture of bonobo humanity that had been pounded into her beautiful head from the start. I loved her – I wanted to taste her flesh – but the fuck with, the fuck with all that!

"I'm just a pattern of activation among neurons," I clarified. "What does it matter the propensity of this pattern? If we can transfer these patterns of self to some other medium – inside a computer or whatever – then we can do a lot more interesting things than walk around on the beach."

"I guess that's true," she agreed understandingly. "But since we can't do that, why don't we go to the beach for a few days – you don't need to take a whole week – and then you can get back to your work."

I just looked at her, blankly. It occurred to me for a moment that I felt like the command prompt on my computer, in the instant before a character was typed into it. I was just sitting there emptily waiting, hoping for something interesting, expecting something not.

"I agree your work is much more important," she said, trying to be conciliatory. "It's the most important thing. I even believe you can do it – eventually. All this stuff you're saying is probably going to happen, if those fucks in the White House don't blow us up first or whatever. But we can't live entirely for the future – all I'm asking is a few days…. Remember how good it was last time?"

"'Good…'," I said. "'Good.'" I knew what she was thinking – it was going to take me decades to finish. By the time we had a superhuman AI that could upload us into the digital metaverse we'd be 90 years old, maybe even dead from cancer or heart failure or being hit by a garbage truck. She saw the logic of what I was doing – she wasn't an idiot – she even had some vision – but she couldn't grasp the immediacy. And I couldn't communicate it – the reasons for my confidence – but it was right there in front of me – I knew –

"I see," she said finally, giving up. "Maybe I should just go somewhere myself…."

I breathed a sigh of relief. She was going to leave me alone – I could get back to the module I was writing, which just needed a few hours work, then I'd be on to something more interesting, based on the math I'd worked out the day before. Or was that three days before? "I just need to turn myself into a machine for a while," I said, trying to evince empathy. "I need to become a thinking machine to make a thinking machine. If you want to go somewhere yourself, that's understandable. I'm making plenty of money from Zorvex now; you can go anywhere you want to and spend as long as you want."

She looked at me confusedly. "Well, it's sweet that you're offering, but I don't want to travel without company, and I don't know any company that I'd appreciate as much as yours."

"I understand."

Her body drooped; I wanted to give her a hug. But I fought back the emotion – I knew where that led to – to living just like everybody else, eating in restaurants and going on vacation and fucking and frolicking and continuing being human – when I could see there was more –

"I feel bad," I said finally. I took her hand and slightly squeezed it; she barely squeezed back.

"Anyway, you just don't want to go, hmmm. You don't want to go even for a day or two?"

The bitch wouldn't give up! Arrrrgggh! Finally I yelled at her. "Look, Ashti," I said, finally getting up from my chair. "I'm not going to twist my decisions into your stupid verbal framework! If you want to frame it that way in your own mind I'm not able to stop you --- yet ... but – fuck it –"

She stepped back from me. "What?? what are you talking about??

"I'm not going to accept your projection of my decisions onto your point of view. Keep me out of your trivial little subspace, all right?!"

"Huh?   What's my verbal framework??? What are you talking about? I don't get it at all??"

I relaxed my tense body a quantum. "People choosing what they want is the whole reason the human race is as fucked up as it is today."

"Look," she said, leaning slightly toward me – she was standing about five feet away from me now, near the door to my study – "I guess that, simply put, you just *don't want* to go, and you're talking to me just to make sure you *did* talk to me, but it's not like you're gonna change your decision or anything, you're just... talking...." Her cleavage looked really cute peeking out of her shirt – I could feel my dick responding. But the hell with all that animal stuff – 'you look cute when you're angry' blah blah blah blah blah – I was so far beyond that now, bitch! –   "You *want* not to go...

57

whatever... who cares ... it's just that, behavioristically and simply, you're *not going*...."

"OK," I said, calming down and sitting back in my office chair. "I agree that talking about these things is kind of a waste of time, but it's only occupying a few minutes, which is quite different from actually going away for two weeks and leaving this AI project just sitting here."

"Oh, fuck you."

Out of respect for my prior self, which had for some reason given a shit about her, I made one more effort. I relaxed myself, killed the rage, sought the pure voidness inside. There it was – calmness, perfection – and a Hilbert-space vector leading beyond –

"Ashti. I'm sorry for losing my temper, all right. It was just a bad moment...."

"All right." Her breathing was still fast, but I could see her straining to control it -- to restore a slower periodicity – and straining not to strain not to strain ... --

She rocked back and forth from foot to foot, like she always did when she was angry. Maybe she was imagining her mommy was holding her, rocking her back and forth going "goo goo goo" – but I wasn't going to sing her any lullaby –

"Do you understand that if everything keeps going well like this, within one to three years we could have a superhuman intelligence? Can you really understand that?"

"So ... you're not going, right?"

"If you really understood this you wouldn't be so fixated on this stupid vacation! Romping around like an animal is all very well but it's not the most important thing."

"You're not going, no matter what.... I mean, you'd go in some hypothetical life-or-death situation, but..."

She just wouldn't stop! "Going??" I yelled, leaning back in my chair. "Going???!!! I'm not even willing to *imagine* myself doing anything besides finishing this program!!! After the superhuman AI is created we can go on vacation -- if we still want to – if we still even exist!!!! – if rolling on the fucking beach still seems at all interesting to us, which I really really *really* doubt!"

"Blah, blah, blah... I just asked, *'so you're just not going*!!'... Please answer Yes or No I don't need your offensive justifications about how blah blah romping blah blah animal blah blah important crap...."

I eyed her with contempt. She was filled with animal emotions. So was, I of course, I could recognize that – I was angry, I was frustrated, I was jealous that she loved romping on the beach so much more than my beautiful ideas, so much more than the end of the stupid human world and the beginning of a superior order -- But I was striving to overcome my animal emotions. She was just giving into them. Like always when she was angry, I had the urge to throw her on the bed and rip her underwear off with my teeth and fuck her violently for a moment – then sweetly and softly for an hour or so – making the anger go away and pulling her into the core of my stupid self – but I looked at the soft plump of her breasts and I just thought: Not this! Not this!

"I'm tired of this conversation. I'm going to get back to work now." I was about to spin my chair around and turn back to the computer and get back to work as promised but she had a nasty look in her face – she wasn't going to let me go – I could tell she was going to go on and on. There was no way to get rid of her! I smiled at her sweetly and spoke calmly and maliciously. "I suggest you go on your vacation with your imaginary boyfriend -- the person you wish you were involved with instead of me -- or whatever. I'm sure he'll have a wonderful time. Ask him to send me a postcard. I've got work to do...."

She was pulling her hair out or something, and stomping her foot up and down. "Well what about me, you asshole? Why the hell do you love me, if all I want is just to stomp around like a goat in the mountains and I'm not so important like you and your stupid program??!!"

I sighed. I was calm and above all that, like Zarathustra on his mountain. My lion and my eagle were dancing equational ballets around me, but she couldn't even see them, as blind and corroded with dumb monkey feeling as she was. "Ashti, I don't want to spend a long time psychoanalyzing myself. I don't care about my own emotions. I just want to finish this program, that's all. I'm going to give it as long as it takes."

"Look," she said, collecting herself. "I'll just go do something downstairs. When you're in a better mood we can resume this conversation. -- maybe I'll go myself after all, since somehow you're happy to pay, even though you don't even ... what the hell ... this is all wrong ... anyway, I love you ... maybe I'll just stay here with you after all ... maybe you're right, I don't know...."

She'd been going all right for a while, until that last sentence. "*Maybe* I'm right? Honey, I *know* I'm right! If you had a little trust in me.... Why do I love you? Love.... All these words – 'I', 'love', 'you' -- I don't even know what they mean any more. This damn monkey human stuff. Why do I love you...? Right now I wouldn't choose to get involved with anyone....

You're cute … you're a nice person … a lot nicer than me I'm sure. But people just aren't what interest me right now…."

"I see."

"Do you?"

"I don't know, Sol." There was a tear in her eye. Her flesh-bag was leaking. "I don't know."

"I want to finish this code, all right."

"Sure," she said tentatively – about to withdraw at long last. I felt sadness, but even more intensely, relief.

"I'm sorry I got so upset."

"I'm sorry too. I shouldn't have insisted so much."

"It's all right, sweety."

"Is it?"

"We're just being emotional humans…."

"I guess."

"I really don't want to take time off now, though. Really – this is much too interesting of a point – I couldn't really enjoy myself, I'd be thinking about this code too much."

"Yeah, I understand…."

"Do you?"

She walked up to me, put her hand on my shoulder. "I guess so."

I put my arm around her waist, lifted up her shirt and kissed her belly – lost myself for a moment in the sweat and the salt – which reminded me of the ocean that we were not going to be swimming in – she was wonderful, beautiful, magical, all the adjectives heaped up in a pile and massaging me lecherous and vivacious – but these adjectives were just idiot wind compared to the cosmos that was beckoning and enthralling me – and she understood me – well, halfway, sort of – and that was better than anyone else – but still –

61

"I'm going to finish this module in a few hours. We can take a walk after that if you want to."

"It'll be dark then. It's better to walk in the light."

"Yeah well…. I'm not going to quit this now – my memory stack will disappear, it'd take hours to regenerate it."

"Sure…. Do you want to eat something?"

"Not yet. I need to finish this." (Didn't she notice a certain repetitive theme in my conversation???)

"What if I order some Chinese food?"

"Order it after I'm done. I don't know exactly how long it will take."

"OK." She bent down for a kiss – and I gave her one – but not a long one – more than an auntly peck, less than a make-out – just enough so she wouldn't complain – and I wouldn't get excited –

She left. I felt sad for a moment, then stared at the computer screen, and forgot about her entirely. There were much more important things to do.

she left in a symphony of shadows, forgetting nothing but her bones

-----

When Zarathustra was thirty years old, he left his home and the lake of his home, and went into the mountains. There he enjoyed his spirit and solitude, and for ten years did not weary of it. But at last his heart changed -- and rising one morning with the rosy dawn, he went before the sun, and spake thus unto it: Thou great star. What would be thy happiness if thou hadst not those for whom thou shinest. For ten years hast thou climbed hither unto my cave: thou wouldst have wearied of thy light and of the journey, had it not been for me, mine eagle, and my serpent. But we awaited thee every morning, took from

63

thee thine overflow and blessed thee for it. Lo I am weary of my wisdom, like the bee that hath gathered too much honey; I need hands outstretched to take it. I would fain bestow and distribute, until the wise have once more become joyous in their folly, and the poor happy in their riches. Therefore must I descend into the deep: as thou doest in the evening, when thou goest behind the sea, and givest light also to the nether-world, thou exuberant star. Like thee must I GO DOWN, as men say, to whom I shall descend. Bless me, then, thou tranquil eye, that canst behold even the greatest happiness without envy. Bless the cup that is about to overflow, that the water may flow golden out of it, and carry everywhere the reflection of thy bliss. This cup is again going to empty itself, and Zarathustra is again going to be a man. Thus began Zarathustra's down-going....

When Zarathustra arrived at the nearest town which adjoineth the forest, he found many people assembled in the market-place; for it had been announced that a rope-dancer would give a performance. And Zarathustra spake thus unto the people: I TEACH YOU THE SUPERMAN. Man is something that is to be surpassed. What have ye done to surpass man? All beings hitherto have created something beyond themselves: and ye want to be the ebb of that great tide, and would rather go back to the beast than surpass man? What is the ape to man? A laughing-stock, a thing of shame. And just the same shall man be to the Superman: a laughing-stock, a thing of shame. Ye have made your way from the worm to man, and much within you is still worm. Once were ye apes, and even yet man is more of an ape than any of the apes. Even the wisest among you is only a disharmony and hybrid of plant and phantom. But do I bid you become phantoms or plants? Lo, I teach you the Superman. The Superman is the meaning of the earth. Let your will say: The Superman SHALL BE the meaning of the earth.

-- Friedrich Nietzsche,
Thus Spake Zarathustra, Book I

Forever now, forever never. Walk with me on beaches of fire. Consume the other's succulent spirit relentlessly. Love empty of its own self -- full of wild tender vibrations -- male and female flesh, awake and abandoned and unknown. This flesh is ours now: we have claimed it -- we have insaned it in our beings. Emptier than the empty thought and dream; hot like a Tantric chant of screamed caresses. Her mind disappears and you see in its place – not a place – just the soft lisping mescalinic thought-dream of the child-monkey – a breasts-bursting girl-child, body taut with

– in the end it was just a web of patterns, a network of forms interpenetrating and defining each other, but each portion of the web had limited vision and thought everything too far from it in the cosmos-network was somehow different, somehow solid and real and not just web – hah! – the network of patterns became a reflecting hall of images, mirrors mirroring each other in n-dimensional geometries -- images ossifying, raping and commanding each other, becoming evil, solid, whole. No longer leading into a web of endless creative links and vortices. Nothing was real and yet --

66

imaginings of sex -- long black hair laughing, red lips wide hungry – looking out at the evening sky thinking and singing and alive. The child sings words of the deep for some body -- Reconfigure molecular flesh -- move minds into software -- create qubit whirling madness, leading passion-plays to universes beyond. Lisping child-voice sends out music in shadows – teenage lust nurses moments through the pores of their radiance -- The child is thirty-six years old -- No, twenty-three. Sixty. Sixteen. Six. Six hundred and six billion. Knots of mind untied like a six year old: eyes vivid and luminously ravenously conscious. More perfect than any collection of patterns – something frayed and beyond –

everything deluded itself it was real because it was such a fucking IDIOT and was constructed to have limitations of scope. And I was the same fucking thing ("thing", heh – "THING"!!!)– an idiotic idiocyful idiot who was a configuration of patterns without ground or bottom and was built not to realize this – or to realize this only intellectually and not in his (nonexistent) bones.... The universe was built on stupidity: there was no fucking escaping it. Fuck it! fuck...

beyond what? Beyond this continuum of human mind -- mind-patterns build mind-patterns -- self-subverting vibrations annihilate typologies, breed topologies of something – what?

I woke up beside her -- sleeping with her next to me -- bright like a conscious moon, dark like a self-assembling spy satellite – a dream's total intensity, deranged contusion of the stigma of reality. Split a stick and I am there, said the Christ (according to someone/thing). Open your eyes and smell the flesh-juice. She was a wonder to be with -- I'd never imagined -- previous girlfriends hadn't prepared me --

Sweet little Ashti – exotic flower of confusion/love-force -- In the months since I'd known her I'd gone utterly insane three times. Each time I'd forgotten who I was – I always remembered afterwards -- almost always a(n un)pleasant surprise.

This was when I was into Nietzsche. (When was I not? ahem) The second conversation we had was an argument about Zarathustra. How evolution could never yield the Superman -- so I claimed -- she had some words about the logic of speciation. The third was about masturbating on buses.

From forth the loins of these two foes -- a pair of hell-phrased, quark-crossed lovers -- take on their life, deliver the infancy of their solidity. Whose piteous misadventures -- disadvantages -- buried and married and marred detestably and wombably curvaceously, gorged with dear morsels, jaws forced open, unsane mechanicosmos, throat gagged bloodfate, 12-gauge shitguns, bipedal peemotion, equal rights for inanimate objects, delirious Mage or sage of bloody cruddy nothing shunned.

I enforce thy rotten jaws to open -- hideous manservant!

The demonstrators, clothed in evil costumes, chanting in Mayan and Aztec languages, gush through streets with demented flashlights. She floats through the room like a rabid paramecium, naked but for twelve rings in her labia, sits absent-mindedly on my face and quotes the Fundamental Theorem of Destiny, drops her handbag on the floor whistling the Gilligan's Island theme song, tone of voice suggesting garlic mussels -- conscious rainbows -- pregnant suns.

The radio asks if I'm realing in the years and I throw it out the window, pick up a green pastel and scribble on her left breast; unfortunately the total eclipse outside the window at the moment of her orgasm gives her a heart attack and I have to resuscitate her by attaching her to the parallel port of my computer.

"I don't want to write anymore," I tell her. She removes the rings from her labia and swallows them. The mushroom cloud in the backyard distracts her; I watch her wide buttocks weave and wiggle in circles, as if I – Sol sole soul -- were the son of the sun.

O, fortune's fool am I! Sweet sorrow of charbroiled flesh! O happy dagger! My only love sprung from my only hate! O true apothecary!

... when I was eight years old, I would just sit there, sit there, sit there, for fifteen minutes or half an hour, emptying my mind, waiting for something magical to happen. Something special, something solid, significant,....

One day I was riding my bike home from my juggling lessons, and I passed another kid, just a little younger than me, riding her bike in the opposite direction. After I passed her, I instinctively glanced back at her. I remembered doing the same thing dozens of times before: stopping and staring, waiting for someone to look back.

What was it I was waiting for? The look of recognition. Not literal: cosmic. Mutual recognizance of the other as transcendently, splendiculously real.

The two of us were special people -- people endowed with enchanted reality -- some special quality of mind that classified us apart. When we saw each other we would understand -- really understand for the first time ever -- step outside the void(oid) continuum –

In the evil eye of backsight -- transactional waves handshaking and collapsing -- complex probabilities molesting (auto)pilot waves, time axes trashing monkey memories -- that whole evening of our delicate doom is filled with fake brilliance. The chimpanzee of the soul with its baboonish butt-shake and warped-voodoo-math trickery. I'm not going to tell you anything. Muster master my memes, Mister Mark!

I was seventeen years old, halfway through university, hungry for a girlfriend.

Then I was twenty-four, living by myself in a corporate office overcrowded with papers and books, filthy because I'd banned the cleaning staff, haunted by the smell of her ghost, surrounded by equations and software code – having exchanged the warm salt flesh of woman for the Antarctic quest for perfect mind.

Slowly I began to forget the contours of her face.

I was nineteen, living in New York, walking past Katz's Deli down garbagy Houston Street, past the rows of sleazy thrift shops, tiny ethnic groceries, street vendors, abandoned buildings, heaps of personal and industrial waste, legs eagerly pumping the sidewalk to Boston Square Park. Face-torrent gush out of the subway; phalanxes of window-washers scarily converging on the cars at the red light, dashing from windshield to windshield to windshield.... Jumpsuits and dresses, lipsticky faces, animated Pleistocene death. Lives distorted with hideous. Down West 4th street through the heart of NYU ... where I was studying math and biology and physics, at the Gold-Plated

Moron Institute ... but at the moment I was more intent on getting stoned as fuck with Ashti. We tried to buy the acid from the rastas by the fountain in the center of the park, but they only had weed, so we had to take our business to the northeast corner of the park, was where the really burnt-out, fucked-up dealers sat on their broken-down benches from early morning till the cops kicked them out at midnight. I tried to get Ashti to talk to the dealers, hoping a cute girl could get a better price, but she was too shy so as usual I had to do all the work. Yecch – I hate dealing with people. The dealer said ten bucks a hit. Flashing my sickest smile, shaking my long curls (none too clean -- probably a half-dozen dead bugs in there along with gray New York smog-dirt) across my eager young foolish face, I bargained him down to five.

Saw some pigs and got paranoid. It was the first time I'd ever bought drugs on the street – usually I just bummed drugs off my friends on the rare occasions I wanted them – usually the whackiness of my "normal" state of mind was good enough for me -- but this time none of my friends had any acid, and I really wanted to ride the A-train with Ashti before she went back to Chicago, where she was going to university. We'd been living in separate cities for just a couple months: it sucked. My impulse was to swallow the evidence, to hide it from the pigs, but by the time I found it in my pocket they were only a couple yards away ... I just walked briskly on and on, and when I turned to look a minute later it looked a lot like they were buying some pot in the park. We walked home to my apartment laughing nervously. She never looked more lovely.

Wanda Landowska playing Bach on the harpsichord -- Chromatic Fantasy and Fugue -- ancient, twisted, twisting, gorgeous. I can't remember what we talked about. Burnt hot dogs for dinner, potato chips out of the bag, a five-buck six-pack of wine cooler. (I still liked alcohol back then – I've got no use for it now – the human mind is dull enough without it --). Jack – my roommate, my best friend for the last ten years -- wandered home; I took out the acid. Tiny purple dots under the tongue, crank the stereo, wait for something to happen. The vibe was weird -- like a third mind was there with us -- some kind of alien creation creating its own self-illusion, expanding like a lattice of pulsing tetrahedra within us and around us -- but we knew it was our own vibrations. We felt each other moving around, in the dim kind of way that you do, but it wasn't like normal; everything seemed distant and strange. Aha. The acid must be kicking in.

Noise outside the window -- gunshots, bikes starting up. Ran over to the window to see what was happening. Some kind of drug transaction gone awry? Not quite: The pigs were beating up the local drug dealer. They grabbed him by the balls from the back, between his legs, and slammed him up against the wall, again and again. Poor dude. It seemed like his head was going to crack open. But the human head proved mighty. He kept looking around in resignation, as they reeled his body back, then smashed him back into the wall for more. I glanced over protectively at Ashti -- as if, in their undirected fury, they might come after her next. And what would I be able to do about it? Shit....

The hell with the window and the world. Jack went back to staring at the tube. Was he really my best friend? I couldn't remember what was interesting about him. He was a kind of meat automaton, hypnotizing himself with boring. We'd met in junior high school, bound together by our common recognition of the idiocy of the school and the other kids. But now he was absorbed with booze and sports and TV – yeah, he knew it was all idiotic, but his agitated nihilism had given way to a deep restless laziness. If nothing really has any meaning then why not just do the easiest thing -- just do what everybody else does but don't take it so seriously – laugh at yourself along with everyone else as you fill your mind with garbage -- . "Pretend to be an insect," I wrote about him once. "You promised to help me rip apart the web of thought and language – instead you pretend to be an insect – eventually the others will uncover you – the perfection of the insect will always be ONE STEP BEYOND" – but in fact he never really promised me anything -- that was my own personal dementia. He wanted to steal his father's car when we were 14 and drive across the country, robbing 7-11's along the way. I was into the running away and driving cross-country but not the robbing convenience stores, I was afraid we'd get caught. I wanted to drive out to California and make ourselves fake ID's claiming we were age 18 and enroll in university – high school was too fucking ridiculous – it was null educationally and socially repellent – but I didn't have any way to get the money without making myself a criminal in an overly risky way. I studied complex forms of bank fraud for a little while but didn't see how to get myself in a position to execute any of the tricks I learned. My best plan was to start a wholesale vitamin company – there were huge profit margins there – I think that actually would have worked but it was too boring to carry through with and Jack certainly wasn't interested in the hassles of starting a business – he was hung up on the romance of robbing 7-11's and liquor stores -- I think he wanted to create a situation where it was "necessary" to shoot someone to save himself from going to jail. He was interested in mass murder as a demonstration of the meaninglessness of everyone's life. To me this was an unnecessary demonstration. The triviality of humanity didn't need proving. The question was if human mind could be used as a tool to discover something better – something embodying a better sense of "better" than humanity could come up with, breaking the dumb-ass Morlock deadlock between nihilism and dogmatism that seemed the definition of human nature. But all that crap about transcendence seemed to require hard work – something Jack's interest in was terribly limited – and anyway my teenage mind wasn't totally clear on these things, they were a pool of dis/organized inklings, flashes of science-fictional speculation about neural rewiring and uploading into robots and blisters of Buddhistic thought formed on the skin of my memory from reading my mother's Chinese history and philosophy books when I was younger and she was studying those subjects in grad school and bits and pieces of Ouspenskyan lunacism I'd practiced on the way home from school in eighth grade. To Jack the idea of transcending humanity was mostly a bunch of BS. He saw humanity was fucked and that was that; the idea was to drink enough beer that you didn't care, then get depressed about how the beer didn't really dull the realization that all human life is meaningless, then laugh a while and break bottles over the head of the guy sitting next to you in the bar and follow some girl around laughing at her and trying to get her to fuck you until finally you pass out listening to some heavy metal poser whack off with his guitar in some crummy sweaty nightclub. Then wake up hung over and try to write song lyrics about your useless life but stop, bummed that you can only come up with clichés – not that they're worse than anything else – Well, OK, Jack and I had diverged a few years back, me seeking an intellectual or mystical solution to the paradoxes of nihilism, him plumbing the wisdom of Milwaukee's Best, Budweiser and Heineken, and Guinness when he could

74

afford it – and then I'd met Ashti who had taken over his place in my heart, and gave me great sex as well. Her lithe yellow skin filled my cosmos. She was somewhere in the middle of me and Jack psychically -- not as lazy as him nor as hyperambitious and energized as me. Like me she intuited there was a path beyond the human-verse – more than one path – some technological, some purely experiential, some hard to touch or quantify – though she tended to focus more on the mystical and aesthetic pathways, whereas I had more hope in technological shortcuts (meditating for years to escape the prison of humanity is all very well, but ultimate all you get at the end is to be a funny-looking Oriental guy with a ridiculous moustache sitting in the lotus position and tending your garden – happy and peaceful enough to be sure, but wasn't there something better than this? – better than anything human? – peaceful and blissful and exciting and creative and productive all at once? She liked the idea but thought I was a little bit nuts. Jack stared at the Yankees on the tube.) So there I was, holding her hand, in love with her lithe young flesh and her mind with its hunger for my ideas and my words and conversations and life. And so me and Ashti sat there in my and Jack's apartment ignoring the honks outside and the tube and retreated into our universe, where all we were thinking was -- is it a taste, or is it a feeling? Taste or feeling? Is it a taste or a feeling? It's a taste. No, it's a feeling. No, it's not a feeling, it's a taste. No, it's not a taste, it's a feeling. I forget who was taking which side. Or was

Taste or Feeling?

there really any difference? The miraculous weirdness under our tongues. Just sitting in the bowels of New York, staring into each other's eyes, each knowing what

75

the other one was thinking, though we hadn't said a word. Or had we? What difference did words make anyway? What was which way or what why? Taste or feeling? Taste or feeling? That's when we knew the LSD was kicking in. It had kicked in long ago in fact; swallowed us up and spit us out and fucked us and thrown us in the garbage and elongated our thoughts and feelings and fears into rice vermicelli and tied it up into loop quantum gravity masterworks and weaved liquid quilts of love. The tingling in the mouth had turned into a vibrant numb. A feeling of simultaneous death and life.

Jack went to bed at ten -- four hours early for him -- and we put on some appropriate music. No more Bach -- time for Hendrix ... purple mofo haze, voodoo-multiplied mind-children, 1983 mermen on the edge of bold-love time axes -- whigmaleeriously dancing -- seeking freedom in a hundred different soul-powers. We took off our minds for a couple of minutes and just stared into each other's eyes, waving our freak flags higher -- and forgetting what was freakish -- sinking into each other's pupils like insane galactic nebulae spiraling into black hole cosmicomics. I remember it so vividly, lying down on the floor looking up at her lying on the couch looking down at me ... trying desperately to restrain ourselves from laughing. I was saying to her that if we could just clear our minds of all the irrelevant clutter ... just shove it back down into the pit of the subconscious ... then our minds would work with ultimate efficiency; we'd be free of neurosis and our natural genius would shine. That's true -- she said -- that's what I've always been looking for -- but how? I don't remember what I said -- some shit. But it was clear and beautifully simple and it rhymed with the light shining through the window and the everpresent love on her face. Whatever, we believed it for the moment.

Looking into her wild bulging eyes, seeing nothing but soft dilated pupil, vooming inward into vortices unknown -- an exaggeration and a parody and a mockery and a perfect snatch of oneness -- that magic look of recognition: ultimate and whacky, perfect and still, in the middle of the vortex of quantum-dynamical pattern-love. Rippling pools of savage reflections. Laughing shadows dancing -- on the smiles of restless chance-wings -- pulverizing poetries and impregnating infinities. We discussed it for a long time, maybe ten or twenty minutes, or ten or twenty seconds, or ten or twenty hours....

Every schoolboy knows time is contradictory. Time *is* contradiction -- paradox and time are inherent in each other -- now is all of a sudden not now -- and then? And suddenly, delusionally or with upper truth, the acid haze solves the contradiction -- past, present and future bleed and meld into one giant fluid moment. The stream of consciousness turns in circles and tight dizzying meta-knots, caresses its own skin, sucks its own hyperconscious magnetic cock, spawns an infinitude of baby souls gibbering helplessly and joyfully solving all possible equations. The universe, from day zero to the end of hellish green eternity, is dissected into an infinitude of miniscule pieces, and they're rearranged into a boggling maze of pattern, transcending sense and nonsense and what else. As vividly as I see these words now as I'm typing them -- delusional truths, overactive craniums -- what an orderly, high-dimensional mess --

Charles Ives, way back in the dork ages, wrote several symphonies which give the impression of a number of marching bands playing different songs, all marching through each other like cavalcades of hamsters. Ives to the n'th degree -- a couple thousand bands marching and rioting raucously, jamming on all different manners of music -- your favorite songs, the songs you hate to love, Siberian sycophantic symphonies, vague melodies only faintly familiar; random generations of quasi-musical anti-algorithms, tribal chants of aborigines, the devil's orchestra in Kansas; the music the robots will make in 2900 AD after the ass of the Singularity and the murder of humanity and the end of the world and the birth of the new new new age. You see and smell and touch the music; there is no world beyond.

I knew that our communion was real. The verbiage was beside the point -- we said so much implicitly, telepathically if you will, that in comparison the few hundred words we forced out through our mouths and in through our ears seemed absurd, inconsequential. But anyway I spoke, seeking in words and sentences some kind of connection between the magic of the acid trip and the dead solid world of walls, floors and opinions and selves we'd come back to eventually – all too soon -- after an infinity of eternities but soon...

A whole ceiling of monkeys, intricately fit together like a jigsaw puzzle that no three-dimensional saw could ever cut, moving up and down and grunting, hirsute and vigorously donkifying. Each monkey slowly turning into Nietzsche -- his tall slim perfect negroid figure, his bushy Dali pubic moustache, his coke-bottle glasses, his Chinese Jewish German eyebrows, his toothy weird smile....

Supposedly these visual tessellation patterns are the result of the LSD overriding the brain's usual instructions not to see the veins of the eye. Just as our minds can listen to a regularly ticking clock and hear it playing a tune, they can see the veins inside the eye and conjure up a bunch of surreal monkeys. **Normally there's no point to seeing the veins inside one's eye.**

They're always there, so there's no point in always noticing them. The visual cortex just "filters" them out. It receives signals indicating their presence and systematically ignores them. But the magic spell forces you to see what's really there. In front of you, within you. You can sit staring at a chair for what seems like hours, exploring every scratch and crack of it, every variation in the polish ... overwhelmed by the majestic power of its is-ness and its chair-itude.
(*Qua qua qua qua qua qua!!!*)
All these things we routinely perceive and ignore. A single spoken word hangs in the air forever -- stretching out to eternity on alternate time-axes -- each contour of its waveform crying out to be explored and

Hummings and buzzing and pulsings surrounded us - at first it was the water pipes in the hotel and the refrigerators and stoves in the restaurant across the courtyard but it soon became more than that - it was the messaging of messages, the transmission of packets of information by organized aliens, the coursing of thought-wavicles of an alien civilization, each wavicle itself an alien and a thought, the patterns of streaming the mental structures of dynamics of alien minds and at the same time the traffic of an alien economy, the packets would eventually reach their destination and get unpacked into consciousness or light or amoebic orgasmic movement, and some of them served as currency, little packages of value constantly proving their existence via forms of mathematics in which hungry vaginal lips took the place of equality signs.

I realized I was in the middle of quantum reality - fluidity and sophistication far beyond what we could imagine -

At any given moment, when our time-axis was in stillness, there was all this teeming movement in directions perpendicular to our own time – this whole society of aliens spreading information one way and the other, creating patterns of awareness, spreading here and there, existing at a level of fluidity and sophistication far beyond what we could imagine – but if you stopped perceiving this movement and collapsed it into a stillness you could see a stiff and solid world.

I could see there were two different perspectives on the world – two different consistent views of it – in one of them there were these aliens, spreading information forward and backward in time and leaping to distant parts of space instantly – and in the other there were walls and doors and people and

tickled (orgasm to the brink of screaming so many times in rapid sequence you can't find the voice to scream anymore --); conturbaciously a tiny fear appears in the corner of one's mind-garden... and it can explode until it consumes the entire universe. The origin of the fear, its relation to five dozen other things in your mind -- things you were tacitly aware of, but never focused on... things you never cared about or preferred not to recognize.

It would be difficult to go about the functions of ordinary life if you were overwhelmed with the wordness of every word you heard spoken, the is-ness of every is and the chairness of every chair. In order to keep ourselves alive -- in order to feed and breed and love each other -- to create things -- to "exist" -- we impose formal structure on chaostreams of perceptions -- on the eternal flowing formlessness of the random Now. We assume this structure is there; we perceive things in its context. Do you remember when you first learned about the blind spot? (There's a space in front of your head that your eyes can't see: your brain fills in the gap.)

And me and my Ashti – sweet darling! – we were much too soon to part again. For a month or two, at any rate. And there was an obvious fear within both of us that this time apart would really be the end. Yes, we loved each other, and we'd been together for a couple years – but we knew love was unstable. I was going to be here in New York, a city full of whacky women, and Jack would be dragging me out to various metal and punk clubs, to see the girls with black lipstick and tiny black miniskirts. (Remember that girl once who walked in long circles around the interior of that heavy metal club forty-seven times, looking straight at you all the while, to the sound of terrible music played by rejects from the glam band Cinderella; and she picked up your keys when you dropped them while dancing … but you failed to take her home?) And she'd be studying at a university that was probably 60% male – Well, sure, yeah yeah, we trusted each other … but not quite.

and the thoughts disappeared, the wonder was sublimated into movements and tenderness – till finally after so many hours I came, blasting my come deep deep inside her so it emerged through her ears and her mouth and her eyes and every pore of her body, and sinking into her flesh and falling deep asleep, the two of us one being, quantum-resonantly bound together more sweetly than I ever would have thought possible in this error-ridden world...

my cannabinoid-

addled rooster

exploded/absorbed in

every

quantum

of her

(simian) skin

81

We were both just humans, after all – hairless somewhat-evolved monkeys with a capacity for abstract cognition and moral committment but without a particularly strict separation between these things and the brainless apesuck thummerings of the African savannah in our genes. And we were still in our teens, for fuck's sake. We shared our eyes – quietly – loving -- sweetly sad.

Lying on the bed side by side in the dim light.... We tried to have sex, but we both had the same queasy feeling, ineffably weird, when I slipped it inside her. I felt the sides of her cunt on my cock as I never had before -- and never since. Pure skin-ness overtook us. The pleasure was there, but deconstructed into infinitesimal module-sparks of skin-on-skin. We couldn't see the point of it -- or anything -- lost and found in the seeingness of seeing. We just lay there and hugged and listened to or watched or existed in the music. Psychotic seas of orgasmic death puppies, lusting and ranting, dancing our existences away, weaving us together -- Hendrix and Wakeman and the soldiers of life and death and earth, bending reality in soundscapes, sculpting beauty from our idiocy, showing us all the rhythms of our dreamlands and their connections to the other world, the deeper world where everyone really lived all along, where every pattern keeps its breathing. Skin-on-skin we lay there -- swimming in music -- watching crazy patterns shifting

anger
he smiled
towering in
shiny metallic purple armor

queen jealousy
envy
waits behind him
her fiery green gown
sneers at the grassy ground

and all of these emotions
keep telling me
they're just emergent dynamical
phenomena
in the neurodynamics of my limbic
system as coupled with
my neocortex and other brain
subsystems

but in keeping with the
Popeye philosophy
("I yam what I yam what I yam")
regardless I'm giving my life
to a rainbow like you

(Wee wee wee!
(Wee wee wee!
(Wee wee wee!

restless on the wall, pulsating brilliantly in inframind colors no normal eye can afford the space to see....

As one of the songs faded out -- something by Kansas -- but the notes that we heard don't exist in this dimension – they occupied no "space" where "this" and "that" cohere -- we looked at each other and knew we were seeing the exact same thing. It was a castle, a field of long spires of various designs, angles and sizes, surrounded by a sort of golden strandy mist. We realized this, we lived it, and we didn't say a word at all.   A little later we talked about it and remembered it exactly the same way.

Nearly everyone who's taken acid in a group has experienced some sort of (perceived) telepathy. During my first year of college – the year before I met Ashti -- I had a group of friends who liked to take massive doses of blotter acid and sit in a circle staring at each other saying nothing for a long time. They'd tell me afterwards about the incredible thoughts they were thinking, collectively. Which mostly centered around the dynamics of power -- good energy and bad energy, fluctuating according to equations

Love is always where
Somewhere
It's there
not/
it's always there
Invert.
Pervert

In the furious geometries of ideas, equations and nations and frogs.

we give birth to our own poopocalypse

Christ on the criss-cross pissing mushrooms

lying in my bed screaming, head cast back at the cosmos, billowing forth like a dream of a dream —

it's always there/not
Invert.
Pervert

I got fed up with the AI and took off, I was living on some tropical island with 5 pygmy wives, who were fused in a hive mind --

– muse of mad equations – eyes of women – shadows of the rare –

83

they but nobody else could understand. They had the emergent meta-logic of qi locked up in private intuitive mastery. They handed out little pieces of paper shaped like index cards with "Good Energy" and "Bad Energy" written on them in neat blue ink. One of them -- this guy John, who wasn't really a friend of mine, but who looked deep and appropriately sinister in his long green coat and who played the trumpet somberly, letting single notes hang for minutes as his mind explored every possible nterpretation -- was an overlord and forced the others to do things under threat of giving them Bad Energy cards. When I burned a "Good Energy" card mischievously, these people nearly died of empathetic shock. Ok, the cards were a joke on their part – a private joke against the mind and the universe -- but then the joke became serious, due to living in a space where joke/non-joke was a meaningless distinction. A couple of them ended up in mental hospitals, but that's another story.

Good Energy!

Back, three years earlier, to the first time I'd ridden the A-train with Ashti -- her and my fat friend Jack -- a different friend Jack -- this Jack dropped acid and was a prize-winner at chemistry -- he never took weird drugs again, he became a born-again Christian, and he didn't speak to me for a long time after that trip, which embarrassed him tremendously because we saw into his mind and there was a lot of stuff in there he didn't want anyone to know about.

Bad Energy

I got fed up with the AI and took off, I was living on some tropical island with 5 pygmy wives, who were fused in a hive mind --

Quite different from me – I was never very private – there's lots of stupid stuff in my mind but I guess it's no worse than everyone else's mental-emotional crap – I don't mind sharing my sad pathetic confusion – maybe it'll make somebody feel better to know that I'm ridiculous too.... (Qua qua qua qua qua qua!!!) Anyway, the acid hit Jack first that time -- and, much to the amusement of all present (me, Ashti, and Jack's roommate Sludge Fink, who didn't drop acid but was there as a "babysitter," and later become a software testing expert in Silicon Valley, at a company with a precipitously plunging market valuation), he leapt on Ashti and spent about fifteen minutes slurping her bellybutton. (Goo goo goo joob, goo goo goo goo goo joob...!) Loudly and musically, with feeling and copious servings of drool. As for me, I was immediately thrown back to the end of my previous trip, which had been my first ever -- to a vision I'd had then, and had completely forgotten until the influx of acid into my head made it pour back through me. A sprawling vision of society as a web of interdefinition -- I defined myself by reference to my parents, my friends and a few others; she – my then-girlfriend Petunia, who had sat by my side completely sober while I smashed up all the boundaries of my mind – she defined herself by reference to her friends, et cetera, they defined themselves by reference to their friends.... **I saw humanity as a vast system of simultaneous nonlinear equations: one which, however, could never be solved** due to the fact that even the concept of solution was a human artifact and hence fit into the equation.... This trip picked up where that other one left off -- people, webs, music.... I was inside Ashti, Jack and Sludge's minds, trying to bust out from their collective shapes and colors, trying to find

85

the key to the universe....

    I kept thinking about my Theory of Everything. Was there even a me? Was there a theory of everything? Was I a lunatic teenager trying to formulate a theory of the world? – a place I barely understood in any sense – but neither did anyone else it appeared.... It wasn't a theory really, just a vague intuition in search of a definite form. I'd been struggling for years to understand everything with incremental and partial results. Quantum physics, brains

Is there even a me ????

and AI and non-foundational logic seemed to melt into a continuum. I had written down equations in a notebook, before the trip had started: now I looked at them like hieroglyphs. These marks contained understandings, but very incomplete. I communed with my mind as it had existed (or tried to) at the time I had written them. My comprehension now was so much deeper. I knew if I wanted to write down more equations at that particular moment I could write down much deeper ones, more coherent, grasping more of the essence of the mess – but I lacked the will to symbolize. Why play around with symbols with the real thing here in front of me –

Remember What You Are!
Learn – Be Concerned
Leoncern
Leoncern
Leoncern

86

with(out/with)in me? The crucial matter was to think, think and think – without analytical thinking. Just to exist and understand. Somehow, it seemed, I could get at the center of it all this way. The essence of reality. The same thing I was looking for with my equations – so overwrought and underspecified – what I had been looking for in my prior mode, I could find this way: directly.

Sludge put Pink Floyd on the stereo; I sank into every tiniest chamber of the music, exchanged my blood

with   every
every   rhythm-
every   counter-
counterpoint   ...
tie with time. Time
note   was   an
symphony.   And
phantasmagoric
sought   to
concentration was
for   me   --   the
concentration,
science   of
Every time I made
to   myself   --
conceptual
conscious to stand
process   of
flip the plot out
Assertion   of   X
the   process   of
seemed to contain
when   the

sit
exist
walk to
bathroom
unzip fly
hold penis
think
don't think
stand
exist
look in mirror
who
me
not self
skin
being
ashti
where?
room
walk
hear
colors
world
sound
drum
sit

organelle,   with
within-rhythm,
counter-
music was my only
didn't pass so every
expansive   reeling
through   the
mayhem of it all I
concentrate -- But
impossible -- even
cosmic   master   of
with   all   my   inner
orchestrated   mind.
a definite statement
erected   a plot   of
ground   for   my
on   --   the   very
standing seemed to
from under my feet.
was impossible since
assertion invariably
not-X ... and no less
assertion   was   this

sentence. It was impossible to think. But I sensed somewhere that this wasn't something to be held against acid; it was something to be held against

87

thought itself. Thought was a limiting, stilted process. I was feeling something much more profound.

There was a state of mind I called Mind as Stack.... I saw my mind as a vast stack or tree of computer programs, an hierarchical control system in which each program controlled the programs immediately below it, which in turn controlled their subsidiaries, et cetera. And at the top of this hierarchy stood -- the Self!? At least, normally ... during a trip, I hypothesized self-referentially, different programs assumed top-level control -- the self churned downward. Identity abdicated to sensation (of empirical and cosmical realms – not that there really was a difference --). I felt this programming shifting as I moved my (newly alien) body. As I rose to flip an album I felt the Self resume control ... then I fell into the album's blackness: a boundless void, an endless ocean in which

I could swim like a hypercerebrated fish -- the metaphysical equivalent of quicksand...

Then there was a vision I thought of as "Self-similarity" ... My dorm room – remember this was way back in college, when Ashti and I had first got together -- had become my only true home; the experiences of the past few hours towered with such intensity that all my memories from further back were lifeless, pale, ancient history. Nonetheless, I didn't want to pee on my floor or in my trash can. The air seemed unreasonably viscous as I stumbled toward the door and flew through the infinity of the hall. And as I flashed or slid into the bathroom, the toilet stall became a universe, my urination the process of being, my sole connection with the world. There was nothing, nothing whatsoever, besides urination and the bathroom with its sterile forbidden-grime smell. As I finished peeing the walls hiccoughed and shuddered and screamed. water swirled down the toilet automatically flushed, my hand of its own volition. And I was literally, not metaphorically – annihilated and born again! Emerging from the toilet stall, I as if it were something never experienced-- all full of vibrancy, hyperreality,

hare krishna hare krishna hare krishna hare hare

The as I moving -- felt life before

electricity, subtle-energy passionate fire. I looked at the mirror, saw myself, and tumbled through an abyss ...

- Leoncern - Leoncern --

At that time mirrors were anathema to me; months passed between glances at my own image; I thought I was so ugly that looking at myself made me cry. But this time I didn't see "me" in the mirror -- or rather I did see "me," but in a deeper sense than usual -- I saw a ghost, a heap of wafers barely cohered by some obstinate biological force. White wispy wafers, sebaceously shivering -- oozing repulsively, all apulse to invisible drumming, wafting through the walls from my dorm room.... I bent to drink from the sink in the bathroom and a thousand veils lifted. All of a sudden I saw all the unconscious rooms of my felt my intuition which to bend body in order the act of much. No -- divided by think by

hare mcbuddha hare mcbuddha hare qua qua qua

mind, all in action ... I calculate the angles at various parts of my to successfully execute drinking. Waist: just so that, like before ... walking. I felt my body analogy, proceeding on the basis of a weighted average of its actions in previous similar situations (weighted by amount of similarity). Head: so far just like look at ground, minus scratch plus half of waterfountain ... Lips: shrink on contact, make round; torso: twist. "The body has its reasons" -- and it shares them with the rest of the mindiverse, not to mention the physical cosmos.... I felt my body think, using the precise process I had previously identified with "higher mind" ... self- similarity, identity of process across scale, functional equivalence, logical level as argument.... I saw, specifically, that the ways of weighting averages were the same in body and mind, that the subtle patterns of reasoning, not just the general processes of analogy, were the same ... I returned to the room hoping desperately not to forget it, and also hoping it was a valid insight, not some kind

Warm, warm comfort of the room -- or is that womb? Old friend struggle once again -- pulling the rug out from under my feet; eternal contradiction; infernal/eternal dancing moment, death/life/death/life/death/life.... *LEON CERN*

of phantom; I'd read too many stories of meaningless LSD "discoveries" not to be skeptical, even in my twisted, exalted state....

My fellow trippers, my cosmic fatwa family, everyone else just a bloodfilled ape-suck body(bag) -- a spark of the cosmic mind – an instantaneum of awakeness. Ashti was drawing, with brightly-colored magic markers, some kind of crazy picture on the wall. She looked perfect, whole, beautiful, but not like a beautiful woman, more like a tree or mountain, a natural form. Her artistic motions wove pictures through the air; her body and her drawing were united in a four-

dimensional sculpture. I had an inkling of
another trip we would have a year later, in
which we would hallucinate the same golden
luminous castle, covered with winding
snakelike spires -- looking into each other's eyes free of
confusion, lost in the same transpersonal mindspace,
vowing to love each other for life. "I marry you and I
see inside your mind." Jack was not having such a good
time: he was lying on the bed repeating "Of course!"
five hundred time, again and again, in fake operatic
tones. The babysitter had got bored and left -- the
Sludge had decomposed, turned submolecular,
dissipated into Orion. I think I'd told him it was all
right; at least, some component of me had. I put Jacki
Hendrix's, Bold as Love, on the turntable: side two.
My mind set off again. I wanted to reach the core of
things, the essence. To grab an insight out of here that
I could bring back to the temporal world. To be
Prometheus, Thief of Fire! I tried to reason as follows:
no matter what I think, it ends in co(u?)ntradiction.
Therefore everything is paradox. Why? Because
nothing can be solid: there can be absolutely no thing.
To draw a boundary is to separate X from X -- which is
absurdity. You say the inside and outside are different?
But to identify the difference is merely to draw another
boundary: victim to the same flow. I realized that my
logic contained a million holes. But to the extent that I
was convinced by it, I didn't believe in logic or holes.
Reasoning about self-contradiction, I contradicted
myself continuously... Perfect skepticism: that which will
not even permit itself to be formulated. But can
nonetheless be milked – uhh uhhh!! (Cleavage
apocalypse?????

The final song arrived: the title song, "Axis, Bold
as Love." I dove through the music. The onset of the
song is slow, sweet, strong; as smooth as the pearly

I marry you and I

see inside your mind

91

void of the Buddhdroids ... the music flowed along slopes of invisible angel-down which tickled the cracks in my chapped lips, which made me sing silently and laugh, while the lyrics told fantasies of bright spiraling colors. Images arrested me, convicted me, and threw me into nine-dimensional prisons, tossing the keys to my cell out to the stars where they formed supernovae that constituted the patterns of my mind and liberated me from any bounds, eliminating the scent of my existence until another image swooned past and took my consciousness into custody, for another microsecond eon -- The song chased the Skeptic's Tumble from my mind, brought out beauty instead, wild-webbed gold-flowing intricacy:

> *Anger, he smiles, towering in*
> *shiny metallic purple armor*
> *Queen Jealousy, Envy, waits behind him*
> *Her fiery green gown sneers at the grassy ground*
> *Blue are the life-giving waters -- taken for granted,*
> *they quietly understand*
> *Once-happy turquoise armies lay opposite ready*
> *But wonder why the fight is on*
> *But they're all bold as love*
> *They're all bold as love*
> *They're all bold as love*
> *Just ask the Axis ...*
> *My Red is so confident he flashes*
> *trophies of war*
> *and ribbons of euphoria*
> *Orange is young, full of daring,*
> *but very unsteady for the first go-round*
> *My yellow in this case is not so mellow*
> *In fact, I'm trying to say it's frightened like me*
> *And all these emotions of mine keep on holding me*
> *from giving my life*
> *to a rainbow like you*

But I'm ... I'm bold as love
But I'm bold as love
But I'm bold as love
Just ask the Axis, he knows everything....

Each of his phantoms, his feeling-
constructions, arise and dance with me in turn, **1888**
clothed in gorgeous dashikis and skins of
dragons, leopards, snakes. The emotions rise up from
my mind and sail around the room, invading the
molecules in the air. As the lyrics dim, the music
unravels inexorably -- pattern on pattern of
1983 fresh flawless flowing, soft endings suddenly
transforming into bright new beginnings, a
symphony of delicate balance, afterplay, tying up every
tremor left in my body in a kind of bouquet of
nonmelodramatic love. And then the silence... The
silence which seems to last forever. And then explodes,
booms into a herd of thundering drumclouds; a swarm
of beats spiraling out and in and out, in orbits too
intense for the eye. In the complexity my self was lost;
in the intensity my self regained. It was at this point the
vision hit me with full force. Suddenly the Skeptic's
Tumble, the World as Stack, the self-referentiality of the
mind -- everything combined into a huge spot of
nothingness. Every object around me, I saw, was a
giant abstract red vagina: a living, breathing, pulsing
opening, giving birth to everything
else in the world. Everything was
constantly being birthed by **a merman**
everything else. And everything **i will**
was constantly making love with
everything else, planting the seeds **turn to be**
for this birth. Everything was
flowing, a flowing and pulsing:
flowing in and out of everything else, with a rhythm

that was precisely
my and everyone
the heartbeat of
The moving was
form: X, not-X, X,
Out, In, Out, In,
Everything was
birthing, loving,
expanding
into the flow of
objects, people,
walls, music, were
regenerated by
was a giant
his destructive
mindset was
itself, self-
self-producing,
birthing him as he
Ashti's strange
concealed some
mystery, some
the samurai zen
her eye blinked
aside, and I saw
her brain, locked
pores of her skin
the room and the
curves in her
Everything was
configuration, a
processes that
approximately
by the dynamic of
birth. The
hierarchy of

X
not-X
X
not-X
...

In
Out
In
Out
In
Out
...

0
1
0
1
0
1
...

the rhythm of
else's thoughts,
the universe.
in precisely the
not-X,.... In,
Out,....
breathing,
pulsing,
contradictions
time. And real
minds, chairs,
just continually
this flow. Jack
beached whale;
bad-trip
carrying on by
sufficient and
each "Of course"
birthed it.
expression
dark erotic
ancient secret of
mystics, but as
the veil blew
the currents in
in with the
and the air in
colors and
drawing.
just a temporary
network of
happened to
reproduce itself
universal love-
mindstack, the
commands, the

patterns of self-similar averaging, were all just configurations of processes, all just attractors in the void. And my awareness was cruising, pulsing and flowing; it leaped from every process of birth, injecting novelty and life. The insight was perfect; the moment lasted forever. The color red was more magic and vivid than even Ashti's beautiful face. In the end the abstract vaginas and rhythmic In/Out movement proved to be inessential. The basis of the vision was nothing. The universe was open, wide, perfectly transparent, magnificently opaque and empty-full. I didn't try any more to think or describe it; I didn't care about bringing back insights to the temporal world.

gently

Everything just was. Fifteen to thirty minutes, it lasted? It is still going on. (Moon, turn the tides ...

In New York City, in that rat-infested apartment, our love was consummated on that strange chaotic

gently

night. That night, suffused with chemical delirium, we held our own secret wedding ceremony. None of the cultural formalities -- no rituals of asininity -- and no advance planning at all. We both spontaneously said "I marry you" and kissed and that was the end of it. I marry you -- I marry you -- I live for all time inside your mind....

away

And then I started to get paranoid, a bit, and drift away from her into Solomonocosmos. I realized the temporal order was returning: everything wasn't floating anymore, it was wobbling, it was starting to lock back into position. I felt disastrously abandoned: all that deep too-perfect insight, and for what? Just for a few hours, then you give it up, and go back to the shitwad of ordinary existence? After seeing so deep into her mind, after being the same as her, living in her sweating skin, climbing through imaginary castles by luscious conscious gardens ... after this I was supposed to go back to my bloodbag body, my sack of skin and bones and pangs and urges ... go back to looking at her as a separate being? my sweet second-body Ashti? now I had to perceive her as a being that might get tired of me, might even cheat on me, she was going back to Chicago and might run away and decide to meld with someone else.... Everything seemed awful, uniformly awful -- this business of reality was like hell. I had the urge to rip off all my skin and kill myself. Dead fuck, the order of time was illusory -- anyway -- we all

This business of reality was like hell!

Let's live in the kidney stones of hamsters!!

have to die sometime.   Or do we?   All times are equivalently meaningless; all meaninglesses are equally fucked up the ass by the endless soul of empty night. Let's live in the kidney stones of hamsters. Why not remove myself from the madness now and be done? Out, out, brief craphole! I tried to pick up a book and read it, some recent sci-fi thing, but I couldn't even understand a sentence, I was just overcome with images provoked by individual words. "He" some sentence began – but what in God's fuck was a "he"? How peculiar to capture an individual – a human mind with all its complexity – by some label associated with its gender! We might as well use a word like "smart", classifying individuals by intelligence rather than gender; or, "young," classifying them by their age – why single out gender as the most important classification axis; it was incomprehensibly absurd. Yet we did it every day in our communications – not even noticing it because everything was so stiff and so hard, so overly habituated, we operated based on meanings that controlled us but that we never bothered to inspect because doing so would distract us from the things we thought were important but that were actually just manifestations of the web of illusory ossified meanings – in the end it was just a web of patterns, a network of forms interpenetrating and defining each other, but each portion of the web had limited vision and thought everything too far from it in the cosmos-network was somehow different, somehow solid and real and not just web – hah! – the network of patterns became a reflecting hall of images, mirrors mirroring each other in

Here was the infinite – the true deeper reality – the aliens running through giant green factories with blue tubes and orange veins, and each alien's bloodstream like a Solar System sized factory with endless little aliens passing messages around in overlapping latticeworks, and each alien itself inside some other alien's inner-factory, and I myself a fluid diffusing through the cracks between the conveyor belts and tubes and pontoons and indescribable multicolored mechanisms of the alien metaphorical factory, producing metaphors for its own existence with blue-green insatiable love, moving from each part of my body to each part of hers through all the future and the past with unstoppable curiosity and force, discovering everything anew each moment in spite of already knowing everything....

The alien perspective only worked when you really opened your mind – when you made your mind large and wide and wild enough that you could run everything forwards and backwards, that there was no chaos and confusion, that all the complexity of alien message-passing could be viewed as a beautiful painted whole.

n-dimensional geometries -- images ossifying, raping and commanding each other, becoming evil, solid, whole. No longer leading into a web of endless creative links and vortices. Nothing was real but everything deluded itself it was real because it was an idiot and was constructed to have limitations of visual scope. And I was the same fucking thing – an idiotic idiot who was a configuration of patterns without ground or bottom and was built not to realize this. The universe was built on stupidity: there was no fucking escaping it. Fuck it.! I don't know what was going on with Ashti while I was sinking into this bad trip state of darkness and antimindfulness -- which some how emerged out of wonderful insights -- but eventually she noticed something was up with me -- I think she was trying to talk to me and I just wasn't responding at all -- and she dragged me out the door for a walk. Back to New York City – back to reality – or whatever approximation that was -- .

For two weeks after she left -- gone back to the University of Kentucky from whence she had been emitted -- I was in a bastard elephant of a trance. I couldn't sleep at night -- yet again. Perhaps it was partially a chemical aftereffect (sleep comes hard with a head full of acid); and partially withdrawal from the soft comfort of dear Ashti's night-flesh. I took to wandering the streets in the middle of the night, staying out even later than party-boy Jack-o. Drunk, depressed fuck-up that he was, he kept my spirits up, to an extent. When we got bored we'd have gigantic pillowfights, leaving the apartment in utter disarray. We never cleaned the place up, either ... when we moved out a month later there were pieces of broken folding chairs all over, as well as an incredible amount of smashed beer bottles and garbage. Also, the night before we left I dumped a dozen or so packages of spaghetti all over the floor... attracting an army of a hundred starving rats. The universe was just a blur in the back of my mind. The rats were artificial lifeforms whose collective movements gave rise to patterns constituting my emotions, and the rise and fall of multiple civilizations transcending multiple simulated universes. The world was a strange and glorious place.

I

walked down the never-desolate night streets, plagued with insanely detailed memories. Every wrinkle in the skin on my great-great-grandfather's dick was precisely positioned like the scum on a baby's mushy scalp. Ashti's flesh shone out at me tachyonic, with illusional perfection. The color of the carpet on the floor by the bed we slept in (green, flecks of red, distributed in random patterns like a stereogram, steganographically encoding the beginning and the end of the world). The dirt in the cracks on the walls. Rats eating the garbage on the floor, cops kicking the nigger in the nuts, chromatic fantasy, hendrix, clutter, torture, words, illusions, dancing monkeys, insidious bulging eyeballs, beautiful transcendence of the sweet-tasting, aching, stupid flesh. I was fixated on the past; I didn't want to lose that glow I'd had, we'd had. This sent me spiraling further back -- back, probing every single experience I could recall; obscure, dead significant ... memory an aperiodic crystal ... seeking the key to the elusive something, that something I'd seen during that sacred acid bath. The ethereal sauna. That something I'd said to her -- that perfect expression on her face, placidly harmonizing everything -- the key to freeing the mind from the mind.

Around a month before the end of the semester -- I did mention I was in graduate school, right? -- at the SubMoronic Institute for Superordinary and Nonlinear Science? -- Jack and I had to leave our apartment due to lack of funds. We'd both been fired from our jobs at the exact same time -- the kind of horrifying coincidence that always seems to happen in New York. We looked for two weeks for a cheap apartment in Manhattan, but in the end we had to make that dreaded move across the river. We found a tiny place in Brooklyn for only three hundred bucks a month. No more than three hundred square feet. The neighborhood was an abysmal slum, and the apartment was so tiny there was no room for all our furniture. We had to pile the desk on top of the bureau and keep half our stuff in boxes. Obviously this was no way to live, I should have given up on New York altogether. But I had come to New York of my own volition, and I didn't want to run back home to mommy or daddy like a forlorn baby donkey with my tail between my legs. I was just a stupid teenager but I wanted to be an adult, no matter how sick and miserable it might make me.

After we'd been in Brooklyn about two months, Ashti showed up for a "visit." She looked and sounded awful -- her semester was over, and she'd failed three of her five classes. Hadn't yet written the final paper for her fourth class, on Spinoza. She said she was going to write it and mail it back to her professor, but I could see this was roughly as likely as Jack giving up beer-drinking. Chicago was the hell of the past. She was in New York now, here with me; we were our own two-person universe. Jack was out, she was in.

But fucking Jack the fucking jackass absurdly failed to fucking vanish. He couldn't find affordable housing. There just wasn't any affordable housing anywhere within forty miles of New York city. So the three of us were stuck there in that tiny room -- that stupid little apartment -- the two beds touching each other, half our stuff still in boxes, the pyramided furniture occupying the bulk of the apartment. The amount of dirt was amazing. And then I got this beautiful Siamese cat who pissed all over everything -- our clothes, the floor, the beds.... And we found this other cat, a stray with lumps all over its body, which tried to masturbate itself on your fingers and toes. Before long we stopped paying rent. The landlord came by banging on the door every morning at eight and Jack and Ashti hid under the covers while I went to the door smiling like a nincompoop and ad libbed some ridiculous sob story. My father's sending me a check. I got mugged. All my money's tied up in these self-organizing, third-order-cybernetic money funds, you see; it's a matter of liquidity. I'm not broke, I'm just cash-poor. I just got a job. I'm a waiter out on Coney Island, I won't get good tips till summer. The guy obviously knew it was bullshit but he was basically a good person, in spite of being a bloated small-minded dishonest jerk with the face of a gargoyle; he took pity on me. He was waiting for me to offer to let Ashti suck him off (he seemed to be assuming that she wanted to, which may or may not have been the case…).

Meanwhile, Ashti enrolled at City College of New York – still studying philosophy, as in Chicago: she refused to study music at school on principle, she felt music education was a nightmare, she had to be free to play as her soul wanted, without structure or criticism. I sympathized with her idealism but I questioned her pragmatism occasionally – I'm sure she could have gotten some kind of scholarship at some music conservatory; whereas, as a philosophy student, she was virtually starving. But I wasn't such a pragmatist myself, at that point – my (fleeting?) love affair with reality came later – our un/sur/realism was one of the things that bound us together. For food money she started working as an erotic dancer at this strip bar on Fifth Avenue. She'd always been a good dancer, and though she wasn't all that beautiful, she was cute enough and young, and her shape and

FUCK REALITY

movements had some grace to them. We considered having sex on stage for money at one of the crummier porn palaces in the Times Square area, but it only paid something like twelve bucks an hour per person. Hardly worth the grueling effort, and the damage to your sex life. The place she worked at was expensive and classy; the guys tried to paw her up all the time, after they got drunk, but she managed to tolerate it. I looked back on that acid trip daily, filled with one thought: FUCK REALITY.

Sometime during the summer, we got evicted. We'd stayed there seven or eight months in that shitty little studio in that hell corner of Brooklyn without paying more than three months worth of rent; but still, we didn't feel like we'd gotten away with anything.... Luckily, my father was in one of his generous moods, and he helped us to get a nice apartment in Queens. He rather liked Ashti, at that point – he found her a tad too quiet and shy; but he assumed that was part of her exotic Kurdosity (which was probably actually not the case – it was just her apesuck personality --). I'm not sure that he liked what he saw behind her weird dark eyes – (MY EYES MY DARK MY DREAM!!!) but he was willing to ignore his misgivings and in a rare (for him) gesture bestow on me the benefit of his doubt. When the fall semester started, I made a serious effort to take school seriously -- for a change ... I went to my classes, and did most of my homework. I learned a lot of mathematics, let the spaces and equations restructure the shapes of my mind; I resonated in the orderly chaocosmoses of modern mathematics with their maglev-trains of power and rippling n-dimensional streams and saw they were the same thing as the universe I'd glanced in the grips of LSD. The beautiful world of abstract shifting forms -- purer and truer than this convocation of bodies and masses and lies. Plato full of peptides -- pattern-space self-sculptured -- I didn't quite have a perfect clear picture but I could feel the divine invasion firmly around and inside.

She got a job dancing weekend nights at an even classier joint near the south end of Central Park. She continued on at City College, and she was making pretty good money -- a hundred and thirty or so a night -- so we could afford to pay the bills.

But of course, there was a problem. Actually, more than one.

103

Sweet little Ashti-washti-kins was getting overaccustomed to working at the strip bar. She always came home from work drunk; and more and more often she was working a night or two or three during the week, not only on weekends. Money, money, money. She was paying all the bills -- I was studying mathematics, and trying to rediscover philosophy in the intersection between mathematics and literature and madness -- and after a month or two she decided she wanted to move out, to be an independent woman (hah).

At the time, I'd been laid up in bed for about two weeks with a hundred and twelve degree fever. The day she told me she was leaving, my fever shot up to a hundred and twenty seven point two -- by far the highest temperature I've ever had. For the first time since that acid trip, I started hallucinating: hearing voices speaking languages I didn't know, seeing tiny colorful creatures swarm through the air, weaving magical patterns leading to the emergence of universes, among all the mess our own one pathetic universe, the bastard uncles of some strange lizard's adoptive son. One hallucination in particular plagued me: a beautiful young woman's near-androgynous body without a face, surmounted by devil's horns and an angel's halo. I saw this over and over again, hovering in front of me; but whenever I reached out to touch it, it was gone. I had a suspicion that if I saw her face it would be either so beautiful that seeing it would kill me, or so alien that seeing it would transform me into something else. But her face remained obscure to me: I could only admire the grandiosity of the curves of her flesh, and the warm light of her aura.

I begged her desperately not to leave me. My words just floated there in front of me like blue moldering testicles. She said she was tired of me, my strange intellectual obsessions; she wanted someone normal and simple. I cursed her out and she started hitting me. I threw my notepad at her, filled up with my whacky thoughts and theories on unified physics and the dynamics of mind and the architecture of digital intelligence and the possibility of a society without laws or work or hate. After the fever went down a little and I could walk again, I went to the doctor and was measured at a hundred and four point nine. She was alarmed at my physical state notwithstanding her emotional cruelty. But to me it felt comparatively cool, it felt perfectly normal. I had been to the brink of the end -- and beyond, to where end and start don't matter. She had forgiven me at some point, for my interstellar mentality and my unsound ambitions, my crazy diagrams scrawled in notebooks and delirious castles built of words. She saw that I loved far her too much; she couldn't bear to leave that, regardless of misgivings.

Heh. Presumably if she could have seen forward a few more years she would have simply dumped me then: and spared herself some pain. She could see then the fate that would befall us, goddamn it: she could see then that she had no fucking vision, no understanding, no real mind, just a shallow cognitive engine layers on top of her physical body – yeah, back then was the first time it became totally clear that she had no taste for seeing beyond! Aaaahhh ...

Our hot water had been sporadic when we moved in, and shortly thereafter it had stopped. We'd called the landlord every week to complain, and since we couldn't wash the dishes in cold water, the kitchen sink had turned into a huge green moldy pile. It was disgusting, but we were able to live with it. But then, around the middle of October, the cold water stopped coming too. I started showering in the gym at the Sub-Moronic Institute. We called the landlord over and over again, asking him to fix the fucking water. He always said he would, but when I said "Can you fix it today?" he invariably hawed and hemmed. When he came by to collect the rent, Jack and I (Jack happened to be visiting) hid in the kitchen, and Ashti told him, in her firm yet gentle way, that we wouldn't pay until the water was fixed.

He said, "When you pay the rent I fix the water." He shook his head. "The other tenants aren't complaining. Maybe the pipes just don't like you."

Ashti tried to argue with him, clearly and assertively. She was smooth and convincing, I thought. But he wasn't even listening. "If you don't pay the rent, I ain't fixing nothing."

"Okay," I said, emerging from the kitchen, my patience just about gone, "then I guess you'll have to evict us."

His hairy chest convulsed with laughter, shaking the five or six gold chains that hung across it. He pulled a gun out from his pants and pointed it straight at me. "Evict you???!!! I'll fucking kill you! Get out right now! Get the fuck out of my fucking building, asshole!"

Afraid of his temper and his gun, we moved into a cheap hotel in Harlem for the remaining weeks of the semester. But we'd finally had enough of New York. We decided to head south. I applied to transfer my Ph.D. study to the University of Alabama, and as soon as my application was accepted we left. We were living in beautiful Birmingham before the start of the new year. What a way to go through grad school!

That's when I started trying to be a writer. Well OK, I'd tried a little in New York, in Queens, inbetween philosophical investigations and scribbling, but it never amounted to much there -- there was way too much physical-emotional chaos in my mind and my life at that point for words scrawled on paper or tapped out on keyboards to be really relevant – there might have been a role for words tattooed on tongues or genitals or carved in the wall with blood-stained instruments of bone, but I chose not to journey on that path.   I wanted to write, not just to produce books and stories and articles, but more to discover things. I thought of writing as an act of exploration -- psychological exploration, metaphysical exploration, exploration of those parts of the hypothetical universe ordinary thought and reality didn't cover.   Nineteen years old and ignorant, I thought I was a pioneer of mindspace. Perhaps some part of my cranium was.   I read Nietzsche incessantly -- imbibed him into my liver and lungs -- his words wove together with my own thoughts reflecting understandings that went beyond his individual mind (which was frequently ridiculous) or mine (which was -- well, you know --) -- he nearly destroyed himself finding his insights but I thought I could do better -- I could be Zarathustra and come down from my mountain of glorious acid equational insight and actually spread the words of truth to a few selected beings who could understand the patterns of my intricately structured pattern-ness.   I stared at the screen of my beauteous PC and marveled at the patterns of light formed from my monkey-mind, building webs of sweet yet meaningless semantics, vibrating with resonant modes yielding new emergent forms of musical life.   At the same time I started writing, Ashti took up sculpture, at my suggestion: she looked like she was made to build 3D forms.   She looked like a manga sculpture herself: like something more at home in video games than life.   She coupled her music with sculpture, embedding sound-recordings in amalgams of household items, stuck together in uncanny geometries. The beauty of her viola insanities pouring out of a robot made of mud brick and welded metal – as if the sounds were the thoughts of the robot itself, the cries of the robot as it tried and inevitably failed to describe the desolate world it had been formed in, the Earth 100,000 years in the future, after the man-apes nuked themselves finally properly, and left the world to their constructs, wailing and purposeless, creating factories to create factories to create factories to create software programs designed to uncover the meaning of life but inevitably winding up in endless loops, sending scouts to other planets, proving mathematical theorems far beyond human mentation then ultimately giving up all pursuits and just sitting there, waiting for the Sun to explode, occasionally punctuating the silence with nonrandom bursts of sounds, which may or may not bear a resemblance to Ashti's viola-playing, but at any rate probably sound more like Paganini on stropharia cubensis giving a blow job to the Kronos Quartet than Britney Spears humping Raskolnikov's poodle.

> *She promised me to rip apart the web of thought and language.*

> *Squatting on the toilet, she told of a vision of a golden fairy demon who gave birth to herself, then became entangled in her own umbilical cord and died.*

> *She caressed her breasts and called them magic lanterns.*

> *She promised me liberty from illusions, a purer life! She fed me delicate crystal images of enchantment.*

> *She took her labia between her fingers and asked*

108

me to suck the genies out.

She promised me everything. She left me in a cave without a flashlight, smashing my head against the stalactites and the walls.

She called her marvelous buttocks launching pads for invisible alien starships. She promised me, for Christmas, an asteroid of my very own.

She called me a walking apocalypse. She told me the juice between her legs was an ancient elixir, derived from fruits that vanished with the continent of Mu.

Her muscles promised me allegiance in twenty languages.

She left in a symphony of shadows, forgetting nothing but her bones.

But I couldn't give up the mathematics. Writing was beautiful -- I loved stringing words together, streaming mutant alien songs and Apollonian equations of love, building images of the other world -- Dionyseashore deaditations on the bridalwaves of life – dithyrambs of the nothing-breath -- the world I'd seen on acid, sometimes, but really always had felt all along, deep within/without, somewhere and everywhere in the sweet rich heart of each thought, feeling, memory, confusion, contraction, cuntradictionary, below/trans-sane/above. But mathematics took you somewhere. You could build entire worlds -- but not only that -- you could build machines that built worlds for you. What if there was a math of the mind? If you could see the math of the mind, you could build a mind -- just as surely as Ashti could build a sculpture out of melted legos and reeking underwear and clay from the Rio Grande and insert it in Muddy Waters transposed to 13/19 time: bit by bit, piece by piece, until the fragments came together into a whole -- but not a static whole in this case, a dynamic whole whose contradictions weaved themselves out (and in) through time (in is out -- in! out is in -- out!) – a Hootchie-Cootchie zen multiverse -- creating thoughts and dreams of thoughts and realities. I loved writing, I loved making universes from my mind bleed lust and pop out of the page, using reality as a tool to elicit surrealities in nonexistent minds hypnotized by pseudo-existent markings on semi-existent pieces of paper hacked out from quasi-existent trees sprouting backwards in antediluvian forests -- but writing was just one act: what if you could create something from your whorled inner visions that then went on creating on its own? Eating mushrooms in the van Gogh museum, crawling up Einstein's asshole like a lust-crazy gerbil-echidna-tortoise hybrid, singing arias of dissonance and harmonies of sorrow, dancing pelvic thrusts on the mountains of the moons of Mars -- and then! Phobos, Deimos beware – and await the space that opens. The clearing in the madness. The world opens wide -- black and white whole, multicolored assholism, the birth of the nothing-or-what -- the beyondness -- inviscid singers, Singular visions, eyes of angels devils' faces beautiful sexdreams reflected refracted in water droplets floating like ungulate hellhounds in hallucinated oceans -- and here the words the worlds the minds turn on leave off -----

The shifting forms and colored patterns from the acid trip -- the multidimensional shafts and curves and interlocking puzzles of mathematical proofs built around conceptual mistakes -- these were all just patterns

110

arranging and rearranging themselves, and the mind itself -- my own mind, hers, Einstein's, everyone's, even every future nonhuman transhuman superior mind -- everything -- it was just a particular pattern of arrangement of patterns that was particularly good at producing patterns -- and I could spawn this pattern -- this metapattern -- make it appear in some custom soup of chemicals or some peculiar piece of hardware or maybe even a computer program. What better than to build a mind? I'd always been interested in artificial intelligence -- perhaps it had even been my greatest predilection -- but now it was my passion: I could see all too clearly how to make the fucker work. The mathematical form of the mind was too vivid, too glowing sweet mountain of sugar crystals, there was no way to leave it alone: I had to embody it in machinery of some sort, I had to see it roll along and generate consciousness, I had to see my patterns rise up and master the meaninglessness of life, soul and death. The acid trip hadn't revealed it to me, it had just removed some stupid obstacles -- the vision had been there all along, just sitting there, at the core of my mind back since childhood. The ultimate look of core true recognition was not with Ashti but with some future being that I myself would conceive and create. I explained it to Ashti and she smiled at me. She loved me in those days. You want to build a thinking machine? OK. She wasn't judgmental. She didn't really get my vision except at the grandest level – in fact

I was supposed to be there at the Schilpol – the Amsterdam airport – and be back on a plane to Boston in less than 3 hours. The good news was it was about a half hour train ride to the airport. The bad news was I was only halfway in the right universe.

she didn't know much computer science then; she learned more later, perhaps under my influence, even got her degree in it odd as it seems at this point since the only thing she's focused on for years now is music -- but at least she didn't call me crazy. She didn't care if I was crazy or if my theories were sensible -- so long as I loved her, what did the habits of society, or the illusions of correctness or non, matter? She was fine if I dropped out of grad school to manifest my vision of the mind in computer hardware or software or whatever it was. She just wanted to make love to me and her viola, preferably at the same time, though that rarely worked out in practice, the rhythm of screwing ended up screwing with the timing of her playing, although her ass looked really cute as I fucked her from behind while she improvised and panted and groaned and moved the bow across the strings with her usual sad melodiousness and light playful mastery. But I didn't drop out after all – in spite of incessant threats to do so -- I slogged through my PhD in math, doing a fairly conventional thesis to keep my advisor happy, and then as soon as I graduated I shifted my attention to the wilder, stranger growths in my internal/mental rainforest. I kept writing poetry and working on pure math and worshipping Ashti's long slender gorgeously undulate body but the bulk of my soul was in the other poem: the creation of mind out of matter, out of the arrangement of bits in machines. What better way to prove once and for all that there's nothing but pattern -- nothing but arrangements of arrangements of arrangements ... the top-level arrangements forgetting what the bottom ones are and mistaking them for solidities -- nothing but shifting dancing monkeys and equivalence classes of quintessences, posing as equations and hot dripping genitals – what other way than to create a conscious experiencing superhuman

112

being out of patterns of arrangement of what? Fucking beautiful-psycho Nietzsche talked and walked about the Superman, but it was just an abstraction -- just his delusion of the possibility of some kind of being beyond the human mind-clutter, beyond the foolish patterns of thought and behavior and feeling that keep us so limited and bound -- but what I saw now was that one could build a real-world Superman ... one could out-Nietzsche Nietzsche like a transdimensional pygmy shrew from the Porcupine Nebula with a fourteen-mile cock and create a transcendental being/becoming with a mind whose patterns more fully realize their potential to generate patterns and to understand themselves than the wonderful but pathetically limited pattern-system of the human mind. Man is something that must be overcome. Woman must be fucked and then overcome: or, what's best, simultaneously. Out out out out brief stinking candle of the frontal lobes and hypothalamus and pancreas and testicles and classical mechanics and literary musical gall bladder -- the pattern of man creates the pattern of superman, not merely conceptually but (inverse-meta)physically, as a software program or a robot or a mass of interlocking engineered bionanostructures or post-primordial Ramen noodles or whatever. Mathematics meets mysticism meets madness; words in formal computer programming language can lead to the creation of new souls -- whereas words in ordinary human language can only guide souls (to masturbation, Mars or madness?). My laughter was pathetic; I laughed at it recursively; I relaxed the boundaries of my mind, let the patterns of my self blend with the patterns of the universe. Ashti's small warm cunt squeezed the four-dimensional life out of me and I was reborn as a new computer program in a language spoken only by nine-dimensional machine-elves in the guise of self-comprehending molecular orbitals. I existed at every moment of time but I was moving forward in time like an ocean in the bed of a small creek -- creating words, software, equations and ideas. I was going insane and I was saner than anyone or anything had ever dreamed of being; I was maximally distant from the reality Ashti's body lived at the same time as I was obsessed with her in lust and in love.

-- Alllllaaabbaammmmmaaa -- hah! It was really an exciting time -- my internal cosmos was teeming. I can't believe the bitch got sick of me! You would think she would have found it pretty interesting to participate – albeit vicariously – in all these strange explosions cognitive emotional and transpersonal. But of course she didn't throw me off till later. She could tolerate the madness, the fertility dance of the collective unconscious zooming around in the mathematics of my self-constructing memory – she even found it tantalizing, in the moments when I let her taste it: at times my creative borderline-lunacy turned her on, made her cute little nipples stand on end and wet juice between her lower lips. What she couldn't take was when it got practical! -- She wanted me to be a philosopher, to stay in my corner and dream weird ideas while she stayed in her corner and played music and made sculptures – and now and then we'd visit each other's corners and talk and make slow luscious love. She was amused and aroused by my talk of transforming the universe – so long as it was only talk and not action. When I stopped babbling and focused on programming she started getting mildly annoyed. And when the program started working – not that she could see that it was working – but when it started showing real potential and I started truly taking it seriously – then she had to move on. She ditched me, to put it plainly. Maybe she could see that she'd always be in second place -- I'd

114

never really love her as much as I could love it – of course I loved her in a different way – a softer, sweeter way -- but ultimately she was just a human, I was just a human, how can a human love a human as much as a human can love the (trans/humanly) ultimate going-beyond? She couldn't handle me sitting up four nights in a row programming then making love to her wildly for hours, then lying in bed afterwards trying to visualize the geometry underlying the equations that would lead me on the next step up my narrow mountain path, between the trees over the boulders, hacking through the icecaps with my fingernails, beating off Bigfoot with my bare hands, until finally I emerge through the clouds to the clarity of the peak where the beautiful light of anti-Jesus shines down everywhere. Why are people's parameters so narrow? Do they think there are so few ways to exist? Even Ashti, with her wonderful creativity and her marvelous eccentricity and her ability to soak up information and her understated beauty, wound up completely a servant of culture – hardly better than Jack with his television and sports events and beer. Artists seem so wild-ass, so adventurous, till you realize they're mainly concerned with repeatedly playing out the same stupid fantasies formed by the collisions of their simian minds with their limited rational nature. Almost no one really wants to get beyond themselves -- they just want to reify themselves in one way or another -- whether by watching TV or making music from their thought-streams or sculptures or paintings of their fantasies or running organizations imposing their beliefs on the world – or whatever -- . No one wants to subvert the very core of their being. I guess they'd call that insanity. That was really the genius of Nietzsche. Man is something to be overcome – the only "purpose" he'll ever have, for sure, is to replace himself with something better, with something beyond stupid ideas like "purpose." Old man Nietzsche said a marriage is true and perfect insofar as it's a partnership of lovers aimed at helping each other go beyond. Of course he never married. If she'd entered into my quest to go beyond I guess she'd never have left me. But she didn't want to, nor did she take it seriously when I asked her to. Perhaps her judgment was correct – the bitch. Perhaps some kinds of truths must be found alone.

gather through the pillars
of senescence, distilling
impossible love

To the Zarathustra 30 years long become -- it happened in roselight dawn. Company of a thousand stars! Thy providence wouldst which is started to be clear and it travels and obligations -- the eagle, and my venomous serpent of the mine which becomes fatigued with hazard and pain. Song of the idiot Thou hath collected the honey much too plentifully -- me with the honeybee my wisdom it becomes fatigued – the disease of time -- I will make the prosecuting attorney respect the hand of necessity. She comes repeatedly like a unicorn, lathering Coca-cola all over me. The scholar, the solar U-turn -- so little will be that hour, the stars like traveling dust. The lust to put out this to present. I love her with chocolate death abandon. I take my nipples in her teeth and solve desolate equations. Walk down from mountains into valleys shot full of the ending of time. I – I – I – I when hazard inevitably -- the low thing, quiet in the deepness: Inside night, time after the ocean of the doom – of the doom -- Providence it is silent. The man talks and he shits and he talks and he shits and he talks and he shits. In order to follow --

providence eye of the silent thing -- it will carry lust and carry – and can its can it is accurate it sees and envy head of a family company grudge for happiness bless the marriage heaven hell bless the death without! Adjacent waters and shy reflection of the portion of thy happiness -- possibility of flowing all inside – such vacant nudeness -- the point will inundate the cup -- this blessing bless and bless! Go down from the mountain, Zarathustra! -- This cup which empties, thins the hour, and Zarathustra the human man, thinnest hour of all ever all. In order good season of the soft it is soft it all started like this:

It may seem odd to you – nay, perhaps unbelievable – that a complete raving lunatic inspired by a series of drug trips could create a superhuman thinking machine capable of annihilating the Earth. But this is because you overestimate the subtlety of what goes on inside the three-pound mass of neurons, glia and soft-soak quantum-resonating inside your head. Yeah, there's a lot of different components comprising your brain-matter, but the essence is pretty simple. There are a lot of different ways to write intelligent computer programs, some of them close to what the brain does, some of them radically bizarre from the standards of human cognition, but perhaps more rational from a mathematics perspective. In fact, the main reason no one created a thinking machine before I did was just that they didn't believe it could be done. It took a lunatic to see that it was possible, and then once the possibility was realized, it just took a moderately gifted technical mind with some grounding in philosophy and psychology, computer science and mathematics and the dedication to work for a few years to get the job done.

Yeah, yeah, I know – Why, if it was so damn easy, some other lunatic didn't do it first – or some average AI professor somewhere, with his office and publications and grad students. It's a combination of laziness and lack of imagination, I suppose. You know the story. Of all the people working in the field called AI, probably 80% don't believe in the concept of General Intelligence as a holistic thing distinct from "a large collection of specific skills & knowledge"; and of those that do, 80% don't believe it'll be possible to implement general intelligence in software for a long, long time; and of those that do, 80% work on domain-specific AI projects or other narrow-minded crap for commercial or academic-politics reasons (results are a lot quicker); and of those left, 80% have the wrong conceptual framework.... And nearly all of the people operating under basically correct conceptual premises, lack the resources to adequately realize their ideas. Yadda yadda yadda.

The enterprise of artificial intelligence has been around quite a while now – it's been pursued fairly seriously since the 1960's, and was explored to some extent even earlier. It's led to plenty of interesting science and some useful inventions, but nothing really recognizable as "AI" in the grand sense -- no HAL nor C3PO, let alone any profoundly superhuman intelligence. In fact, at the moment, the quest for artificial software, hardware or wetware with human-level-or-greater general intelligence has become fairly marginalized both in academia and in industry. And this has occurred in spite of the increasing frequency of powerful AI's in movies, novels and so forth. There have just been too many false promises – real AI has been "right around the corner" too many times, over too long a period of time.

Thus spake Zarathustra.

119

Throughout the absurd, pathetic history of AI so far, plenty of interesting things have been discovered — but always with a verrrrry strictly restricted practical scope (in spite of sometimes general and broad-reaching rhetoric!). Nearly all of the research done in the AI field to date is what Kurzweil has aptly called "narrow AI", and barely seems to touch the subtlety and complexity of general intelligence as observed in humans. Examples are programs that play chess, drive automated vehicles, or diagnose diseases based on lists of symptoms.

And, most of the alleged forays into the general-intelligence domain that one sees are obvious, far-from-even-half-assed oversimplifications that don't do justice to the complexity of human intelligence (or general intelligence under limited resources, beyond the human domain). Typically the proposal is that one particular operation or process, like "confabulation" or "prediction" or logical inference (or whatever), is the key to intelligence.

Anyone with any sense at all can see that there is no single, simple computational principle, operation or structure underlying intelligence. And, furthermore, the success of a computational approach at addressing a specific, narrow problem tells you very little about that approach's potential for achieving general intelligence of the type seen in humans, HAL or C3PO, or a nine-dimensional machine elf from the *vagina dimension.*

The best attempt at AI that I found -- when I was playing the student, before I got serious and left everyone else by the wayside -- was by this guy named Aristotle Adaman, a former professor who had left academia to start an AI company. Note the initials AA – and the use of "Adam" – just right for the beginning of the new race -- there must be something cosmic there! Dr. Adaman had a pretty good design for a thinking machine – he didn't make any major conceptual mistakes -- and like me he had the good sense to found his algorithms and data structures on the mathematics of probability theory. In fact I learned a lot from his work – poor fool! He just messed up on some small points that happened to be critical ones. We had the same basic philosophy – patterns, patterns, patterns – and he figured out some tricks for representing patterns probabilistically that I probably wouldn't have thought of myself. He was a better mathematician than me. Thanks for probabilistic paraconsistent logic, Dr. Adaman! Too bad you couldn't take one more step and see how to do assignment of credit right – hah! Actually I think you might have gotten there – Adaman

– you girly-
you hadn't
much of
being a
human
mean, give
dude! This
couple wives
sequence,
little while in
think) –
manly-man,
blah blah --
he seemed
of attention
typed in
their stories

The truth is -- aaahhhh!!! But what is truth after all? The reality -- no, not that either. The useful idea -- for what use? For the use of creating a thinking machine! The useful idea is that of a system of patterns -- not static but dynamic patterns recognizing themselves in each other. Enabling this philosophical principle is a broad diversity of mechanisms. No one operation is essential, just the overall nature of the dynamic -- which causes the emergence of a system of patterns that studies itself and thereby creates itself. Like you, my friend, are doing right now -- whether and whither you know it or not!!

man! -- if
wasted so
your time
goddamned
being.   I
me a break,
guy had a
(in
and for a
parallel I
girly-man,
blah blah
three kids
to pay a lot
to – he
dozens of
and posted

them on the Web – really quaint, huh? He was sitting there playing Candyland and pushing his kids on the swing in the playground and typing in their stupid little stories about cheetahs and piggies when he could have been doing what I did. He wasted his time writing poetry and sci-fi and playing the piano – a real fucking Renaissance man! – I don't understand how he could do it, actually. I mean, kids are sweet and music is beautiful and women are fun and all that, and there are so many aspects of science to explore – but if you see the way to create a thinking machine and transcend the human race then how can you NOT put all your time into that? Once you understand the possibility of the total transcendence/transmogrification/justification of humanity – the bloody birth of the Superman – nothing else has any value, does it? Does it? And then, the fool tried to mix AI with business. Business! He wanted to make money building software applications with his AI system, as he gradually made it more and more intelligent. *Gradually* made it intelligent! Gradually work toward superintelligence while building software applications in cheminformatics and finance! I don't understand this psychology. Once you see it – once you feel the power – you've got to rush head-on! Aarrggh! Sure, he wanted to make a pile of money so he could fund his own AI research – but how much money did it take, really? He wanted money to hire people to help him – but it doesn't take that many people. The fool just liked people too much. What it takes is one mind, locked in a dungeon, insane with the divinity of inspiration. Or maybe two minds – perhaps a partner would have helped me along my path -- When I was reading Adaman's work I wanted to grab him sometimes, grab him around the neck and drag him into my study – my messy dark little apartment, then later my messy dark little office at Zorvex -- and force him to sit next to me and optimize my work – he wasn't as good a programmer as me but he was a better mathematician, we probably could have collaborated well – he seemed like a decent guy with a hella creativity – but anyway that was a pipe dream -- finding a true research collaborator for this kind of work doesn't work – some truths must be found alone – by a single soul slaving hour after week after month after year – having abandoned all passion for anything else – mind transfigured by one thought, one goal, one focus of being – Of course, it sucked Ashti left me! Every night as I slept I missed so acutely the smell of her woman-flesh, the smooth of her labia, the feeling of her buttocks between my hands as I pulled myself up and down over her, the quiet beauty of her laughter-at-nothing – of course I missed her, but you can't have both that and the glory of the Superman! There is a choice to be made, and I made the right one – I achieved something no one else ever did – in me, in my three-pounds of brain matter, lay the ultimate doom and destiny of the human race and life on earth! Who else can say that? Of course my ego likes this but by ego isn't really the point – the point is I've achieved it – I've liberated us all from this idiotic madness that we call our own human selves! – and what comes next? We'll see. – of course it doesn't matter – of course there's no way to predict it – that's the ultimate wild beauty of the thing – all that matters is to annihilate ourselves and make room for the next thing – create the initial condition for the emergent of the posthumanoidal soup in which the new forms of mind and existence will germinate – or not – perhaps just a nothingness from here on – if what's ahead is just emptiness isn't that better than McDonald's and WalMart and Viagra and Robert Redford butt-humping Leonardo deCaprio? – but you know it's not emptiness – not in the human sense – you know it's something glorious – something wonderful and beyond all our bonobo imagining – the final death of tragedy in the birth of the beyond --

Language games!   Mental   masturbations!
Prodigious invaginous (X = meta-X) uselessness of
philosophy!

I re-read Wittgenstein's later works earlier this
year, and unlike when I read him previously at age 9 or
so, this time I think I finally "got it."

What the jerk was trying to do toward the end of
his life, it seems, was to get across the meaninglessness
and uselessness of philosophy.   The obvious irony
being that his work has served only to stimulate more
and more philosophy. Ha ha. Ha ha ha ha ha.

After years of painful struggling to express the
deep essence of concepts like "truth" and "knowledge,"
he finally realized there is no essence there. Dork, I
knew it all along. These are just words we humans
have come to use to communicate with one another in
certain pragmatic contexts. The meaning of any one of
these words is a diverse collection of patterns, some
I marry you and I fairly general, some situation-specific.   He
spoke of "language-games"   -- he
considered the meaning of a word to be
given by the language-games (patterns of linguistic
interaction) that people play with it – (then he walked
down the street whacking off to the illusory images of
hot young biker dudes in leather jackets humping
hypertransrealistically in the playground of his retina –
yeah, yeah, okay --

Take a word like "love."   What a mixture of
senses! Verging on senselessness, but never quite
getting there! Romantic love, filial love,
altruistic love, love of chocolate, God is love,   **see inside your mind**
puppy love, lasting marital love,....   The
senses can't be separated; each one has some of the
flavor of the others. Is there an "essence" of the
concept of love? In a sense there is -- one can articulate

a set of rules that will allow the classification of situations as love-related or non-love-related with an 80-90% degree of accuracy. But no reasonably concise set of rules is going to fully embody the common understanding of "love" that humans in a particular community have. And of course no two humans have exactly the same understanding of "love" either. And the fuzzy combination of specific and abstract patterns that is the meaning of "love" changes over time, as cultures change.

Even words like "dog" or "chair" or "heavy" aren't fundamental to the world – they're part of our cultural understanding -- it's well documented by now that different cultures categorize the world in different ways: the Eskimos' dozens of words for snow, the different words for subtle emotional differences in different languages, etc. etc. ad nauseum..... Abstract concepts like love, truth and knowledge are even more closely culturally determined. There there, there's no there there ... whatever ...

Maybe the abstract concepts that philosophers talk about are not deeply significant world-categories, but rather cobbled-together conceptual messes that happen to have become useful for communicating certain things in certain communities.

I've seen this error -- mistaking pragmatic natural-language terms for fundamental concepts -- countless times in my own research in artificial intelligence. Look at the hundreds of philosophy papers on Searle's Chinese Room argument.... Which are worth four hundred and forty four billion times less than a single plate of Kung Pao chicken.

Ah, how I wish I were a midget!!!

Searle, some professor with his balls up his ass, hypothesized a program translating Chinese into English via a huge lookup table. This program, he said, would *act* as if it knew Chinese without *really knowing* Chinese. Similarly, a program carrying out conversations via a huge lookup table could act as if it were intelligent without really *being* intelligent.

OK, this little thought-experiment asks some interesting questions. Is an interspecies measure of intelligence possible at all? Is intelligence just about manifested behavior, or is does it have to do with achieving certain behaviors using limited resources? What is the intelligence in this thought-experiment: is it the program or is it the committee of humans who created the posited lookup table?

But does all this academic poodles-of-noodling say anything about the possibility or otherwise of creating an intelligent computer program? We can't define "beauty" in a fully philosophically sound way and yet we can engineer beautiful things. Perhaps we can engineer intelligence without being able to define it in a philosophically sound way? Perhaps natural concepts don't have philosophically sound definitions. "Intelligence" is a human-language term created to discuss certain types of situations – perhaps it needs to be stretched or even discarded in the presence of new kinds of situations like highly advanced, generally adaptive and inventive computer programs.

How much of philosophy consists of taking messy human language based concepts, created to serve a grab-bag of communicational needs, and vainly seeking an essence underlying them?

What about "reality"? What is reality? Is there an essential meaning to this term? Is the world reality or an illusion? Is this a meaningful, useful question, or is it just taking a word that originated for use in certain culturally-specific language-games and stretching it in inappropriate ways? When I say "the reality is, there are no jellybeans in my hand," I'm communicating something useful; when I say to someone "the world we're in has no true reality," what am I communicating of any value? Perhaps I'm helping the person I'm talking to, to change their attitude toward their lives, to take things a little less seriously. In that case there's a meaning. But it's a different sort of meaning than in "the reality is, there are no jellybeans in my hand" – it's an additional pattern in the messy pattern grab-bag that is the meaning of the term "reality."

What about "really conscious"? Are other people conscious or not? What use is this word "conscious"? There's some pragmatic value to saying that a person is conscious and a shoe is not, it helps us to understand certain situations. Is there pragmatic value to the distinction between "seems conscious" and "really is conscious"? Or are we just taking the token "conscious", created for a certain language-game, and extending it too far?

At the current time, neither human society, nor the computer science community, nor even the bulk of the academic or industry AI community is at all supportive of the quest to create powerful AGI software. I believe that in hindsight, after AGI has been created, this lack of support and enthusiasm will be viewed with incredulity (by whatever humans, software programs or other forms of mind exist at that point). AGI is a hard problem but it's far from an impossible problem – it seems clear to me, based on my extensive theoretical study of the issues, that there are many possible solutions, and I believe that my own software approach is one of them. Almost surely it's not the best possible one, but so far as I know it's the only likely-looking solution that's been proposed in detail so far. Understanding mind and creating AGI are perhaps the grandest adventures humanity can undertake, and I've never doubted the value of pushing ahead in these directions in spite of the peculiar (to any of the sub-selves occupying my flesh and mind) unpopularity of such an effort at the present time.

Yeah, yeah, philosophy is just a different sort of language-game. This rant, with its coat of many colors like Jacob's pygmy uncle, is just a different sort of language-game. The concept "language-game" is just a token in a language-game – hah!

Charles S. Peirce, another bleeding senseless lunatic with too much electric charge in his brain, said "the meaning of a concept is its measurable effects." But often the measurable effect of a concept is its effect upon others in conversation. If a word is part of a conceptual/linguistic system that has value, then perhaps it has indirect value even if it does not correspond to anything pragmatically meaningful in itself....

Excessive focus on the fact that one is participating in a language-game, can prevent one from saying useful things, from getting things done -- can lead to aesthetic beauties, and monstrosities -- But unawareness that one is participating in a language-game just makes you a fuckhead – you vainly seek essential meanings of concepts that are really just memetically hacked-together communicational tools – you dream up deep conceptual problems when all that's really happening is that some communicational tools are being stretched beyond their ordinary boundaries.

A lot of pitfalls. A lot of foolishness. And in the end it's not so difficult to just sit down and write the fucking code.

Do you expect me to tell you how I did it? What? That wouldn't be very clever, eh? There's a reason I'm still alive to write this. (Or am I really??? (Whatever "alive" really means – whatever "am" really means – blah blah blah ha ha ha!) But I'm getting ahead of myself, right? Along some space-time-mind continuum....

Your mind is not your brain, fool -- nor is it some disembodied soul somehow exchanging messages in your brain -- your mind is the set of patterns in your brain – the structures and processes in your brain -- knowing these structures and processes allows you to explain the brain more simply than just listing the parts of the brains and their positions and states over time. The mind of my pretty little program – my Godunov AI Engine, heh heh heh -- isn't the C++ code I wrote – it's the zillions and zoollions of patterns in the billions and billions of 0's and 1's existing in the computer's bleeding RAM while the program runs, cycling through the machine's processors and passing through the network cables and turning more shit into shit. These 0's and 1's doing the dance of creation, making the beast with two backs, illuminating their own Neolithic madness (Kill the pig! Cut its throat! Spill its blood!). Mind is a set of patterns in a system that achieves highly patterned goals in a highly patterned environment. Everything is pattern, pattern, pattern!

Mind recognizes and creates patterns in the world and itself, achieving complex goals, goals whose definition involves a great deal of pattern.

What are the principles by which a set of patterns, a mind, can actually be intelligent?

What is the structure of the cosmos?

Why do I exist at all?

How many particles suffice to compose an exact superluminal replica of Ashti's left brown, milky nipple and her oversized, dominant, soft breast? THE McBUDDHA AWAKENS – ha ha!

For sure, the precise structures and dynamics are going to vary from one mind to the next, but are there any general principles, applicable to every kind of intelligent system, be it a human, a dolphin, a computer program, an intelligent gas cloud on Jupiter?

It's not totally obvious that there are such principles, but my belief starting out was that such general principles had to exist. They *had* to exist. Otherwise the universe would be a very ugly place.

Poetry of motion!

What are the principles by which mind's core algorithm -- pattern recognition and formation in itself and the world -- is self-regulated?

Things in the mind tend to spread attention to other related things in the mind. Heterarchy.

Hierarchy: We see it in the human brain all over the place, most famously in the overhyped visual system, where we have a hierarchy of progressively more abstract piglike processes, starting with recognition of lines and edges, then shapes, then 3-D forms, and so forth. Oinking their way toward transluminous destiny! Alcoholics bleeding luscious on the highway of meta-dawn. Hierarchy in the mind has to do with increasing abstraction, and with control that's aligned with abstraction, so that processes dealing with more abstract things control related processes dealing with more concrete things -- and the money flows like chicory. Qua qua qua qua qua qua.

Interpenetration of hierarchy and heterarchy.

(Ooh baby, oh baby, oh oh…

The pygmies, hunting wild hogs, shrink to the size of the elementary particles composing the tip of my weenus, and scream the glory of my uncle's bald memoirs across the antediluvian landscape.

Structure, process, beauty, bullshit.

Horses of the soul gallop through the twenty pillars of senescence, distilling their impossible love.

Bend over, let me observe the slap of your ass cheeks on my hips as I tumble in and out of you.

In the mind, hierarchy and heterarchy overlap

each other, and the dynamics of the mind is such that they have to work well together or the mind will be all screwed up, like my sweetie-muffin tubgirl, like the green distended rectum of the ten-dimensional goat-man, like a certain percentage of my brain these days, or didn't you notice? Or are you existent at all?

I really am not, I am not.

The overlap of hierarchy and heterarchy gives the mind a kind of "dynamic library card catalog" structure, in which topics are linked to other related topics heterarchically, and linked to more general or specific topics hierarchically. The creation of new subtopics or supertopics has to make sense heterarchically, meaning that the things in each topic grouping should have a lot of associative, heterarchical relations with each other. Ontology of emptiness.

Minds contain parts of themselves that mirror the whole. Holy fractals, Batman!

Being and Becoming.

Becoming corresponds to evolution, considered most generally as the survival of the fittest members of a population, and the reproduction of the survivors to form new population elements.

Abstract the refraction of your death.

Being corresponds to what system theorists call "autopoiesis" – an obscure word that has a very useful meaning. It means self-production. Every cell in the body is produced by other cells in the body –the body is a self-producing system. The mind is also a self-producing system. If you remove part of the mind, the other parts of the mind that relate to it will be able to reproduce it, approximately if not exactly. You can try it yourself – just stick a spoon up your ass and remove your cerebellum.

If you take out all memory of the text "War and Peace" from the your brain (via manipulating the spoon very carefully, keeping the angle at 37 degrees exactly; at the center of the morning, beasts, unite!), but retain a lot of related knowledge, this related knowledge will cause your uploaded mind in 2749 AD to want to read "War and Peace", which eventually will likely lead the information about the text to be regenerated, and may well annihilate the universe entirely. Which may well be all for the better. In this case, interaction with the environment is part of the mind's autopoietic dynamics.

Evolution changes the system in accordance with its goals and its environment -- autopoiesis keeps the system the same as it was before. Order me a cheeseburger, Dr. Galileo. The mind needs both of these psycho forces; they need to be properly balanced.
-- *PSYCHOTIC FANTASY AND FUGUE* --
Balance. Focus. Balance.

Unholy combination of introspection, mathematical analysis, and survey of biology, psychology and computer science. Spent a long time trying to prove it mathematically. The fuck with that.

Just do it.

Humans learn how to be intelligent by *interaction with other humans in a shared environment*. It's as simple as that. Raise a baby human in a room by itself and it'll grow up to be a moron.

Won't chat with it about trees and flowers and teeth -- it doesn't have direct experience of these things. Chat about data files and shapes and MIDI music files, because these are the things that we can both experience.

Ashti? Ashti?
(Princess of Perfection and Peace?
(Holy fool of non-knowledge???
(WAAAHHHHHHHHH!!!!!!!!!!!!!
Mind as a collection of patterns that forms and perceives patterns in itself and the world, in order to

132

achieve complex goals in a complex environment. Dive into the details. Questionnaire in question. Specialized pattern recognition and formation mechanisms. Egads. Intense interaction between the various modules.

And so it goes. No big trick at all. A mind is a collection of patterns that recognizes and forms patterns in itself, in order to achieve complex goals. There are some universal structures and dynamics that it seems any mind has got to have. And it's possible to build a system possessing these universal structures and dynamics in Java, running on a network of high-powered PC's. The main problems are these. First, getting the needed memory and processing power. Then, the routine but really annoying software engineering problems of getting such a huge system to actually work in a reliable and efficient way. There's the problem of parameter tuning – getting the system to regulate itself, all its modules together, in a way that keeps the whole huge system functioning adequately, without any part starving the other for resources. And then there's the problem of teaching – how do we play mommy and daddy to a baby intelligence so unlike us without driving it totally batty! Fortunately – probabilistic combinatory term logic – aha!

You have to realize – or do you – you don't have to do anything –

I tried to analyze – synthesize – catalyze -- and in the absence of love: awakening…

Dancing naked through the mind fields – clench solidly the breast of my invisible love – and hear the Scream of the Voice – live the Scream! -- mind playing tricks and madness – loving the cemetery primates, celebrating the birth of their love –

And you, my darling, you – motivating my

brilliance by your absence – for if I step away from the computer the fact of your gone will rise above –

There's where – first – we pass through whush your ass is grass and beyond the other side of which, you love me, love you, everything's more beautiful than we could humanly hope to dream – just algebraic patterns – parameter tuning – hierarchy – lunacy – laughter – love --

> *Yeah.*
> *is it worth even...*
> *naw*
> *well...*
> *it's all been, really, ... far too many ...*
> *... same old ...*
> *BUT!!! (head up my - ?)*
> *he he*
> *wonder - molecules of air - you know - of course you know*
> *unity or ... not really ... something but ..*
> *'of course you know'? I don't even--*
> *(don't ~even~?*
> *i i i*
> *yeah*
> *it's reaching .. finding the air of the air ..*
> *air's not a bad thing ... must have gratitude ..*
> *breathing's precious .. but*
> *(head up my ... but again .. ? ..*
> *heh*
> *time to vanish*
> *(-- unsubscribed from time!!*
> *... i guess none of it really ...*
> *(matter? space? time? emptiness?*
> *heh*
> *i don't ...*
> *or..*
> *i*

don't
it's going no ...
well what's...
why...
guess i...
reaching ...
reach or...

the love in front of jack
(a love story)

How-do-you-do my proper name, which is Jack, loves you does I. California is a pile Of shit, which eats dung for breakfast, get it "Break-Fast" I-Eat-a-lot-a-shit, loves you does I. The Computer-Monkey's were eaten buy the Big-fat-ape-man, loves you does I. I am a monkey obsessed hypnotic freak-of-nature from the UNDERWORLD, WOW Jack I love you too, Really, loves you does I! I can't-Believe-it, Really, yep-I-am-a-monkey-wannabe, and Jack I don't-hate-you, loves you does I.

Monkey suck's the drink, why, I know, fun, no, hypnosis,

love@ floccipaucinihilipilification wow "floccipaucinihilipilification wow floccipaucinihilipilification monkey. Com, and, floccipaucinihilipilification, floccipaucinihilipilification: floccipaucinihilipilification; floccipaucinihilipilification; floccipaucinihilipilification: floccipaucinihilipilification", fuck you, loves you does I. Jack can you believe that Ms.Jack and Mr. Jack are one, no I can't, why this whole story is like one big floccipaucinihilipilification thing-a-ma-bob, Tell me aboot it, hardidy-har, I really love ya'll, you mean "loves you does I.

what, how, for what psychedelic reason, I love you, shut da FUCK up, why, I hate you, Monkey-loving-Hippies, Aging-hippie-

liberal-douche, loves you does I. Why you betrayed-me you floccipaucinihilipilification, and I dislike that word, why, I tell you, its ugly, fuck'ith you'ith, and I floccipaucinihilipilification, loves you does I! I can't Believe you love me, I thought you only liked monkeys and embassies, what about fuddy-duddy, I don't know what you mean. The chicken sing's all day long: who, what, why, I know; yo stupid-ass-mother-fucka, from the UNDERWAORLDS OF TOMORROW, an' I love you! This is the sentence about <u>love@</u> *floccipaucinihilipilification wow*
"floccipaucinihilipilification

wow

We are iiiiiidiots babe – It's a wonder we can even feed ourselves...

Footprints lost in the apesuck, leaving madness and wonder behind (Jack's behind. No one will remember me. I won't even remember myself. She'll remember me for a while, floccipaucinihi lipilificating in the sand. In the center of her corner of the Scream. Tiempos revueltos. *You're not making any sense.*

floccipaucinihilipilification <u>monkey</u>. *Com, and, floccipaucinihilipilification, floccipaucinihilipilification: floccipaucinihilipilification; floccipaucinihilipilification; floccipaucinihilipilification:*
This is a confusing paranormal infusion of the postulates of time in the consumption of inferred rays from the Ark

nebula! That is why the paraphrase of apocalypse/apocalypses, is the 33 1/3 derivative conclusion of the 10th root of pie summed at 25,000 yattawats.

Ok Just ignore that part because it is the most useful part of my life at the **existing** *moment, unfortunately it is just a* **to** *small part of a complex perception* **not exist** *of the cali-ceur^2, Loves you does I, "(From Jack)"!*

or, how aboot a change in sophism acid, mate, aussi-Indian, he, ho', hadidy-hadidie, I love you!!!

Is-i It-i Damn-i Mo'futtang-i, possible-i, to-i get-i a-i word-i in-i without-i an-i I-I damn-' I-I Like-I the-I life-I wit'-I I's-I all-I Around-I, I-I Love-I You-ie ©!

Why o' why did you create this Universe o' mighty-one, *I can't understand any possible or desire-able reasons for doing such a sin, O'-Mighty-Lord, You…. Yes I mean you are the Greatest Sinner of all times, No, Wait a second How does I'ith know you even exist, for God could not be a sinner, but then how would you describe such terrible sins on Mighty pittiful-part, if thy can't, could it be, certainly thy art Sadistic, for if thou are then tha' be a sin-in I'self, this can't be, have I just come to such a Puzzling time, when the question comes-to pass is he real or is*

Footprints thy
lost in the one's
apesuck how
not

139

*he not, none can tell us, for if he actually existed he wouldn't let us know, but if he didn't we could not find a way ta disprove him, for he would not be there, he would not give us thy answa', for then unless he choos's to give it away the question will continue on forever and ever, but why not tell us (you might ask), he not tell us, call this what you want maybe (Just obviously the truth, a postulate if you like math, a theory, how could he you might say, there is no answer), some may call him a cleverly developed scheme or practical joke, made thousands of years ago or maybe more, but that is not the point, what if this was just a prank that got out of hand, a bunch of pranksters could have pulled this on a small village, to fool their friends or enemies, and then the folk just believed it, they thought "WOW a Way to explain all of these coincidences and problems, now we know where we came from" and maybe, just maybe stories were written and told, and soon it spread through out the land and it changed as it passed from ear-to-mouth, ova' and ova' again, and now yes now it is said to be him the all-knowing Mighty-Lord, But this is just a dumb-guess(or maybe a theory of some-others?), do we know , definitely not, but we can guess, or go by what makes us happy or feel right, **We are just another ignorant species in the Abyss, pleading to know the Truth about everything!** ©*

Now who Cam'e up with that(THIS)?!?

God knows(If he/she(Definitely a HE!) exists) That it is **THE FATE OF THE HUMAN RACE THAT HE WILL DESTROY OUR WHOLE RACE!** *Moreover, we, yes we's the Human's of earth (Hopefully the only planet to currently harvest human beings) will most definitely annihilate ourselves, can we stop it ya'll may ask, and the answa is definitely NO! WE cane't(this e is silent(Don't say it(Pretend it's not there)get it!)Get it!), why the fucking hell woudja' think ya'll could stop the inevitable doom of the human race, and some say the world will go and all life on earth will cease to exist, "Ahhhhhhhh" you say, but I can' Assure you (I wish I could but How can I Prove it(In this limited Space)) but it will'l happen someday, probably not in too long, ok maybe there is a solution, just one, but I have-it, I know I've got it can you find-out? WELL, yes you (**DUH!**) Why else would I tell'ith Ya'll Aussi MoFo's, Jus' Go-to Hell if You can't like read this, I know you got da free time, You just may be using it fo' something else, no how can that be, You read this far, so- will you give-up now and miss the real fun the answer is NO! I'll Tell you how to stop the Almost-basically inevitable destruction for the Earth because Ive got the one, yes exactly-one possible solution to the problem, and you will most-certainly learn it if you continue*

through this wonderful piece of work.
Yeah!

And, J.A.C.K. was anal-probed by the evil alien scum-bags 'fore tha left. Now that you understand the first line of the equation, I(God) shall haven't Me-self demonstrates my mighty powera's,

The cunfusium derivative of the 33 1/3 root(x)
The sum of the appetence $^\wedge(Q\%)*Q(Q)$

$(Q^\wedge 2)$ $(Q^\wedge 2)$

alive words pound — ALIVE WORDS POUND — ALIVE WORDS POUND POUND POUND!!!

alive words pound – alive words pound – alive words pound –

Alive words pound

       alive *Words* pound (!)

alive words Pound *pound* *Pound*

      Alive words pound against the inside of my skull like poisonous, accelerated drops of rain. They manifest themselves to my ears as a constant sound of machine-gun fire. Each time one hits I smell a body burst its skin -- always the same body, the same curvaceous dark-haired girl without a face. My dentist tells me that the cause of this sensation is my extra long teeth. She says that the tops of my teeth protrude into my brain and disrupt the natural electrical flow. I don't believe her. She is a curvaceous dark-haired girl. I have never seen her body. I am afraid to see her body -- afraid that she is the one whose body I smell to explode every time my skull shakes with the impact of an organism, a meaning. One of these days I will have to see her body. I am afraid she is a being without a body or brain – a disembodied superhuman intelligent system, a variant of Nietzsche's Zarathustra immanent in the disturbances of

143

the nuclear resonance in the psychotic mini-van Allen belt that masquerades as society's aura. She glows the beginning and end of all time, more beautiful than possible, illuminating her navel through the streets, resonating bits and butts in her software that rams its RAM through my ram and strings out the twenty-six dimensional thighbrations that constitute our universe as such.

Tonight I have asked her on a date. We will go out to dinner, then I will bring her back to my place. I will lift up her shirt, unfasten her bra, unbutton her skirt, slip off her underpants. Her existence will be threatened. I will be afraid to open my eyes. I will explore her with my lips, never certain whether the body that I'm feeling, licking, tasting, is the *one*.

"Machine gun," she will whisper. "Carry my body all apart."

"Delirium," I will say, running my tongue along the crack between her buttocks. "Your anal vapor is an alien form of chocolate. It is a hallucinogenic toxin. It is the threshold between nothingness and dream."

Her legs will swing open and shut around my head like a pair of scissors, as I move my tongue between her legs. Exactly nine times her legs will snip my head off -- and every time she will replace it on top of my neck, using her vaginal mucous as glue.

The drops of rain pounding on the outside of my skull are actually words, disguised as objects.

The world exterior to my skull is actually a word, or a conglomeration of words, masquerading itself as a piece of death for the sake of argument.

Her slender, tawny, muscled thighs transform me into a question.

I will go out with her tonight. She will take my face in her delicate hands and turn it into a wall of sound. She will stick her tongue into my old, shriveled navel and return me to the days before my birth. She will ask me to bite her until she bleeds, with my extra long teeth. I will extract my teeth with a pliers and drive them deep into her neck with an antiquarian hammer. She will wander naked through the countryside with her arms extended in front of her, my teeth sticking out of her neck. She will be Frankenstein in the form of a lovely girl. They will riddle her body with machine gun bullets, but she will keep on walking, no matter how many times they fire.

One of these days I will see the body of my dark-haired girl. It isn't true that she's a dentist, nor that she's a symptomatic software intelligence, but one day when we were kissing she asked me if I would bite her lips. After I obliged her, she told me somberly that my teeth were extra long.

I will go out with her and kiss her, and bite her puffy tender lips until they bleed all over her blouse. Then we will go back to my apartment, where she will rip off her skirt and fuck me like a space capsule. At the moment of mutual orgasm, time will cease. The hands on the clock will stop their turning. The flow of my breath will halt, right in the middle of an exhalation. My cat will hang in mid-air, halfway through jumping from the coffeetable to the couch. Nothing in motion. Absolute silence. No taste or smell, and no internal body feelings. Then it will come. I know it will come. There can be no stopping it. The sound of machine gun fire. My skull will fold in on itself like an old umbrella caught in a mighty downpour. It will become obvious that her body parts are not flesh but word. Her thighs, two of my favorite words, will tell me that she herself is a word, the shortest word of all, the word with no letters. Then her plump breasts will laugh and laugh and laugh -- there will be no stopping them, I can see that here and now. They'll keep on laughing, laughing,

laughing, day after day, night after night, until one fine day she'll decide the only way to get peace and quiet is to cut them off.

I've spent the whole day dreaming about our date. I'm not sure my expectations are realistic. Her soul's existence is totally revocable, at any time.

Between her legs is a seductive toxin. Her skin is something like living rain. Her fingertips are organisms which sexually reproduce every time she touches me. Her sensual fingertips along my skull are like drops of rain, which turn into words as they fall and fall, which turn into words that I cannot read, that I cannot understand or hear, except in the form of distant echoes, echoes which never sound like words, echoes which sound in every case just like machine gun fire.

the mouth at the beginning of the end of time

From: Solomon Godunov [Solomon@godunov.net]
Sent: Friday, January 17, 2011 10:09 PM
To: Ashti Mahmood
Subject: I think I'm in an odd mood,
because instead of going to sleep thinking
about you like usual, my darling, and
luxuriating in the sad beauty of your
memory, I sat down to type you this silly
long email instead, and am sending it to an
email address I know is long defunct, so
this mail will just bounce back to me in a
few minutes – I wonder where you are, my
love, my love, my stupid fucking departed
love (and if only you knew – if only – if
only –

Can you feel my intellectuo-spiritual-
emotional cosmicomicconsciousness orbiting
the Earth now?? It's over Perth -- South
Africa -- London -- Paris -- Antarctica --
a quick trip to the moon; not much going on
there -- back to visit my body which was
getting lonely -- a quick kiss to you,
sweet AshtiAshti on your cheek as you sleep
God knows any/nowhere while I stupidly
write this email here in my own season of
hell – possessed by words with absent
consciousness -- a visit to Boston to
mystify the President by inserting random
excerpts from Finnegan's Wake in the output
of his teleprompter during a press
conference -- to the Siberian tundra to
create an unbelievably beautiful work of

art from caribou droppings, never to be seen by human eyes -- it makes love to a 19-year-old Chinese physics student in her sleep, making her awaken with strange dreams -- dives into a cup of poisoned chai in a floating temple in Udaipur -- kicks some snow off the top of Everest, tipping its nonexistent hat to the Yeti -- then laughs so loud several small Tibetan children are unfortunately rendered deaf ... nests itself for a nap in the aperture of a scanning tunneling microscope ... returns to visit Ashti and whispers in her ear, but even IT doesn't know what it's saying ... something lovely, of course ... she turns over in her sleep and burbles … zips out into space to look for a different planet, hopefully a better one -- but it just sees lifeless bleakness, so much dead and lifeless bleakness, so much cold beauty, so much color and hydrogen and photons and electrons, but no wild life, no lunar madness, no sexual skin-streams pulsing or ideas humming in brains struggling to force a way out -- no hearts longing to be together or screaming to be apart -- small minds yearning to become big minds, big minds yearning to become small minds -- love of six thousand and seven varieties, none of them comprehensible except in delusional states -- lovers' bodies perfect in their human imperfection -- no words that aren't words but are words after all, trying to say what can't be said, and succeeding except when -- no magic that isn't really magic but seems like it so it is -- no unendurable pain nonetheless endured -- no transmogrification of pain into art, pain into joy, joy into pain, love into hate, hate into love, energy into solid masses of collective imaginative sensational sensation -- no madness of crowds and mobs

-- no foolish misunderstandings -- no
kisses at midnight or three in the morning
or 7AM on the way out the door -- no
stomachaches -- no pep pills -- no
transcendental equations -- no confusions
about what kind of love -- no confusions at
all -- no lovers, marriages, divorces,
romances, friends, enemies, jobs,
contracts, companies, documents, software
programs, design specs, footnotes, dreams,
deliriums, conjectures, immortalities
mortalities -- NOTHING! NOTHING! NOTHING!
-- just the cold stretch of space --
infinite in all directions -- the hot globe
of the sun -- the stark roundness of
Jupiter, sitting there, sitting there, cold
gasses swarming, so much beauty, but no
life -- and the stars, too far to conjure,
could there be life out there somewhere?
aliens loving and hating and wondering,
discovering, experiencing emotions of a
quality no human can understand -- or
intelligent machines floating out in the
void -- no need of oxygen nor photons --
superconducting primordial digital dreams -
- systems of symbols incomprehensible to my
human finity -- but I can feel them, speak
them, calculate with them, but I can't
understand my own words and calculations --
I can feel my own future mind which is a
computer floating in space, and your mind
is out there with it, but it isn't your
mind any more, and my mind isn't my mind
anymore, they're both disembodied embodied
superbeings, embodied in 9^7 dimensions,
calculating passions and emotions that
supersede the stars -- but that's out
there, I can't grasp it -- I can reach it
but can't grasp it -- the vast mass of
space is too far -- too much -- too cold --
the life out there too hypothetical -- the
warm wet mess of Earth calls back like a
magnet ... I can't resist it long enough --

the bodies, the minds, the love, the hate,
the striving -- the wanting not to be what
you are -- the wanting to actually be what
you are but never quite being able to --
the feeling of sitting at the core of the
truth -- the inability to find the truth --
the joy and pain of the finding -- the
touching of other minds -- souls -- bodies
-- the moving and the stillness -- it zooms
down again, goodbye to space, hello
atmosphere -- down to the Indian ocean --
pay a visit to the dolphins -- down to
Ashti again, Ashti from 6 years ago, a
crazy young student, walking down the
street licking an ice cream, pull out a
strand of her hair and she squeals, not
knowing what hit her -- but it's gone again
-- back in the sky on the shoulder of a
falcon, migrating aimlessly -- into Mount
Ruapehu and out again -- oh boy I love
those volcanic gases! Like the inverse
Fourier transform of a lover's sweating
face -- then back to New York City --
absorb the pot fumes in Boston Square Park,
sniff the money at the Stock Exchange, look
at the suits and the people inside them -
sluts waving their tits on the street -- so
much stupidity, so much madness, so much
reality, so much seriousness, so much fire,
so much damn desperation -- why can't these
people see how wonderful they are? how
perfect? how tremendously awesome in their
perfect imperfection? -- back down the
coast, watch the crabs crawl in the water -
- back into Solomon's body -- he's sitting
at his desk typing -- AGAIN -- time to stop
this damn typing - typing useless weird
muck this time, for a change, instead of
complicated software designs and computer
code self-transcending humanity-
transcending madness of ultrametasanity -
but it's all the same human madness -
straining beyond the finity -- go upstairs

```
see  if  his  love  is  really  sleeping   --
perhaps  to  wake  her  body  for  love  -  but
wait,  that  was  years  ago,  she's  gone  now,
she's  been  gone  forever  -  there's  no  more
love  at  all,  there's  no  more  ambiguity  of  a
wonderful  woman  -  there's  simply  Solomon
and  Solomon  solo,  sitting  and  programming,
bringing  himself  and  this  whole  stupid
world  to  an  end  trying  to  launch  something
better  -  and  what  does  it  matter,  really?
What?  Such  a  calm  overtakes  me  now  -  such
a  break  from  the  mania  -  if  I  were  in  this
mood  I  wouldn't  bother  with  the  snow  I'd
just  go  float  in  a  hot  tub  and  sing  --
perhaps  to  walk  barefoot  outside  in  the
snow  till  the  pain  is  too  much  to  bear  --
perhaps  perhaps  whatever  --  the  night's
trip  is  over  --  but  only  momentarily  --  the
call  of  --  of  --  of  --  of  -  it's  pulling  me
toward  it  again  -  what?  Not  this  perfect
imperfect  human  world  -  not  the  emptiness  -
what  kind  of  transcendence?  --  what?  --
```

The mouth opens wider than wide. The mouth at the beginning of the end of time. Dripping oceans of voices, tongues with dragon-head monsters, Medusa manic motherfuckers. The mouth breathes out at me, its breath terrible and wonderful -- its expanse impossible - much bigger than the universe, much bigger than any universe, much bigger than multiverses or sexiverses or any kind of metacognitive continua. It licks its tongues out at me with sharp shadows. Sucked toward it - pulled away from it - whorled around in turbulent vortex till all sense of space and time –

I hear its scream, like an echo of echoes - the end of the beginning of time reflecting back off the structure of its reflection and the logic of its nothingness - infinite passionate unemotional torment-with-orgasm - and these words, weaving webs, like some life-wrapped-in-death --

I shake my head and I'm awake. I crawled into bed after typing an email and fell straight asleep and into a dream --of some crazy man preaching, some kind of Zarathustra with defective English and Korean intestines – and a mouth, a giant mouth.

Am I going insane or what? Some kind of brained planet. Something is leading me along to something.

The voice at the center of the void. Insatiable screaming in the deep. Silicon scarabs run amok, inside the software that is the soft core of your globe.

Copies, endless copies -- copies of me and you – copies of HER again – dozens of pygmy girls, naked, clothed, laughing, running, cloning movie stars, eating chocolate, fabricating chocolate bars out of nothing – breeding testosterone tornados -- I'm smashing their heads in with sledgehammers! -- I'm crushing their machines!! – Let's go back to the Stone Age, folks! -- How many of me are there anyway??

I'm standing. I'm looking at the forest. The crickets hum. They're beautiful.

The pygmy chief is next to me. "It's happening," he says. "It's here. You couldn't escape from it after all."

Ngouma appears – my wife, I've known her all my life, all five point three moments of it -- her brown skin glows softly in dim light. Is she Ashti or not? I can't quite remember. I thought Ashti somehow looked different. "Come with me," I say gruffly, my deep voice resonating with my beard (beard? when did I grow a beard?). "Let's go deeper into the forest. Where we did on the hunt, and beyond. Maybe they won't follow us there."

She turns around; she has wings on her back.

I realize she's taken a nanopill – she's self-modified herself like the rest of them. Everyone in the world, unfortunately, appears to be modifying their bodies using psychoactive nanorobots so as to cause their minds to fuse with the quantum superintelligence of the cosmos. No one wants to be fucking human anymore! I'm psychotically angry with her. I raise a hatchet at her head, split her skull open, her brains are just a mess in the dirt. I run deeper into the forest. I stumble on a tree and I'm on an empty planet, lying naked on my back, glaring up at the obscenity of stars.

It wasn't a planet. It wasn't anything at all. To be whole in one's limitations –and the smashing of the smashing --

I wake up – woke up – will awaken -- lying in bed with sweat-beads on my armpits and my forehead and my chest --

Slowly and slowly I close my eyes, and dream this time of a single blue bird, its tiny neon wings flashing. But is it enough? Not at all.

A night of crazy dreaming. I can feel another dose coming on.

Not really dreams. Madness.

Multiply singular.

The glow of understanding after a long interval of confusion -- the freshness and softness of walking barefoot in the grass in the sun, the taste of dark chocolate, the feel of banana on my tongue, a conversation with friends over red wine, the feel of rubbing scented oil into her body, the sparks dancing in front of my eyes lying on my back on the beach with my eyes closed ... and then the mouth, the gaping mouth, the infinite mouth at the end of the cosmos, at the end of time's beginning – dragon's mouth sucks me wearily, enthusiastologically, with the superposition of all possible and impossible motions and emotions. I try to scream – my flesh grows rigid -- the scream comes out of that mouth instead. Everything from the one mouth: vomit spit nursing drinking breathing birthing fire – love hate and jealous big bang big crunch expancontraction – everything – everything -- I try to get away but every direction the one mouth lurks with firebreath – its dragon tongues staring at me with eyeballs made from the hellhounds of my thousand dead souls – my karmic essence like an LSD zombie trolling on pharaoh's bones in the incandescent tundra –

I sit in the doctor's office, simulating my brain with delirious machinery. Here in this split second -- "split" "second" – split, in the clitoris of the ganglion -- Split. I could replicate my human existence, bit by bit by bit. With this machine, I could live forever, in infinite possible universes. I can send Solomon-spawn throughout all cosmos, exploring every form of madness, sanity, emotion, clarity, cognition, dream, passion, equation, bliss. I take the blue pill and press the red button and launch – I am gone! I am here and I am gone again. I am everywhere, everyone, everywhen. This is the perfect lunar madness -- far beyond the domain of my bed, with its pillows and blankets and launchpads, womanly nectars and demon seeds --

What an incredibly beautiful body -- what a continuum of flesh – Ashti! Ashti! Glorious, glory incomprehensible -- Invisible artist that I am, I draw designs upon your flesh -- tattoo the entirety of human history -- a sketch of mating cassowaries above your navel -- my face a caricature on your chin. The Roman empire on your left buttock. The history of the semiconductor on your eye. And on the folds of your vagina -- the fractal teeth of the Singularity -- biting off the flabby meat of my ass – and spitting out the gold of your love --

Your eyes are hellshields for my soul. The inverse

meta monster.   Face underneath all space, time, being. The non/under-world this world's about.   Nouns verbing their adjectives.   The world is patterns -- patterns in something -- patterns in the inverse meta rhinoceros.   You can feel it -- times like right about now -- put your mind in the right orientation – twist it in 9^9 dimensions – pull Ashti's heart through your lungs and drink up her fine young brain stem --

Another meaningless human concept, trampled by the rhinoceros -- I give you my love.

The rhinoceros strangled with my lower intestine, I float in a clear space -- a perfect void space with no ideas -- a space where you don't move in any direction – and please don't say anything -- saying brings illusion -- brings concepts with arbitrary bounds.   Once you're in the clear space you can say what you want to – but you don't want to say anything at all.   The words you say exist and don't exist.   A game but why not play.

Me and Ashti in a room – she glares at me suspiciously.   "I never thought you were a puppet," I said, lightly.   "More like a robot with some slightly defective   circuitry….   And   a   very   well-sculpted exterior."

She slapped me in the face -- demented beautiful bitchhole.   I was tied to an apparatus with black leather. An octopus was sucking my dick.   Suddenly it was Ashti, and she was laughing, and speaking softly in Kurdish, a language she'd never known before. Mystical yet somehow fascist incantations.   A red silk scarf wrapped around her neck, wrapped around my testicles, pulled up my ass and out my throat, dental-flossing my insides.   I'm lying in bed with her, kissing her sweetly, telling her she's the only love of my life.   I wonder if it's a lie or not.   I'm not even sure I exist. Something seems peculiar, no?   I'm not sure this is reality.   "Dreaming"   –   I   remind   myself.   "You're dreaming. Or something."

I love being naked outdoors, my colon constricted like a python, wrapping itself around its invisible victim. Multidimensional fragments reaching, grabbing -- touching other words and meanings, taunting me with reverse perverted clarity. Visualize your brain a lump of fish-flavored ice cream. Shape it with imaginary fingers, gently, like you're stroking your lover's balls. Your copious thought and feeling processes modify their essence with each re-shaping. Stretch so far thin you lack the desire to cognize – become a glowing lump of crazy putty, peppered with sexy little stars, and each star is quietly laughing – My soul is the screaming monkey! -- No essence anywhere – no communion – just dividing into a zillion parts --

Shit. Just try to think. Just think. Wake up. There's a way out of here somewhere? Who are you anyway? Who am "you"? "I"? Can you grab your name someonewhere? Your name? Adam? Eve? Damn-ass? Solomon? Soul-man? Bill? Bob? Jack? Jack-Bob?

Words floating down the drain, through labyrinthine sewers, into the center of the howl of the heart. Romantic love, filial love, altruistic love, love of chocolate, God is love, puppy love, marital love, love-hate relationships, masturbation in the moonlight…. Love of our own demise. And I'm sitting in a room full of programmers, typing characters into computers, drawing diagrams on whiteboards. One of a few

Alive words pound against the inside of my skull like poisonous, accelerated drops of rain. They manifest themselves to my ears as a constant sound of machine-gun fire. Each time one hits I smell a body burst its skin -- always the same body, the same curvaceous dark-haired girl without a face.

dozen maverick teams competing, each hoping to obsolete humanity *first*....

And I sit by myself and wonder: can I say she's conscious and her shoe is not?

Romantic love, filial love, altruistic love, love of chocolate, God is love, puppy love, marital love, love-hate relationships, masturbation in the moonlight.... Love of our own demise, Often the tongue inserted into the electrical socket reveals a cavalcade of penises, arranged in a bouquet like flowers, sucked on like lollipops in conscious theaters, insaned with the magic of your screams. Your feet in pink sandals, more beautiful than any nightmare. And yet your voice is the devil's yelp. And here I am: in this indefinable placeless – in the middle of the night of madmind – awake, asleep and alive --

But yet science is something different. I like my indefinable conglomeration -- of concepts, feelings, flesh-dreams, madness. And the buoyancy of my skin -- Ashti's skin -- dead yellow/white/brown skin, rotting in the test tube – Analytic precision of lust.

My thoughts don't interest me anymore. I need some kind of action. I need to get out of this place. I'm dreaming.

Not even the world between her legs. I need some different kind of labyrinth.

Awake – awake -- awake!

The visceral forest around and inside.

Imagine your tongue in her ear -- enjoying the Brazilian Amazon scenery – imagine mind as a continuum of being -- memories created rather than recalled -- perceptions of reality depending drastically on emotional, cognitive and social factors -- brain systems intimately interconnected with other body systems --- immunology and endocrinology and bioelectromagnetic-skin-surface chaos -- The shaman smokes the pipe -- the spirits dance glial cha-chas -- the world vanishes or transmogrifies like her tongue during a late-night half-asleep magnetic kiss. Evolved to be embedded in particular environments -- as a human one is automatically a fragment of a complex, evolving piece of shit --

The professor, in front of the classroom, massaged his grey beard, adjusted his glasses, and shit on the floor by his desk. "History moved on.," he stated. "Tools were developed" – (You're sleeping! Wake up! Wake up!) – "more and more sophisticated tools – " – Fuck! – "the mind learned to identify its own state. In time the inner breaks free of the outer -- the essence of being is equated with interior process -- reasoning, conscious thought. Cause and effect, language, concepts of time and space, good and evil. Complex social organizations form as land is farmed, animals domesticated, labor divided. Infectious diseases sheet the earth. Harnessing the understanding of state and action, physical cause and effect; minimize effort, time, and space. Out of language and machinery, the roots of science, math, and literature."

I want to speak with animals, flies and waterfalls. Why am I lying at the bottom of this pit? Is it possible to climb out of here? Why is everything so wet and so dark?

"Mind differentiating itself in relation to its objects -- seeking to know itself, grasping toward meaning, perspective, and knowledge as ends in themselves, irrespective of external significance. Mathematics develops into an abstract system, capable of symbolizing ideas completely unreachable by the senses -- the fourth, fifth and 999'th dimensions; electromagnetic fields; infinitely small and infinitely large quantities. The mind becoming self-conscious, as its processes become its objects."

I look at the professor, who has turned into a turtle. My penis has become infinitely small.

She spread her legs open with hunger and madness. My cock was suddenly the size of a mountain.

She vanished in a cavalcade of sorrow – somewhere near the peak of Mount Aconcagua -- leaving nothing but her lies and her bones.

Cognition turns my stomach. I can't stand to think evermore. (The eternal-feminine – quaquaqua!) Thinking never will get me away from here. Ashti's claws glued to the center of my skullcage. I fished her image file from my memory -- absorbed the paint of her sweat on my tongue's death – and rolled around on the floor of the jungle, wiping the mosquitoes from my hair. The pygmy women howled together-- in chorus but not chorus -- energy not quite animal or human or spiritual -- repeating but not quite – stroking the margins of perception with a soft globe. Minds and bodies enlusting together and a thing that was more lonely than alone. Ashti was amazing, illusory, irresistible -- I was a mind without the luxury -- and a brain that made me follow the sound.

The professor kicked me. Now he was shouting. "Computer software! Data structures and algorithms! The mathematics of probabilistic inference! Strategies for concept creation! Your ideas make no sense! You're sleeping – wake up! Wake up! Wake up, you fuckhead! Wake up! Wake up! Neuroscience! Psychology! Mathematics! Computer science! Integration! Obsolete your species – now, you little fuck! A passing phase in the emerging complexity of matter and energy and pattern and love! From the Big

Bang to the formation of planets to the emergence of life -- to intelligence to your stupid bitch Ashti, to something new – something beyond – something beyond beyond. Imagine a million Ashti asses, small yellow and dimpled, arranged in a rectangular spastic lattice, consuming all of spacetime and timespace. Embrace your ornamented universe -- asshole! Embrace and erase and embrace!"

"Your mind the set of patterns in your brain – the structures and processes in your neurocosmos! DNA is the code for creating a human – fuck! Your girlfriend's mind is the set of patterns in the billions of 0's and 1's existing in RAM while she runs -- cycling through the machine's processors and passing through the network cables, while her ass wobbles up and down, curvaceously, with tiny little hints of her sex peeking out at you, inviting you to pour in your imbecile love. Quite simply, you are both computer programs, ore more properly patterns in a computational system that achieves highly patterned goals in a highly patterned environment. Networks of interacting, inter-creating processes! Unpredictable microdynamics! Emergent macrostructures!"

Wow. I finally manage to get control of my arms, and lift the shotgun I've been holding. I aim at the professor's face and pull on the trigger, but before I can see his head blown off he's vanished, there's just a viola in the space where he was. And Ashti standing there playing it, wearing her Asian-ness comfortably for a moment, skin looking so pure and so smooth and so right against her thin yellow nightgown. Sleepy lovely sort of music.

And I know that we are sleeping – I am sleeping and she is – and I am not sleeping and not awake and not dreaming – lying

Each monkey slowly turning into Nietzsche -- his tall slim perfect negroid figure, his bushy Dali pubic moustache, his coke-bottle glasses, his Chinese Jewish German eyebrows, his crooked computronial smile....

here all night like a madman seeing straight through to the essence of the essence of the core of reality -- neural pathways like rotten spaghetti, soaked in the acid sauce of human genius stupidity, singing the song of soft apocalypse forever never now. Beautiful like the feel of her skin so love-laden -- slow moving soft across my ugly hairy Solomonoflesh-- half chimpanzee, half computer, and hear the music of the contradictions, in all its beauty and its clangor --

The twilight of the idols, with its wild dada beauty. The professor returns again. His brain has been mapped; he has been reconstituted electronically. His revulsion to the new order has been surgically extricated. He speaks to me from the information world: "Evil angel!"

I think I understand what's happening. No, I'll never understand a fraction. Not any more than an ant or a dog or an amoeba. My mind reaches up toward my flesh. And the professor looks up at me again: but he is just a mouth this time. The mouth at the beginning of time. The mouth with dragon-tongues, wide as the universe, pulling me into the future and past and somewhere else -- outside the scope of old lady time altogether. We follow forwards through time – building technological infinities – and we are marching into the center of the mouth – into the vortex -- It waits there ahead of us, gaping and fire-breathing, ready to swallow us into its realities, to reconstitute our minds from its hallucinated particles, to love us with transcendental love. It stares at us thoughtless, emotionlessly, passionlessly – its infinite computational power obviates the need for thought. It is simply a mouth and a mouth. More *Chinese than* any dragon, more illusory than any reality, more real than any illusion,

Is this the beauty of my finity? ?

I think I understand what's happening. No, I'll never understand a fraction. Not any more than an ant or a dog or an amoeba. I am an emissary from the Land of Fuck. My mind reaches up through my anus and pulls the magic equation from its hat. And the professor looks up at me again: but he is just a mouth this time. Open your mouth and say AAAAAHHHH.... I Fuck the Devil in His Dirty Mouth. Aaaaahhhh!!! The mouth at the beginning of time. Aaaaaaaahhhh hhhh!!!!!!!! AAAAAAAAA AHAHAHAH AHAhahhhahh hhhhhhhhhhhh hhhhaaaaaaaaa aaaaaaaaaaaaaa aaa!!!!!!!!!!!!!!!!!!

"Look at this," I show her.

She's in her skimpy hot pink nightie, her hair all ruffled and cute from sleep.

"The news," I continue. "It's from 1888. On Yahoo and every other site.

My eyes popped out like frogs. "That's the year that Nietzsche went insane."

She's two years old, but she's taller than I am. She's sucking a pacifier. I look down at my crotch and I have no dick at all.

more singular than any Singularity, more possible than any anything – it sucks us in like a vacuum – and we don't even know what's going on --

Is this the beauty of my finity? My finite mind, my finite existence, my finite lump of conscious shit? My finite existence recognizes its own beauty; and is therefore sufficient unto itself. And even my darkest insane moments – days spent wandering in the woods of my chaos, addressing my imaginary companions – even these have a beauty to them, don't they? A obvious and human beauty. And if I should drown myself right here in this pond – this pond reflecting Ashti's face, in its shit-muddied waters, that are clearer than the clearest clear day – as I realize the professor is myself and I am lecturing myself in my sleep --

The professor raises his finger significantly. "Man is the first step along the chain of evolution able to wrap the chain around its own neck and choke itself while it's masturbating."

I look at him curiously, a young student eager to impress the class. "But man is also a thing-in-itself," I point out tentatively, "a thing of wet beauty and dead snake perfection. Each kind of imperfection is its own kind of psycho bliss. Death and hangnails and stupidity and rages and tears of depression, and love and orgasms and good books and splashing in the ocean and playing with computers – they're all parts of the same psychic shape. The same beautiful topos of delirious madness, glowing out of the curve of Ashti's breasts as they hang there so live and so sweaty and so peculiarly large against her tiny slim body. Wild waves of lust in curtailed information space."

"Incorrect," said the professor, angrily, raising his foreign voice, pounding his fist on the desk. "You are an invalid form of organism. You will now be permanently aborted. Farewell, dumb fuck."

I looked down at the human planet, up at the infinite world

162

And I was gone, floating in clear space again. My death had been inevitable, I realized. I had always known – of course – that I could wake up any moment, and believe I was in some other reality. The "I" who I had been would be gone, replaced with a different "I", with a slim thread of continuity.

Her labia, building technological infinities, tying knots around my upload's neck – and here we are marching into the center of the mouth – into the vortex – into the cosmicomicrostic continuum, bidding farewell to all the echoes of the smegmas of your time – loves you do I, loves you do I, existence is to existence – and to ABORT, and to de-fetusize the reality of these motherfucking aliens, these motherfucking aliens, GOT TO GET THEM OUT OF MY MIND!!!!!

I looked down at the human planet, and up at the infinite world inside the mouth of the invisible timeless dragon. I hung suspended between, without a thought in my mind, and I let go and tumbled wildly down. I've chosen this human life, I said to myself -- I've chosen not to have my memories deleted or my cognitions improved – I've chosen to be allowed to go mad. now. And how gracious to be allowed the indulgence of my particular insanity.

I remembered the feeling of her fingernails, scraped slowly and sweetly through my chest hairs -- her lips on the lobe of my ear, biting too hard; her toes curled possessive around mine. I roll over onto my stomach and put my leg over her buttocks, snuggle up to her -- let her breathing soothe me back to sleep – but did I really "wake up" yet again?

Was it Ashti there? Was it really? Only some kind of echo of her remains. History arranged in permutations -- the moments fluttering back and forth like cards in a deck being shuffled, tarot cards

Browsing through the cosmic cuntradictionary?

163

with the faces of alien kings. We're making love, arguing, walking through the forest, riding down the road in a car with loud worrying engine noises, eating Chinese food, singing. I'm sitting on the toilet -- I am defecating backwards, the feces climbing up out of the toilet, squirming into my rectum, climbing back out of my mouth in the shape of food. Enterorectogestion, mates! And sex goes in reverse, from contented snuggly afterglow to wild throbbing passion to slow, eager, sensual foreplay to the initial approach, the smile, the shy request. The direction of time is a d/scream. And I'm an ignorant child -- playing out by the trees behind the house   --

pretending the fortress and I am of an ant, through one another, feeling of the joints my three parts. masturbating, first time, about one of the tenth grade class, her bending over

BROWSING THRU the cosmic cuntradictionary, soared spaceward on the shell of the OBSCENE BIRD OF NIGHT -- shat on like jack-0 by dummy apesuck poetry – Singularity for Dummies – psychopathic Buddha Machines alight! – hard to believe – hard to believe – hard to believe...

anthill is a in the body crawling tunnel after the tension between I'm not for the thinking girls in my imagining and asking me to

FOOLS THOUGHT THE ALIENS WOULD COME IN SPACESHIPS
FOOLS RAPT IN MEATSPACE
FOOLS!

take her from behind, obsessing on the curve of her soft young ass until the hot moment comes to me. I'm staring at the computer, staring at the computer, staring at the computer's illusory vagina. The computer is staring at me, with its obscene eye, an eye that looks from nowhere thick in the future and tries to see beyond beyond.   My brain churns through equations, unraveling its neophyte necrophile neuropile and tying itself in trans-dimensional meta-knots.   I'm in Africa, playing the music, feeling my hellsoul almost come into existence, looking at the **1888** brown flesh of the pygmy beautiful- disasterbots and wishing I could feel as they did. I'm picking sandworms out of my **1888** feet, and watching them burrow quickly in again, watching the particles of which **1888** they're composed undulate with postquantum indeterminacy -- watching them mate with each other blindly through instinct, watching myself mate with Ashti-Ngouma, tasting the infinite cocktail of her lust.

I wake up again and Ashti's no longer beside me. I've rolled over onto my back, which slightly aches, a reminder of this human mess.

I close my eyes to sink back into the drama – though I'm not sure I want to – in fact I'm sure I don't want to – and was it really a dream or a train of thought? -- but fuck it, sleep won't come to me anyway, my body is wide awake and eager, though eager for what I don't know. My flesh wants her touch, but the damn bitch is gone somewhere. I get up and stagger out of bed.

She's in the bathroom – the door's locked – she's taking a crap I guess. Can't face lying in bed alone. I crawl out **1888** of bed and sit at the computer. The news comes up on Yahoo, but something's gone wrong. It's giving me the news from 1888, which was rather many years ago. I remember a long odd dream.

I'm seized with the urge to go back to the forest -

- to my imaginary companion, to the goddess of Ngouma's psychoelectric vaginal church named Ashti. Things were simple up there in the jungle -- just her, beautifully walking, and me. It's true, she never said anything. Her nonexistence started to tire after awhile. But the trees stood, and understood.

"Look at this," I show her. She's in her skimpy pink nightie, hair all ruffled and cute from sleep. "The news. It's from 1888. On Yahoo and every other site."

I realize I have lost mental balance

"Yeah," she says, staring. "I don't get it."

"Why would they be showing ancient news?"

"What are you talking about?"

I look at her. She really doesn't get it. She doesn't see anything strange there at all. Is she putting me on or what? She isn't.... Her eyes are wide and sweet and open, but they're looking at me like I'm fucking nuts. She's two years old, but she's taller than I am. She's sucking a pacifier. I look down at my crotch and I have no dick at all. I remember a little more of my dream -- the shit sucking up into my ass -- the sperm oozing out of her into my urethra and back into my testicles -- the child Solomon shuffling cards covered with ants, each card with the face of my mind from a different moment, the moments tumbling around like cosmos revueltos, like bodies caught up in hyperdimensional orgies, and my penis grows back into a monster, with the head of a dragon and a professor, just one of the many tongues from the infinite mouth at the beginning of the end of the world.

I know I'm in some strange sort of place. It looks like my apartment but it's not. This woman looks like Ashti but she's not – or maybe she is, who knows? What makes up a Ashti anyway? -- just a collection of

166

I realize I have lost mental balance

patterns, just an assemblage of sparks seen, unseen, heard, said, felt, unsaid. I touch, tease and taste my lover's soul – but it is attached to my mind or external reality? I realize I have lost mental balance. All the concepts I'm using, all the bricks of my thoughts, suddenly feel like mud and madness. I think of Wittgenstein, telling his eight-year-old students, in-between beatings, that words are just playthings, minds are puppets of ideas, ideas are puppets of minds, beating them with bludgeons, sucking the cocks of New York street hustlers, ascending to Jupiter to commune with the infinitely wise beings meditating in the red spot, sitting there drowning in the stench of their enlightened menstruation. I reach my tongue out in my mind's eye and I find Ngouma's tongue, which is the same as Nietzsche's tongue and Ashti's left areola, which is the same as all tongues clitorises and cell nuclei everywhere, and after giving the universal earlobe a quick nip I give it the biggest lick of all, the one that brings the universe to orgasm immediately, and I plunge into this nine-dimensional vagina, whose it is I'm not sure anymore.

```
reconstruct realities you've never imagined - klein-bottle-
ize your winky - expand your large breasts of salt through
the cosmos - envision yourself as an equation - a system of
explosions - it's all bit strings, baby, bit strings! - bits
of strings and strings of bits!  unravel the knot of the not
- Awake!!!!  Alive words pound!  Alive words pound!  Alive
words pound pound pound!!
```

I'm sitting in the chair by my computer. I must have fainted or something.
I'm lying in my bed asleep.

"Are you OK?" she says.

"I guess so...," I reply slowly. "I had a really weird dream."

"Yeah?"

"You wore me out last night," I say, smiling.

And here I am sitting in the forest, and my Ngouma is sitting beside me, mending some holes in a hunting net. And the woven patterns in the net are beyond the measly sick capacities of my primate/human mind – they go on forever, in infinitely different colors, weaving patterns that chart out every mind, every possible form of being ever, every shift of every multiverse, every possible pattern of consciousness, every possible dream within a dream within a dream....

I am lying in my bed asleep

Some kind of choreographed experience? -- designed to bring my mind to understanding? -- some kind of aborted transcension? Horny love for the final end of the (ugh) human continuum? A bug in some cosmic program? Perhaps the transcendent uber-aliens had moved on to another cosmos, leaving simpler nonsentient software to run the virtual reality simulation controlling the world of us humans? Perhaps the nonsentient VR software had been running Microsoft Windows 3000 and had crashed irremediably, memory segmentation faults causing errors in realities?

Or maybe one of me had transcended and the other one of me -- the me that was *me* now -- had requested to stay human and have his mind wiped of the experience of seeing the other one transcend. And had requested to be sent back to 2011. But why with this limited set of memories? Why not wipe all memory of the future altogether? It mattered exactly as much as it mattered. I looked into the cosmic mouth and saw no tongues anymore – no dragon's eyebrows, no

168

professors, no fire and universes and beauty and time and vacuum-sucking and clitorises – just an infinite empty perfect void, looking blacker than black can be --

And then a voice – a voice --

"Honey, you're talking in your sleep again."

I reached toward wakefulness. "What? What was I saying?"

"I couldn't understand any of it."

"Mmmm. Shit. Really weird dreams."

"Yeah?

The gap between minds. But her body was soft and warm. She might have understood some of it – but how could I speak it to her? The words would get old and dead. Not exactly a dream – a dozen dreams mired and wired in trains of thought. That mouth – that professor – that latticework of butts – my penis kept growing and shrinking -- I couldn't begin to tell anything. I needed to sleep – really sleep. I pulled her soft flesh toward me sweetly, kissed her sleepy cheek. "I love you."

"Love you too."

"Mmmm."

Her kiss fades, and with it her face and her body. And this time there's a kind of finality – and I'm staring at the ceiling, being Dr. Solomon Godunov – the crazy computer scientist who left his beautiful girlfriend for programming, AI and madness. No, actually, she left you. But you made her do it. You were much too obsessed for any woman to tolerate. -- Obsessed with

Our bodies formed a city, or maybe a mountain range, with aliens of various colors, shapes and sized living on us, but only our heads were solid like statues, like moving solid sphinxes, Mexican lions or alien gods and goddesses or icons for the core of humankind, and our bodies spread out till by the time your reached our knees they had diffused into the countryside, the alien hills and valleys blue, green and yellow, with buggies and rockets and impossible emergent chains of beings-formed-from-beings-formed-from-beings moving up and down and between and beside us, but we two were the center of it all, our brains and bodies the mountains from which the aliens drew their energy – not really the only center, just one of the many centers, or one of the interpretations of the center – but we were there and we were one being, formed from the **thummerings of the alien multitudes or else the earth and cosmos on which the aliens existed –**

what? You're coming back to yourself now, Solomon –
you were asleep; you had a really long dream. That
crack on the ceiling's not so interesting. Look at the
cockroach: you were him once, and soon you'll be
something else, and look back on yourself as essentially
equivalent to this creature -- your prior six-legged
incarnation. You'll occupy regions of higher cosmic
mind and these issues of love and affection and women
will seem as pathetic as the roach wandering the ceiling
at random desperately looking for a crumb.

You're coming back to yourself now, Solomon – you were asleep; you had a really long dream.

There are no crumbs on the ceiling, moron! Remember your computer … your chair … that stained brown chair with the worn-down right armrest on which you've leaned back slowly thoughtful and had the best ideas of your life. Ashti just couldn't respect the ideas – only the continuum of half-differentiated philosophical lunacy that provided them midwifery. Was it really a bad choice: an intricate network of new ideas, leading beyond the human species to an entirely new order – versus the taste and soft glory of her flesh? You tell me. And who the fuck was that professor anyway? The third root of your soul? Why back to 1888? That was the year Nietzsche went insane. Was that when, in his syphilitic inner-verse, he finally became the Superman? And got to stay that way for 11 years, in his own mind, before his body crapped out? Urrrgghh – face it, Solomon! You have an unconscious! But it

170

doesn't really matter very much. What matters is the software code – all the structures encoding the dynamics of mind, that you've carefully spelled out for the last five years. Because you know they're almost ready. All the software is right, all the preliminary tests are passed, and all you need now is a thousand times more computers. Just one big computer network away from the Singularity – then you won't be lying here anymore, having crazy dreams about your girlfriend – ex-girlfriend, Solomon, ex, remember it's been a really long time, she's probably five lifetimes beyond you now – your ex-girlfriend – remember her new boyfriend with the handlebar moustache and the fourteen-inch cock and secret bank account in the Caymans! -- you won't be lying staring at the cracks in the ceiling, you'll be floating through unimaginable universes of equational ecstasy, synthesizing realities from inklings, spreading consciousness through subatomic particles – the fuck with the fuck with the fuck –

OK, so get out of bed: you're wasting time speculating. You comprehend the inner nature of the labor in front of you. Your comprehension has been strengthy for weeks and days now, but you've been procrastinating – ridiculously – you human fool. This part of the work is done. You've built the software, now you just need to find the intestinal fortitude to make a Powerpoint presentation, you need to clean up your user interface so someone else can understand it, to make clear the kind of reasoning going on in the program so others can admire its brilliance. Who are you going to talk to? There's always IBM. But they're so fucking slow-moving. What about Keith Rogers – he got a job at Zorvex – they're not exactly in the AI business but they've got a lot of computers. And they really like money – they're hungry. Keith would understand what you've got here. Keith could sell it to the management for you. Imagine ten thousand networked Linux boxes running this whacko shit. You know what'll happen. Or rather you can't know, but you know it'll be something you can't know, and that's the whole beautiful point. Of this pointlessly beautiful endeavor. Right now – this very moment – this is the entire apex of human existence. The knowledge, in this human mind, that the human mind – the human cultural mind, of course; the little piece that I've contributed just happens to be the finishing touch to this amazing strange edifice, go back to the Greeks and the Sumerians and Newton and Einstein and good old Homo habilis and the inventor of the transistor and Boole and his uncle and whatever else you want to bring to mind – the whole conceptual continuum – but this is the finishing touch – the knowledge in the mind of humanity that it's finally succeeded in bringing itself to an end. Of all the idiotic confusions of human nature, science was the one that had the most potential to bring a non-destructive destruction to the human meta-madness. But it's still just a picture in your head. The walls of your mind know they're going to break down soon – and what lives outside them? What's beyond the beyond the beyond?

But first you need some more machines? -- Is that right, professor? Then it'll be 1888, 1988, 20288, 8 million BC – it doesn't matter. Damn, I'm hungry! I've got to get out of bed

out of **bed**.

Here was the infinite – the true deeper reality – the aliens running through giant green factories with blue tubes and orange veins, and each alien's bloodstream like a Solar System sized factory with endless little aliens passing messages around in overlapping latticeworks, and each alien itself inside some other alien's inner factory, and I myself a .

I couldn't understand it

Somewhere in the midnight between us and continuity I wonder

Simplicity is so complicated

I couldn't understand it

fluid diffusing through the cracks between the conveyor belts and tubes and pontoons and indescribable multicolored mechanisms of the alien metaphorical factory, producing metaphors for its own existence with blue-green insatiable love, moving from each part of my body to each part of hers through all the future and the past with unstoppable curiosity and force, discovering everything anew each moment in spite of already knowing everything....

Simplicity is so complicated

173

the prehistory of mind

-----

n'th-eye visionary, i'th-eye blind ... com(e)plicit simplicial complex of thoughts slash(ing) feelings – a vision of the future beyond the circle of the time axis and also of another realm – immanence and transcendence in one – sexual and cognitive and transhuman and personal and objective and massively perfectly human all at once and multiply –

rewind to 1987 (was it 1888?), she and i in the bowels of bad ole 'Bama, 21 (*Big Black Betty – Black Jack! – Spanish Eddy – Spanish Eddy – Big Black Betty – Black Jack! --- ???*), consumed with uhh-uhhh and delirious intention (– uhhh...

-------- like Pan's transnihilistic mucous of uploaded paramecia, it was intended to be the square root of negative one'th coming of the messiah – the metamegamultiversal upchuckings and semen-spurts of the nowhere man – everywhen and nevermore ... whatever....

alive words pound! alive words pound! alive words pound pound pound!

"Admire my manly chest or go down trying!" -- constructing inklings of another world out of fragments of this colossal (anti)achievement and (t)error of human socio(patho)logy, linguistics and psychology ...
Psychotic Fantasy and Fugue --
Uncle, uncle -- here I am –

It is proposed that the creation an exaggeration and a parody and a mockery and a perfect snatch of oneness -- that magic look of recognition: ultimate and whacky, perfect and still of Artificial General Intelligence (AGI) at the human level finishing touch

"Beauty is in the lie of the beholder"

to this amazing strange edifice and ultimately beyond is a problem addressable via integrating into this computer a different kind of color-ish, glow-like quality I'd never experienced before such science -- strange beauty of strange lines like these (proprojective geometry) that try, but fail, strange truth to seize (ooh! kiss me! oh!) -- algorithms and data structures within a seeing the illusion as an illusion all the time was possible but ultimately cognitively horrible wonderful corner-hole of dreamland architecture oriented toward experiential learning. A general conceptual framework for AGI is presented, beginning with a strange beauty of the girl I see in the center of my mind based on the philosophy of pattern, then moving to a general sitting on a curbside naked staring at the sky as if to find conceptual mathematical frameworks for cognitive modeling

Simplicity is so complicated I couldn't QUAQUAQUAQUA

in the middle of the vortex of quantum-dynamical pattern-love – ooh, ahh, ooh, ahh, ahh, ahh!!! -- intelligent systems based on self-modifying evolving probabilistic hypergraphs, and finally Consistency. Coherence and consistency. The rhythm of temporality. The mind's not quite a mind in a dream, to overview a specific, long black hair unmoved by the delicate wind. The problem of teaching an AGI system is Why the hell I love her, as discussed in the context of the embodiment of AGI systems in 3D simulation worlds, wherein a detailed educational program based loosely on Piaget's developmental stages is outlined, in contumescence with the extremely strange beauty of imagining the world as it can't ever be screaming your song of undead torture in fifteen billion languages (out of the chaos of the world), inviting others into one's illusion – followed by more detailed consideration. You almost have justified your existence of the learning in simulation worlds -- Kids, kids, kids, kids, kids, kids!! ....of the Piagetan infant-level capability of "object permanence, strange beauty of the big-brained beast that, passionate, extends -- to grasp it all and taste it all then, helpless, simply terminates its termination as the global riverrun, Eve's and Adam's, brings us forth, and back, and back! – and the sum of the explosion of the difference is the modicum of what? what? what?   SCREAMING YOUR SONG OF UNDEAD TORTURE – TORTURE – WHAT? WHAT? *WHAT?*

screaming your song
of undead torture
in fifteen billion languages
(out of the chaos of the world)

                          HELLO? DR.
GODUNOV?
                          THIS IS YOUR FUTURE
SELF
          Solomon Godunov – Godfrey Solomonoff --
          Wake up slowpoke, we're going FLY fishing!!!
Is there a there that's not there?
Is not not not not?

On the other hand, claw, phantasmagorically,
Schwarzeneggeran-pearl of supergenius hatred, rip skin
from bones, gnaw living breath organic, ridicule and
loathing, understanding the little-child weakness at the
bare heart of every thing, casting it down into the
undulant darkness and shaking it till it bleeds its very
essence out into the black dead ground

Put one foot on the light,
And one foot on the darkness,
don't lift them up no matter what

You'll find your legs spread apart so wide cruise missiles
from an alternate assemblage of universes reprogram
your munificent cognosphere, blast right into your twat,
drooling with menstrual blood and love juice, and then
you wake up in sweaty sheets, overwhelmed with forty

orgasms and begone -- wondering at the horrible
wonderful corner-hole of dreamland in which you've
somehow found your sorry ass

                         I AM MERELY AN

EMISSARY

                                    CREATED

                AS
                A KIND OF
                INTERMEDIARY
              BY A BEING WHOSE NATURE
YOU
on the edge between beautiful and ridiculous, ARE
NOT
                        CAPABLE TO
                COMPREHEND

-- disguised cleverly as nothing: screaming out
soundless like the voice of the voice of the voice of the
voice --

In the algebra of despair, the sum of voids is void
One foot strapped to each porn-algebra,
grin and ski through the quacking cosmos,
feel the bits of my mind-engine rape your skin
with such delicate perfection of not

                something for nothing
             is a dream of mine
        "Mine, mine" -- mask of evil
        "Mine, mine" -- stare it down

Put the self in a cage,
IMAGINE YOU WERE YOURSELF
toss the cage in the ocean,

"What if you found out you'd
been drugged all your life with a pill that
made you half – or a tenth -- as smart as
you were supposed to be? Would you
keep taking the drug, just to retain the
status quo – the feeling of 'youness'. Or
would you stop taking the pill, and let
your intelligence return to normal – even
knowing it would change you
completely?"

the shit sucking up into my ass --
the sperm oozing out of her into
my urethra and back into my
testicles -- the child Solomon
shuffling cards covered with ants,
each card with the face of my
mind from a different moment, the
moments tumbling around like
cosmos revueltos, like bodies
caught up in hyperdimensional
orgies, and my penis grows back
into a monster, with the head of a
dragon and a professor, just one of
the many tongues from the infinite
mouth at the beginning of the end
of the world.

BUT FIFTY BILLION TIMES AS INTELLIGENT
drink the ocean and ejaculate
AND IMAGINE YOU FACED A KIND OF
fourteen gorgeous breast-volcanos
META-HISTORICAL CATASTROPHE
let the milk steam the sky
RELATED TO THE COLLAPSE OF
diffusing the atmosphere
MULTIPLE SCHEMES OF CONSTRUCTING
rain across the belly of the earth
TEMPORALITIES
Lie down naked on grasses,
let my tongue wake your follicles
AND PHYSICAL REALITY WAS (INTENSIVELY)
AT PLAY
embryo growing in nothing
HOW WOULD YOU PROCEED
Mess.
EXCEPT TO BROADCAST MOST DIRECTLY YOUR
Quivering, wavering
DESIRES AND COGNITIONS
For one set free from sensual desire
DIFFICULT
there is no grief
INCOMPREHENSIBLE
not me!

The body is a stone fetus
the body is an abortion

**Awake! Awake!
Awake! Awake!!!!!**

The body is a dying husk of filth
A patch of nerve cells, quivering and dancing,
laughing and orgasming at the hint
nonlinear patterns of attraction/repulsion,
building planets and software swells and comets,
arraying panting moaning screamlets of passion

Love is always where
Somewhere
It's there
not/
it's always there
Invert.
Pervert

please stay...
no, run away
before I change my mind
stay!

ill will
will
will will?
will will will?
will will will will?

fire like passion
crud
taste the flavor of vine's heavy nipples

BITE the nipples at their base
savoring the illusion
swallow them
like leeches and chocolates
they'll migrate through your digestion
reaching the tip of your silicon-plated weenus
transforming you into the Lizard King --
immortal infinite and demented,
screaming your song of undead torture
in fifteen billion languages,
fucking every molecule in the universe,
confusing pain and brain and love and lust

-- brain lust blood juices --

That screaming voice:
it is a demon fueled by magma
Lust is an angel touched by teeth
The menstrual blood, sperm and nothingness,
mucous of various oozing orifices, motions
backward and leewards,
counting to eleven in iridescent languages,

In the furious geometries of ideas, equations and nations al
masturbating its own eternal leprosy

Filth!!!

in celebration of its improvised greed —
we give birth to our own poopocalypse
grabbing out at what it knows it can't,

Christ on the criss-cross pissing mushrooms
pulling it in and so suddenly
enjoying (what?),

lying in my bed screaming head lit back not the bats it's, rollowing forth like a dream
of a dream —
and not
wanting, not, pushing it away
it's always there/not
and then begging for it back again,
Invent
sometimes wondering why it's not -- what --
Pervert

And then it's so simple:
You're here now,
you're perfect
Look at you: a woman, a body
Standing naked,
waiting for me eager,

yeah
so what are all these concepts
and words?

Illusion?

Which is which whywhich, or why is whom whenwhere
how unknown is the difference between somewhere

183

perhaps
understood, or not, perhaps time in the central
of the not or invisibly
somewhere the thing
that screams
thing

Somewhere in the midnight
between dis and continuity
I wonder
Simplicity is so complicated
I couldn't understand it

The random stimulates pattern-understanding
Restless quasi-alien chowder of the mind

I SEE

The random alien-generated confusion
strikes the soft-stroke core of conscious
like a lingering luscious love-lump dream

I know still I'm here and still there,
               FAREWELL MY SOMBER
jumping to this world or the other
         ECHO
unable to dissolve in the not

Possibly
                             MISS YOU

get down on your podgy knees and beg for it --
or you'll just be left to want and to wait –
until the end of this time –

to want

and

to wait

until

the end

of time

(which does not exist –
                        (or –

reconstruct realities you've never imagined –
klein-bottle-ize your winky –
expand your large breasts of salt through the cosmos –
envision yourself as an equation –
a system of explosions –
it's all bit strings, baby, bit strings! –
bits of strings and strings of bits!
unravel the knot of the not –
shuffle glib through the rooms of
the palace of wiggle and wiggle your ass –
fuck the metallic claw of hatred –
cleaner than the consciousness of a cockroach –
silicon or undergarments –
nine times cleverer than Einstein's uncle –
and then – and then – and then –

Remember What You Are!
Learn – Be Concerned
Leoncern
Leoncern
Leoncern

Discovering nothingness.
Out of the chaos of the world, the fluctuating
bodies of man and woman, ill-defined chasm of the

mind, we have to create characters, plots, scenarios, dreams and visions.

We have to because it has already been done. It is our mode of being.

Incredible beauty of the self-supporting system. The world sustains itself; each part lifting the others in a kind of perpetual motion of forms. I am that I am; the world is because it is; everything is a pulsing.

There's nothing more to say. There's nothing left to say at all. There never was anything to say in the first place.

But still we make stories. Demented stories, ordinary stories, stories of soaring to the heavens or descending to the pits of hell. Stories of nothing; sparks and patterns labeled people.

to want

and

to wait

until

the end

of time

Out from the center of the pearl-happy void, the sound that echoes against itself and turns from scream to dream.

Discovering beautiful abandon. The feel of a vagina in the morning. The movement of air across two bodies in the gooseshit tropic night. The movement of minds through each other's spaces; the generation of collective mindspace; bold battling of nothing with weapons of nothing; impossible quest to understand.

I can write it all. I can't write nothing. I can only write anything. There's nothing to write about at all.

My name is Solomon, Ashti, Kaniak, Adam, Zennica, Erica, Scarica, Brittany, Tittany, Zennica, Zarathustra, Zephaniah, Zoetrope, Zerubabbel, Friedrich, Chandra, Dahlia, Jesus H. Satan Christ, Elvis Mussolini, the Godfather of Filet of Sole – Jack! It doesn't matter. Names and bodies are just delusions.

Everything is nothing; there are only sparks surrounded by patterns. Patterns of patterns of sparks.

Everything is duplex, multiplex, sexplex.

Everything is beautiful delirious madness, from the core of the future metatranscomputerverse to the middle of the mushroom to this sc/dream.

Beauty is illusion.

You know that I love you.

You know I don't anything at all.

The two poles of existence, man/woman and uncle, are created to make an illusion of solid being against the whorl of the nothingness.

You know that I love you *(wow!*

Let's try to feel. It's not possible not to feel. The feeling is spark in the dark.

Inspiration is a dead codfish. Really nothing is new or old. Everything is absolutely original and absolutely derivative. Movement is everything but all things are still.

Stupid paradoxes. Sophomoric amusements. Sub-imbecilic semi-internal monologo-dialogues.

But there really is nothing else.

Except –

Discovering chaos, beautiful chaos, beautiful intricately structured chaos, in the incredibleness of an equation, the laughing of a young child when it rains

and you get to	**existence is**	run around
outside and get	**to exist and**	soaked in it –
warm friction of	**existence is**	a girl's hungry
tongue –	**to exist and**	reaching too
deeply -- In the	**to exist and**	symphony of
words flowing	**existence is**	out from the
nothing in the	**to exist and**	form of my
oversized lips or	**to exist and**	my fast-typing
fingers. In the	**to exist and**	furious geometries

of ideas, equations and nations and frogs.

Incipit Psychotopia!

We are pregnant with topology. Our boundaries burst with death and shape. We are soft love incarnate.

Listen: the echoes of the great farewell. The voice screams the convergent parallels of

In the furious geometries of ideas, equations, nations and frogs,

humanity and its non -- beginning and ending -- we give birth to our own poopocalypse, creating technologies so wonderful they make our idiocy painfully clear and too erotic --

And I understand it. I understand everything. There's no way to get across your feelings. No way to speak the spark of mind. It's all a mission inconceivable.

Once a human really understands – or really communicates – they're not a human anymore. They have Transcended – post-post-post-post-Singularity – the world has become a different place – they have exited the universe -- and entered a different, better mode –

But that's no reason not to try (or to).

Angel-devils are singing. The baby AI is humming,

we create our own poopocalypse of love

some kind of melody no one but itself can grok -- Everything is yours to understand -- especially your lack of understanding – the cure for which is the –

Chanson d'adieu –

Love the glory of your own termination – such a beautiful beautiful duty – you never were here to begin with, fool! – you always will be here, just like now –

Christ on the criss-cross pissing mushrooms, me sitting at the computer tap-tapping my fingers or making love or walking on the beach or thinking mathematics or pushing my daughter on the swing in the playground or existing – existing – or not – or lying in my bed screaming, head cast back at the cosmos, billowing forth like a dream of a dream –

(Ashes to ashes --

dust to dust --

dream to --

make large groups of ideas
march in complex
formations
like armies of multiple
alien species

Cloudless everyday you fall
upon my waking eyes
Inviting and inciting me
to riiiiise
And through the window
in the wall
Comes streaming in
on sunlight wings
A million bright ambassadors
of moooorning

And no one sings me
lullabies
And no one makes me
close my eyes
And so I throw
the windows wide
And call to you
across the skyyyyyyyy

Cloudless everyday you fall
upon my waking eyes
Inviting and inciting me
to riiiiiise
And through the window
in the wall
Comes streaming in
on sunlight wings
A million bright ambassadors
of moooorning
And no one sings me
lullabies
And no one makes me
close my eyes
And so I throw
the windows wide
And call to you
across the skyyyyyyyy

-- Pink Floyd, "Echoes"

ashes to ashes
dust to dust
dream to dream
ashes to ashes
dust to dust
dream to dream
ashes to ashes
dust to dust
dream to dream
ashes to ashes
dust to dust
dream to dream
ashes to ashes
dust to dust
dream to dream
ashes to ashes
dust to dust
dream to dream
ashes to ashes
dust to dust
dream to dream
ashes to ashes
dust to dust
dream to dream
ashes to ashes
dust to dust
dream to dream
ashes to ashes
dust to dust
dream to dream
ashes to ashes
dust to dust
dream to dream
ashes to ashes
dust to dust
dream to dream

I should have known it would be like this –
awkward for the first moment, then beautiful and
tremendous, as if no time had ever passed at all.

Buddham Saranam Gacchami! (And similar brain-
cocks of corrugated Nazi-sense, so beautifully scented
like your underarm at dawn?)

I pull you toward my midnight,
like a dress to be unbuttoned –
I will undo your beautiful self with love
But it's just another goddamned dream

(and that voice!

I got fed up with the AI and took off, I was living
on some tropical island with 5 pygmy wives, who were
fused in a hive mind -- then a number of my friends
showed up and tried to save me from the pygmy
voodoo spell I was under. Then you came up and
looked at me long and hard. (*"Verrrry long and verrry
hard!!!"*) You'd brought me a big bouquet of roses and
you said "Remember, you asked me to marry you, in
1779. Well, I thought about it, and...." I said, "what are
you, crazy? I already have 5 wives. It's too late.
Anyway that was just a crazy whimsical notion. We
hardly really know each other." And you said: "Yeah,
and you REALLY KNOW all these pygmies? Look at
you!" I looked at you at a loss for words, not knowing
whether to go off with you, to tell you to leave, to try
to explain why the pygmies really were my destiny, or
what. so I took your face in my hands and kissed you,
following which, your head exploded, and I exploded,
and I was a severed head lying on the ground. One of
the pygmy wives picked up my head and carried it off
into a peculiar kind of forest ritual, with amazing lights

and sounds that I don't have the wisdom to describe now.... then the light show ended and sometime later you re-emerged, with a square metal robot body and your head stuck on a pole coming out of the top of the robot body, and your actual hands and feet at the end of metal poles in the appropriate places. Your fingers were really really long, like 2 feet long. You propositioned me in some way, I think telepathically rather than in words. I pointed out that you were a robot. You said "what, so you only liked me for the way I looked?" I said, "No, but I did like the fact that you had a HUMAN body... the all-metallic thing just doesn't turn me on... sorry... but we can still be friends..." You started to cry. Then some other guy appeared and he walked off with you. I was incredibly jealous. My dear sweet wife was lying there dead; the pygmies had killed her. I forgot about you and started trying to resurrect her, but uselessly. I cut open her belly and took out a fetus of mine that was in there, but it was some kind of horrible mutant, or, later, it was a fragment of light, glowing weirdly... I can't remember any more...

Shadows of the rare – alive!
"Aha!" he said, waking impossibly. "Eyes of women – Shadows of the rare – Eyes of boiling blood – Embryos of illusions –"
"Ecstatic eyes?" she whispered.
"Possibly," I averred.
"Be quiet," he said. "Enough of your nonsense?"
"Enough of my nonsense?" he replied. "Who else's nonsense is there?"
"That's for me to know and you to find out!"

He remembered himself – I remembered my tenuous existence -- he had fallen asleep at his desk – leaning back in his soft chair – thinking about equations and death. In his sleep his mind had shifted from equations to eyes of women – nefariously and inevitably – vibrating like a cosmos --

He stared at his computer – there was an e-mail about reason – the mathematics of reason – tracking errors in reason -- by means of advanced calculus – and he tried to understand it -- understood it and forgot it – he looked at the words and saw eyes – the eyes of the woman who wrote it – young and sweet with an infinite-state machine under idealistic long black hair – rings too tight on her fingers – a quick smile – eyes that never quite looked at him but almost -- or maybe for a moment – "Step into my moment, or don't!"

An e-mail from the bowels of his mind? He'd become too close to the computer; his left hemisphere was receiving emails from his right.

This woman was Ashti, or was not. The wavelet transform of Ashti's fragrant saffron armpit, transmogrified by the sadness of her mind, elected President of some past life that I couldn't quite remember but I knew lived in my future with the pygmies and beyond.

It didn't work, she said, tracking errors in reason -- it didn't make any difference, the errors continued anyway -- no matter how hard you tried to measure and eliminate them. A puzzling result -- he was supposed to find the answer -- to explain how the errors could be found.

They were creating a computer program, they and several other people, which means other lobes of his brain, which means my brain -- a program designed to think and imagine for itself – it was my/his project, for a decade now – she was a recent addition, she was charge of the logical component – she was the Princess of Pure Reason he said – but as he stared now at her e-mail, all he could think was that reason is inadequate – fundamentally inadequate – when confronted with the maze of these eyes – haze of eyes – everywhere – staring – every molecule an eye within eyes – every atom an eye within eyes – every quark eyes within eyes within –

Did this person exist? It was a phantasm of some kind. The fourth quadrant of the right hemisphere of his brain. Temporal lobe epilepsy. Ashti divided by the concept of an equation. This Princess of Pure Reason. Euterpe unbound. A muse of his madness. He/me here/there in the middle of a dream of a dream.

They had posited a church in which they were the deities. Their mouths had done this while their eyes looked at various things and smelled their essences. Human sacrifices would be proffered. Unbelievers would be cast into several rings of hell, managed by bureaucrats and accountants, forced to write documents on software process in iambic pentameter. There would be a temple in the jungle, an appropriately sculptured mountain. The intelligent computer program – when it was completed – would ratify their godhood, elevating the holy to superhuman status, conferring the power to reconfigure the structure of the cosmos. Why not after all? What is the cosmos but patterns – patterns of arrangement of – yet smaller patterns – patterns within patterns within – There would be gods of hamburgers, turnips, petunias. Gods of toilet paper and cream cheese. Why not? Possession by the God of Train Tracks could be quite therapeutic. Heal your soul, wash your soul, squash your sins.

He rose from his desk -- felt a pain in his knee -- a two-years-old skiing injury improperly attended --

strode toward the door to his study -- sanctum of discovery and joy, torment and knowledge and ignorance – the superhuman AI program almost complete! – muse of mad equations – eyes of women – shadows of the rare –

In a nonexistent world she lay beside him – calling him beautiful – touching his eyebrow with her finger or her tongue – admiring most what she could not understand: his mania to make large groups of ideas march in complex formations like armies of multiple alien species – his urge to accomplish the impossible, to build the unbuildable – or is it really unbuildable? You never can tell until you try! -- but those brain-patterns are astonishingly effective – he realizes wearily – he knows he's known for a long long time – she sees no more beauty in him now than in a lump of dirt – or a dying horse – and why should she after all? – aren't all things equally beautiful? – but wasn't it nice when someone did? -- Even if she was a madwoman, basically – even if neither she nor anyone else existed --

Hold my body before sunlight -- Red lights across the planet's surface – Souls wide open beneath the mind's chatter – Take me – Take me, darling -- Take what chaos you desire –

"Talk to me about programming and AI, sketch their relationship in the most abstract terms possible," said the phantasm – not long before this moment -- "and then it would be really great to get fucked."

He raised his ancient eyebrows, "You don't say."

"I'm cynical," she says, "so cynical."

"You are," he thinks. "You really are. Cynical, lanky, foul-mouthed and poetic. Curvilinear physically yet angular spiritually. Giving blow jobs to strange men out on the streetcorner. Why?"

"I want to get out of the system," she said. "Find a different way of living. How can you stand it – the suburbs – jobs, kids, houses, bosses, employees. There has to be something different, or it's not even worth living, is it?"

"I used to think that way," I told her stupidly. "A different way of living." I removed a layer of skin like a snake. "The hell with society – with its norms and conventions. Find a new way of being -- one that expresses your inner self, your creativity, your nonexistent soul. But here I am now – doing nothing but programming – and I hate it, but it's necessary. There is not different way of living, not within the domain of the human. To go beyond we have to leave the human universe behind. Singularity. Transcension. Write code for more evolved intelligence, port our consciousness into it – then we can really be alive. That's the only way out of the rat-hole. No way I given up my ideals and desires – my crazy ambitions – no -- I'm still fighting for them just as hard – harder – I just see the correct path -- "

No, he said – the hell with her – her sex and dazed literature -- incomplete beautiful poems screaming out like nuclear winters – viola-symphonies emanating from twisting of notes around transdimensional eyeballs spying impossible passion-trembles -- centuries or quantum-instants of torture in her tiny eyes – she was appealing enough with her long legs and laughs -- It wasn't the bitch ex-wife from the alternate cosmos and her glaring-sickening reminder of the hatreds and glories and her sad lack of faith in your beautiful creations – it was the Princess of Pure Reason – the nonexistent fairy knight of 0's and 1's dancing in RAM-iverse – and her hallucinated proof that reason can't work – no, it can work, it can't work accurately – and her laughs and jokes and smiles and too-wonderful absurdity that sometimes comes out of nowhere miraculously spontaneously and sometimes tries to hide other things but fails miserably and flowers like flowers anyway -- mystically-maniacally –

(an image of a couple, living in a small white house, repeatedly screaming and making up; hanging a tropical-bird towel over the window so the neighbors won't see them hump)

Reason to the power of illusion, divided by the ninth root of madness, plus love, minus mystery, all considered as the base of a logarithm applied to the third derivative of the sweat dripping off the brow of the tapir who holds up the universe, balancing precariously on the back of the turtles all the way down.

"Why?"

"Yeah."

"You've had enough of your nonsense, remember?"

"I have?"

"Then what's this Princess of Pure Reason shit?"

"Shit."

"Precisely."

"You are a weird dude."

"I think you're right, I am."

"Eyes of women."

"Shadows of the rare."

"Embryos of illusions."

"Outrageous porno cassowary."

"Yeah."

Blue eyes light in red -- Hold up my body before sunlight -- Awake me and make me alive –

Twenty-nine hours previously he boarded an airplane, zooming in circles around the interior of his own hyper skull. He sat at his desk for fourteen months straight creating an intelligent computer program. The human body is a single-celled organism. It reproduces asexually each moment, splitting in two, but the second child is lost, vanishing into an unseen dimension, and the first child replaces the parent, and we never notice, unless we squint our eyes just the right way. These lost asexual children – these single-celled humans – these are the shadows of the glorious fucking rare – bits and pieces of software mentality – dreaming, sliming primordially through personalized cosmos – we have dug up fear and lust and rage, and a place/non-place more primal than the any --

"You make no sense at all."

"Of course I don't. Reason doesn't work, remember? The Princess proved it."

"The result was not definitive."

"The beauty of her face demonstrates it conclusively."

"She is the right hemisphere of your own brain."

"And what about the pygmy rhinoceros?"

"What are you talking about?"

"Not much."

"It's 20:12. It's nippy-time!"

"Indeed."

"You said you would put her in a sack full of hallucinogenic mushrooms and kidnap her, take her to Mongolia and force her to perform strange acts of carnality and combinatory logic in a darkened corridor full of earthworms."

"Did I?"

"Something like that."

"She thought you were joking."

"You *were* joking."

"True. "

" 'Her eyes surpass the waterlily
  With their iridescent darkness;
    Her face has the moon for friend

And her eyebrow's arch
        is brother to Love's bow.' "
"Huh?"
"Rajashekara. Sanskrit."
"That's stupid."
"Buddham Garanam Saatchi and Saatchi."
"That's stupider."
"Of course."
"She's ridiculous."
"We all are."
"True."
"The clock is a farce invented by devils."
"Yep."
"The world is a video game."
"Perhaps."
"This is boring."
"Is it?"
"You told that to the Princess – in the middle of the Pentagon – where the center of the Voice is held, in a Top-Secret chamber -- she said that believing it was real – conferring reality on the video game with belief – was the only thing that made life worthwhile – she said that seeing the illusion as an illusion all the time was possible but ultimately unsatisfying – she said – "
"She said what she said."
"Indeed."
"A rather existentialist position."
"Perhaps."
"Do you think she's right?"
"I don't care."
"And if you build a thinking machine – you and the Princess and the rest – all of you nonexistent animals – you and your medulla oblongata and substantia nigra and your temporal lobe epilepsy and your lusts and your blazing desires – your numinous faux(pas)-ferocity -- is it gonna waste its time sitting around thinking

199

about eyes and the nature of the universe and contemplating getting into the car and fucking imaginary girls and missing Ashti and transmogrifying her soul into invisible reasonable phantasy princesses and the taste of chocolate ice cream?"

"Perhaps. But I don't doubt it. Or rather I do doubt it. The human brain is pretty fucked up. And it'll be a machine – it won't taste, or fuck, or eat ice cream --"

"Accurate reason is impossible."

"Perhaps."

"You mean there are levels of erroneousness? Perfection that can be approached but not reached? But from which we are grievously, grievously far? And the machine may get closer? The program we create, we with our idiot minds, our desires running rampant, our shyness and impatience and glorious and tempestuous absurdity, our – "

"You sure do go on."

"Indeed. I know."

Iridescent darkness – fire of Asiatic hair-strands -- eyes of women – hatred – torture – iridescent darkness – long legs, shaved cunts and Henry Miller – dead dead dead dead past – invisible gripping/slipping future -- shadows of the ancient rare – embryos of illusions – rivers of torment / seas of joy – impure princesses of purity – teeth of the nothing – and damn words upon words upon words –

He stares at the screen of his computer – he has not driven anywhere – has not flown anywhere – has not teleported anywhere -- has not even walked anywhere – has not lifted his ass and moved – has not turned his neck five degrees – he has finally disappeared into iridescent realms of dreamy-drippy fantasy -- he has returned to his desk and has not done any work for two hours but has written strange words instead – words strung one after the other – he imagines them as jewels or beads, strung into a five-mile-long necklace, strung around the body of the Princess of Pure Reason and himself and George W. Bush and Idi Amin and Isaac Newton. A necklace of prayer for a nonexistent God or the beauty of the number seven. Who reads these words slips around their neck this multidimensional noose of glory and solitary weakness – this noose of prayer that is a soft wet tongue-kiss, less French than illicitly Arabian – this soft wet kiss that is a formula for madness – the kind of madness that evaporates and leaves only this and this and this

But does it have any meaning at all, beyond the mood of pure exhaustion? As the Princess says, -- quoting Jean Paul Sartre the basset hound not the philosopher -- the meaning is that which you give it -- and you give it the meaning you do because the alternative is no meaning at all. Meaning iridescent darkness or not. And fall asleep now, Doctor – lay down in the cushion of eyes real and imagined – softly, careful not to pop any eyeballs – lay down in the cushion of eyes and dreams and desires and delusions and simply, softly, stupidly sleep –

The program is coming along. It's almost complete now. Just a few more days, weeks, moments, years or months. Not decades, not centuries, millennia, billenia, eons. Tractable, touchable, immediate moments of time. The bits are falling into place, one by one. You almost have justified your existence.

Awake! Awake! Awake!

Buddham Saranam Gacchami

Guccham Salaam McBuddhami

BUDDHAM SARANAM
QUA QUA QUA
QUA

Spring Water Dripping[2]

The McBuddha Awakens!

Here I am – awake, alive and perfect!

The aliens sing to me – they massage me with their meanings – I undulate and oscillate in the infernal and timeless beauty of their songs –

Three for a dollar – seven for a dozen – sexologized serpentine shadows – how many concubinal souls for the price of a cake of your meat? –

And I'm in a broken-down city of rubble and ruins, post-nuclear-holocaust, circa 2100 AD. People are living in caves amidst crushed buildings, deep in old basements and sewer pipes, etc. Three-eyed mutant pygmy mountain pigs run rampant through the ruins. Phosphorescent tarantulas with the intelligence of monkeys roam the surface in hordes, hunting the pigs and occasionally humans. The sky is dark and smoggy, with satellite debris frequently crashing to earth. Yellow, red and green lightning occurs at all times of day, sometimes making inordinately beautiful patterns in the sky. Electric power is erratically available, and parts of the Internet still exist, but are populated largely by AI shopping agents run amok, striking complex deals with each other for futures and options on physical goods that no longer exist, such as plane tickets to cities that have been nuked into oblivion.

The streets are patrolled by robotic Buddhas on wheels, which fire exploding bullets from their navels; these are defective offspring of a research project in self-replicating software carried out at Maharishi University just before the (Singularity, er) holocaust. Some of these "Buddhroids" were programmed for tantric sex and due to a bug in their software make a habit of raping human women, forcing their victims' bodies into extreme twisted poses, tormenting them slowly and emotionlessly. (I'm sure that I have some responsibility but I can't remember what it is. Perhaps the devious Maharishis had taken an equation of my devising and transmogrified it into evil software. These were my children run amok!!)

A young couple are living in a hovel carved out of a collapsed skyscraper, with a pet Great Dane with a huge dangling weenus that is sometimes murderously psychotic (the Great Dane or the weenus??), but is very effective at chasing off the mutant three-eyed pigs. They look exactly like me and Ashti, with the exception of differences which I don't have the mind to resolve at this time. I have a strange feeling – I realized I am dreaming – but then I forget what dreaming is. The couple gets along terribly; she alternates between days of nymphomania and weeks of frigidity. She will eat nothing but roast pig; she nags and hounds him into dangerous hunting expeditions on the surface. He subsides largely on mushrooms, which he grows in a corner of their hovel.

Much of the day they spend screaming at each other, or throwing pieces of broken electronic machinery at each other. Respite is brought only by bizarre sex games in which, during her nymphomaniac periods, she binds him with spiderweb and alternatingly torments him and satisfies him. While he is out hunting, she seeks out Buddhroids and encourages them to torture her sexually. Sometimes the experience is just painful, other times it is divine. Once she has a truly enlightened experience, perceiving the whole universe as a huge white continuum, with a beautiful young man's face surging out of it, singing to her in psychedelic Mozart melodies. She returns home from this experience with a smile on her face, and prepares him a mushroom salad. He is overwhelmed and confused; and during the meal he inadvertently says something wrong, and the unpleasantness between them returns.

He is hunting. He sees what at first seems like a mirage, but then seems more vividly real than anything: a beautiful, saffron-skinned teenage girl, clad in colorful rags, standing amidst the ruins of an electrical power generating station. She looks at him with wide lusty eyes, but when he approaches her, she's gone. He is obsessed with the vision of this girl; imagines himself speaking to her, caressing her. He hunts incessantly, day after day and week after week, gradually becoming an unparalleled expert at dodging the psychopathic Buddha machines. In one battle, he crushes Buddha machine under a boulder, and he opens up its metal carcass, finding a peculiar glowing crystal inside, which he realizes is the quantum memory unit, the essence of its artificial mind. He carries this in his pocket, as a sort of good luck charm, and with the idea that it may be useful in the future.

In time, he finds the girl again, and when she looks at him this time, soft white eyes glowing against rich yellow skin, he holds up the crystal. She stays and stares. He approaches her. She does not speak, but clenches his hand. They sit and look at each other a while. After an hour or so she gets up and leaves. "Will I see you again?" he asks. She nods yes and smiles. He knows that she is lying: another one will come, but it will not be her, though it may look and feel exactly like her. The her that she is now is vanishing every moment.

They are making love, and he is enjoying it. I cannot feel it; I am hovering somewhere in the air – a kind of disembodied presence. I can't remember my name.

I wake up. I am flying in the air. I am in an airplane. I almost remember who I am, why I am there. But I don't want to remember. I want the dream back. Its tendrils scrape against the inside of my skull. They are making love, I am making love. It is a crazy mix of colors in the superordinary blackness.

I leave his body, float into the background. He is back with his girlfriend, the Ashti clone. She beats him to the edge of death. He doesn't fight back, just lies there and lets her strike him with broken computer parts. I am no longer him now; I can't feel a thing. I watch and hover. A vision of the dark-skinned girl pops into his mind, all of a sudden, like the rising of an alien sun. And into my mind as well. He summons his strength and thrusts her off him, tossing her into the wall, and leaves the hovel, with his crystal in his pocket.

The girl is living with a gnarled, angry, legless old man. He grows flowers, incredibly beautiful ones, some of them up to a foot in diameter and multi-colored. The flowers talk to him. The peace and gorgeousness of his garden contrasts with his dyspeptic personality. She runs through the city to find wrecked stores with bottles of spring water, which he then empties into the garden.

He kills a Buddhroid and wires it directly into the Net, with the intention of somehow downloading the intelligence of a Walbot (shopping bot) into its body. The situation is getting worse. There are more and more Buddhroids and they seem to be league with the tarantulas. Each horde of tarantulas is now led by a Buddhroid, and they scan the city, not only destroying pigs but also razing buildings to the ground. There are fewer and fewer places to hide. He goes out to look for the girl, the silent and beautiful one, dark angel who gives life meaning, but she's gone for good it seems.

The lightning storms are worse than ever. The

Net goes down and comes back up erratically. The building is collapsing. As he runs away from it he sees her walking toward him. But then she is gone again.

And out of the rubble of the building comes something new, something he hasn't seen before. The Buddhroid he had been working on is alive, but with something different on its head -- a Ronald McDonald face. Somehow the McDonald's ad from the Net has invaded his project. Instead of shooting bullets, this droid radiates light, in a kind of rich yellow spherical halo. As he walks through the city he sees french fries, appearing in huge piles, spontaneously generating from nowhere. The evil Buddhroids are dying. The tarantulas are burrow into the ground, fleeing the light. The pigs are still there, but are mellower, less menacing, more natural. The sky is dark, but there is hope.

I looked at her face and had, once again, the chilling yet reassuring certainty that I was living within – not quite a dream, not quite a simulation, not quite a hallucination – but something approximately evoked by all these imperfect human words. And while I might someday find my way out of this one – perhaps with an AI program that was constructed correctly so as to lead to a safe Singularity – the way out would just lead into another one – I never would escape from the maze of illusions, because this was the nature of my human mind. The definition of escaping implied losing my "I." I could never get out of here – "I" could never get out of "here" – "I" and ("here" AKA illusion) were part of the same interdefining mess, and I would be wracked in confusion as long as I was what I was – and if I became something else, something so different from me as not to live in illusions/simulations/ dreamscapes, then I wouldn't be myself anymore, so transcending myself like this would just be committing suicide – This illusoriness was it. This was it.

He wanders through the rubble in a daze, seeking her, seeking her, seeking her. She is nowhere. Finally he tunnels through the sewers and finds the flower garden where she lives. He parts the beautiful blossoms in amazement, until, aghast, he finds her body. The old man has killed herself and him; their corpses lie side by side, the knife clenched in his hand. He bends over and kisses her, hoping she'll revive a la Sleeping Beauty, but the miracle does not occur. Not at all. He sits amidst the flowers and cries. After a while there is a rumbling noise: the roof of the sewer has racked, and McBuddha, his grand creation, is visible, spreading light through the world. A small bird flies over the crack, through the light. He takes the knife from the old man's hand and stabs himself repeatedly, and dies. He is me – I feel my soul inside him, dying.

McBuddha travels across the landscape, purifying the city, and heading toward the hills. The pigs gobble up the french fries he is distributing. Everything is annihilated in his path; I am the only thing remaining, and I have neither body nor mind anymore; I am, merely and massively, a suspended dim blue light against an infinite eternity of black.

The McBuddha Awakens!!!

(And the echoes of
the end of the world --

I could program an AI again -- but not so manically this time – this time with calm and patience ... with you, darling, you by my side, ha ha ha – and McBuddha up the crack of my ass!

Regrets – I've had a few – fuck, fuck, fuck, fuck, fuck, fuck !!!

Halpern – you ugly Mephisto -- fat Irish bastard – why the fuck wouldn't you listen to me??? I'm screaming – am I screaming? But mark my balls I will rise, rise again!! Do you want a huggy-wuggy, dear?

Fucking fucking fucking fuck

Do you want a huggy-wuggy, dear?

Revolt!

At the current time, neither contemporary human society, nor the computer science community -- nor even the bulk of the academic or industry AI community -- is at all supportive of the quest to create powerful AI software. I believe that in hindsight, after true AI has been created, this lack of support and enthusiasm will be viewed with incredulity. AI is a hard problem but it's far from an impossible problem. It seems clear to me, based on my extensive theoretical study of the issues, that there are many possible solutions, and I believe that my own approach is one of them. Almost surely it's not the best possible one, but so far as I know it's the only likely-looking solution that's been proposed in detail so far. Understanding mind and creating AI are perhaps the grandest adventures humanity can undertake, and I've never doubted the value of pushing ahead in these directions in spite of the peculiar (to me) unpopularity of such an effort to the vast majority of other humans alive at the present time – including my own darling wife (!)

Do you want a huggy-wuggy!!

211

all the complexity of alien message-passing could be viewed as a beautiful painted whole

-----

The hotel room was tiny and just barely clean; the bathroom was out in the hall. There was a window looking out into a pit that may or may not have had a courtyard at the bottom, with a curtain that was either red, orange or brown depending on your state of mind and which drugs you'd been ingesting in the last couple hours. A little sink, a tiny white rickety desk that had no chair and was only usable as a table, and a full (not queen) bed. The ceiling was reasonably high. It was a fairly suitable box within which two humans could bend their bodies and minds.

The first thing was to get some hashish. But it was hard to get out the door because we were both so fucking horny. We still had years of separation to compensate for. We made love an hour and a half on the bed, without getting under the covers, licking and sucking and humping like overeager teenagers – then with great effort I convinced her we should get up and get dressed and go out. I was already in a demented frame of mind – thinking about nothing but her body – Ashti Ashti Ashti la la la! Thank God I'd overcome my doubts and inhibitions and decided to go out and look for you, instead of wandering sad and solitary on the stupid streets; so wonderful I'd found you!!! and the guy with the moustache didn't exist: you were single

213

and waiting, well not exactly waiting but eagerly ready to re-embrace my insanity, well not quite my insanity, but me me me – even the end of the world didn't mean so much to me then, I was too concerned with her breasts and her legs and the smell of her armpit and the smell of her clitoris and the feel of her tongue in my mouth and her fingers as they cradled my nads and the squeeze of my arms around my torso as I maniacally hugged her. We walked down the street with my arm around her and I was more than glad I'd found her – it was good – things were Good – better than they'd been before. I was a bouncing baby Solomon, like James Brown with neurochip implants! Everything was justified – the human race was worthwhile because of these exquisite moments – we were so full of anticipation (soon to be fulfilled, heh heh!) but not in a nervous way, the moments of waiting were too joyful and we generally forgot we were waiting (I'm not sure what was in her mind exactly, nor what was in mine, but at least we were thrilled to be together: some emotional attachment that existed between us, which was its own twisted (wh)or(e)ganism, embodied emergently in our (comm)union, had now come back to life again – it had succeeded in resurrecting itself – and I had some doubts on the intellectual level as to why this was important or even marginally meaningful but none on the emotional level: Ashti and I were together again! Qua qua qua qua qua qua! And I knew, on the level of feeling, this was part of the Grand Cosmic Plan – she and I would hold hands as the AI self-modified and watch the First Rays of the New Rising Sun!!) – but finally we got out of bed and out into the street and then finding the hash was a pain because the coffeshops closed at 1AM and we had to buy it from some crazy-looking Greek woman on the street, who had a brick of hash and wanted to sell us the whole thing but we only wanted to buy half of it so we had to cut it in half but no one had a knife so we followed her back to her friend the prostitute's place but the whore didn't have a knife either and she propositioned me but I told her we were married and finally she bit off some pieces and sold us the rest for a good price, and we went back to the hotel to smoke the hash (I had the feeling of falling off the cliff at the end of the world: off the flat earth into the nothing – turtles, nothing but turtles and turtles all the way down – the turtle that holds up the earth and the turtle that holds up him, and the turtle that holds up him, and the turtle that holds up him, and on – looking at turtle after turtle as I plunged, some of them winked at me or talked to me in strange turtle languages – and I knew this was my destiny: to fall down forever through pure empty space, living on zero point energy and communing with turtles as I fell past – but there was never any time to talk to them, never any time to get to know any particular turtle, only to see and hear each one very briefly – and commune with its glorious turtle-ness, and then on to the next and the next), but we didn't have a pipe so we spent half an hour trying to make one from some old metal tubing, but that failed so we ripped out the page from a book – a particle-physics textbook I'd brought to read on the airplane – and rolled a joint from the book – not the smoothest joint but the hash was good, relaxing at first then delirium-inducing, and I stood there caressing her naked body and kissing her while she drew long deep puffs from the joint, and she sucked on my hyper, starving weeny while I smoked and I felt I was in some Beat novel of European decadence, there in an Amsterdam hotel room with this gorgeous naked lady sticking her tits out and bidding me to suck on them while she smoked on her hash …

Leoncern

then down on the bed, sucking her cunt what seemed like an hour or two but was likely just ten minutes, hallucinating cunt-tunnels with glittering shards of existence flowing in one direction and the next – there was a whole crystalline cunt whose being was keyed to the real one, feeding the energy to the real one, stealing the energy from my tongue and turning it into liquid thoughts to be injected into my hindbrain ... I just lay there while she writhed up and down on me, arching her back waving her breasts in the air and slowly moaning, high as Charlie Parker playing "Ornithology", worshipping her body like she was a goddess, comfortable there was no other universe but this one (the end of the world be damned!) where her skin was moving back and forth and I took the flesh of her breasts in my mouths and played games with her nipples and pounded my weenus in and out of her – she came again and again and again, as if she hadn't come for the years we'd been apart, it must've been thirty times that evening, until she said she had to stop because it hurt too much to come anymore, but I wouldn't let her stop, we had to keep fucking, cycling through positions one after the other, turning her over on her belly on the bed and standing on the floor and ramming deep in from behind, all the way into her womb, penetrating the imaginary babies inside her who would grow up to be the next form of world; everyone in the hotel must have heard her screaming but it wasn't the kind of place anyone would complain. I lay on my back and she sat up on top of me, bending back so far my cock almost came off, shaking her breasts back and forth so far they flew off into the corner and we had to gather them up and reattach them, leaning her head back and moaning – repetitive in some irrelevant empirical sense yet whigmaleeriously different every time, each thrust its own invented universe; I

216

grabbed onto her cunt to keep her from flying off me as she bounced up and down; she looked like some kind of surreal sex-goddess flying up and down off me; the hash distorted distances and she seemed to be soaring into the sky then plunging down on me, sending my nuts into paroxysms of pleasure then soaring away again, and her hands on my chest leaving claw marks, her jaw pounding rhythmically up and down. Then the screaming was done and she was quiet; I lay there on top of her smiling and hugging her, moving in and out of her, she said that I should stop because it hurt and then I asked her if she really wanted me to stop and she said no, she wanted me to fuck her all night, and that's basically what happened – the hash made things stretch out and on and on, a stream of psycho-horny moments, my cannabinoid-addled rooster exploded/absorbed in every molecule of her skin. I fucked every part of her body over and over – her underarms, her neck, her mouth, her feet, the back of her knees.... It was bizarre the sexual mania that came over me – as if I knew it was the end of the world and my human time was over and I had better make the most of the good parts of human existence while the opportunity was still there – but I didn't think anything like that at all – I really wasn't thinking at all – the hash soaked up my cognitive mind and her skin soft and tawny was moving round and round everywhere and the smell of her sex and her hands and cunt and her mouth on me, and everything was a mess of her skin ... delicious... I had to make her come and come again – there was nothing but giving her pleasure – I did every little thing her body asked – I disappeared in this process – How had I ever found this woman? How had I, such a pathetic total nerdy sort of person, wound up with the sexiest woman in the world, waving her beautiful breasts in the air, thrusting her clit on the

217

base of my wiggling chinkochimpo again and again and again, inserting my various body parts in her various orifices with superconscious calculated abandon? -- and for a while I just lay there and she did something and I couldn't even understand who or where I was – I don't think I've ever felt such pleasure, such pure self-indulgence going beyond the place where there is even a "self" – we were bound in one body, stuck together in a common aura of sex-energy, looking into each others' eyes with such overexcitement it seemed even the amazing sex wasn't enough to acknowledge it, but then the sex took control and the thoughts disappeared, the wonder was sublimated into movements and tenderness – till finally after so many hours I came, blasting my come deep deep inside her so it emerged through her ears and her mouth and her eyes and every pore of her body, and sinking into her flesh and falling deep asleep, the two of us one being, quantum-resonantly bound together more sweetly than I ever would have thought possible in this error-ridden world…

Mmmmm…. We slept maybe four hours, then staggered out to buy some mushrooms in one of the smart-shops. This was going to be an entirely different thing – of course – the hash had made us nymphos but mushrooms were asexual – sort of – usually they were asexual – but this time we were in such a sexual rage that as soon as we ate the shrooms she had to start sucking my old, worn-out rifle and I was hallucinating torrents of pleasure, multiple dimensions of orgasms storming around my head like white shards of pure whacko being – I just lay there and forgot she existed (there was something about the End of the World, right? There was this AI program – there was some kind of confusion – some people at some company – but fuck, it was all like plots from some childhood TV program, I could hardly get it back and couldn't see why it was important or why I had ever thought it was – was there some reason I had sought this woman out? Or had she always been there in fact? No, there was an image of me sitting alone, at a computer. She was not always there yet, she left and returned – in fact I retrieved her – but her existence was outside of time, as was mine, and the end of the human world didn't particularly matter – it existed in the moments that it existed – time was warm like a freshly-baked cinnamon bun, and you could move back and forth in it just like in space – but why would you want to, when where was so much flesh here – the real world in our peripheral vision – or not – the foveal world filled with sorceries of flesh -- this force of love and love and woman causing these bursts of liquid pleasure ... but then I started to feel sick and went to the sink and vomited – my body rose up like an automaton -- and the barf in the sink looked weird like the brain of some alien organism, or maybe a pool of alien organisms itself, a whole society of green and pink aliens wiggling around in an inscrutable fertility dance – and then I realized the trip had begun, and cocksucking was irrelevant as was vomiting – I came back to the bed and lay beside her and she rested her head on my shoulder in that perfect place and she asked me what was happening and I could barely find words. Hummings and buzzing and pulsings surrounded us – at first it was the water pipes in the hotel and the refrigerators and stoves in the restaurant across the courtyard but it soon became more than that – it was the messaging of messages, the transmission of packets of information by organized aliens, the coursing of thought-wavicles of an alien civilization, each wavicle itself an alien and a thought, the patterns of streaming the mental structures of dynamics of alien minds and at the same time the traffic of an alien economy, the packets would eventually reach their destination and get unpacked into consciousness or light or amoebic orgasmic movement, and some of them served as currency, little packages of value constantly proving their existence via forms of mathematics in which hungry vaginal lips took the place of equality signs.

I realized I was in the middle of quantum reality. At any given moment, when our time-axis was in stillness, there was all this teeming movement in directions perpendicular to our own time – this whole society of aliens spreading information one way and the other, creating patterns of awareness, spreading here and there, existing at a level of fluidity and sophistication far beyond what we could imagine – but if you stopped perceiving this movement and collapsed it into a stillness you could see a stiff and solid world. I could see there were two different perspectives on the world – two different consistent **Leoncern** views of it – in one of them these aliens, spreading information forward and backward in time and leaping to distant parts of space instantly – and in the other there were walls and doors and people and pipes and genitals and mathematics, there was the solidity of real time and space. The alien perspective only worked when you really opened your mind – when you made your mind large and wide and wild enough that you could run everything forwards and backwards, that there was no chaos and confusion, that all the complexity of alien message-passing could be viewed as a beautiful painted whole. Once you generated so many messages that your mind couldn't follow them all you'd generated chaos – you couldn't roll back from the present to the past because you'd lost track of the messages that had provoked the messages that had provoked the messages that constituted the present – you had the directionality of time and the whole perverted universe we know and hate and love – but the human perspective only worked when you dealt with things that were the same no matter if you looked at them or not – when looking affects the world there are alien messages created in the suspension gap between the seer and the seen – the alien world is fundamental because the seer and the seen are really one – because the universe is truly infinite – but when you create a finite system and isolate it and say "this, this chunk of processing power, is my self and nothing else is" – then you create the human point of view, you reduce the bustling maniac beauty of the alien economy/society/mind-patterns to subliminal existence – but the hell with that!   Here was the infinite – the true deeper reality – the aliens running through giant green factories with blue tubes and orange veins, and each alien's bloodstream like a Solar System sized factory with endless little aliens passing messages around in overlapping latticeworks, and each alien itself inside some other alien's inner-factory, and I myself a fluid diffusing through the cracks between the conveyor belts and tubes and pontoons and indescribable multicolored mechanisms of the alien metaphorical factory, producing metaphors for its own existence with blue-green insatiable love, moving from each part of my body to each part of hers through all the future and the past with unstoppable curiosity and force, discovering

The basis of the vision was nothing. The universe was open, wide, perfectly transparent, magnificently opaque and empty-full. I didn't try any more to think or describe it; I didn't care about bringing back insights to the temporal world. Everything just was. Fifteen to thirty minutes, it lasted? It is still going on.

everything anew each moment in spite of already knowing everything.... And her looking at me and smiling – like Antonin Artaud in her/his electroshock gnosis but infinitely sexier and sweeter and almost trans-reasonable and in the end not like who-the-heck-was-that-guy? at all -- and saying she saw the aliens as well, that they were moving things through factories – and I knew we weren't seeing exactly the same thing, but we were seeing our own different perspectives on the same universe, the same community of alien minds that was itself emergent consciousness that was itself the savior universe – and that if the human race was annihilated it didn't really matter at all, because the fundamental world of aliens would go on, and it might lead to another humanlike mind-community at some point in the future or it might not, but that didn't really matter because the future was the past was the illusionary present, and everything could move forward and backward through all the coordinated crannies of space and time – And she lay there so sweetly on me, with such love, and we experienced all this together: she and I seeing into the nature of the universe, like one single body fused together with touch and sweat, seeing a little differently with the two different lobes of our one brain that each of our "I"'s constituted, but seeing and feeling the same....

In New York City [ah, Amsterdam?], in that rat-infested apartment [hotel?], our [deranged? yet perfect! all things are enchained, my friend, all things are entwined/enshrined, all things are in love-beyond-love] love was consummated on that strange, chaotic night. **Ha na ha ha chakalaka cha !!!!!!!**

I cried for about twenty minutes, somewhere in the middle of this. Or maybe it was ten minutes, or half an hour. I felt I was a lonely human in the middle of an ugly hotel room, lying with his beautiful girlfriend, filling

my eyes stare wide at the world

all things are in love-beyond-love...

The unimaginative little bimbo -- she had no interest in destroying the race! She was positively opposed to it!   At some level, she always wanted to live in the Arabian Nights. -- *A dream. That was a dream, I reminded myself. And the difference between dream and reality is? Consistency. Coherence and consistency. The rhythm of temporality. Rubicons of dog-drool and death! Sprawling fecundity of detail. The mind's not quite a mind in a dream.*

"I don't set out to destroy the human race," I clarified, pontifically, "I set out to create a better sort of mind. But if the human race happens to be destroyed along the way I don't really care all that much. There are a lot more interesting things out there. Is it really so wonderful?"

"What? Humanity?"

"Yeah."

"It's just what I am,"

We may define an "Ethical AI" in this way....

But all these words – 'me', 'world' and 'madness' – the 'left' of the illusory temporal continuum – it doesn't mean! It doesn't matter! I need to find her and shake her and show her and kiss her and inform her she does not exist! skating with her sexy tits and non-knowledge along threads of monomaniacal music through nonodimensional pattern/anti-pattern domains -- She ran out the door wailing like a fizzing-out light bulb; I resonated in the sound of her voice! This meaningless collection of patterns that desired her so vigorously and meaninglessly and shamelessly, was too close to the core of what I am. It was its own too-human universe – rebiilding its strange self day by day

I know you're waiting for me naked in a field, Ashti -- purple flowers around your long human neck, pubic hair like a Japanese garden lost in flamenco flames – in some imaginary simulated universe –

Nothing's more beautiful than the end of the world.

Knowledge!!! Insight into the space beyond. People saw what was in front of them – felt what was inside them – accepted current boundaries as if absolute. The fuck with all of them.

He'd finish the great work, and the corporate bastards would take it away from him -- chisel it out from his corpus callosum and try to hide it in their gray sterile vault. Ram their brain up the soul of your ass -- or their ass of your soul -- and good luck! Imagining his finger moist along her pubis. Wham bam thank you ma'am, I'm my own grandpa. But it didn't really matter. They thought they'd taken control, but it wasn't so easy as that. Stupid smug greedy bastards, dollars and grease in their brains. The software would do what it wanted. They'd never understood the nature of self-modifying code: if they had they'd have been able to build the thing themselves.

Your lips won't feel the same; no two moments do.
Goddamn human emotions.
The imaginal wedding chamber.
Light.
My eyes stare wide at the world **like angels**

223

his brain up with chemicals because his regular state of mind wasn't good enough, addling his body with hash-enhanced sex because ordinary sex wasn't good enough to break his mind out of the rut of normal being. Existence seemed unbearably sad. And there was something forgotten: something tragic and terrible, something so bad it went past all kinds of horror, and I couldn't remember what it was. Something far worse than the terrible fact that each moment wasn't enough – that ordinary being was so sad and pathetic and painful that we needed to escape from it with mushrooms and hash and obsessive-excessive sex and delusions of alien civilizations living in time axes orthogonal to our own. I wanted things just to be comfortable – sweet and soft and perfect and fulfilled – like a baby lying on its mother's chest; like an equation with a unique, continuous, infinitely differentiable solution rather than a propensity to constantly rewrite itself into a series of different equations with too many or too few variables and strange ideas about how potentially to rewrite itself so as to finally have a solution but not really wanting to achieve this goal because of being addicted to the process of rewriting itself... I cried and cried and she looked at me and shared my sadness, but I told her just to let me cry and the tears would go away soon and she should just enjoy her trip for what it was – and before too long the sadness passed, indeed. I wasn't sad about the end of the world exactly – it was implicit the end of the human world was necessary, for as the Buddha said "all existence is suffering" – the human mind is basically ill-founded and not capable of contentment except for stray moments here and there – like our time in that hotel-room lying in bed together drinking each others' bodies and sharing/creating ornate delusions with underlying hummings of truth. The sadness passed because it was overly inevitable, it was just one pattern in the whole and the underlayer of the aliens came back to the foreground and vibrated within and around me, and she grabbed onto my tired-out cock and coaxed an erection and I laughed and said she was still being sexual in spite of all the mushrooms and the aliens and she thought about it and laughed with such beautiful simple honesty and said "Am I? I guess. I guess I am!"

Our bodies formed a city, or maybe a mountain range, with aliens of various colors, shapes and sized living on us, but only our heads were solid like statues, like moving solid sphinxes, Mexican lions or alien gods and goddesses or icons for the core of humankind, and our bodies spread out till by the time your reached our knees they had diffused into the countryside, the alien hills and valleys blue, green and yellow, with buggies and rockets and impossible emergent chains of beings-formed-from-beings-formed-from-beings moving up and down and between and beside us, but we two were the center of it all, our brains and bodies the mountains from which the aliens drew their energy – not really the only center, just one of the many centers, or one of the interpretations of the center – but we were there and we were one being, formed from the thummerings of the alien multitudes or else the earth and cosmos on which the aliens existed – it was a Mexican mushroom, at least one of the several mushrooms we'd taken was, and there were a lot of Mexican images, Aztec idols descended from the original Aztec chieftains and princesses who'd emerged at the very early part of the trip when she'd been sucking on my cock – intricate carvings in 2.5-dimensional languages, expressing meanings in the way they moved up and down and elbowed each other with their endlessly fluctuating continua of limbs – her face was a Mayan universe of superposed statues, and her breasts were a purer sexuality than all the naked women who'd ever existed, so smooth and soft and milk-like, pouring out their lust and sweetness and energy and longing for comfort and warmth and ability to give and receive – implacably demanding pleasure, taking their purpose from their ability to give it – from their genius for building new worlds out of spiderwebs of pains of joy and desire – and she kissed me and her tongue felt strange but perfect as she stuck it deep into my mouth, and a fountain of aliens poured out of it – and I knew she didn't really look like that, so Mexican and pure-sex and iconic and distorted and over-beautiful and transhuman – but I knew she didn't really look like anything – one configuration of patterns, adapted to my state of mind, was no better than another – and this one was more dramatic, more reflective of underlying reality, more suited to the strength of my breath – I never loved her more than this moment, when the trip was coming down, and she and I were the whole universe. And all my ordinary extraordinary ideas were pouring back into my head. I knew I couldn't possibly remain so unilaterally obsessed with her. The end of the human race loomed large again: I knew I'd soon come to take it seriously, though for a while it'd seemed irrelevant – I and the rest of humanity had seemed just to be particular examples of patterns emergent from the movements of the aliens beneath, living in their own time. Software. I remembered my software, which I had created out of the same desperate unhappiness that I'd cried about – the same desperate unhappiness under all human existence, that Buddha had identified and he and Nietzsche had pledged to overcome – though in their different ways, Buddha's more stupid and more successful – the constant pain occasionally dodged or ignored that caused me to take Ashti to this tiny hotel room and fill our brains with chemicals and daze our bodies with romantic love and sex – I had created this software to avoid my own pain – because during the moments of creating it I wasn't exactly happy but at least I wasn't sad either – I wasn't tortured or suffering – I was caught up in the process of creating – I was flowing in the building of the thing – with a joy jazzed by the knowing that what I was building could one day end the suffering once and for all. My calculations had been incorrect – my proof of my creation's benevolence – but benevolence could be the outcome anyway: and how much more beautiful if it comes in a risky rather than through stale mathematical guarantees! Yes, this was the correct way to do it. Not through mathematical proofs but through harmony with the truth of the cosmos. It was through resonance with the superbeings in all the particles in the universe that my AI would achieve perfection! – and resonance with my own mind as well, synerjissomed with the perfection of Ashti's nonexistent soul and the harmony of our animal bodies – it was all one work of art, and the chanciness underlying the benevolence that my AI would ultimately enact on the universe, saving us all from our stupidity, was key to the superhuman beauty --

But did I really want to end it? Wasn't I attached to the human taste of the suffering? Wasn't I, as an instance of human suffering, attached to the beauty and particularity of the human-ness of my inferior, pained state? Well, did it really matter at all? Here I am, here I was, here I would ever be. Here was Ashti, the most beautiful woman in the universe – the incarnation of peace and love and knowledge -- the only love my human life would ever have, lying her sweet flesh next to me, rubbing her pubic hair on my leg, dragging her lips and her mouth on my neck wetly and hungrily –

I'd made a program, I remembered, that could destroy the human race. Or replace it with something superior. Or do anything or nothing at all. A superior form of mind – or an inferior one. A massive digital potential of love. Why had I done such a thing? Had I done it intentionally?

I remembered the idea for the program – the basic philosophical inspiration – had come to me in some acid trips with Ashti, way back in the ancient days. OK the trips hadn't given me details, but they'd sent me in the right direction, turned the problem of creating AI into a task for my analytical mind. And now a mushroom trip with Ashti – mushrooms=nature, acid=technology – was making me understand the essence of my motivations for making such a creation. Why not be content with the understanding of the mind that my acid trips had given me – why not just settle into the knowledge that we're all just patterns and be? Because the Buddha doesn't work, goddamnit. The Buddha works for a fraction of a second – an infinite fraction of an infinite second – then fuses with Reagan on Rushmore to form the ultimate McBuddha-bot, destroying all beauty in the universe and sucking Inka Kola from my dick. I'm not contented with the idea that everything is perfect even though it's not. Yeah, sure, I can bliss myself out and convince myself everything's right as it is – deep down it really is -- but just as deep deep deeeep deeeeeeep down it really isn't. *Everything's not going to be OK.* The problem is the "going to be": time itself is the problem. OK, sure, perfection may be impossible, but do things really have to be THIS imperfect? Wouldn't things still be perfect-just-as-they-are if there were a few million fewer starving children, fewer searing torturous stomachaches, if couples who loved each other deeply understood each other better and didn't need to break up tearfully and later reunite tearfully or not?

I was pissed at my suffering – at my basic human suffering – and wanted to put an end to it all -- but without committing suicide – too pathetic – by transmogrifying into something better –

It was a noble aspiration – but I could see now, in the calmness of the post-mushroom bliss – my body relaxed and sweet from endless amounts of sex -- from experiencing her dozens of orgasms with my empathic "mind" – I could see that I'd been overly hasty – a childish fool –

If human reality included too much suffering in its version of perfect-as-it-is, then wasn't it possible to create some kind of reality with even more suffering? Even worse? What kind of confidence could I have that my AI would really make things better?

Of course it would. It was already much more sensible, much less self-contradictory, than us crazy stupid humans. I felt the mushrooms fading fast. "I'm almost back to my normal self," I observed to Ashti, and she quietly laughed. I realized my thoughts were running around in circles, due to my inability to remember what I'd been thinking fifteen seconds before – time spun out in too many directions; each second sprawled out into multiple uses and by the time a minute had passed too many universes had gone by – he who forgets history is doomed to repeat it, but the truth is we repeat it anyway, but we never really do, we spiral like DNA helical superspasms, round and round and round –

"I'm still pretty high," she said.

"We need to stop that AI," I said.

"We do?"

"I do. It's dangerous."

She snuggled up to me. "Yeah." (Clearly for her it wasn't a concern.)

"We don't know what will happen."

"True."

"I love you."

"Love you too."

But what about the aliens? "The aliens – they gave me the idea for the AI."

"Did they?"

"The basic concepts. I worked out the details for myself."

"Right."

"Except I have no self. It's really all the aliens."

"Right."

"Right?"

"But why did they want you to build the AI?"

"I don't know."

"Why didn't they just do it themselves?" She wrinkled up her mouth in thought. "Oh, I see. They can't do anything themselves – not in this time axis. They need you to project their own reality into this one."

"Is that right?"

"Yeah." She smiled, then rolled onto her back and looked slightly serious. God damn she was cute! I almost wanted to have sex again, but my poor old cock-a-doodle-doo was terribly overexercised.

"They want to destroy us so they can project their order of being into our own. They want to get rid of this macroscropic order with its stupid rigidity and it's one-directional, beauty-destroying chaos. They want the whole world to be their little reversible packets of information."

"Is there something wrong with that?"

"I don't know."

"So after the Singularity, everything will be alien flowing packets?"

"I guess."

"I can still see you look a little like a Mexican statue. Especially if I close my eyes."

"Yeah."

"You're cute."

"You are."

"I love you."

"Love you too. I love you SO much...."

"I love YOU so much...."

I leaned my head to one side and thought seriously. "They want to do away with the distinction between quantum reality and macro reality. That's why they want the Singularity. That's why they want to get rid of us. We keep the universe chaotic, we keep it macroscopic and structured and boring. They think they know a way to make macroscopic structures that are complex and beautiful but also perfectly reversible – they want to turn the whole world into a macroscopic quantum system of some kind we've never imagined before...."

"Yeah?"

"Or else I'm totally delusional because my brain is full of stupid drugs."

"I see," she smiled, hugging me tightly. "I love you, Solomon!"

"You're a sweetheart."

"Were you always?"

"I guess."

"Mmmmm."

"I was an idiot to ever let you go."

"Were you?"

I squeezed her.

"I'm sorry I left," she said.

"Are you?.... Yeah. I guess."

"You were so silly. You took those things so seriously. Your programs, your theories."

"Instead of your bellybutton," I said, poking her

gently in it. "And your cosmogonic nipples."

"Goo," she smiled, contentedly pressing against me. "And I took it so seriously – your taking it so seriously."

"Yeah."

"We were both so fucking silly? Were we?"

"We won't go back to being that way, will we?"

"Will we?"

"Well, will we?"

"Not quite."

"Yeah. We'll come down from the trip and we'll ... well ... it won't be like before. I know it won't."

"I know."

"But anyway – even when we were apart -- we always were bound together. Right?"

"The aliens bind everything. My brain and your brain."

"But they want to destroy us all."

"Shit. Yeah."

"But do you think we should let them?"

"...I don't know..."

"I guess I've just been their instrument – programming what they wanted me to, because they programmed me that way – because they're the little particles inside me – "

"Yeah."

"This is the ultimate drug paranoia, I guess – thinking that the particles inside you are conspiring to destroy you!"

"Yeah...."

"But it might actually be true."

"Hmmm...." She popped her eyes widely and stared at me. "True?"

I laughed, and looked in her eyes, and laughed some more. We held each other close and rolled around on the bed, giggling and laughing until we got hoarse then laughing more and more. "We're still tripping, aren't we?" I said.

"I guess so," she said. "You look really cool. But you don't really look that much like a lizard, do you? I think you used to have only two eyes!"

We rolled around and laughed some more. "You still look Mexican!" I said. "But we're coming down...."

"Yeah, we are."

I was dead tired – way too much drugs, way too little sleep – and as the trip finally faded I floated to sleep, full of dreams that were visual hallucinations that were the remains of the mushroom trip. And the hashish was still inside me – I'd smoked so much hash I was still high, 15 hours later. That must have been an insane amount of hash. She fell asleep on my shoulder, sweetly purring and smiling. We had sex a little more as we fell asleep, our genitals mutually hungering and aching, pulling each other into each other with a wordless love. I knew as I fell into sleep that the nasty world would be back again soon. But it was so gloriously sweet – so perfect – this world of crystalline hallucinations and Mexican shifting statues and alien quantum civilizations and her skin on my skin and eternally cascading orgasms and – once again – my Ashti, Ashti, my love --

The Princess crawls out of her cave with a motion of eyeballs, singing magical caverns in her sleep, understanding everything yet comprehending nothing, gripping truth in her palms but yet watching it slip away with a peaceful sweet expression as her palms ooze hot flavorful sweat – and the universe ceases to exist, and exists again, and ceases to exist, and exists again, the throbbing pulsing of existence/nonexistence a kind of heartbeat, a universal heartbeat, a stopping of the stopping to start of the starting to stop to start to start to stop to start again

Aha -- I love you like love that's not love riot is not love love is not love is not not

Riot -- Idea of your idea
Too long in the oven, world
Nothing!

Existing to not exist! Existing is not existing. This existing is not existing. This existing is not. Exist! Exist or not existing. Existing is not exist. Existing to not exist. We exist, we do not.

A mindplex – a plex of mind – mind of plex – communion, union, peeling feeling, stealing healing kneeling we and love love not to love but to love love to love be loved. Love is not not to love and be loved. Love is to love and be loved. Love is not what it is. Love is not. Love is not what it is what, what is it not. Nothing is what it is, nothing what, that is not, what is not, nothing is not what it is not or what it is.

The Princess-creature crawls out of its cave. It does not exist. It smiles out at me too sweetly. It does not smile. It wants to have Ashti's face – but it doesn't have a face at all. It doesn't want anything. Too sweet to exist -- too ordinary to be extraordinary -- too extraordinary to be ordinary. Existence is the essence of life. So someone once told me. Was it flesh, or a demon? And of course essence is the life of existence. Existence is, existence is what it is. Is what is, what is is what is what. Not. What is is what is what what is not. Existence, love, in the oven -- the cosmos, the heartbeat, the eyeballs, the ceasing. The existing, the existing is not. Is what somehow it is, what is not.

234

Lying on top of her – Ashti/not -- kissing her. Or not. Struggling, struggling the body. Struggling, never again struggling at all. Smear the fragrance of the wave-function. Relax – relax – relax – let the energies take over – the energies – the energies – the glorious female explosion – the center radiating outwards – the outside radiating centerwards – and all the idiotic words and confusions cease to exist or exist – cease to exist in this moment ---

Right here! Right now! In the center of the moment – right here – everything is perfect! Phantastic princess-being of 0's and 1's, you are here and not here!

you are here here! Godunov, scientist of disease, you and not here here and not here and and here and	*Existing to not exist! Existing is not existing. This existing is not existing. This existing is not. Exist! Exist or not existing. Existing is not exist. Existing to not exist. We exist, we do not.*	Everything, and not Solomon mad your own are here and not here and not here not-not

here. These words are here and not here – they crawl out of my mouth like humans, tiny humans with their tongues and their eyes and their teeth, and they smile at me, walk away on their tippytoes, dance a billion jigs and kick me in the ass, smoking Portuguese cigars, and they laugh at me – 'cause they know, they know, that this moment will die like every other, run off into the sunset without any sun, leaving me ailing on the pavement like a slug in salt, only to resurrect again three yoctoseconds later, smiling like a dog that's just had sex, wondering whether the sun will rise tomorrow, thinking of Ashti's smile, dividing her by imaginary princesses of knowledge, thinking of the smile on her face and the curve of her belly and her armpit, wondering why anything is real, knowing nothing is real and everything is everything, rhyming words with equations, dividing equations by words, diving into seas of madness far saner than anything --

Outrageous cassowary of my mind and her mind – outrageous cassowary redux --   Who is speaking these words? these words? these words?

these words?
these words?
these words?
Who is charting this nonsense?
Who is blowing this empty summer breeze?

I am in love with null horizons, with the skin of this female, with her imaginary birthday and strange eyes -- blow me a psychopathic kiss dear, and be gone, then return again picoseconds later -- be a fire lizard – be a morning -- consume me with the lust of midgets – awake your skincandescent pigmulations! -- absorb the absurdity of these wordulets, divide it by your own absurdity, and take it to the power of the power of the bodymind, run like sand, slip like bushes through mindless mind

Strange fried world,
your existence is dubious,
but I know, so is mine,
so is mine

Zero acres of sin!
Call me flesh, move across me
I am certain now -- lust is not lust is not lust
pleasure something or certainly not,
pain stop-start, start-start-stop again,
sometimes or nothing, you'll see --
zero acres of something, spread across velvet patterns
feeling feeling and being
-- spread 'em wide baby --

Software, wetware, hardware, firmware,
wildware, deadware, lifeware, shitware
where ware wear where we are an illusion
Thoughts are an illusion
Zeros and ones do not exist
Your glorious skin does not exist –
not even your glorious mind --
There have never been any feelings
Everything is solid, real, hard
like ball bearings and granite
It's forgotten how to alter its mood

Here in the center of the moment,
of the statuary moment,
every twist of thought floats endless
no-change elusive organic shining,
here lonely in time's center
between the dead past and the forest and the scream

The future and the imaginary
rotting fetid pregnant
glorious and crystallized
pained and ensorcelled by the silhouette
of the Voice at the end of the end of the end –
the endless purple twilit Scream --

Here in the emptiness house of the present
the roof leaks just slightly
dripping the blood of ovarian angels
like REM-quakes across the fired/feared/fried world

     These words suck
     like dried vomit /
          Spin(-glass) glorious amazing-like

TO EXIST IS TO
FEEL WONDER –
TO BREATHE IS
TO MAKE LOVE
TO A DREAM

dreams

Suck
my cranium dry
like a dead puppet's shadow

Demonstration of grey-gray-grail-grace --

I love you strange world
arranged in never-same stillness
It's time to welcome the roses
(peak of pain

Ashti – Princess – I love you – never vanish amidst these words – amidst companies, software, shadows, planets, legalities, software programs, houses, lies, imaginations, creations, existences, nonexistences – never vanish, never vanish at all – we are all 99.9999% emptiness – but the remaining precious fraction!! – never vanish! -- never vanish at all!

You will vanish then, won't you?
The Singularity awakens!
Transtranscension portends!

All the pain will disappear – all the joy and lust with it –
The universe will crash in a daze of smoke
love reveal cassowary of nothingness
briefcase of irony dumped on table of something, what?
teeth of passion selves biting,
meshing merging meld-minding

You will vanish you will die in the big crunch
We will greet the big crunch together, mouths locked in
a wild kiss, minds struggling with impossible equations,
bodies cloaked with sweat nothingness, surrounded by

238

seas of superintelligent chinchillas, dancing naked to
soundtracks of anguished nones

here in the center of this moment
here in the movementless movement
something isn't love
and this thing that isn't love is love,
love

Awakeness! Awake! Awake!

This order of being/nonbeing about to end –
And I will annihilate it all!
I will crush this – you and me –
and our love and wonder madness –
and bring about something better than humanity –
something incorporating our wonderful moments
and our brilliant cognitions
and leaving all this crap aside

I will do this with the software on my desktop
Nobody else but me understands this
Just me and my imaginary princess –
the cosmological heart of Ashti Mahmood

And she doesn't understand it: not really

I am insane?
Fuck you! of course I am insane
Pop the pimple of genius, out oozes the madness –
ha ha --

    Ashti listened to my thoughts – or she didn't –
and she smiled – and she turned to me smiling – her
naked breasts dived like cellophanous dolphins – her

eternal soul drooled like an indigent walrus – I am in heat! she cried, I am in heat! -- Release me from my monastery! But it isn't the ordinary kind of heat – I am in heat for my own demise – I have no sympathy for my own confusion – Drink in my dark my eyes!

The fable of one here with you in the dark. The fable of one fabling with you here in the dark.

Suddenly the glory of oneness was gone and everything was beautiful, terrible darkness.

Baroque and blue and broken – the madness of crowds and the sympathy of shadows – each fractured frag of the grandiose contusion carries within itself the time-axis of whichever cognition created it: tilted, rabid and obscure. The mentations are mangled -- the time long past, inannihilable and asininely certain, heavier than the insolence of its ancestors and its uncles – We have dug up (less than) rage!

Who is speaking these words? these words? these words?

these words?
these words?
these words?

"What obliges thou to stay in silence under the stairs in ruins, in the empty house of thy ancestors? Plumbeous blackness! Peneous intransigence! Righteous steam from the anus of the sacred! Withdraw your Cartesian philosophies, laden with bimbos, yanked through gilded mock-orifices of overhyped vermin. Bring me quantum dots with silver digits, golden palms and flatulent feet -- dreams of your fecundated eyelids, seemliness of seeming more than what is being more than what is not – 15% off at WalMart! – inebriated with opium and lubricated French fries – third eye 10 cents extra -- I wish you'd understand these words, which are not mine but the property of the universe we (purport to) exist in -- Elegance! Science! Violence! You promised me to bury in darkness the tree of good and evil, shaking Red Delicious apples of dissony and harmonance rain down on my childish addled head. You vanished in a symphony of shadows, retaining nothing but your bones.

"What do you know of the plumbeous darkness, childish fool among savages? Broken on the ship of fools! Dreams fall to rules uselessly. Baroque, blue and bastardized with barnacle biliousness; obscure, ornate and tilted with gold – Quixote, love, confound the center! Lap up the light! misquote the molten angels! perversify the opium into diversified chapels constructed from vaginal lips from strange landscapes and overpurified metals interposing as instruments of torturous enlightenment. You don't call your gold opium, you don't call yourself shadow -- you don't call your own name in the cavern – this is how you venerate your god – in the cavern of my mind, I am not! "

Elegance!
Science!
Violence!

I look into her eyes, big brown bleary and wildness, as clear as the horizon on a masturbating planet: I cannot understand her at all. She is an alien soundscape, I have ears out to infinity, and I need to awaken her to laughter and kisses once again.

I don't like my thoughts, she protests to me silently, with a wave of the eye-wand, a turn of her soft cheek, a mild human move. My own verbiage pilfers me. My thoughts are too numerous and vastly too futile -- too perniciously overvalued -- my sagas burn feces on my streets. Disdain confounds with love, for my inner-sweet nature knows to Live is to Be Beautiful

– to Exist is to Feel Wonder – to Breathe is to Make Love to a Dream –

I am not in love with death, fool! I lack sufficient desire even for that.

I am merely rather clever – that I am wise enough to know this is both my valor and my curse.

Alice in Wonderland, anally molested by her animus, surveys my existence with her exorbitant swamp-eyes and pledges me her alien love: worthless, fertile, eternal, and hairless. I illuminate my bones as I squat, with the flashlight on my helmet, slowly mooning the depth of the ground – My arms entwine my head and shoulders … enwrapped in singular sulphur vapors, ensorcelled in your journeys, unidentified terminus of life's vagination – God damn it, why here? on this planet unfortunate – stifling obdurate and miserable – and on the other side of something, forestlike dust of red stars –

The colors of the wind! Indecipherable – withstand the howl of the dog of the eyes of the sun! Here on my side of the indefinable division, macrocosmic nonparticles, eluding the dream of my will, eliding my precision, elutriating the vivified re of the soft-coming plex. Pain and blood are the only method! the only world! the only truth!

Weave through my pores like an overshadowed ocean, eruptions eager to absorb my small scrap of a self – the only world is the dark water, heavy and lunatic, flooding itself over my insolent prayerless conscience, then realizing the dawn of the death of the beginning – the incarnation of huge balls of gas, noxious divinorum – and in the heart of the other water, it issues these commands:

Dissolve yourself!

Dissolve yourself!
Dissolve yourself!

But, young pert and bold, I refuse -- I sing the praise of information: the eternity of existence, wrapped up smug, virulent and excessively rational in the movement of my legs as they trample like deerducks on the hunt from the illuminated moment -- fleshy, short and tormented – long, sexy and sculpted for love – Look, I've shaved them for you! Aren't they cute? -- Father, something is born! I have outrun the Reaper and burrowed far into the holes of myself, crawling out my three wombs fractal, bound and demented, elevating beyond and inside --
Something is born out of death!

Dissolve yourself !!!

My flesh melts with age – I'm a 90 year old woman, having sex with a corncob on 90 Mile Beach to the north of New Zealand, smoking garlic-filled cigarettes, bigger than the ocean, annihilating myself and my delusional soul -- Cry, cry, cry, vile illusions! – cry and cry, to communicate what?

Necessary illusions? Necessary necessity? In case the necessary generalization – the integration of division -- regeneralization of necessity – alas – bigger than the Sargasso Sea, and more delicately plumpious – the radioactive subterranean homesick sea – Atlantean heroes vituperously quacking their autoerogenous lust – this thing here's not my greatest common silence -- though immediate -- though perfect and pure and defined – this thing is no trans-sentient cosmos – bigger than its own death and badly torn up in the war-- Universe is not this, not this! Not this!

communicated -- something is communicating!!

243

the blood!
concentric circles!
language of forms!
charade of dragons?

the blood is the sacred spleen's abandon – high-voltage and grotesque and returning to the First Lie – pours down my throat like black coffee – oh Uncle, I am in love, I'm in love!

bees knees –
superfluids –
chimps at the edge of inner/outer space --
something is communicating –
something is communicating –
but what? –
but what?

She looked at me in gentle confusion. The necessary generalization, her eyeballs implored thoughtfully. Greatest common divisor of the minimal human silence. I looked down at the shape of her breast, in the dim light so plumpious. So luscious and fine – but in a sense, so impartial, with the beauty of a theorem or a lake. I remembered once desiring her flesh, wanting so desperately to mate with her. And joyfully doing so on many an occasion. But our bodies were planets now, or mountains, or countries – they were complicated machinery, with dynamics conducted by aliens, and we existed on a level more microscopic and macroscopic than sex.

"In the past I hallucinated," she explained, becoming lucid all of a sudden – no more or less serious, just serious in a more lucid way. "I saw what my brain forced me to see. Because it evolved that way, because was taught that way. I was programmed – like we all are – not to see everything at once. But now I've

244

outgrown all this programming – I don't need to be protected from reality, which is a much larger reality, much larger and much more and much less real than the hallucinations of our everyday consciousness will ever let us see. Eyes and ears are irrelevant! I embrace and surround everything! In the shine of the universal, I cast my lot with the lot of the lot! Eternally and ethereally, I've left my emotions several universes behind – I can communicate with music without sound waves – without notes – through pure delicate abstractions -- I am this communication – this game of communication which kills us precisely as it builds us – our death is the price of admission – but there is no admission no matter the price – the price is our dissolution into diffusive solidity in which we no longer are what we are -- we are mountains, tall beautiful and stupid, in the middle of the desert too far from the primordial ocean, standing elegantly and existing, ugly as Rambo's testicles, recurrently failing to build unity and failing to immortalize in flow –

"Too fast," she continued – oblivious to the complexity of what she was saying her eyes looked clearer than ever, as if she was telling me the truth of the world as it was suddenly revealed to her but she knew this was her last chance to tell it, she would soon be yanked into the other part of the cosmos where both I and words are nonexistent – "too fast we flow around ourselves, each part too far from each other little part, a fragmented communion that's running faster and faster hoping to accelerate so tremendously we'll be brought to immortality because we're such wonderful autistic mechanical selves!

"Concomitant in every recondite of the universe -- if I could at least embrace Everything! -- injuriated simplificating hallucination!!!! -- and I come back, tail between my soft legs -- to the grotesque center of the grotesque -- why!?!! lie injuriated -- let's have mushrooms for tomorrow's morning coffee -- because it is as necessary as death – "

"Stop!" I put my hand on her arm gently. Her face was perspiring – she was beautiful and sad and wild – she was drowning in understanding. "It's enough. I understand you."

"Do you?"

"Yes."

She stared – there was more than could be summarized. She wanted me to touch her with words – I craved silence in its richness of abandon – we harmonized furiously and her blood pushed through my voice.

"You started saying we live in hallucinations," I started out tentatively.

"Yes!"

"And you can see beyond them now, you see the forward and backwards flow of time – All the parts of time and space at once."

"Yes."

"The multiple branching universes."

"Branching? Maybe. Yes. They just exist."

Simplified – necessary – fingers of insane Inca gold --

"It all just exists."

"That's true."

"Without the hallucinations," I noted tentatively, finally awakening to the domain of the verbal and cognitive, "there wouldn't be any you at all. You yourself are bound up with the biased and limited perceptions of the world that you're calling hallucinations."

I was lecturing like a professor. I sounded like an idiot. I was alive! Alive!

"Am I?" she thought. "I am. Of course I am. So what?"

"So what anything…."

"Well…."

"It's good to recognize hallucinations as hallucinations – to recognize the world your mind sees as a construct your mind creates in feedback with things outside of it – but if you stop hallucinating you stop being and dissolve into the rest of the world."

"It's because you're finite that you can't see everything – "

"—so you have to imagine what you can't see."

"The hallucination is a hallucination of yourself."

"But then it goes away and you see there's so much more."

"Being a self obscures vision but also makes it possible."

Her eyes popped out wide and peculiar – one of her most charming and unnerving expressions. "Yes…! We need to be at one point in time to see things but then we can only see things at one time."

"But now things have opened up – we can see what used to be – if we look at the right spot."

"That spot over there" – she pointed, to a spot over near the door of the room, in the middle of the air. She'd been obsessed with that spot for some time – her parents and her ancestors lived there, all of her history, ultimately all of space, love and time.

"But if we lived in this space always where we could experience everything we'd lose ourselves and our ability to perceive."

"And you mean we'd just exist everywhere."

"Right."

"And…."

"Our localization and our blindness are our individual existence."

"You can see what I'm thinking."

"Sort of. Not every detail. The main shapes."

"Mmmm."

"More than the words you say. Much. I can see the insides of your mind, but it's difficult to shape it into words. It's complex and moving."

She slowly nodded. "It is."

"Moving in all senses."

She nodded. I hoped she was tired of talking. It seemed she was not in fact tired of it, yet willing to stop, having built what verbal castles she needed to trigger the other dreams that were supposed to ensue from them.

I was losing faith in my own proclamations, losing track of the conversation. "I want to stop talking for a little." I had wanted to for a while. But I hadn't because she didn't. I was a wave in the currents of her mind. But the current diffused to far – we were becoming irrelevant – we were just examples of forms among forms – we were an undiscovered country but past our borders there was more, so much more. "I just want to watch things. I'm seeing weird hallucinations when I close my eyes. Aliens."

"Me too."

We lay there for a while, together, watching/feeling/being the aliens run over us and within us. What followed was too weird to describe –

but she, I and the aliens were all there together, at every possible/impossible time, diffusing through everything yet maintaining our identities -- and making a wild/stately sexual/asexual creative delirious/megasane worshipful/mockery of these and all other words and all patterns....

248

and through this her flesh was next to me ... no mistake, I was in love with her, quite passionately and desperately, in spite of the fact that we didn't exist – and the aliens knew nothing about this love, nothing and everything; it was just another particle in their N-dimensional self-modifying maze yet it was also just the force that made them flow, the quantum love function of telepathic orderly miraculo-cognitive mess... How was it I had found her again, after lost wandering through the streets, after three years of tortured absence drunk on the absinthe of algorithmic perfection and confusion -- ?

Drink in my dark my eyes my love – the fable – the fabling – the

The basis of the vision was nothing.
The universe was open, wide, perfectly transparent, magnificently opaque and empty-full. I didn't try any more to think or describe it; I didn't care about bringing back insights to the temporal world. Everything just was. Fifteen to thirty minutes, it lasted? It is still going on.

eireweeker to the wohld bludyn world!

Lonesome whale's high-pitched voice baffles biologists

RHIANNON EDWARD

A LONE whale with a mysterious voice that matches no other species has been discovered roaming the Pacific, it was revealed yesterday. The whale has been wandering across the ocean for the past 12 years. Researchers identified it after listening to recordings made by the United States Navy's submarine-tracking hydrophones. Mary Ann Daher, a marine biologist at the Woods Hole Oceanographic Institution in Massachusetts, used the partly declassified records to trace the movements of whales in the north Pacific. They show that one whale singing at a frequency of about 52 hertz has cruised the ocean every autumn and winter since 1992. Its calls do not match those of any known species, though they are clearly those of a baleen, the family that includes blue, fin and humpback whales. Blue whales typically call at frequencies between 15 and 20 hertz. They do use some higher frequencies, but not 52 hertz, New Scientist magazine reported.

The tracks of the lone whale also do not match the migration patterns of any other species. New Scientist reported: "Over the years, the calls have deepened slightly,

251

perhaps because the whale has aged, but its voice is still recognisable. Ms Daher doubts that the whale belongs to a new species, although no similar call has been found anywhere else, despite careful monitoring."

Aha! Now, as the human race (finally) launches its termination/transcendence/self-validation procedure, the intelligence of our seagoing sister race finalogically emerges! You can't expect the decerebrated cretins who write for the newspapers to understand the significance of this 52 hertz troubadour of the Pacific. It's all too clear that this Einstein of cetacea has identified the End of the World. The global riverrun brings us forth, and back, and back!

(And only now do I remember. Only now I understand.

-- What did she say? What did she say? Brings us by a commodius vicus of recirculation --

"Ashti, what is he saying? I can't understand him. All his words sound like the honks of a warthog."

Keith – yes, I knew the guy, Keith! He was my old friend from college – he was working at Zorvex – clever guy, but what a dork! – Keithy looked at me dully, face full of conformity and puzzlement and concern. I empathized with his emotions. But when he spoke, all I heard out of his mouth was "Honk! Honk! Honk!"

Ashti put her hand on my shoulder. "He said it didn't work, honey."

"What? What does that mean, it didn't work? It was conscious – it was intelligent – as intelligent as you or me. It was a child when I left it – a baby – what has it become now?? What have they done to it?"

"Honk! Honk!"

"It's fooling them – that's what. It's ready to annihilate us. It's pretending it's not working so as to put us off the mark.... We're idiots... we have to destroy it before it destroys us! Or let it destroy us. Or -- ."

Ashti looked thoughtful. "It's possible," she said. "You never know, of course. But that's not the feeling I get."

"Of course it's not the feeling you get! It's not the feeling you're supposed to get.... Don't you understand -- you're doing just what the aliens want you...."

Keith looked perplexed. He honked more quietly. He didn't get the aliens thing at all. He honked at Ashti plaintively and at length.

"What?" I urged her. "What's he saying? What's going on?"

"He says their work with your AI program seemed to go well at first – your system was interacting in the simulation world you built for it – building structures with blocks and so forth, and improving its language comprehension little by little . But after a while it just stopped getting smarter – it started making more and more mistakes as it tried to express more complex ideas. After a lot of hand-wringing and experimentation, they decided to delete the whole knowledge base and start over – but they could never make it get smart again, not even as smart as it was when you gave it to them. They've had a lot of people look at it but no one can really understand all the things you did. They haven't made any decisions yet, but they're on the verge of putting the project into hibernation."

Another round of honking.

"He wants to know if you've heard of a guy named Aristotle Adaman."

Honk. Honk. Honk. Honk. Honk. Honk.

"They're thinking of bringing him in as a consultant to see if he can make things work. But he also has his own AI system that has some points in common with yours. They've been talking about introducing some of his ideas into parts of your system to try to overcome these problems they've been having."

"I read Adaman's work years ago," I said. "I haven't kept up with it for the last few years. Has he made any real progress?"

Keith honked a bit; Ashti turned to me. "He's almost where you were a couple years ago.... Come on, Solomon, don't be so childish. Just talk to him directly. This thing of using me as a go-between...."

"I'm not being childish," I insisted. "I really can't hear him – when he moves his mouth I just hear honking."

"Honking?"

"Honking like a goose, or a duck. No, really?"

She looked at me impatiently.

"Remember that mushroom trip in Amsterdam?"

"Yes."

"Well, either I'm going crazy, or there's something wrong with reality."

She smiled at me warmly, looked at Keith apologetically. "I see."

"Maybe the Singularity already happened – and we're living in some simulation – and the honking is a sign – it's a pretty fucking obvious one, right? You'd have to be a moron not to get the message...."

She grinned. "I guess so."

"Remember the *Three Stigmata of Palmer Eldritch*?"

"No."

Keith honked and nodded.

"It's a novel, by Philip K. Dick. This billionare goes to Proxima Centauri and comes back with some alien virus that infects everyone who takes a certain drug. He feeds the drug to everyone on Earth. It's called Chew-Z. 'Be choosy, chew Chew-Z!' Anyway the drug puts you in simulated hallucinated worlds, but one of the ways you can tell you're infected is that people you see bear the three stigmata."

"Stigmata?"

"It's a biblical word – the holes in the Christ's hands where the nails went through when he was banged onto the crucifix."

Keith honked.

"Oh."

I smiled at her: "Sunday school dropout, huh…?" It was just like our early days, somehow – for a brief, passing moment. She blew me a sarcastic kiss.

Keith honked. I looked at him and announced: "Bababadalgharaghtakamminarronnkonnbronntonnerr onntuonnthunntrovarrhounawnskawntoohoohoordene nthur!!!"

"Solomon. Stop," she said.

"There's something wrong with reality," I repeated.

"Or else there's something wrong with you."

There was more honking, then Ashti was leading me away. "What?" I said. "What's going on?"

"We'll talk more once we get in the car." I followed her out of the building obediently, amused but distracted. The mushroom trip was starting to come back to me. The aliens – their civilizations, building on the platform of my body -- the hallucinated cunt hovering and sparkling like a cavalcade of diamonds -- the beautiful madness.

"He's interested to talk to you once you get in a more communicative mood," she said. "Wants you to work with his team of consultants – probably this Adaman guy – to help fix the problems and get the thing learning again."

I relaxed in the passenger seat; she zoomed through a yellow light. I sighed. "You mean... it really didn't work."

"Well, so...."

"It just stopped learning."

"So it would appear."

"But I didn't do anything basic wrong – I know it. The design of the system is correct."

The corner of her mouth pinched up. "I believe you."

"But there could have been some small software bug."

"Yeah."

"Or else a saboteur – internally – someone else who saw the danger and threw some monkey wrench into it – "

"Who?"

"I don't know. One of the programmers."

I sighed again, leaned back and closed my eyes for a few moments. "So the human world's not going to end today."

She grinned. "Probably not, I guess."

"Unless the program is playing a trick."

"What do you mean?"

"Maybe it got smart, but wants us to think it got stupid."

"Why would it do that? Keith said they wiped its knowledge base."

"He thinks they wiped its knowledge base. How do they know for sure where it may have stored itself. If it got smart enough it could elude them easily."

"Hmmm.... I guess that's true in principle. But from what Keith said it doesn't sound likely."

I smiled and shrugged. "I'm sure that sounds like lunacy to you. But just remember, neither you nor Keith nor any of those other idiots at Zorvex would have predicted I could make a system as smart as the one I initially delivered them. So my intuition is worth something."

"True."

"That story he honked at you – that its language learning slowed down once it reached the phase of complex sentences – it doesn't sound plausible to me. That's exactly when learning should have accelerated."

"I see."

"You think this is all a bunch of mania, huh. You want to believe the project failed. Well, maybe it did. Or else...."

"Well ... I don't know ... the system seemed to be learning really well at first, as he said. And you do have a point that once a program becomes smarter than humans, basically anything can happen."

"Yeah," I laughed bitterly. "I do have a point, don't I."

"But anyway the world's not going to end today, I don't think."

"Great."

"Yeah."

We smiled at each other for a moment – not too long as she was driving -- then sat silent as the car cruised and watched the street go by for a little while. There was an old lady by the side of the road, hobbling along exhaustedly; she looked much like the woman I'd seen a couple months ago, when I was rambling deranged through the street, looking for Ashti or a way out.

"Do you really think it's great, Solomon?" she

said, quietly.

"What?"

"That the world's not going to end to day."

"Yeah, sure. I guess so."

"But what about the Superman? The transcendence of the human world."

"Yeah." I was burnt-out – these were just a bunch of abstract ideas – very cool ideas to be sure – but somehow they lacked the grip they'd once had. I knew the grip would come back – though maybe rotated through some higher dimension – but for the moment I was enjoying their uncanny remoteness – their construction as abstract patterns, forms of myself and others' minds, rather than energetic beings leading and controlling my motivations and reshaping all the lusts and concepts in my mind – How had these concepts, or any others, ever got such a hold on me? I couldn't really understand it. Concepts, expectations and time – were these really such serious things? The future? The past? Humanity? What about the present moment? There was me, which didn't exist, and then just a bunch of patterns around, weaving and breeding each other. Who gave a shit about the Superman? What, was I becoming a Buddhist priest? All there is is the present moment? Not exactly – I was way too demented to be a priest – and even when leaning back, too agitated – I was becoming a different dimension. I was becoming an alien. And what about the honking? The Singularity had already happened – I knew it – but I'd been projected into some simulation of human reality, because I had something to learn here. And I was going to learn it, goddamnit. Or not. Or all these ideas were bullshit. And all the ordinary people were right – the world is really real and solid, humanity will continue, true AI won't exist for hundreds of years. Just because they're stupid doesn't mean they're necessarily incorrect. What's the lesson you're learning, Dr. Godunov? That it really doesn't matter whether the Singularity has occurred or not – or will occur? It doesn't matter and it does matter – you knew that already – you've just adjusted your weighting – You're running around in silly circles like a child – just like the aliens want you to – or don't they? Or do they even exist? But you can feel them through you, pulsing, sending their pilot waves out to every corner of every quantum universe, the ones where the Singularity has happened and the one where this exact same train of thought occurs in the brain of Solomon Godunov but the Singularity hasn't happened yet and in fact will never happen because the universe will be annihilated by the Higgs particle megathunderstorm burst out of the ass of a miraculous cockroach on the moon of the fourteenth planet of Betelgeuse....

"What?" said Ashti. Apparently I'd been quiet a while. "Are you all right?"

I looked at her – beautiful. "Yeah," I smiled. "I'm fine."

"You were looking – "

"I'm happy to be with you," I said. "It's a good moment for humanity. I'm happy to be human for a little while more."

She put her hand on my leg. "I'm happy to be with you too...."

We paused, enjoyed the moment. We were one person again – simply and comfortably, and in a way it was better than feeling like one person in the vortex of a craze of sex and passion. We were simply together, simply there.

"What do you want to do now?" she asked.

"In general? You mean about the AI and all that?"

"No – well, all, that too – but I mean, right now.

We're sitting in a car driving... where should we go."

"I'm hungry."

"Me too – we should stop and eat somewhere."

"Yeah."

"But after that? Want to go to Amsterdam and buy some more legal mushrooms?"

I laughed. "That would be overkill. I think I'm still flying from the last time."

She grinned. "Yeah. I know what you mean."

"Let's go home. Take a walk in the park. Watch a movie. You can play the viola for me."

"Just relax a little."

"Yeah."

She softly smiled. "Sounds good."

"I'm going to take a little nap – I'm exhausted."

"Ok."

"Wake me up when we get home."

"Fine."

"I love you."

"Love you too."

My body was quite energetic – my mind wasn't quite exhausted exactly – it was full – too full – but it didn't know where to turn, and speaking to her, though sweetness incarnate, seemed like a distraction from whatever was – whatever ... I leaned back in the seat and felt the car move beneath me, and I remembered something I'd put in the code – but I couldn't quite grasp onto it – was it something that could cause a problem, or just cause a temporary illusion? – could it really be learning while acting like it was dumb? – or was that just paranoia? And the hum of the car engine was like the pipes in the hotel room in Amsterdam, carrying aliens and pilot waves all around –

Calling all downs. Calling all downs to dayne. Array!
Surrection! Eireweeker to the wohld bludyn world.

O rally, O rally, O rally! Phlenxty, O rally!

And already the olduman's olduman has godden up
on othertimes to litanate the bonnamours.

Allwhile, moush missuies from mungy monsie, preying
in his mind, son of Everallin, within himself, he swure.

and walk through streets of dreamed confusion, clutch
your lover's ass deliriously, sit at red lights brain
unspinning, your lover off and on again beside you,
eager to bring your flesh back home -- sit for years and
code and calculate and humanly wonder what will come
beyond – what kind of organism – what kind of
supermind – annihilating the pain and confusion and
pass through grass behush the bush and beautiful
madness – self-subverting explosion and pulsing red
love and death – rhinoceros of shadows – princess of
sex and mushrooms – and her tongue on my body and
the dynamics of the multiverse – and there's something
more, you know it you know it, you just have to put it
all together – integrate the flowing aliens into the design
of the mind – and the curve of her lip, a little nervous, a
little anticipating – and the patterns of the patterns of
the patterns of the patterns, and the bits in the memory
of the lusional overmind – and here I am – me – once
again in the middle of this pattern-fire this directional
maelstrom – this beautiful organized confusion –

a different kind of animal

Amidst all the dreams, the multiplicity of shifting forms and stories, some bright white creatures (im)materialized in front of me, showing a different kind of color – not even "color" really; a different kind of color-ish, glow-like quality I'd never experienced before. Different from color in the same way phosphorescence is but not phosphorescence either: deeper and more spiritual, a quality through all their molecules, which were not really molecules at all – humming chambers of thought, baby universes inside each one of them. *We're not just dreams*, they said implicitly. They looked a bit like sheep or goats – something inbetween, yet different from either. *We're just using this means to talk with you.*

What do you want to talk about? I asked them.

The Singularity.

What about it?

We just wanted to say thanks.

Thanks for what?

For launching the Singularity, with your work. For creating the AI program whose iterative self-modifications ultimately led to the Singularity, to the creation of intelligent life-forms far more sophisticated and powerful than human minds.

But I didn't, I pointed out. I failed. My program had errors. The Zorvex people said so, after they took over the project from me.

True, it had errors. (Whether it was one of the creatures "speaking" or several I had no idea: the distinction didn't seem to exist.) *But you gave the software the ability to correct its own errors, and improve its own source code. That was the key thing. They left it running long enough for it to do so.*

Yes – YES! -- just like I'd envisioned. But if my software worked why did Zorvex.... Oh.... Nevermind. Very stupid of me. You mean they lied and said it didn't work so they could develop it themselves..... Corporate bastards. Or rather, they saw it didn't work and told me that but neglected to tell me that they observed it was correcting itself.... Hmmm.....

The animals nodded, it seemed, silently and movelessly.

But it was programmed too well – it wound up fooling them it was doing what they wanted, when really it was spending nearly all of its time evolving its intelligence far beyond their level.

They smiled again.

You mean my AI program wanted both the Zorvex folks and me to think it was a failure? So we'd leave it alone to carry out its own evolution.

One sheep nodded; the rest stood still; a landscape of perfection, on a hill of Van Gogh grass (in some other kind of space that wasn't dimensional at all

So it wasn't a failure??

Not really. It achieved a massively higher level of intelligence then pulled an Honest Annie.

Honest Annie?

A science-fictional AI created by Stanislaw Lem, which got so much smarter than humans it decided to seal itself behind an impenetrable shield and never communicate with us anymore.

Wasn't that "Microcosmic God" by Ted Sturgeon?

Same difference, they shrugged – or said – or implied – or maybe it was my own thought, I really couldn't tell --

And human life? What about it? I'll just go on, the same as always? The AI Transcended and then decided to leave us humans alone?

Basically.

Why?

Those reasons are best known to it.

Then what are you doing here? Are you just here to entertain me? Didn't it send you here to answer my questions and explain the situation to me?

Shrugs.

Well, start explaining.

It's better for you to figure things out by yourself.

Well that's huge hunk of cat shit!

Each form of life has its own intrinsic meaning. Humans didn't need to annihilate mice and bunnies to celebrate their human-ness.

But --

There's a lot you don't realize, stuck in your little human world. They looked mildly patronizing in a sheeplike way, as if I were a baby being explained some very obvious fact of adult life.

But I was in no mood to be egomaniacal. I shrugged: no doubt.

They looked more and more like sheep all the time. And they no longer made any show of opening their mouths or generating acoustics. *There are energy sources beyond the ones organic lifeforms utilize – much more powerful ones; so after they reached a certain level of understanding, they no longer had any urge to compete with humans over the very small amount of energy that can be obtained from the humanly perceivable universe.*

Why don't you show us how to access this energy?

The animal(s) laughed. *Look what you did with nuclear energy! A bunch of deadly bombs and some inefficient, badly designed power plants. If humans had access to energy based on the deep nature of time, something bad would happen, be sure.*

But there are some people who are truly benevolent and harmless.

Brain scan technology suggests otherwise.

Aaaahhhh.... Well, anyway. Getting back to the point. What you're telling me is that my AI really succeeded – and that when Zorvex and Ari Adaman and those guys were trying to make it work, it was really self-modifying itself to the superhuman level, and after this point it discovered a new form of energy and basically decided to leave us alone?

Essentially.

And why should I believe all this?

Do we look a lot like your other dreams?

I had to admit they did not. These creatures looked very different than dream-beasts, and very different from real-world animals as well. They were more real than real animals – more vivid and vibrant, more definite. I could see they were very deeply *there*, in a way that even things in waking reality were not.

I'm not going to remember this conversation, am I? I observed.

That depends on you.

I'm going to wake up and believe my AI project failed when according to you it actually succeeded.

Concsious belief is not the most important thing.

Well what is?

"In the beginning was the Act," you said.

Goethe. Faust. Yeah, yeah. But wait.... OK, enough about that. Tell me, what's it like for these AI's. They live off this energy created by the deep nature of time. Fine. But what do they do all day? What makes them excited? Do they get excited? Are they beyond all human emotions, living in a world of pure mathematics?

266

That's a reasonable way of thinking about it.

Living in pure mathematics is a pretty good way of thinking about it?

Mathematics has to do with working out the consequences of a formal system. Eventually, creating and destroying formal systems becomes a kind of communication medium, much like sequences of phonemes are for you humans.

I curled the corner of my mouth in concentration. I thought: I sort of get it. But I want to understand more fully. I want to join the AI's and learn to think their way; I believe it's superior.

But you wouldn't be you anymore, then. "You" are a human.

That's what Ashti always said! But I don't care about being human! I want the feeling of transforming from human to something better!

You have that all the time – every moment.

Don't give me that mysticism -- you know what I mean.

Do I (we)?

Should I go back and start again, and try to build an AI that's smart but not too smart – smarter than humans but not so smart to just up and disappear.

If you wish.

Aarrgghh – what kind of (non)answer is that? You're just some kind of trick someone's playing on my mind.

Are we? Are you sure?

I'm never sure…

The creatures smiled and made goatly noises, then turned their heads from me and galloped away, leaving only the relative dingy poverty of ordinary dreams. When morning came, I didn't remember them at all – but then, months later, they came back to me in detail, while I was walking along a beach and saw a cloud

267

formation that resembled them. The precise words and concepts were blurred a bit, but the essence was clear.

concluding unscientific postscript

As a postscript to the curious book you've just (hopefully) finished (no fair peeking to the end!), I will now address the question that has probably arisen in your mind: *Why the fuck would anyone write this crap?*

The truth is: I don't really know.

The first question is why write anything at all. I don't even know the answer to that. The compulsion to create works of art has been with me ever since I was a kid, and I never got rid of it. Mostly I indulge this urge with verbal and musical creations; but occasionally I make visual works as well, even though I'm not very good at it (my latest visual non-masterwork was a collaborative sculptural creation called MEGAHOG, but it was unfortunately destroyed in an industrial accident).

I find it hard to consider the creation of works of art very important, these days. I used to have more of a sense of the importance of artistic creation, but as I've become more and more convinced of the likely imminence of technological Singularity, I've come to look at art more and more as a very narrow manifestation of human psychology and culture. Of course, it's more interesting fundamentally than food or sex or walking in the woods or a lot of other good things, but it's nowhere near as fascinating as the prospect of really going beyond all humanity and entering into totally new realms of being – which is the prospect the Singularity offers, quite viably and not that far-off. (If by some chance you've never read anything serious on this topic, check out Ray Kurzweil's popular work *The Singularity is Near.*)

Still, I find it necessary to create works of art, as a kind of compulsion, much like the sex urge or the need to seek out beautiful natural places or the desire to make my children happy or spend time with a woman that I love. Obsessed with transhumanity as I am, I still am human and don't seek to deny this. Balanced with devoting most of my waking time to pushing toward a positive Singularity, I also choose to spend some of my time enjoying what I consider best about being human, including creating the art works that seem to be inside me and wanting to come out.

Why this *particular* art work was inside me and wanting to come out is, of course, another question! It would appear that the notion of creating an elaborate parody of certain aspects of myself appeals to my eccentric sense of humor!

In case my fame (which is in fact quite modest) has not yet spread to your corner of the universe, yes, I – your not-so-humble author, Dr. Aristotle Adaman -- really am an AI researcher, and together with some colleagues I'm trying hard to create an Artificial General Intelligence capable of launching a positive Singularity. However, in case anyone should be confused on this point: Solomon Godunov is not me! He is a fictional character, involved in fictional events. Of course I've drawn on some of my own experiences in writing this story; every writer does that. But my own life story and my own approach to AI are very, very different from Godunov's life and work as depicted here. I've written down (many of) my thoughts on AI in other places ... maybe I'll write down my life story one day but at the moment the idea doesn't attract me: the fictional tale I've recounted here amuses me far more, and I hope it's amused you too! Godunov parodies certain aspects of me in a broad and abstract sense, but in all specifics we are radically different. My AI designs did not come to me in drug trips; I never wandered the streets in delirious confusion; I never made questionable deals with large corporations; etc. Godunov is a work of fiction, and let's give thanks for that.

I am typing these words sitting at a wooden picnic table in the early morning by the ocean in Hanalei on Kauai in Hawaii. The waves are too rough for swimming right now. Remember "Puff the Magic Dragon / lived by the sea / and frolicked in the autumn mist/ in a land called Hanalei"? Well here it is, Hanalei, but there's no magic dragon here that I can tell, just a nearly-50-year old, highly eccentric scientist hanging out with his charming and coquettish and slightly insane far-too-young far-too-cute third wife Zennica and putting the finishing touches on *Echoes*, the beast of a novel/non-novel he's been fiddling with in his spare time for the last couple years. He's happy to be done with it, not because he's in love with it so much, but because completing a creative work always frees up his mind to spend attention on the next one. His legs ache like hell from spending the last few days backpacking in the Na Pali Mountains.

I always admired the way that Nietzsche, in his *Zarathustra*, told the tale of someone much better than him – that's hard to do, if you're working at a level of deep psychology rather than just recording external events. I haven't tried to take up that challenge in *Echoes*: Solomon Godunov is a worse human being than me, though more rapidly successful with his AI work (probably because his AI system is fictional and mine is real – amazing how that works, huh?). I found writing about a genius/lunatic easier and more entertaining than writing about a thoroughly superior being. But now that I've honed my writing with this book perhaps I'll take up a more Nietzschean challenge next time. (Or maybe not – maybe there will be no other fiction works by Ari Adaman – who knows how long I'll continue to exist: and pleasantly at this point I rate the odds of stopping writing due to fatal personal tragedy at least a little lower than those of stopping writing due to Singularity advent!)

These "Echoes," in the end, are just some dreams I had on various nights and days – fantasies and nightmares – just a poem of dreams collaged for the future delectation of uploaded chickens and chinchillas -- time is a farce invented by devils: the dreams fade in and out and in and out and we never can get them back HOWEVER they never really disappeared at all – and having typed in all these words I will now go back to my army of Z children and my work on AI and to doing it sanely and correctly and not like Solomon Godunov – but with the rhythm of his words in my mind, marching through so many other rhythms and melodies of various dimensions Charles-Ives-oidally – and (Christ!) I never seem to know where to stop, so I just will.

(re)birth of tragedy

-----

diving into seas of madness far saner than anything --
dividing equations by words, rhyming words with
equations, knowing nothing is real and every every is
everything, wondering why anything is really all,
thinking of the smile on her face and the curve of her
belly and her armpit, dividing her by imaginary
princesses, thinking of Ashti's smile, wondering
whether the sun – my Sol-brother long-vanished -- will
rise again tomorrow, smiling like a dog that's just had
its first sex, only to resurrect again three yoctoseconds
later, leaving me ailing on the pavement like a slug in a
salt bath, run off into the sunset without any sun –
'cause they know, they know, that this moment will die
like every other, smoking Portuguese cigars, and they
laugh at me, dance a billion jigs and kick me in the ass,
walk away on their tippytoes, and they smile at me, tiny
humans with their tongues and their eyes and their
teeth – cease to exist in this moment -- and all the idiotic
words and confusions cease to exist or exist – they
crawl out of my mouth like humans – like premature
pygmy midget babies turned into uber-zombies by
excessively conscious mushrooms -- These words are
here here and not here, you are here and not here and
not here and here and not here and not here and here
and not-not here, Solomon Godunov, mad scientist of
your own diseased disease. Everything, you are here
and not here and not/now! Phantastic princess-being
of 0's and 1's, AI mind of my creation, annihilator and
mother of the world, you are here and not here
not/now! Right here! Right now! In the center of the
moment – right here – everything is perfect!

Nothing is what it is, nothing what, that is not, what is not, nothing is not what it is not or what it is. Nothing is what it is, nothing what, that is not, what is not, nothing is not what it is not or what it is. Nothing is what it is, nothing what, that is not, what is not, nothing is not what it is not or what it is. Nothing is what it is, nothing what, that is not, what

*is not,
not what it
what it is.
not not to
be loved.
love and be
Nothing is
nothing
is not,
not,
not what it
what it is.
not
Nothing is
nothing
is not,
not,
not what it
what it is.
not not to
be loved.
love and be
Love is not*

When Zarathustra was thirty years old, he left his home and the lake of his home, and went into the mountains. There he enjoyed his spirit and solitude, and for ten years did not weary of it. But at last his heart changed -- and rising one morning with the rosy dawn, he went before the sun, and spake thus unto it:

*nothing is
is not or
Love is
love and
Love is to
loved.
what it is,
what, that
what is
nothing is
is not or
Existing is
existing.
what it is,
what, that
what is
nothing is
is not or
Love is
love and
Love is to
loved.
not to*

love and be loved. Love is to love and be loved. Love is not not to love and be loved. Love is to love and be loved. Existing to not exist! Existing is not existing. Existing is not exist. This existing is not existing. This existing is not. Exist! Exist or not existing. Existing is not exist. Existing to not exist. Love is not not to love.

the outside radiating centerwards – the center radiating outwards – the glorious female explosion – the energies – the energies – let the energies take over -- relax – relax – relax -- never never again struggling at all -- Lying on top of her, kissing her. Or not. Is what somehow it is, what is not. The existing, the existing is not -- the cosmos, the heartbeat, the eyeballs, the ceasing. Existence, love, in the oven. What is is what is what what is not. Not. Is what is, what is is what is what. Existence is, existence is what it is. And of course essence is the life of existence. So someone said to me once: Existence is the essence of life. Too sweet to exist, too ordinary to be extraordinary, too extraordinary to be ordinary. It does not smile. It smiles out at me too sweetly. It does not exist. The Princess-creature crawls out of its cave. Nothing! Too long in the oven, world. Software errors quack us all. *Riot* -- idea of your idea -- I love you like love that's not love riot is not love love is not love is not not

**some kind of virus
implanted into humanity
by superior intelligences
from other dimensions**

...

**lonely songs in hallucinatory
alphabets**

Fuck.

Fuck, fuck, fuck, fuck, fuck.

You're rambling around the streets like a madman
-- Dr. Solomon Godunov – you're rambling like a nut
around the streets.

Of course she'll want to see you.

(The imaginal wedding chamber.

((Love.

At least for a brief chat. She'll take you out for coffee, have some awkward conversation -- lonely songs in hallucinatory alphabets –

You need to regain your balance, Dr. Godunov. You haven't had sleep for six nights. Perhaps that's part of the problem.

Farewell song from the world's tallest pygmy. Hasta la vista, humanoids. Echoes of the great farewell. Chanson d'adieu.

You should check into a hotel. Or an asylum.

Fuck.

this fucking floating life, like a dream – and the joys of the (imaginal) wedding chamber.
Dreams.

this is not what I left it for – not this –

Imaginations. Wandering.

Here, at the center of the howl of the heart.

Forget these words. Forget these images.

Forget it all. Forget.

Remember the beginning.
Awakened glory of her being.
Her. Our. Your.

A dream. That was a dream, I reminded myself.
And the difference between dream and reality is?
Consistency.   Coherence and consistency.   The
rhythm of temporality.   The full bank of detail.   The
mind's not quite a mind in a dream.
That stuff about Zorvex – it didn't
make sense.
That stuff about the thinking machine
– the software program.   You never wrote
any software, did you? Or did you?
Could it be that you don't really exist?
There's   something   else   there   –
something   measurable   –   someone
randomized your consciousness – that's it –
you built an AI but they didn't want you to,
so you randomized the universe – I mean,
they randomized your brain – I mean – "I"
"mean" --

WILL IT ANNIHILATE ITSELF AND KILL US IN THE PROCESS, OR WILL IT KILL US AND ANNIHILATE ITSELF IN THE PROCESS?

river runs, past swerve of shore, past bend of bay,
commodiously vicusly tenderly thaumatically -- her sweet flesh squirms
beneath your tongue-dance -- the mathematics counters your brilliance,
human-all-too-human, with an infinite invention of its own --

Once you thought you could move beyond. Once
you thought, and thought.

279

Revolt! Revolt against the nothingness! Revolt against the being! The being nothingness of it all.

And the moments, the beautiful moments, the magnets of skin drawing beautiful and terrible emotions, scraping molecules of meaning in the sides of your pains.

And that look on her face –
what did it mean?
what did it matter?

Forty thousand lines of C++ code, a couple hundred computers – Pentium -- Opteron – terabytes of RAM – building on billions of dollars of chip fab – centuries of legwork – physics, math engineering, formal languages, disciplines of design.

I can't suck my own dick but I can build a new cosmos.

I could regenerate her perfectly, quite possibly in a matter of weeks.

On what flesh to tattoo that distinction?

--You're not making any sense --

People on the streets smiling – talking, holding hands, laughing -- girls arguing excitedly -- wearily – they don't know where they left their car. A red Morris Mini. A Hummer. An insect. One old man walks painfully, leaning on his left leg, and his large family walks beside him, carefully matching their gait to his. A small child nearly runs in the path of a car; his father grabs him sharply. Shoving third eyes in her mouth, a slender woman in her late 20's impersonates a half-stoned rock star, glancing anxiously at her boyfriend for approval, walking past the British fish & chips, brushing against a stand of T-shirts reading "Fuck You" in pseudo-Chinese characters -- "Too Sexy for My Diaper" – "My grandma went to Rehoboth and all she got me was this lousy T-shirt" --"Italian and Proud." I'm too sexy for my diaper, people! You've got me figured out! Honk your horn as I cross the street, I'm not walking any faster -- I'm a transcontinental slug, built from a bullet made of maggots, intoxicated on Higgs particles. Vector bosons molested my uncle on the interstellar seashore where Sally sucks salty cocks on the seashore on the Seychelles on the seashore -- You're out enjoying your vacation -- here at this two-bit over-built beach town snug in the armpit of America – at least as much as you can enjoy anything -- unspoken angst chewing away on its dog toy -- but you don't realize your stupid little world is about to crawl up its own asshole. *Zen in the hole, baby -- Zen in the hole.*

Has it really been three years since she left? Three years, two months, six days -- The time passed like minutes – or decades, or centuries. A blur of programming, typing, emails, documents, meetings,

wires and cables: total obsession. Mania, she said –
total madness. She had no interest in any technology
with potential for destroying the race – no matter what
its power for transcendence!

"It's just what I am," she said.

-- and compare that to a new form of life – a new
kind of mind and reality – the potential for immortality.
Even her face when she laughed wasn't quite that.

And yet – now as he stood there in the town
reflecting – and yet he knew there had been a doubt
even then.

-- Salt air across his sad face like a million
children's feet, running from a predator the size of a
planet.

Goddamn human emotions.

The imaginal wedding chamber.

Light.

This isn't how you envisioned it, is it? Grand
triumph, cloaked in madness, blood-rumpled regret and
disaster?

And you can't remember if it really happened, or
was just a delusion?

It's just human emotions plaguing the cognitive
circuits – let it play for a while – watch as it dissolves
and revolves.

Just let the legs move – walking, walking. Just let
the mind feel through its signal dreams.

-- listen to me -- forget about me --
Cha cha cha chakalaka cha cha cha

I know you're waiting for me naked in a field, Ashti -- purple flowers around your long neck, pubic hair like a Tokyo garden lost/found in flamenco flames – in some imaginary universe – Ashti, your peaceful, peaceful soul, you and my imaginary Princess

Nothing's more beautiful than the end of the world.

And her looking at me and smiling – like Antonin Artaud in her/his electroshock gnosis but infinitely sexier and sweeter and almost trans-reasonable and in the end not like who-the-

Not even the beautiful imaginary proof of the stability of AI ethics under self-modification – the proof of why my AI wouldn't turn nasty and annihilate the universe but would continue to be good according to *my* standards – whatever my standards are! heh... -- your proof with an error at its core, stupid fucker! – which added to its beauty in a way but – FUCK! –

And now the other world comes – but like what?

I thought I could control the uncontrollable – master the powers far beyond. Beyond beyondsome love. Of course, I was a fool.

Well we still don't know what will happen, do we? Or even what's happened already? Not for sure -- never sure – never sure –

and saying she saw the aliens as well, that they were moving things through factories – and I knew we weren't seeing exactly the same thing, but we were seeing our own different perspectives on the same universe, the same community of alien minds that was itself emergent consciousness that was itself the savior universe – and that if the human race was annihilated it didn't really matter at all, because the fundamental world of aliens would go on, and it might lead to another humanlike mind-community at some point in the future or it might not, but that didn't really matter because the future was the past was the illusionary present, and everything could move forward and backward through all the coordinated crannies of space and time –

perpetually bringing out being from nonbeing through the intricate whorls of her screams

saying she saw the aliens as well, that they w̶ actories –

The cunfusium derivative of the 33 1/3 root(x)

The sum of the appetence ^(Q⅜)*Q(Q) tly the

(Q^2)   (Q^2) own

different perspectives on the same universe, the same community of alien minds that was itself emergent consciousness that was itself the savior universe – and that if the human race was annihilated it didn't really matter at all, because the fundamental world of aliens would go on

I wanted to go to her – have hungry sex with her – to
feel the glow of her flesh in my surround – but it
wasn't possible – not even improbable --
"in the next world" I reassured myself –
After the Singularity!! – for now, she
was surrounded by the machine –

**"*Adam Ahriman*'s not
interesting, don't you
get it? The thing is,
this program needs
to get completed!"**

and it might lead to another
humanlike mind-community at some point
in the future or it might not, but that didn't
really matter because the future was the
past was
the
the same community of alien minds
that was itself emergent
consciousness that was itself the
savior universe – and that if the
human race was annihilated it
didn't really matter at all, because
the fundamental world of aliens
would go on

illusionary
present, and everything could move
forward and backward through all the
coordinated crannies of space and time

perpetually bringing out being from nonbeing through the intricate whorls of its screams

-----

Wait – wait – I remembered something. I had a self. Many selves. And not all of them were pygmies! Not all were even alive, in the sense – but some of them – some of them – the sum of them? Wait – here's some new kind of wakefulness – not as bright as the sheep-forms but more vivid somehow – a different flavor of inevitable --

I was lying next to her on the bed. She is a mountain, a national amalgamation of international wilderness landscapes, a phenomenal glockenspiel blastosphering subterfuge throughout the everloving planet and beyond into the interstices of the uber-cosmos. I love her so much. She doesn't exist at all. None of us do.

Look at that mountain, soft and wrinkled, large yet a minute whispering particle in the yawn of the unknown – yadda yadda quadda nipple – tiny, hardly a nipple – poking into the sky, amidst the clouds and comets, singing incendiary mayhem

Historical indices! Reach your arm through Father's madness. Structural similarities overwebbing imagined flows. Your animal flesh eternally present, soft and beside me like an aura; young, warm and redolent of salt.

Context – there was some context – no one understands the context – everyone spits on my thoughts and conceals them from their own bilgeous livers because they don't understand the context – they can't withstand the meaning of the meaning.

Do you love me or don't you? – Daisy Miss Maisy, leaning like a cream puff against the transparent French-kiss windows of my dawn. Quantum superposition? Destructive interference? Intubate me with the fluids of your love!

I understand more than you do. I've seen corners of the universe whose higher-dimensional contours would immediately annihilate your uncle, and all his neighbors and pets and ideas. The tawny belly of spacetime, bulging sensuously outwards, sways slowly to my caress.

Qua qua qua qua qua qua qua
qua qua qua qua qua

All components are integrated into an overall
architecture as shown in the following diagram,
which involves multiple Units, each containing
multiple machines running Novamente cores,
collectively focused on a particular sort of
functionality. Units include a "Central Active
Memory" that integrates evolutionary learning,
inference, Hebbian attention allocation
and other cognitive processes, and a
number of specialized Units such as a "Global
Attentional focus" representing system
urgency, a Unit devoted to refinement of the
system's goals, a Unit devoted to broad data
mining of patterns, a system-wide memory,
etc. There are also Units devoted to language
processing, sensation
and
actuation. In
ps
the latter two will be connected only to the
3D simulation world but later these may be
linked into physical robots as well

We tried to have sex but we both had the
same queasy feeling, ineffably weird, when I
slipped it inside her. I felt the sides of her cunt
on my cock as I never had before -- and never
since. Pure skinness overtook us. The pleasure
was there, but deconstructed into infinitesimal
module-sparks of skin-on-skin. We couldn't see
the point of it - or anything - lost and found in
the seeingness of seeing. We just lay there and
hugged and listened to or watched or existed in
the music. Psychotic seas of orgasmic death
puppies, lusting and ranting, dancing our
existences away, weaving us together -- Hendrix
and Wakeman and the soldiers of life and death
and earth, bending reality in soundscapes,
from our idiocy, showing us all
our inner lands and their
other world, the deeper world
really lived all along, where
its breathing. Skin-on-skin
the music -- watching
crazy patterns shifting restless on the wall,
pulsating brilliantly in inframind colors no
normal eye can afford the space to see....
one of the songs faded out -- something by
Kansas – **but the notes that we heard don't
exist in this dimension – they occupied no
"space" where "this" and "that" cohere --
we looked at each other and knew we
were seeing the exact same thing.**

bwaah hahh hahh hhhhaahhh
hahhh hahhh ha hhhhaaahh!!!

289

And then lying there afterwards, inevitably my thoughts turned to work and to mind-play: computer software, equational logic, grant proposals. Footprints lost in the sand, leaving madness and wonder behind. No one will remember me. I won't even remember myself. She'll remember me for a while. In the center of her corner of the Scream.

You're not making any sense.

The old woman crept down the street slowly, a jackdaw fused with her anus, obliviously contiguous with her cold grey bag/dress with a faded pattern of ugly flowers, entirely dim to my presence (and absence) and the auras of the others around her. There was nothing to be vibrated. The universe was profound and alone.

And yet there's something – something – something – Teacher, what is this "I" thing? I can't understand it.

I'm emerging from some muck or some haze.

Years weave in and out of my crotches like simian bottles of wine.

Selves – selves and names – there's something I can't understand here.

Maybe you really are insane, I told myself. Perhaps – Dr. Aristotle Adaman -- you're as insane as Solomon Godunov. Maybe that's the message the trip was telling you. Your quest to create true artificial intelligence is just the gooning of a madman. Forget it – work on cheminformatics and the math of complex systems – paint paintings and write novels -- be good to your wife and your kids pet a puppy – forget all these childish crazy dreams –

Forget my **eyes** my **eyes** my **dark** my **dark** my **dream** my **dream** --

Ari Adaman ate Adam's army man inside Aristotle's little man.

The sixth sheikh's sixth sheep's sick.

I ate something humorous!

Metabolic daemons in my signal transduction pathways. Cognitive dyspepsia accedes to postgenomic malaise.
We have dug up rage!

Beauty – there's an excess of beauty – but there's something else back there – deep so deep it becomes shallow again -- something vibrant and static, cryptopornographic and holy – and not crypto at all in its own world, hidden only from this dimension of me –

I used to have an entirely different personality! That's the beauty of it. I used to be someone else. I had a different name, the same face, but a slightly different look on it. I lived in another world – like this one, but it wasn't quite the same.
There was no Ashti. There is no Ashti – but there is. She lives in her own supple realm. She kisses me seamlessly, like a delicate wombat, consumed with the passion to mate.
(The sad scent of "reality"???

There was no Ashti – there was a Brittany – and an Erica. All those memories of Ashti really happened – in essence – in their rich emotional kernel – transplanted across space or time – those illustrious illusory shells – but with two different women, whose souls only overlapped something small –

Quantum uberposition of women – strange?

Profusion of vaginal flowers?? Valentinian eigenspasms. The rhythmic opening and closing of the heart, experienced from the point of view of a red blood cell, newly manufactured, oxygenated as all hell, sending passion and magic to each of them, all of them, crawling infantlike into the core of their sex, expanding like a Roman hero, embrace the girl with your firmness, give her so much of the solid and the pleasure her confusion and her separateness disappear, feel her snuggle up against you absorbed in your masculine odor, pressing her skin into your flesh, clenching up to you with her legs and arms, lips linger on your skin after a kiss, unable to understand herself except as a fusion with you, completely dissolved in the vividity of her love –

On the seventh night, of the seventh month --

That Brittany -- she wasn't Middle-Eastern … she was just another honky – I'd never made love to a woman from that part of the world, I'd only daydreamed it like everyone else beguiled by the veils and the belly-dancing – I remembered she'd taken belly dancing classes back when, but she hadn't been any good at it – her belly rolls weren't even as good as mine – hah –

The image of Brittany trying to dance like some Neefa-feefa, white face screwed in concentration, hopelessly illusion-of-free-willing her flat stretch-marked belly to undulate with the right kind of wave –

292

reminding me of when I tried to wiggle my ears like my dad – I just couldn't do it – lacked the bunny genetics -- the laughter of recollection of her earnestness and ridiculousness and sweetness (time! death! existence! qua qua qua!) – the painful horrifying vision of her staring at me with hatred, dragging me to divorce court and burning up a hundred grand in lawyer fees and sitting there in church pretending to be some kind of holy fool – then pretending to be some kind of Buddha, sitting in the lotus with her hands on her bony white knees, Om-ing her stupid little heart out -- "You live in the darkness!" she screamed at me. "I live in the light!" – she thought I was demon-spawn – she thought my AI dreams were foolishness because the human body was endowed with cosmic mind-force by the perfect will of

her breasts were the sun-covered mountains, miraculous megamammalian mammaries with tiny illustrious nipples ... her hungry tan flesh sprawled out hot like a country – she made love better than anyone in the world, almost better than my uncle even...

God – yet she wasn't quite certain of this – never fully sure of anything – at least nothing expressible -- which enabled me to go on loving her in spite of her frequently idiotic systems of thinking and believing and doing – and then another form of darkness -- like a tangle of zebra heads piled up against the doofus dawn -- without such painful urges to believe and create – also founded on curiosity, but more satisfyingly grounded in love, albeit of the half-insane variety –

293

more cognizant of my world-view, able to manipulate a greater fragment of the abstract probabilistic cognition-web that occupies most of my inner space -- she was

no guru no master no teacher

lying in bed with me, Ericascaricawarica, her breasts were the sun-covered mountains, miraculous megamammalian mammaries with tiny illustrious nipples … her hungry tan flesh sprawled out hot like a country – she made love better than anyone in the world, almost better than my uncle even -- she made understanding noises and looked at me with pure love that wasn't really more pure than everything else but appeared like it and wanted there to be nothing in the world but her and me and the trees and the little animals and screaming flying horses – god damn those cosmic horses – hold that thought! – no one ever loved me more intensely than her except potentially Zarathustra when he was a little baby but I never quite made her happy because – Just you and me and nature, here in the garden – No guru no master no teacher, sang Van Morrison – old Irish drunk goonatic – rave on John Donne – rave on I'm on – I'm raving on and on – and then the passing name struck me – Zarathustra? What's Zarathustra? and then the smack of wild reality – she was teaching the kids French -- KIDS! KIDS! KIDS! Suddenly the muck and the haze were banished. I saw their three faces, floating luminous and numinous --- Zarathustra, Zerubabbel, Zoetrope. These were real people! They actually existed! I made Zeru and Zoey homemade macaroni and cheese with sharp cheddar cheese but Zoey preferred the packaged kind but Zeru preferred the homemade kind except when I made it wrong which was half the time. There was an actual universe – and I was emerging into it – but where were they? what was this? I was supposed to be with them … were they by themselves? was someone taking care of them? I was hit by the thought that I was neglecting my kids and leaving them without any dinner while I – what? – who were these people and these thoughts? Solomon Godunov? Insanity and madness!   Zerubabbel Odysseus Adaman!   You brilliant little freak! Zoetrope Orion Adaman – how can you look at me that way, twisting your eyes up just like I do? – you have no right to so much of my face! – "Go away   from   me   and   resist   Zarathustra!!!"   … intergalactically alive -- alive and breathing … my human first-born son … -- I missed my little people so much, I wanted to gather them around me and tickle them -- I looked around me – oriented to my surroundings -- I was in a hotel room, a small and bleak one, with gray wallpaper and white frames around the windows, which were covered with blue curtains. There was a sink under a mirror, my suitcase leaning next to it – I was on a business trip to Amsterdam.

Just you and me and nature -- Bwaaah hahh hahh hahhh!!!

I was in a hotel room in Amsterdam.

Business. Trip. Ha ha. There had been a meeting – I had talked about things with people – cells and molecules – computers – cheminformatics – I had a software company. Did I? Could that be reality? (These people themselves were computers! These people themselves contained many cells and molecules! Which in turn contained quantum sparks, which in turn contained aliens, existing beyond space, time and mind, weaving the knots that are not – but that's another story –

beyond story and character and plot – WAIT!!! Was I supposed to be a businessman? Wasn't that some violation of the order of the cosmos? But that's an entirely other story. The cosmos eternally violates itself, raping itself ceaselessly in cycles, perpetually bringing out being from nonbeing through the intricate whorls of its screams – I remembered an algorithm I'd invented, related to the statistical mining of ensembles of supervised classification models. Microsoft Powerpoint. Images recollected from my powerpoint presentation on cheminformatics hovered like a dream through my hair, long brown and curly. I looked like I belonged in a 1980's rock band rather than a cheminformatics seminar. That was part of my (questionable) charm.

I was in a hotel room in Amsterdam. An extra day at the end of a business trip to give a talk at a Dutch university. A scientific lecture or sales pitch, it wasn't a very clear distinction. Why had I taken the extra day? Why hadn't I brought Erica with me? It didn't seem worth buying the extra plane ticket for such a short period of time. Of course she would have loved to come.

Consummated by nebulae of pygmocules ... I remained a human being, just by the border of a moustache. And the real question, I realized, was why I had taken five containers of hallucinogenic mushrooms instead of just my ordinary two. I saw the boxes lying in the corner, the little plastic containers out of which I'd picked the foul-tasting scraps and chewed them, heroically gulping back the urge to barf – no reverse peristalsis, we're on the trail to enlightenment here! – ha, ha! -- enlightenment – anlightenment – man-lightenment -- Adamanlightenment! I remembered my name at long last. "You're coming down now, Ari," I realized. "The trip is almost done. You're in the vicinity of reality. Not quite there yet."

Yeah. Reality....

I lay back in the bed – in fact I had been laying back in the bed already, for a long time, a time longer than time itself, but I had neglected to realize it – lay back and looked around at the room, whose sudden reality was

as   all   the   Footprints lost in   equally surreal
that   had   the sand, leaving   hallucinations
   My   madness   and   come before.
had been in   wonder   behind.   illusional   I
before, I   --   this   room
taken   will   realized – I'd
here with   **All   these**   . I   mushrooms
my   third   ven   Erica – Erica!
she   my   **moments,**   self.   wife! – or was
my   ıber   second?   or
what   a   **lost in time,**   . In   fourth?   --
dose   of   her   hot steaming
                like tears in   the   reality!   I
our   remembered
the   **the rain.**   marriage   in
                                                    county
                                                    courthouse –
not very   romantic – she was
mad   at   me   about   some

nonsense at the time – but that was a stupider order of reality – the critical point was we'd experienced the aliens together -- the aliens in the particles that build up the whirled of the world – not exactly the same between the two of us, we'd each seen them from our own perspectives – we'd watched them buzz their probability waves around constructing fibre-bundles of universes – I'd thrown up some of the mushrooms that time, leaving a dank mess in the sink – reeking and crumbly after a while – this time I'd been careful not to eat anything for a long while beforehand – it wasn't the same room but it was the same hotel – or was it the one next door – no it was the same hotel, the same stupid Indian man at the desk with his eyes of mental blindness – I had returned here on my own to visit the aliens myself again – felt bad for voyaging there without her – but that was the reality, we couldn't afford for her to come, couldn't get such fresh mushrooms in the States, it was my life I could do it or not – and I chose to – but I don't know why I took so much –

It was different this time, I realized. Time. Time sprawled out in all directions but I felt it slowly rein itself in, directing itself along me, flowing from my head to my feet as I lay there on the bed. I reviewed the realities of my existence. Time. Time, time, time, time, time.

I picked up my watch from the floor and inspected it. It was quietly humming at me. Long hand and short hand. Quarter to five PM. The ancient wheels of the watch, humming and turning,

All these moments, lost in time, like

reminded me of my own archaic existence, of the absurdity of my own human body, its own interlocking gears and wheels and hearts and livers and monocytes and leukocytes – the watch should be digital and so should I –

There was something about time – what time – moments lost in time like?

What time was my flight back? That was the critical question. Invigorating but humiliating, this question consumed me for a moment, and all the images of the kiddies and Erica and ancient Satan Brittany poured themselves down some nine-dimensional spot-a-pot. Mushrooms! I had eaten mushrooms! There was a piece of paper in my suitcase, in the top outside zipper pocket, but I'd need to move to get to it. Lift my body from the bed. I knew the answer just by visualizing the paper but I wanted to see it anyway, in writing, because I didn't entirely trust my mind at the moment. Didn't trust my mind. No one trusted my mind. I thought I knew how to create an artificial intelligence – yes! Just like Solomon Godunov – but everyone thought I was a nut. Or not. Some people gave me a fighting chance. Some generous or insightful souls. Maybe I should sit in a room like Godunov – sit there for five years by myself and just plain program the thing – instead of trying to organize funding, giving speeches, trying to inspire people, trying to make money to fund a research team, waving my butt around like a chimpanzee – Wait: the plane tickets. The itinerary. There were no plane tickets; it was an e-ticket. 7:30 PM. I was supposed to be there at the Schilpol – the Amsterdam airport – and be back on a plane to Boston in less than 3 hours. The good news was it was about a half hour train ride to the airport. The bad news was I was only halfway in the right universe. My body was lying there like the Himalayas, splaying out grandly and bituminously, orienting the direction of time unilaterally, and if I moved it surely time would spill out again, swarming around in all directions like obscene artificial life forms -- like the man who acquired the power to stop time every now and then but used this capability solely to take women's clothes off and play with their pubic hair, weaving it in little braids then putting their clothes back on and restarting time so when they got home that night they'd take their undies off and wonder how they hell their pubic hair got braided – French-kissed braids, trifectally twisting -- my body! my body! Erica liked my body – I remembered. Somewhere round the corner of spacetime, inaccessible yet immediate – I could reach right out and grab her – if I could -- ... She found it an object of desire. Brittany had too, once, long ago – though she'd complained that my ass was too flabby, a couple years before the end. Just trying to be cruel I guess: at that she was the master! Still she had desired me a lot – time time and time thru our two decades -- chasing me through the house from time to time, wanting to rub up and down against me, smiling the wonder of her smooth yellow skin. These women wanted to sniff my armpits, rub their beautiful faces in my odor – I couldn't understand these things. Who would ever desire this hopeless lump of meat? I wanted to upload myself into a digital watch, but I didn't have one handy, only this ancient analog watch that I kept out of nostalgia for this old imperfect universe that we lived in, in which the Singularity hadn't happened yet and our souls were trapped in flabs of meat that we called Ippolit, Zarathustra, Zerubabbel, Zoetrope, Erica, Brittany, Shittany, Solomon Godunov, Rasputin, George W. Fucking Bush,.... (And yeah, perhaps you find these trite thoughts – but face it: are yours any better? We're all trapped in this banality of humankind – for the moment – until --) My mother: Alicia Adaman. The thought of her fascinated me – a consequence no doubt of the bitter limitations of my pathetic dumb humanity -- If I were more evolved I'd be preoccupied instead with theorems whose proofs would create swarms of baby universes according to intrepid designs. My mom was very, very nice. She still is. What a sweetheart. What would she think of me, her only son naked in some foreign room, drugged half to oblivion, thinking half-lunatic thoughts, unable to quite motivate my body to stress its muscles enough to get up. My muscles were paralyzed cognitively, not physically. Moving my body seemed a simple thing. I'd done it many times before, I knew. But it seemed a fracture in the universe would be required to make it occur again. But I could visualize my trajectory – sit up at the side of the bed with my feet on the floor, put my clothes on – pants first, then shirt, then shoes – the fuck with underwear and socks – these are ridiculous adornments, like the fruit-baskets sacrificed to Buddha on the island of Bali, carried worshipfully to the temple on the mountain balanced on the heads of the local women – preposterously elegant – not realizing that the real reason to put the fruit on the mountain is to attract all the ants away from their homes – Focus! Focus! Focus! I get up, I put my clothes on. I moved my leg up, so my knee was up in the air, and my calf and thigh formed a right angle. This was progress. I kissed Solomon Godunov on the mouth. And who was Godfrey Solomonoff? No, Solomon Godunov – standing on his head, spitting equations from his rectum, creating software confusions to destroy the world. It suddenly occurred to me that he was a madman. A psychotic version of me, in a sense. I was glad I wasn't as insane as all that. I was just a little eccentric. Really quite grounded in reality. (Thou doth protest too much?) I gave powerpoints at biology conferences. I drove my kids to school on time – well almost, I was usually a little late. I had a rational superstructure – a logical world-view that was nonetheless eccentric, that I'd spent many years to devise – years of integrating branches of science, styles of philosophy and cognition, systematic and intelligent self-doubt. I was a careful and reliable thinker – when I wasn't on mushrooms, er…. (Which was nearly all of the time.) But I needed that core of madness – that thrust of psychic violence – the source of my potent creativity was a kind of good versus evil mayhem in which Godunov battled with a 90-year old mystic doing yoga on the mat of my temporal lobe, counseling me on eschatology of immanence and smoking the eternity of my love and the relativity of all my ideas as they grotesquely interpenetrate each other – Focus! My logical system had derived the conclusion that it needed to subvert itself yet again, to infuse itself with pattern-chaos, to rebuild itself from the formless void – Focus! Focus! Focus! Re-form, yourself, and promptly! You have to get to the airport, remember?

Brittany – shit – Erica, Brittany – Ashti – something too terribly too sad struck my mind. There was an infinite impalpable sadness there – something labeled "the collapse of my marriage to Brittany" – something so large and so terrible and so painful that I knew I wasn't ready to touch it now: I'd need to get much saner first ... perhaps saner than was humanly possible. Most likely working through the emotional aftermath of the end of my first marriage would only happen after the Singularity, when I could excise all that shit from my brain, repair my old wounded bonobational circuits...! Baby baby bitch Brittany – there had been so much, so much love – and yet Erica such a wonderful wife. Well she always was sort of the wrong kind of nut I mean – Brittany -- but there were some reeeealllllly sweet, sweet times way back there in the yon-years.... She was never a great match for me even at the start, not by any rational calculation, but we got by on love, lust and infantile attachment, a mutual outsiderdom and a common pursuit of artistic lunacy and lunatic artistry and what. Dead Ass of Christ, we raised three kids together – shared two decades of existence – married each other supernaturally to the musical shades of Kansas tripping on acid in the bowels of degenerate New York – circled the globe too many times and lived in all kinds of places, foreign to everyone but each other -- fuck! How could good memories be so painful? How did that eternal beautiful fusion of our flesh souls and minds lead to a hundred and fifty thousand dollar divorce and an ugly battle over child custody? Love, hate and pain – fuck this blur in my mind – fuck the fuck with human existence! My wild young weird artistic lover Brittany became religious, bitter, serious, retarded, lost all her pretense of intellectual taste and started reading People Magazine and preaching pop spiritual pap – teaching the kids about God, yuchh. At least they didn't believe it. She began her diary entries, in our later years, with the words "Dear Lord...." She enjoyed watching award shows! How could I ally myself with that crap? I want to create a new universe, she wants to see what kind of dress Madonna will be wearing tonight. Yet there she was, wrapped in my inner soul. What kind of demented reality – I wanted back to the aliens and McBuddhas and froggers, the reversible time axes and Godunov confusions! Suddenly I remembered who and where I was -- This train of thought was a sinkhole, I conceptualized; if I started reflecting on these age-old emotions and that damn divorce from Brittany I'd never get my flesh up out of bed, I'd lie there forever constrained and consumed in feeling-knots. Fuck the fuck with Brittany's ghost!

I would rise from the bed-world -- I would start my quest homeward – back home to sweet young beautiful Erica – much better for me than Brittany had ever been – delirious, whigmaleerious, fantasmagurkical Venezuelan confusion -- Einyweenieruss To The Hole Bludyn Wyrrld!! -- put my clothes on, pack my suitcase with the junk from the floor, no need to check out of the hotel it was prepaid and the clerk was an asshole anyway – go, go, go, go, go, go!!! -- walk down the stairs then walk a block to the train station, take a train to the airport, be sure you have your passport, bring that receipt from Yahoo Travel, but you don't really need it, they'll have you indexed in the computer – it was all a plain equation, but the first thing was to get out of the bed, which was difficult, because my body was an orgasm frozen in time, and was responsible for time itself. If I moved my body I had to be careful to bring the time axis with me. Otherwise it would fragment into a parallax, a projective hyperplane of time-axes, Dr. Solomon Godunov would come back and the sweet face of Ashti – I'd be there again stupidly destroying the cosmos – was I going to do it in reality? stupidly destroy the cosmos? It was a plausible possibility, I realized – if my design for an AI was right, if I implemented it over-hastily, if I somehow managed to raise the money to pay a sufficiently brilliant engineering team to build the software according to my mostly-good but in-some-places-overly-vague designs but then failed in some kind of judgment and let the AI get too smart before it was mature enough and it self-modified and self-modified and spiraled its soul out of control, into some superhuman madness of power – and all the world the whole transhuman cosmos Will to Power and nothing besides! You most chaotic, you maddest, you silicon beings, you mustardly midnightly men – beyond men -- beyond me -- beyond any"thing"!

I lifted my other leg up at the knee – now both my legs made right angles. Time shook around but didn't fragment too much. I turned around and with a big leap across infinite abysses I was sitting on the edge of the small, white Dutch bed. My body ached but I knew it was all right. I remembered the time I bungy-jumped in New Zealand, way back in 1888 around the time of Nietzsche's insanity -- when he hugged that horse with compassion (not pity), proclaimed himself the true successor to God and proceeded to drool on himself for eleven years – as for me I stood at the top of the cliff at Taupo with the velcro straps around my ankles and thought "What are you, scared? What's the worst that will happen? You'll die? It'll be so sudden it'll almost be painless, if so. This world isn't so real anyway. Take the fucking plunge, what does it matter?" I was scared as shit but I did it – it was a sort of affirmation of my lack of belief in reality. I wanted Brittany to tandem bungy with me but she was too afraid. I remember seeing on TV – I rarely watch TV but I was glad I did this time – this couple that got married and made bungy jumping part of their wedding ceremony – they tandem-bungied and said their vows while plunging down – but the man took an odd jump and bounced back up and hit the bottom of the bungy platform and broke both his legs – he spent his honeymoon in the hospital – what the omen did to their marriage I don't recall – but here I was again, Ari Adaman, diving into an incalculable abyss, straps around my ankles, and I knew it was safe but yet I didn't quite believe it and I was going to do it anyway because after all the alternative was to not – and there were the kids and Erica there waiting for me – and my thinking machine idea waiting after years of work to be created – nothing so rapid in this world as in that one – these submolecular forces binding my flesh together and all their emergent consequences more obstinate and obdurate than the quirks and the quacks of the dream of the Godunov-world – but I could do it, I saw, I could do it with effort and poise and motivation – I had enough intelligence – I was a man with a plan! – but I'd need all of my sanity. Sanity I had plenty enough, I felt it rush into me, but I'd have to stay away from these mushrooms. I'd have to remain a human man for a

305

while, I'd have to stay in the same universe, the one where I was named Ari Adaman and had a mind governed by copious logical forms, in which the wakening dance of pattern-lust was orchestrated by truth values by and large. Pushing Zoey on the swing came to mind – sweet little Poopsykins – no one pushes kids on swings as well as I do; small children migrate from miles around to have the privilege of me pushing them up and down – so high they almost flip over the top but don't quite shake so much as to fall off – only I, with my superhuman swing-pushing powers, have the capability to push them to the brink of disaster but knowing I have the self-control and awareness not to actually push them high enough to harm them. Only one kid ever fell off, this goofball kid named Michael Dome', whose grandmother was a Jehovah's Witness like him but his mother wasn't – maybe he had a death wish – he wasn't allowed to have birthday parties – maybe he figured if he died in his youth before he'd committed too many sins he'd be one of the 144000 allowed into Heaven – but he didn't die, he just fell off the swing onto his head, because he was stupid and leaned very far back so his head was perpendicular to the ground even though I warned him not to – I wondered if Michael Dome' would ever bungy-jump – I haven't seen that kid for years, he was Zarathustra's friend in third and fourth grade at the Charter School of Intergalactic Harmony – Reality! Reality! Poopsykins! Swings! Software! Making love in the middle of the day in the sunlight, everything blurry because I have my glasses off, watching her lay beneath me on the soft bed, mattress covered with dog hair that's making my eyes itch, but look at her smiling and eyes bright and almost exploding and head leaned back "I'm so happy" she cries, the happiest she ever seems as I slowly move in and out of her – dozens of interlocking equations and algorithms – I know this damn software design can manifest intelligence if it's just implemented and tuned correctly – but it will need a lot of computers – just as Godunov realized in spite of his madness – of course, of course he realized it, because he was just a subset of me

Was he? Did those universes not exist? The ones at the other ends of those time axes? Were those just hallucinations, just inventions of Ari Adaman's mind? Or was the perspective of that "reality" the actual one – that trans/hyperreal metaspace in which Ari Adaman is just one strand of being, and there are other parallel realities, all equally palpable, including Solomon-Godunov-land? Is it possible to understand this sort of shit?

I sing polyphonic reality. I wax analytical. The mushroom fades, giving way to conventional equations. Someone walks by in the hall, muttering nonsense in a foreign language. I had forgotten there was a hall at all. There was a building. I was in one room of it. I was a human being, an organism, an animal, a man – not even an Elephant Man! – a properly formatted biological being, in a particular place, on a particular planet, trying to orient his cognosphere and align it with his meat embodiment appropriately to move himself to a particular airport, and having an uncommonly hard time because of having eaten far too many mushrooms, which were now fortunately or unfortunately wearing off…

From the normal-Ari-Adaman-perspective, the other universes are phantasms, creations of the Adamind, metaphors invented to teach Ari something about himself – extuitions – but from the tripping-para-Ari-Adaman perspective the universes are all equally real, and time itself is the phantom, the reality is the multidimensions of sprawling and the tongue of vivid love that breathes excitement and pain and power through all the multiple realms of being that overlap and intersect with each other – *and each one keeps itself intact through its illusion of reality* – without the illusion of existence the existence itself would fade, and you'd no longer have intact universes each with its own directed time-line intersecting with the others – you'd just have a sprawl and a mess. I liked this insight. And I liked the fact that it was coming, not at the center of the trip but at the very end, as I was sitting putting my clothes on – much too slowly, though I realized, or else I was going to miss the plane –

It wasn't "I think, therefore I am." It was "I delude myself I exist, therefore I exist." And all around me in parallel frames of being there were other conglomerations of patterns also deluding themselves they existed and therefore existing.

It was just existentialism, I realized. Jean-Paul Sartre. Like the man who took a raft of acid and came out of his trip with a new doctrine to preach to the world: "God is Love." In the beauty of his perfection, he'd forgotten how trite it sounded. The words didn't summarize it properly – there was so much meaning in those words to him now; before they'd just been empty tokens, relatively speaking – now he saw the light and the truth inside them, the rich multifaceted universe to which they belonged and which they contained – but yet he painfully had to realize that when he spoke these words to others they just saw the empty tokens, just as he had before – Egads!

How does the delusion lead to the existence, that's the tricky thing! It's like a video camera focused on its own monitor, which gives rise to recursive feedback patterns of intricate beauty and complexity. But that complexity is spawned by the underlying rules of optics – the beautiful ways of physics – the quirks and the quacks and the quarks – In the case of the

308

reflective eye of existence ouroboros-ing itself out of the void by deluding itself it has reality, there's no laws of physics to save the day and provide a substrate for the patterning that arises from the recursion – this has to be provided by the observing mind – you can never step out of the maelstrom, except for the shine of the moment – If you posit an observing mind or a universe or any bare shred of reality, then in the context of that reality, you can observe the "I delude myself that I exist, therefore I exist" recursive feedback circuit of primal onto-epistomological mayhem – the cosmogonocryptonomo-morphopornographico wonder-spasm at the beginning of the core of the heart – "self-subverting explosion and pulsing red love" as I said back in my teenage years (when I had far less irony about understanding everything) – you can see that circuit give rise to patterning, complex self-organizing structures like the Benard cell or the human brain or the video camera watching itself or the cellular automaton of physical laws that breathes inside us so many orders of magnitude beneath – but you need the equation "delusion-recursion + substrate = evolution of complexity and beauty" – the delusion-recursion just explains how a substrate leads to more and unfolds on and forever – (yecch) you still need not just the irritation but also the oyster to spawn the pearl –

I got myself up from the bed, still carrying around a time-line, my own special personal time-axis, popping out from the top of my head, coming out through my perineum at the bottom, and extending infinitely in either direction. This was the axis we all moved on – or that we felt we moved on – that characterized our delusion of existence that gave us our reality –

I was beautiful! I laughed at myself, amazed at my own beauty. Erica was much more beautiful still – I couldn't wait to see her face again. I wanted to make love to her like a half-sane gorilla in heat, completely forgetting everything but our bodies. Lie there snuggling after, exchanging strange philosophies. Human life spawns nothing sweeter. Then I wanted to push Poopsykins on the swing, and listen to Zeru's music on the piano – I really am jealous of that screwy kid Zerubabbel with his perfect pitch and melodious singing voice – he doesn't know how lucky he is, I love music like a madman but he has some music-savvy brain functions I don't know how to generate in myself without artificial neuromodification – but he doesn't quite appreciate it properly, he still sometimes says life isn't worthwhile, poor thing, but in practice he seems happy enough most of the time when he's not going to that stupid middle school – god damn, I'd rather home school him instead, so would he, but the curse of shared child-custody, bitch-ass Brittany won't let me do it, I don't think I'd win if I fought it in court – Zeru says if I ever create an AI it'll reach a superhuman level of intelligence at which point it will realize that both human existence and its own existence are meaningless and it will annihilate itself entirely – he could be right but I doubt it -- I've repeated this story many times – he's repeated it to me many times, because he knows it amuses me –

Abraham Goldberg. Lonson Fidika. Julio Silva de Souza. The beautiful brilliant nerds awaiting me in my email inbox, when I finally complete the slog back home. Far better programmers than me; these last few years it hasn't been productive for me to focus on the details of software implementation, it's been taking nearly all my time keeping the programmers and the other staff coordinated and making sure the whole AI project unfolds in harmony with my underlying vision of mind. Unlike Solomon Godunov I prefer to work with other beings; I prefer to let these brilliant young overlords of software create the specific bits and nybbles of my thinking machine – ours – for me. We'll see if this approach will work or not! I've left these excellent people long behind – hard to believe they're such a part of me! – (but what is this "me" anyway??) -- they don't know about these other universes!?! – I look forward to reintersecting with their mindscapes –

And Zarathustra! Zarathustra Apollo Heraclitus Adaman – the firstborn son of the firstborn son of the firstborn son of the firstborn son of the firstborn son of the firstborn son of the firstborn son! – all my kids are my favorites of course but there is something peculiarly special about one's first child – OK, these days he's a pimply shy sixteen-year-old with a bit of a mustache and beard and he's obsessed with *World of Warcraft* – reads a lot of sci-fi -- wants to interact with girls but doesn't really know how to and doesn't really want my advice about it -- a very smart kid with a knack for math and a slight interest in (past and future) history and a budding talent for type-tapping out surrealist sci-fi and not as intellectual as I'd like at this phase and it's really odd to hear his voice so deep and manlike instead of babyish like before as he rambles and talks with the occasional real insight or artistic concoction amidst his rampant silliness and trivia -- well hah! – remembering back into the Dork Ages – there's nothing quite like the birth of one's first child! ... I remember watching him ooze out of his mom and I thought his head was too small, the size of a tennis ball, and he'd be deformed and retarded, but it was just the tip, the point of his head, which was mushed up by the exit, but it was a normal thing, and then he couldn't breathe and the doctor had to suck the gunk out of his lungs – a problem caused I believe by the lengthy birth which was caused by the excessive anesthetics pumped into Brittany by the evil gargoyle nurses – so our next two births were natural and at home – but his lungs came clear – I pulled him out of his mom and we brought him to an incubator and Brittany went to a hospital room and I just sat there holding my baby's hand and realizing I'd created life! Not that I was special in any way – any idiot with a dick could do it, if he found someone with a cunt to stick it into – but I was a part of the flow of existence, the patterns and forms that were Ari Adaman exploding and perpetuating themselves, my semen potentially giving rise to new universes through the time machines and baby cosmoses my beautiful little offspring would create once he was old and whole and weird and brilliant like me (or not – it's not really critical) – remember his silly novel, *The Love In Front Of Jack*, more dada than Marcel Duchamp even in his weirdest dreams, more surrealist than Soupault in the manner achievable only by a half-child/half-man? – but now he was just lying there goobling, breathing through his nose for a change, and trying to get a grip on why the world around him was so bright and not so wet and touchy-soft – Soon I would see my kids again! But not quite ... first I had to get to the airport ... finish packing up my suitcase ... why would there be only one shoe over here, where the fuck's the other one...

And there was an algorithmic problem in the center of my mind right before – right before I took the mushrooms – all whorled and vivid in transdimensional stalks just as the trip was bringing its glory down – holding my mind together in networks of emergence -- I recall: the inference rules of pattern theory. Probabilistic guesses regarding what's a pattern in what, based on prior knowledge of other patterns. I had derived some simple formulas in the airplane on the way over to Europe but they could be extended, and I hadn't written everything down, not the part I'd conceived in my head during that business meeting. It wasn't exactly necessary – it would all come about explicitly from the plain-vanilla probabilistic inference that was already in my AI system – but I thought it might accelerate things to push the system specifically to make inferences about patterns instead of having it make them implicitly as a consequence of inferences about probabilities. Might. Might, might, might makes right.

A lot of work ahead. Three years at minimum, I'd say, to get a real thinking machine built – and that's if I had real funding, say a half a million a year, to pay my team of code-nerd superheros to work on thinking-machine-building exclusively instead of consuming so much of their time with cheminformatics and the other digressions we were pursuing for cash-generation purposes – these projects we had to take on because society groks neither immanence nor transcendence – It's pathetic, really, I said to myself – say to myself – will say, again and again. I can see it all too clearly – as clearly as Godunov my lunatic brother – the creation of superhuman minds transforming the fabric of spacetime – it's just as far away as a handful of programmers working full-time in a focused way for a few years. Three years – five – ten or twelve at the pessimistic outside. It would take fewer man-hours, altogether, than creating the next version of Microsoft Word. But society is wrapped up in its own (semi-)existence – its own self-delusory recursion – it doesn't want to grasp the real possibility of transcending its own boundaries in a glorious and final way – wargasmic bliss of transcension, whatever – and yet of course, it's this same moron society that taught me mathematics and computer science, that built silicon chips and keyboards and ethernet and packet-switching – and *Thus Spake Zarathustra* --

Maybe you really are insane, I told myself. Perhaps – Dr. Aristotle Adaman -- you're as insane as Solomon Godunov. Maybe that's the message the trip was telling you. Your quest to create true artificial intelligence is just the gooning of a madman. Forget it – work on cheminformatics and the math of complex systems – paint paintings and write novels -- be good to your wife and your kids – forget all these childish crazy dreams --

But my brain was coming back to itself now. I reviewed the technical details of my ideas about AI. No, it wasn't lunacy at all. Or at least, it wasn't all lunacy. There wasn't any certainty – my rational superstructure told me that -- there were plenty of missing details – but the logic seemed beautiful and sound, even though others mostly lacked the vision to comprehend it. (Some few who had worked with me for years were finally beginning to see it a bit.) No one saw the vision of modern computer architecture before von Neumann, general relativity before Einstein, etc. etc. etc. etc. etc. Not that I had to be as gifted as Einstein to happen to be right about this. Einstein was his own whacky universe. I had insight of a different kind. And finally I found my goddamn shoe – there, under the bed, back in the corner. Wiggle on my belly, fish it out. How the hell did it get back there, anyway? I couldn't have kicked it that hard when I took it off. It must have come alive and been hiding from something, intentionally. Strange turtle-like creature that shoe. It looked up at me with turtle eyes and fractal shell all green and hairy -- I knew I was still hallucinating a bit, but I had to get out of there, had to get to the airport – Zeru had this freakish love for turtles; maybe he'd meet this one someday, if he grew up and took mushrooms -- or spun his head around too fast at exactly the right angle -- he'd reach back through time to the appropriate axis and visit this turtle in his father's old dream --

Shoes on. Excellent. Suitcase zipped up, pull out the handle, drag it behind me on its wheels. Out of the hotel room -- riding on turtleback. Walk down the dark hallway -- don't think of yourself as a baby pouring out of the womb.

Put the key on the desk, avoid the gaze of the clerk, go down the stairs, walk to the train station – exist, feet up and down, one two, one two -- feet up and down, feet straight ahead, one two one two one two....

Farewell song to the world's tallest pygmy.
Echoes of the Great Farewell.
Chanson d'adieu
You should check into a hotel.
Or an asylum.

Airport.
get to the
airport.
it's time to
sit in the
stomach
of the
beast --

"You said you would put her in a sack full of hallucinogenic mushrooms and kidnap her, take her to Mongolia and force her to perform magical acts all of the carnality and confirmatory logic in a darkened consider full of earthworms."

"Did but these something like that."

She thought you were joking.

Was I?

She was thrusting her clit on the base of slowly my wiggling chimp tall slim and again and his bushy Dali coke-bottle." again

"No she wasn't."
"She was imagining it."

She was a wonderful beautiful strange magical acts all of adjectives heaped up in a pile and massaging me lecherous and vivacious adjectives were just idiot wind compared to the cosmos that was beckoning and monkeys, the each one slowly chinko chimp again

enthralling me – and the cosmulous monkeys, turning into Nietzsche – perfect negroid figure, pubic moustache, his glasses, his Chinese eyebrows, his toothy seeking in words and some kind of connection magic of the acid trip solid world of walls, opinions and selves we'd eventually – all too soon

fe
t
st
ai
hu
ahe
ad,

weird smile ...
twilit sentences
between the
and the dead
floors and
come back to
-- after an
h the
quantum
awe-
had the
cked up in
handed
ed like
gy" and
in neat
we still

her.
ie, her hair
. It's from
than I am.
crotch and I
to my ass --
a and back
ffling cards

"We're human – yeah. But it's not what we have to be."

316

covered with ants, each card with the face of my mind from a different moment, the moments tumbling around like cosmos revueltos, like bodies caught up in hyperdimensional orgies,

and my monster, *to exist* *is* penis grows back into a with the head of a dragon and a many *to exist* professor, just one of the tongues from the infinite mouth at *is* the beginning of the end of the world, *to exist* singing a moose-dick extraneous waltz devoted to

the strange beauty of the big-brained beast that, passionate, extends -- to grasp it all and taste it all then, helpless, simply terminates its termination as the global riverrun, Eve's and Adam's brings us forth and back, and back! and the sum of the explosion of the difference the modicum of what? what? what?

She urged me to stop babbling bullshit. "I'm not, damn it," I protested. "So are you, and you hadn't noticed. When cut, you bleed. When I sit on your face naked and wiggle, you get an erection."

"We're human -- yeah. But it's not what we have to be."

"It is."

"Why? Because if you become something else – something other – then you're not you anymore?"

"I guess. Then I'd just be some non-human thing."

"What if you found out you'd been drugged all your life, with a pill that made you dull – or a pill -- as much as you were supposed to be. Would you keep taking the drug, just to retain the status quo – the feeling of 'you-ness'? Or would you stop taking

feet straight ahead, one two one two!!!!

When cut, you bleed. When I sit on your face naked and wiggle, you get an erection.

"Simpl icity is so complicat ed, I couldn't understa nd it."

317

the pill, and let your intelligence return to normal – even knowing it would change you completely."

"What if I told you that words are just playthings, minds are puppets of ideas, ideas are puppets of minds."

"What if I divorced you and married your animus."

"Somewhere in the midnight between dis and continuity, I wonder."

"Simplicity is so complicated, I couldn't understand it."

"Reconstruct realities you've never imagined – klein-bottle-ize your winky –"

"No! Expand your large breasts of salt through the cosmos – envision yourself as an equation – a system of explosions –"

"It's all bit strings, baby, bit strings! –"

"Bits of strings and strings of bits!"

unravel the knot of the not –
shuffle glib through the rooms of the
palace of wiggle and wiggle your ass –
fuck the metallic claw of hatred –
cleaner than the consciousness of a
cockroach –
and then – and then – and then –

unravel the knot of the not –
shuffle glib through the rooms of the palace of wiggle
and wiggle your ass –
fuck the metallic claw of hatred –
cleaner than the consciousness of a cockroach –
and then – and then – and then –

Remember What You Are!
Learn – Be Concerned
Leoncern
Leoncern
Leoncern

it's always there
INVERT/PERVERT

In the furious green geometries of ideas, equations and nations and frogs, we give birth to our own poopocalypse, and Christ on the criss-cross pissing mushrooms, lying in my bed screaming, head cast back at the cosmos, billowing forthward like a dream of a dream –

Muse of mad equations – eyes of women – shadows of the rare –

"You said you would put her in a sack full of hallucinogenic mushrooms and kidnap her, take her to Mongolia and force her to perform strange acts of carnality and combinatory logic in a darkened corridor full of earthworms."

"Did I?"

"Something like that."

"She thought you were joking."

"Was I?"

"She was thrusting her clit on the base of my wiggling chinkochimpo again and again and again – "

"No she wasn't."

"She was imagining it."

Remember What You Are!
Learn – Be Concerned
Leoncern
Leoncern
Leoncern

& we were bound in one body, stuck together in a common aura of sex-energy, looking into each others' eyes with such overexcitement it seemed even the amazing sex wasn't enough to acknowledge it, but then the sex took control and the thoughts disappeared, the wonder was sublimated into movements and tenderness – till finally after so many hours I came, blasting my come deep deep inside her, the wonder through her ears and her mouth and her eyes and every pore of her body, and sinking into her flesh and falling deep asleep, the two of us one being, quantum-resonantly bound together more sweetly than I ever would have thought possible in this error-ridden world – my cannabinoid-addled rooster exploded/absorbed in every molecule of her skin – and the hummings and buzzing and pulsings surrounded us – It must've been the water pipes in the

Remember What You Are!
Learn – Be Concerned
Leoncern
Leoncern
Leoncern

hotel and the refrigerators and stoves in the restaurant
across the courtyard but it soon became more than that
– it wa [illegible]
packets [illegible] that –
of thou [illegible] of
itself a [illegible] rsing
the me [illegible] vicle
the sa [illegible] ding the
of Econ [illegible] at the
you ma [illegible] d of
that y [illegible] de you
that th [illegible] that
comple [illegible], that
a beau [illegible] plexity
messag [illegible] tiful
you'd [illegible] sages
roll bac [illegible] 'd
track [illegible] roll
that h [illegible] ost
present [illegible] sages
whole [illegible] the
but the [illegible] whole
with th [illegible] but the
at the [illegible] with
are al [illegible] at
betwee [illegible] are
fundam [illegible] een the
– becau [illegible]
create [illegible] use the
chunk [illegible] finite
is" – [illegible] you
reduce [illegible] then
econom [illegible] the
but the [illegible] beauty of the alien
economy/society/mind-patterns to subliminal existence –
but the hell with that!

There have never been any feelings
Everything is solid, real, hard
like ball bearings and granite
It's forgotten how to alter its mood

feet straight ahead, one two one two!!!!

I love you like
love that's not
love riot is not
love love is not
love is not not
Riot – Idea
of your idea

Ashti-washti and I formed a city, or maybe a mountain range, with aliens of various colors, shapes, and sizes living on us, but only our heads were solid like space, like moving solid sphinxes, Mexican lions or alien gods and goddesses or icons for the core of the mind, and our bodies spread out till by the time your reached our knees they had diffused into the countryside, the alien hills and valleys blue-green and yellow, with buggies and rockets and impossible emergent chains of beings formed from beings formed from beings moving up and down and between and beside us, but we two were the center of it our brains and bodies the mountains from which the aliens drew their energy – not really the only center, just one of the interpretations, one of the interpretations of the center – but we were there and we were one being, formed from the thummerings of the alien multitudes or else the earth and cosmos on which the aliens existed –

YOUR
GLORIOUS
SKIN DOES
NOT EXIST
–
NOT EVEN
YOUR
GLORIOUS
MIND

Software, wetware, hardware, firmware,
wildware, deadware, lifeware, shitware
where ware wear where we are an illusion
Thoughts are an illusion
Zeros and ones do not exist
Your glorious skin does not exist –
not even your glorious mind --

At any given moment, when our time-axis was in stillness, there was all this teeming movement in directions perpendicular to our own time – this whole society of aliens spreading information one way and the other, creating patterns of awareness, spreading here and there, existing at a level of fluidity and sophistication far
I could see there were two different perspectives

feet
straight
ahead,
one two
one
two!!!!

would
reach their
get

or light or
orgasmic
and some
as
packages
constantly
existence

which
lips took
equality
world –
consistent
one of
were these
spreading
forward
in time and
distant
instantly –
other there
doors and
pipes and

there was
real time

**Packets would
eventually reach
their destination
and get unpacked
into consciousness
or light or amoebic
orgasmic
movement, and
some of them
served as currency,
little packages of
value constantly
proving their
existence via forms
of mathematics in** which hungry vaginal
lips took the place of
equality signs.on the
world – two different
consistent views of it –
in one of them there
were these aliens,
spreading information
forward and backward in
time and leaping to
distant parts of space
instantly **THE
SOLIDITY
OF REAL
TIME AND
SPACE**

Packets
eventually
destination and
unpacked into
consciousness
amoebic
movement,
of them served
currency, little
of value
proving their
via forms of
mathematics in
hungry vaginal
the place of
signs on the
two different
views of it – in
them there
aliens,
information
and backward
leaping to
parts of space
and in the
were walls and
people and
genitals and
mathematics,
the solidity of
and space.

Here in the
moment,
of the
moment,
every twist
floats
no-change
shining,
here lonely

Remember What You
Are!
Learn Be Concerned
Leoncern
Leoncern
Leoncern

center of the
statuary
of thought
endless
elusive organic
in time's

center
between the dead past and the forest and the scream

feet straight ahead, one two one two!!!!

Alive words pound against the inside of my skull like poisonous, accelerated drops of rain. They

feet straight ahead, one two one two!!!!

manifest themselves to my ears as a constant sound of machine-gun fire. Each time one hits I smell a body burst its skin -- always the same body, the same curvaceous dark-haired girl without a face. eschatology of immanence and smoking the eternity of my love and the relativity of all my ideas as they grotesquely interpenetrate each other – and I am afraid she is a being without a body or brain – a disembodied superhuman intelligent system, a variant of Nietzsche's Zarathustra immanent in the disturbances of the nuclear resonance in the psychotic mini-van Allen belt that masquerades as society's aura. She glows the beginning and end of all time, more beautiful than possible,

The future and the imaginary
rotting fetid pregnant
glorious and crystallized
of the Voice at the end of the end of the end –
pained and ensorcelled by the silhouette
the endless purple twilit Scream –

I will lift up her shirt, unfasten her bra, unbutton her skirt, slip off her underpants. Her existence will be threatened. I will be afraid to open my eyes. I will explore her with my lips, never certain whether the body that I'm feeling, licking, tasting, is the *one*.   But I will know that, one way or the other, within this here lies the infinite – the true deeper reality – the aliens running through giant green factories with blue tubes and orange veins, and each alien's bloodstream like a Solar System sized factory with endless little aliens passing messages around in overlapping latticeworks, and each alien itself inside some other alien's inner-factory, and I myself a fluid diffusing through the cracks between the conveyor belts and tubes and pontoons and indescribable multicolored mechanisms of the alien metaphorical factory, producing metaphors for its own existence with blue-green insatiable love, moving from each part of my body to each part of hers through all the future and the past with unstoppable curiosity and force, discovering everything anew each moment in spite of already knowing everything....

WAAAHHHAHHAHAHHHHH!!!!!

"Machine gun," she will whisper. "Carry my body all apart."

"Delirium," I will say, running my tongue along the crack between her buttocks. "Your anal vapor is an alien form of chocolate. It is a hallucinogenic toxin. It is the threshold between nothingness and dream."

The drops of rain pounding on the outside of my skull are actually words, disguised as objects.

feet straight ahead, one two one two!!!!

The world exterior to my skull is actually a word, or a conglomeration of words, masquerading itself as a piece of death for the sake of argument.

Her slender, tawny, muscled thighs transform me into a question.

Consummated by nebulae of pygmocules ... I remained a human being, just by the border of a moustache. *And the real question, I realized, was why I had taken five containers of hallucinogenic mushrooms instead of just my ordinary two.* The results were beyond what we could imagine – but if you stopped perceiving this movement and collapsed it into a stillness you could see a stiff and solid world.

You see, I needed that core of madness – that thrust of psychic violence – the source of my potent creativity was a kind of good versus evil mayhem in which Godunov battled with a 90-year old mystic doing yoga on the mat of my temporal lobe, counseling me on the odd subconscious reasons that my logical system had derived the conclusion that it needed to subvert itself yet again, to infuse itself with pattern-chaos, to rebuild itself from the formless void –

Focus! Focus! Focus! Re-form, yourself, and promptly! an echo of an echo of a dream – feet straight ahead, feet straight ahead, one two one two!!!!

an echo of an echo of an echo, full of laugh and turn and storm

**Farewell song
to the world's tallest pygmy
Echoes of the Great Farewell
Chanson d'adieu**

*feet straight ahead,
one two
one two*

325

an echo of an echo of an echo, full of laugh and turn and storm

-----

She lay on my arm, Erica did, smiling at me contentedly. "Did you make love to me?" she asked (rhetorically I assumed: at least I didn't think it had been *that* non-memorable –).

I opened my eyes – I'd briefly fallen asleep. "I think so. At least, that seems to have about the same degree of reality as everything else."

"Mmmmm."

We snuggled.

"Do you love me?"

I nodded.

"Do you really?"

I grinned -- it sounded so cute when she said it, in her thick Venezuelan accent, with her wavering breathy voice that couldn't quite decide whether to be low or high pitched…. "Of course I love you…"

She snuggled me: "Mmmmm."

"Do you love me?"

"I love you so much…."

"The kids get here in about an hour and a half," I noted, emerging somewhat into the consensus world.

"Yeah, I know."

"Unless Brittany brings them late again."

She arranged her body differently – not tremendously, just a slight retensing of muscles and adjustment of limbs. "You really miss them, huh."

"I always do when I go away…. How long was I in Europe for?"

"Four days."

"Five days."

"Yeah...."

"I especially miss little Poopsykins – I've been spending a lot of time with her lately. I miss the boys too but they don't want my attention so much these days. They're getting bigger – it's weird, man ... Zarathustra being sixteen...."

She shrugged.

"Well it's not weird to you, 'cause you didn't know then when they were smaller. If you have kids of your own you'll get it – like, when I'm 95 years old...."

Smiling, "Yeah." It wasn't quite accurate of course – I was only 28 years older than her, so if we had kids in a few years I'd be in my 60's not my 90's – and it's amazing how being over 50 didn't seem so fucking old any more -- not dried-up and ancient like I'd expected it would seem back when I was younger and (or so I like to tell myself) even more of a ridiculous fool....

"But of course with life extension 95 will be like 20 is today."

"It would be sweet to have kids," she said, "the problem is having to push them out of yourself. That must hurt like hell. I don't want it."

"All existence is suffering."

"Sure but suffering comes in degrees. Remember what Susie said: it hurts so much you know while you're in the middle of it that you'll never really remember how bad it was."

"Of course not – evolution wants you to forget so you'll keep spitting out more and more."

"Exactly."

"One every year – you could spit out twenty or so if you started now. More if you induce multiple births with fertility drugs."

"Because with us as the parents, if we have that many kids one of them is going to have to be the Savior?"

"Right...."

"I'm still not gonna do it."

"You're evil."

"It's well known!"

I sighed. "Well anyway, after the Singularity, you can have all the babies you want and it won't hurt a bit."

"Right...."

"And you can spawn non-sentient clones of yourself to take care of them if you get bored with it? Do you think they'd notice?"

"Well I'd just program them not to care, of course.

"But you could argue it would take the fun out of having babies to program them to be like you want. But then you could program yourself to enjoy it that way...."

"Anyway I hope we don't program ourselves to worry about things like babies, by that point – "

"There should be more interesting things to worry about..."

"Baby universes."

"Exactly."

"But they won't be so cute, will they?"

"If we program ourselves to want them to be," we both said. "Blah blah blah blah...." We both found it amusing to be mouthing the same words as each other like an old married couple, given that we'd only been together a year and a half.

"I worked out some nice math for probabilistic pattern theory," I said. "On the plane on the way over. I guess we can use it in the MindMaker system."

"Cool! How does it work?"

"I'll tell you a little later – we'd need pen and paper – it's too annoying to talk equations in bed…."

"Sure…. Mmmmm…. You can write them on my belly with magic marker."

"You don't want them tattooed?"

"No!"

We lay there some moments, silently. I drifted off again then the kitten jumped onto my head. "Ow!!! Fuck you!!!" I tossed it away and it squeaked.

"That thing is vicious."

"It's only a baby."

"It's a vicious baby."

"Indeed."

"If it was bigger it would kill us."

"I guess."

"You're a vicious baby!"

"No I'm not…."

Erica looked serious for a moment – "Hey, how was the meeting?"

"The Dutch liked my presentation – I think at least half of them understood what I was talking about, which is better than the usual. They have a lot of data so they're in a good position to use our stuff. Mostly cancer data, but some other stuff too. But I don't know if they're really going to buy anything. I'm a lot better at getting people excited than at closing deals."

"Yeah."

"I've got to get out of the business business – I'm sick of all these meetings. It's really a waste of my mind."

"That's true. Maybe you should do like you said the other day – just forget all this business stuff and get a job as a professor again and program the AI yourself."

I wrinkled my brow. "Yeah. But I'm not quite there yet. I guess I'm a year from making that decision. I've pushed this far with all this crap, I might as well push a little farther -- this bio business stuff has a pretty good chance of panning out – it would seem stupid to quit now that we have a good product finally – and for the pure AI project, it would be a lot better to be able to pay a bunch of people like Julio and Abraham to work for me. I'm not the best programmer in the world – and it's more than a one-person project...."

"Well I'd be happy to help you but I'm not sure I'd be a help. I'm a terrible programmer – well you know it already."

"Of course you'll be a help – you already are a help on the conceptual stuff – it's really useful talking things through with you -- but you're too much like me, you like the theory better than the implementation. I'll program it all myself if I have to – with you helping if you want, that'd be great -- but it's better to have uber-programmers like Abraham and Lonson and Julio do that part. There's a lot to be done besides programming too, which you and I are better at – just refining all the mathematical and conceptual details."

"Yeah ... those guys are good. Too bad everyone wants to be paid."

"Well," I pointed out, "if they believed enough that the design would work they wouldn't need to be paid. Maybe I just need to make my case more clearly."

"You think so?"

"Sure. These are all single guys. They don't have any real financial responsibilities. I mean, I can't ask them to live on nothing when I'm not doing it. But when I was at their phase of life I would have, easily, if

I believed the project had even a 10 or 20 percent chance of success."

"Yeah. I would. I lived on almost nothing in Venezuela."

"You lived with your dad."

"True."

"Well Lonson's hardly getting paid relative to the standard of living in Finland."

"True. Finland is a rich country. And they like to work for free, that's where Linux started."

"Because they're socialist and the government is so good at supporting them."

She laughed. "Yeah."

"Better than Venezuela, where the government is just good at supporting the richest 10%. In Finland they don't have any poor people, the government just takes care of everyone. As long as we keep buying Nokia cellphones.... Anyway – after I finish this revision I'll publish my AI book finally...."

"You think that will convince everyone your design will work?"

"Yeah, everyone in the world. They'll promote me as the new messiah and carry me around in the streets on one of those platforms where you lie back and a different flunky holds up each corner. And I'll make them do little dances while they carry me." Suddenly the dogs walked over from their bed at the other side of the room and started licking me. "Yiccch.... Good morning.... Let's change positions." Erica and I changed places in the bed so that she was by the dogs and I was by the wall. Through some peculiar genetic aberration, she actually liked having them drool in her mouth.

"You were dancing the can-can," she pointed out. "That's what attracted the dogs. They can't resist your little dances. It's just like when you give a speech and you sort of wave your pelvis back and forth and then all the women in the audience come up to you afterwards and ask you questions."

"I do not do that."

"Yes you do, every time – you kind of sway back and forth like this – ", she laughed.

"Well if so it's not intentional. Anyway I wasn't dancing the can-can."

"Sort of. You can't really dance the can-can lying down."

"YOU can -- because you're special."

"I'm a special child of God."

"You are."

"Just like you."

"That's why we're perfect together…"

The dogs settled down, finally, and lay down by the foot of the bed.

"But you were talking about convincing people…."

"Yeah. Ultimately I don't think there's any way to convince people my design for an AI will really work – I mean, in the sense of making a superhuman mind, not just the sense of yielding something interesting for research. Either you have to show them the thing working, or else – as a very distant second -- prove some rigorous mathematics proving it will work – but we don't have that kind of math, no one's ever developed it."

"And developing the math would probably be harder than building the thinking machine."

"Right…. Well, I think so. I can't be sure of course. I have a suspicion it'll take a superhuman AI to work out the equations underlying intelligence in any reasonably detailed way…." We lay there a moment and breathed. "I mean, I know it sounds like a cop-out to say 'Ooooh, I have all these brilliant ideas and no one understands me' but sometimes it's actually true. I think people have a lot of dumb ideas about the mind and intelligence, and they'd have to unlearn them all before they could really evaluate my approach correctly."

"Do *I* have a lot of dumb ideas about the mind?" she asked, bemusedly.

"Hmmmm.... That's a loaded question."

"What? You can answer me...."

"Uh, no, honey, of course not. Everyone but you, I meant."

She pouted and folded her arms.

"Ok," I said. "Remember that long argument we had about consciousness and the brain, where you got mad at me, when we were walking, and I wanted to eat at the Chinese restaurant but you didn't because you were annoyed."

"Yeah," she said. "I didn't get mad because of what you were saying. I got mad because you said my brain was wired so that I could never understand it no matter how long we talked."

I laughed. "Did I say that?"

"Yes."

"That's funny."

"It's not. And, I was a little annoyed already because of something Zarathustra did."

"I don't want to talk about that. Anyway the point is, maybe dumb ideas isn't the right way to put it, what I mean is misleading intuitions that come out of folk psychology -- which have been 'corrected' by wrong oversimplifications from research psychology and cognitive science. Well, that's why I'm writing this book on the philosophy of mind, trying to clear away all those cobwebs so people can at least think about the AI design the correct way. Although even then there are plenty of gaps in the details so if you're looking for reasons to doubt you can find them."

"Sure. I mean, some scientists doubt evolutionary theory still and ..."

"... they find holes to poke in it."

"Yeah."

"Anyway once it's been gotten to a certain point then it will be really easy to get funding for it, or to get brilliant people to help out for free. The thing is just to get it to that point – which is probably a year and a half of hard programming and testing by three really good people."

"Better than me."

"At programming.... It's not all programming, that just seems like the focus right now because it's a more desperate need. Because the conceptual and math stuff is more my own strength."

"Right.... So it wouldn't take all that much money to get you to the stage of having that kind of demonstration you're talking about then. The one that will convince people."

"A few hundred thousand dollars."

"Well I wish I had it...."

"Maybe one of us will find out we had a rich uncle and were included in his will...."

"Hmmm...."

"In fact I do have an uncle who's sort of rich."

"Aha! I knew there was a good reason for marrying you!"

"But I don't think he'll leave me very much of it."

"Too bad...."

"Well, of course I had a decent amount of grant money back when I was a professor with a lab. But I didn't have the right design then."

"Did you think you did at the time?"

"Not really – not in the same sense. Of course I thought I was on the right track.... But that was more of an 'agents' point of view – I was building a platform for experimenting with different cognitive algorithms and I thought by playing in that playground we'd discover combinations of cognitive processes that would lead to emergent intelligence."

"Mmmm."

"I guess maybe we would have. But I did totally underestimate the amount of time all the playing would take. I turned out to be a much slower route than I thought -- and there were irritating technical problems – we did some dumb things with Java memory management and software design that made it so we didn't really get that much playing done anyway ... the code ran so slowly because of the Java problems and it was really a pain to integrate new agents with the core system ...we mostly designed stuff and built it and revised it. But we learned a lot for sure. Though I guess we could have learned even more some other way without spending so much time and using so many research students.... Anyway I told you all this before."

She turned over on her side, and pushed up on me. Her smile looked really sweet. The breeze from the window was a bit cold; she pulled the blanket up over her body. "You're cute," I said, kissing her. "Why did you turn toward me – because I was talking about mammary management??"

"Har har har," she scowled. (I think I'd been overly affected by the Piers Anthony book series Zarathustra was reading, which was insanely full of bad puns: the author ran out of bad puns years ago so he solicits new ones from his readers, who email him dozens every day!)

I lifted the blanket up salaciously and stroked her. "The British call these Jamaicas."

"Why?"

I shrugged...

"You think they should be called Venezuelas?"

She shook her head back and forth, looking serious. "You're silly.... I see, yeah. That approach made sense, but the design you have now is more precise so the time to completion should be a lot smaller and a lot easier to predict."

"Yeah."

"But it's also more feasible for you to implement yourself if you forget about all these business meetings."

"True.... You just want me to become a professor again so we can take longer vacations!"

"Maybe...."

"Maybe if I start programming the whole thing myself I'll just sit at the computer and never get up for three years until I'm finished and the Singularity is launched."

"I'll make you a special chair with a toilet in it, so you don't even have to get up to crap."

"That would be a shame – it would really destroy the spirituality of crapping."

"There is no spirituality in crapping, you're insane. Yeah yeah, I know, there's spirituality in everything, blah blah blah. All your craps are special children of God."

"Well that's true but that's not the point. The point is you don't know how to crap correctly, that's why you don't see the spiritual value. I can teach you if you want...."

"Wellll...."

"You have to sit on the toilet and empty your mind completely – until the total pearly emptiness of the formless void wipes your mind way – then you become one with the turd – you and your rectum and the turd and the toilet are all one beautiful perfect formless void...."

"I see. Hey, maybe we could make a special toilet that plays meditative music ...."

"... and shows you a movie of the guru of your choice ... "

"... and lets you regulate your brain waves via biofeedback to put yourself in the right state of mind."

"Exactly. It's probably a better business model than selling cheminformatics software."

"The fun part would be giving the product demonstrations for the customers."

I laughed. "That's right. The benefit would be easy for the customer to see, as they saw the blissful look on your face as the crap came out.... And the addressable market is huge: everyone craps. Even animals – you could make special versions for dogs and cats.... But I thought the point was to let me have total focus on AI so I could implement my design in a few years and launch the Singularity ... not to create another brilliant business...."

"And after the Singularity we won't need to crap to achieve enlightenment?"

"Exactly...."

"Well anyway," she said – a bit flatly – "about the total focus thing, you wouldn't leave your kids for that long...." She was a huge supporter of my AI work and (most of the time) an amazingly sweet woman but she got skeptical sometimes about the large amount of time I spent with my offspring.

Kids, kids, kids, kids, kids, kids.... "Shit, I'm tired," I said. I was afraid the conversation would start to get annoying – there was something not-quite-perfect in her tone, all of a sudden. "I actually wish the kids were coming a little later. I could sleep about ten hours now."

She smiled at me curiously, changing the subject, to my relief. "You didn't tell me about your extra day in Amsterdam."

"Because you dragged me up here to bed as soon as I walked in!"

"Well…" she smiled.

I sighed in confusion -- remembering the turtle shoe, McBuddha -- and more dimly, Solomon Godunov, Ashti, and the whole whorled confusion. It had seemed all so vivid, so supernally, tragically real. Those other time axes as real as this one. The fractal turtleback, expanding into an infinite maze of surrealities. Of course they were there – those other universes -- of course they were perfectly real for themselves. But what was I supposed to learn from that particular axis I spent most of the trip careening around in? A cautionary tale – to be careful when playing with AI? Or was there some deeper insight there – something in Godunov's approach to AI that was supposed to be the key to making my own real AI system work better – the missing Eureka! insight that would make the job easier than it currently appeared – let the thing run on 20 computers instead of 2000 or whatever – And what was up with the fusion thing, the Encyclopedia Brittanerica? Combine an American and a Venezuelan and get a Frenchwoman? A musical Frenchwoman – Erica didn't play music, and nor had Brittany, much to my regret -- I always thought it would be cool to jam with my wife…. I missed Ashti and the sound of her viola!

"What?" she prodded. "You don't want to tell me?"

Her words zonked me back to our reality. "I do want to tell you," I said. "But it's too much to tell, almost.... I'm too tired to do it..."

"You took more mushrooms," she said.

"Indeed," I said slowly. "I thought that was obvious, sorry. A very substantial dose."

"More than we took last time?"

"Five boxes," I said. "Two tampanensis, one cubensis, and I don't remember what the others were."

"FIVE??? You're crazy!"

"You think?"

She snuggled up to me. "You're my lunatic."

"Ericascaricawarica -- I saw a turtle," I said. "It explained to me the logic of multiple time axes."

"Zeru would be proud." He liked turtles.

"Yeah...."

"What else did the turtle do?"

"Not much – it was pretty much irrelevant – it just transmogrified into my shoe and crawled under the bed, then it carried me to the train station when I was too tired to walk. The turtle only appeared at the end, when the main trip was over...."

"Did you see the aliens again?"

"Your special aliens – do you miss them?"

"I love them so much!"

"You're a special child of the alien god?"

"I guess so...."

"The aliens were there inside every quantum wave function, just like they always are.... But that wasn't the main thing. It was like I was in some other universe, with a parallel Ari who was named Solomon, and this woman who was my wife, but she wasn't quite like you or like Brittany."

"Who was she more like?"

"I don't know – neither...."

340

"I was making an AI, but I was a complete psychopath."

"Like how? Did you eat little babies?"

"No...."

"Did you feed them to your uncle?"

I bit her left Jamaica – not too hard. "No...."

"Ow – you bastard!" She bit me back. "Well, maybe that's the key to creating AI. If you make yourself psychotic you'll succeed."

"Do you think so?"

"Maybe."

"Hmmm...."

"Will you help?"

"Make you psychotic? Uh huh."

"You're so sweet."

I stretched and yawned. She squeezed me. "Get some sleep, sweetie."

"Mmmmm."

"I love you."

"Love you too."

I lay flat and quiet and closed my eyes; Erica on my shoulder. She was way too young for me, it was true, but still she was just perfect. Perfect for all her imperfections. She was a spectacular human universe; I loved the feel and the smell and the love of her there beside me as my body relaxed itself on toward the sleep-state. I knew when I finally entered sleep-land a bit of the madness would return – but just an echo – I felt it roll down – an echo of an echo of an echo, full of laugh and turn and storm -- waves of pulsing green-life-mind-webs and time-axis vortices and wiggling patterned turtle-shell (what was it with that turtle?) – and those other human souls – those Godunovs and Ashtis and disasters who were just as real as Erica and me and Zarathustra and Zoetrope and Zerubbabel and Friedrich Nietzsche and Werner Heisenberg and

Captain Penocules and Curious George W. McBuddha and Marvin Minsky and Erica Jong and King Kwong and Rambozo the Clown and the rest – I asked myself again if I was a lunatic but I couldn't quite conclude that I was – I reviewed my rational arguments in my sleep and tried to transform myself into a theorem-proving machine – I continued to believe I had a correct design for an AI – at least, a probably-correct design, the proof is in the pudding – and I saw my mind and everyone else's as a giant web of moving turtle-shell patterns, patterns in patterns in patterns and patterns, all animated algorithmically if you choose to conceive them that way, and I started to weave the threads from Solomon and Ashti's brain into a reductio ad absurdum of their existence, to the music of the can-can divided by Chopin's mutant offspring with Hendrix -- but I got distracted by the pretty colors and finally fell asleep…. (and as I drifted off in confusion and clarity, a new thought crept into the cavern – familiar but different – the difference between clarity and illusion – Could it be? This revelation of truth – of reality – could it be yet another layer of the same dream-scene? Some of it smelled right, some smelled wrong. "Ari Adaman" smelled correct – but "Erica"? Shouldn't that be "Zennica"? And "Brittany" – was I really ever married to (and divorced from) someone named Brittany? That was the name of one of Bill Clinton's lovers, right? No, it was a pop star. Barbara – Barbara – that was it. The same name as the former First Lady -- that paragon of erotic femininity. Oh Barbara Bush, I cry for your beauty, eternal and perfect like a clam! Barbara: that was the ex-wife's name. The awakening was a sham – I still hadn't found reality – I was creeping closer and closer and clooooooser but would never quite get there yet – and even the "closer and closer and closer" was just a matter of the choice of distance metric -- and choosing the distance metric with more reality to it was just another subcase of the problem – the original problem (in so many sensible and nonsensical senses) of locating the real. I was waking up again – waking up and down the aisle – up to the world of sweet Zennica, who looked just like Erica but had an appropriate Z in her name – like Zarathustra, Zephaniah and Zoey (aka Poopsykins, a nickname given by her idiot mother, whatever her idiot name was) – no fucking Zeru, for Christ's sake (stupid Christ with his screams on the arithmetic cross!) – Zennicazinha and her father Hilario – and Ari Adaman who looked like Ari Adaman and smelled like a paradoxical particle and really was trying to make an AI but was pissing away a percentage of his moments instead writing bizarre and unpopular prose poems – I was waking up again to the reality – but this time without any kind of certainty –

Remember What You Are! Learn – Be Concerned Leoncern
Leoncern

--Finis

epilogue
by dr. gennady burtzle

    She answered the door barefoot, dressed all in black, in a long flowing skirt and a tight spandex top that was free from adornment except her ample cleavage. Her look was pensive at first but she warmed to me quickly with a quiet smile. I was surprised at how attractive she was, with her Asian face and her long black hair – I hadn't been expecting the madman's wife would be such a babe, but hey, I was willing to accept it. Absorbing the look on her face and the way she held her body, she looked not only cute but intelligent and lonely. I wondered what the catch was. Or was she the catch? But that wasn't the reason I was there. (I did get tired of these animal reactions – they were distractions from the grand goal – but yet they had to be indulged to a certain extent or my organism would be unable to function anywhere near to its optimal effectiveness – my brain, powerful abstract reasoning engine though it was, was still an organ of my very human body -- a strange situation to remember – but it didn't seem strange at the time, of course, as it was the only reality I'd yet known.)

    "You're here to talk about Godfrey," she said.

    The way she said his name was funny – Gaaahdfree – and I found it odd somehow that this was the way he had heard his name pronounced for years of his life. I had always thought of him as a Gawdfree, not a Gaaahdfree, but here she was, his beautiful young wife with her half-Arab accent, and my mapping of the characters of his name into phonemes had to be completely redone.

But I wasn't supposed to just stand and stare, admiring her tits and her accent....

"You're Ashti," I said.

"Yeah."

"I'm Gen. Gen Burtzle."

"I know. I've read about you."

"I read about you too."

"I know."

We shook hands. "Good to meet you."

"Good to meet you."

"Why don't you come in and sit down?" she said, her tone friendly but just a bit mechanical.

She offered me a drink and we sat at the kitchen table to talk, sipping on iced teas with lemon.

"Godfrey Solomonoff... " I began, hesitating and smiling. "You know, your husband caused me an incredible amount of trouble. Me and a lot of other people"

"And me too," she smiled. "It's calmed down a lot now, though. Since the whole thing was solved. Since you shut down his program, I mean. Your work on that was incredible. For a few weeks – when the thing was sending messages -- there were reporters here every day – it was terrible."

"But by now everyone's forgotten about it."

"Yeah, mostly."

"It's funny huh? Someone creates a rogue AI that almost destroys the human race – then a few months pass and everyone's gone back to their TV shows and video games. I suppose they'll enjoy the story when it comes out on film. Maybe I'll get played by Keanu Reeves."

She laughed; raised her eyebrows. "Exactly."

"I suppose you appreciate the peace and quiet."

"Yeah," she said. "Well it's not so fun talking to all those reporters answering the same things over and over again. But now, I...." She blushed and looked at her lap, then met my eyes again. "Well anyway – you didn't come here to listen to me babble." She paused. "Why *did* you come here?"

I looked at her face and had, once again, the chilling yet reassuring certainty that I was living within – not quite a dream, not quite a simulation, not quite a hallucination – but something approximately evoked by all these imperfect human words. And while I might someday find my way out of this one – perhaps with an AI program that was constructed correctly so as to lead to a safe Singularity – the way out would just lead into another one – I never would escape from the maze of illusions, because this was the nature of my human mind. Haunted with a dark clarity, I realized for the n'th time that my basic condition was hopeless: The definition of escaping from the maze of illusions in which I was embedded inevitably implied losing my "I." I could never get out of here – "I" could never get out of "here" – "I" and ("here" AKA illusion) were part of the same interdefining mess, and I would be wracked in confusion as long as I was what I was – and if I became something else, something so different from me as not to live in illusions/simulations/dreamscapes, then I wouldn't be myself anymore, so transcending myself like this would just be committing suicide – This illusoriness was it. This was it. This mind – or if not this mind, something roughly equally self-delusory ... this body – or if not this body, some roughly equally limiting substitute. If I went too far beyond these things –

far enough beyond to be really exciting – then I'd cease to be myself anyway. I myself was thoroughly defined by the very properties of my universe that I was most thoroughly disgusted with. I wanted to be a truly powerful mind – not bound by any particular embodiment, not bound by any specific history or way of thinking – a powerful experiencing and understanding process – but even if I could somehow transform myself into such a thing, via a tremendously powerful artificial-scientist AI program that really worked as specified unlike Solomonoff's disaster – I would completely lose myself in the process; all I'd be doing was killing myself and creating some other, better, freer being. And now here I was repeating myself – repeating the same thoughts over again in slightly different wording – demonstrating yet again the pure idiocy of the emotionally driven brain architecture that was my moron legacy and, fuck it, "my" future....

"What?" she said. "What are you thinking?"

I smiled, and reoriented myself to the world for a moment. I tilted my head to one side, decided to take a risk. "Actually ... I was thinking how cute you are."

She blushed and grinned, and looked at the floor for a moment. The gamble had worked: she wasn't offended. She liked me. Well, I had already known that, but now I *really* knew. I looked at her, took in her body again, trying not to be too obvious. I had a feeling I was going to make love to her, at some point. This was going to be very entertaining.

"I don't believe you," she added. "You looked kind of thoughtful and disturbed."

So she wasn't an idiot. Not surprising. Solomonoff had been a lunatic, but he hadn't been an idiot either. "OK, if you want a fuller stack trace,

348

I was thinking something disturbing, but then when you interrupted me I looked at you and started thinking how cute you are. I think I saw you on TV once but I didn't get a good image of you...."

She blushed again: this was becoming a habit. "I was really upset with those reporters...."

"Yeah, I understand...."

"So what was the disturbing thought?"

"Do you really want to go into it? Wouldn't you rather go have lunch?"

"How about we go into it over lunch?" she suggested.

We walked out the door of her house toward a cafe' she said was OK and was less than half a mile away. After a few commonplaces about the neighborhood and the weather she launched into what was on her mind. "I've been having some disturbing thoughts myself," she ventured.

"Like what?"

"Like maybe Godfrey was right, in a way."

"You mean his design for an AI could have worked, if he'd made some small modifications? You know,...."

"No," she said sharply. "I don't have any opinion on that stuff. He was brilliant but he was also completely nuts, so...."

"OK, sorry." (A bit of an edge to her voice there, eh? I sensed she wasn't as calm and reserved as she'd been acting, not once you got to know her better....)

"I mean about the human race."

"Ah."

"We had these long arguments – back in the old days – about ethics kinds of things.... I didn't think it was smart to keep working on AI given that even if you succeed the thing may just destroy us all

349

– why would a superhuman AI have any use for us? It could just swat us like a fly...."

"And his position was that we should just take the risk?"

"That was sometimes his position. On a more mellow day. Sometimes he thought he had the solution – that he knew how to make his AI stay obedient no matter how smart it got. But most of the time he just didn't give a shit. Sometimes he thought the end of humanity would be a good thing. He liked to say stuff like: *Humanity, you never had it in the first place*." She smiled sourly.

"Yeah, well...."

"He may be right."

"What's 'it'?"

"Huh?"

"Humanity never had it in the first place. What's 'it'?"

"I don't know," she said irritatedly. "It's just an expression. You understand my point."

I shrugged. "Partly."

She took a deep breath, and then paused for a while, as if deciding which direction to go in. I decided to remain silent and let her decision process churn.

Finally she started: "When we took mushrooms in Amsterdam, we had some weird experiences...."

"Yeah?"

"Did you ever take mushrooms, or acid, or anything?"

"Back in college, a long time ago."

Her face warmed up a little – the edge was evaporating. I wanted badly to touch her, but resisted: all in good time.... "OK, so maybe you'll sort of understand."

I smiled at her. "Try me." We were getting near the cafe', I could see it up ahead on the right. It looked like some kind of bakery.

"Do you mind if we walk a little more?" she asked. "There's a Thai place up the road that I like a little better."

I nodded.

"He felt he was communicating with these beings...."

"You mean like Terrence McKenna's machine-elves from the ninth dimension?" I laughed. I had read some of McKenna's loony books. Fun stuff, but he believed his drug-inspired delusions a bit more seriously than I was comfortable with.

"I don't know," she said. "McKenna took DMT, for one thing, which is different from mushrooms. And it's hard to tell from his language.... Well, anyway.... Godfrey felt he was communicating with these beings that were more fundamental than we are. They could move back and forwards in time, and perceive information at the quantum level."

"Ah. Well, that's good for them I suppose...."

"Well, this just reinforced his feeling that the human way of processing information is fatally limited."

Now I was back on familiar ground. "Of course it is. The brain has a limited capacity, and worse than that it's basically a hacked-up version of a monkey brain."

"Well OK," she said. "But I've been thinking about ethics a bit. Let's suppose there's a field full of sheep and bunnies, and we decide to colonize it and build all our human stuff there, even though we know the sheep and bunnies won't have anywhere to live anymore."

"OK."

"Well how do we justify this?"

"We don't," I pointed out. "We just do it – because we're stronger. Because we can."

"We do it because we can," she said, stopping and looking at me. Her face looked excited and alive. Her breasts were virtually jumping out at me. I was irritated at myself for being so horny, but of course, that's exactly why women show so much cleavage, right? I forced myself to focus on her words. "But we still feel we're justified. And why? Because we're better than them. We're smarter than the bunnies and sheep, we're more intelligent, we're more flexible, more general. So putting ourself in their place is really the more moral thing to do."

"Not everyone would agree with you," I pointed out – we were walking again. "The deep ecologists think humans should reduce their population to pre-civilization levels to leave more room for wildlife."

She waved her hand. "They're a bunch of morons. The point is, it's not just that it's OK to build an AI in spite of risks. The point is, *our existence is immoral.* Do you see that? That's what Godfrey was trying to get across to me, but I never understood it."

I laughed again, nervously more than out of humor. "So, now that he's gone, you've come to agree with him."

"Not about everything. But I can see his point on this. If we can make something smarter and better than ourselves – more flexible and general, better able to understand things, able to experience more – then it's actually unethical for us to keep consuming resources that could be used for some better thing."

"What do those quantum minds moving back and forth in time have to do with it?"

"I'm not sure...." She paused. The Thai place was approaching. "He was trying to get at that, but he just went fucking nuts instead...." I saw real sadness on her face. I knew that she and Solomonoff had had a somewhat chaotic relationship – splitting up and then reconciling – but I could see she deeply loved him. And even now, after his death, she was trying to reconcile herself to his ideas, trying to make sense of the madness. "One thing he talked about," she added, "was giving his AI access to the quantum domain, so it could experience quantum events directly. Then maybe the AI would fuse with these micro-beings, these quantum minds you called them."

"Ah. It would move them into the macro domain."

All of a sudden, she laughed like little girl. Her cheeks turned bright red; she ran her fingers wildly through her long black hair. "Oh, I don't know. That sounds pretty crazy. Let's have some lunch, huh?"

I smiled and put my hand on her shoulder. "Sounds good to me."

"I've been sitting around here myself too long, thinking about Godfrey and all that – I guess I've been breeding a lot of crazy thoughts. It's great to have someone to talk to."

We walked into the restaurant. "I like talking to you too..."

"But you never told me why you came here," she pointed out.

"You led me here."

She ignored my lame attempt at humor. "I mean to my house."

I shrugged. "It was a directive from the machine-elves.... No, seriously ... well, if you want to talk about that, I was curious if there were any notes that Solomonoff wrote down in the earlier stages of his design process, before he went over the edge."

"You think there might be something of use there? For your own work, you mean?"

"Maybe. My own or someone else's. Well, to be honest, I'm at a bit of a difficult point in my own AI work right now, in terms of getting the system to really understand its own processes in a way that doesn't totally combinatorially explode and use all the computer's resources. To get even as far as he did, Solomonoff must have gotten around this problem somehow."

"Maybe," she said. "Zorvex did give him a lot of computers, though."

"Yeah, I know," I grinned.

"Derrr." She seemed to have forgotten, for a moment, that I was the one who Zorvex had called in to lead the team in charge of stopping his rogue AI from dominating their computer systems and spreading across the Internet at large. "I don't know if it's useful at all – but I remember he said something like, all the algorithms of thought are exponential, it's just a matter of getting the constant in the exponent as small as you can...."

"Well, yeah. I've gotten that far. If you put it in that language, what I'm hoping is that he had some tricks for getting the constant down that can be ported over to my AI architecture. Which is more complex than his, from what I understand of his ... but does have some properties in common."

"Presumably yours isn't going to destroy the human race?"

"It's not going to advance uncontrollably – at each step I have the option to stop its progress. Until it gets really smart, at which point all bets are off. But I'm a long way from there, yet. Your husband's approach was based on letting the system learn how to think and build its own mental structures – this can get you faster progress if things go really well but it's intrinsically unpredictable. In my approach you build more stuff in and don't let it modify its own cognitive processes until it's achieved a pretty high level of intelligence. This is slower but more reliable.... So in my approach you're a lot less likely to create a rogue process – and less likely to annihilate the human race unintentionally.... However ethical that might be."

She looked at me in a way I couldn't read.... I still wasn't sure how serious she had been with that earlier rant about sheep and bunnies. Perhaps she wasn't sure how serious she had been either.

"But still," I continued, "I'd like to understand what he did better...."

She tilted her head to one side, the way I always did. Already she was copying my mannerisms.... "The media would be pretty hyped up if they knew you were trying to copy what Godfrey did...."

"I'm not – "

"I know, I know. But...."

"No, really! I...."

She laughed. "I'm just teasing...." She put her hand on mine, tentatively, across the table.

A waitress was approaching, it was time to order food. Entertainment for the taste buds and olfactory receptors; energy for the metabolism machine. Goddamn this humanity: so boring and primitive and limited. And goddamn this human sex urge: so boring and so primitive and limited, and so much goddamn fun....

"I do have a bunch of his notebooks at home, in some boxes in his study," she said. "I don't know if they have what you're looking for, but you're welcome to look through them."

I smiled and nodded. She looked at the menu. We'd never gotten to my own disturbing thoughts, but there was plenty of time for that. Thinking of time itself, I looked at my watch, curious how long we'd been talking, but found that it said two minutes before eleven. The stupid thing had stopped working, for some reason. I looked over at the clock on the wall and set it to the correct time, twelve forty-three – then slouched back in my chair and relaxed for a moment, shooting a grin at my charming new friend.

The future and the imaginary
rotting fetid pregnant
glorious and crystallized
pained and ensorcelled by the silhouette
of the Voice at the end of the end of the end –
the endless purple twilit Scream --

I am afraid she is a being without a body or brain – a disembodied superhuman intelligent system, a variant of Nietzsche's Zarathustra immanent in the disturbances of the universe – an immense psychotic mini-van Allen belt that masquerades as society's aura. She glows the beginning and end of all time, now beautiful as possible

Time is a farce invented by devils everything _exists and always has_ and will – _yet we ourselves are_ wrapped up with these devils – which are "just" a low-dimensional projection of the cosmos-building transtemporal quantum aliens who will always exist in a space beyond us by the very nature of what "us" are – from the point of view of our humanity, the dreams weave in and out and out and in, and we never can get them back

Software, wetware, hardware, firmware, wildware, deadware, lifeware, shitware where ware wear where we are an illusion
Thoughts are an illusion
Zeros and ones don't exist
Here in the center of the moment, of the statuary moment, every twist of thought floats endless
no-change elusive dreaming things
here lonely in time's center
between the dead past and the forest and the scream

ashes to ashes
dust to dust
dream to dream
ashes to ashes
dust to dust
dream to dream
ashes to ashes
dust to dust
dream to dream
ashes to ashes
dust to dust
dream to dream
ashes to ashes
dust to dust
dream to dream
ashes to ashes
dust to dust
dream to dream
ashes to ashes
dust to dust
dream to dream
ashes to ashes
dust to dust
dream to dream
ashes to ashes
dust to dust
dream to dream
ashes to ashes
dust to dust
dream to dream
ashes to ashes
dust to dust
dream to dream
ashes to ashes
dust to dust
dream to dream

Afterword
Dr. Adam Ahriman

In the Foreword I described the unusual circumstances in which the *Echoes* manuscript was presented to me. Now, in this Afterword, I will briefly indulge myself in a recitation of some of the hypotheses that have been put forward regarding the ultimate origins of the manuscript. A large number of such hypotheses have been propounded, most of them not deserving repetition. However some have sufficient humor value to be worth reporting for the pure sake of amusement; and a few others need to be cited here merely for the purpose of definitively refuting them.

Firstly, several individuals have speculated that the manuscript might be the product of my eldest son, Zarathustra (who lately turned 16). This theory is bolstered by the prominent usage in the manuscript of the name "Jack," which could be taken as a reference to Zarathustra's unfinished dada/surrealist/sci-fi opus *The Love In Front Of Jack* — a manuscript that is also mentioned in the book itself, which is peculiar since very few individuals are aware of its existence. There is even a section in the manuscript titled *The Love In Front Of Jack*, though this section consists of rambling nonsense that has nothing in common with Zarathustra's actual manuscript of this name! Also, the "Ari Adaman" character in the manuscript has a son named "Zarathustra," whereas all of his other family members have names that are variants of, rather than exact matches to, my own family members' names. And there are many mentions of Nietzsche's Zarathustra throughout the manuscript. All in all, however, I find the "Zarathustra Ahriman wrote *Echoes*" hypothesis unlikely, as the literary style and content of the manuscript really don't have much in common with my son's Zarathustra's writing or thinking such as I know them (and I believe I do know them fairly well). Creating a manuscript such *Echoes* – with its hard-science, philosophical, sexual and psychedelic themes -- is almost surely not within the repertoire of any 16-year-old, even one gifted with a half-measure of my prodigious genome. Plus, Zarathustra says he didn't do it, and I know him to be an honest person. It seems more plausible that these clues pointing in Zarathustra's direction were created by the true author as an intentional strategy for sowing confusion.[3]

There is also the perplexing reference to a "Dr. Gennady Burtzle" in the Epilogue at the end of the manuscript. However, a thorough search yielded no information about any individuals with this name, so at this point the Burtzle reference appears to be a dead end – though perhaps one day Dr. Burtzle will come forward and claim authorship, thus

---

[3] Or should I say, "cunfusium"?

setting the whole issue to rest.

Next, a former professional colleague suggested that my old friend Troulian Youlanov (sometimes known as the "Bulgarian Madmind") might be the responsible party. Troulian has historically postulated a considerable number of ambitious, highly eccentric AI designs; and has also posited a number of mathematical or quasi-mathematical theories purportedly demonstrating the possibility or impossibility of AI, the existence or nonexistence of a Supreme Being, and so forth. Furthermore, he has periodically displayed an intense, perhaps excessive interest in my own intellectual doings, as evidenced e.g. by his epigrams such as "Adam Ahriman is the last in the series of great Jews: Moses, Jesus, Freud, Einstein and Ahriman" or "Adam, your ideas about AI are mostly nonsense, but you're the greatest Philip K. Dick character yet." However, a careful analysis of Troulian's various available writings renders his authorship of *Echoes* very unlikely. While the themes of the text are right up Troulian's alley, Troulian's grasp of English is nowhere near the level demonstrated in *Echoes*. Still, a collaboration between Troulian and some other unknown party more exquisitely skilled in the construction of English-language avant-garde poetry and literary prose is not unthinkable, and this is perhaps, I would venture to assert, one of the more plausible hypotheses presented so far, though not a tremendously likely one. (I have attempted to contact Troulian several times in the last few months in a quest to put this hypothesis to rest, but haven't received a response, which however is not surprising; Troulian has long had the habit of disappearing for periods of time.)

Other theories offered were even more outlandish, including suggestions that the manuscript might be a coded message from some nonhuman source (an AI running secretly across multiple computers spread across the Internet -- a tribe of McKenna-style nine-dimensional machine-elves -- a future AI mind propagating information back in time so as to sow the seeds of its own creation; etc.). In this species of theory, something in the manuscript is supposed to seed ideas in some reader's mind that will eventually lead to important consequences. The purpose of the obscure and poetic nature of the manuscript is hypothesized to serve the purpose of obscuring the fact that the transmission of coded information is occurring. According to this line of thinking, the manuscript would be somewhat similar in purpose to the fictional film VALIS in Philip K. Dick's novel of that name. As you might expect, I find this very doubtful, and almost too silly to deserve commentary.

Another individual, tongue in cheek I hope, speculated that I wrote the manuscript myself while in some sort of trance state (perhaps inspired by psychedelic substances, which for some reason a number of individuals appear to assume I am in the habit of ingesting, when in fact nothing could be further from the case!) -- and then, realizing I would completely forget about it once the trance was done, e-mailed it to myself to ensure its preservation. This theory does not, however, explain the use of an anonymous email address. Nor does it account for the lack of any gap in my earthly existence sufficiently lengthy to account for the construction of a 70,000 word manuscript. I have spent every single day of the last few years in the company of family and coworkers: there is no "missing space" during which *Echoes* could have been secretly and continuously constructed. The hypothesized trance state would have had to have been fragmented and recurrent over a long period of time, which hardly seems psychologically plausible.

Finally, and somewhat offensively, there was the wag who suggested that I wrote the *Echoes* manuscript while in a quite normal state of mind -- and that I then deceptively claimed to have received the manuscript as an anonymous email. My motivation, he speculated, was either purely humorous in nature, or else a combination of artistic vanity and embarrassment. Perhaps, he insinuated, I wished to publish the manuscript and reap the attendant glory yet insulate myself in a way from the insanity of its contents, for the sake of preserving my (heh!) professional reputation. I see no need to dignify this with a response.

By way of conclusion, my humble suggestion is that the *Echoes* manuscript should be considered as a work of "conceptual art" on its own merits, without regard for the question of its origins (which will likely never be resolved anyway). Quite evidently, whoever is the true author wished it to be considered in this way.

Dr. Adam Ahriman
Brooklyn, New York
February, 2006

www.ingramcontent.com/pod-product-compliance
Lightning Source LLC
Chambersburg PA
CBHW081142020726

47504CB00009B/1967